In Praise

"You'd think a battered wife's near-death escape to a remote Wyoming cattle ranch would be enough to keep readers on the edge of their seats, but author Nancy Roy's addictive romantic thriller, *There Was A Fire*, is tightly woven with rich characters (a sadistically abusive husband, a vivacious socialite best friend, colorful cowboys, boisterous beauticians, and even a lonely ghost), along with riveting plot twists and steamy liaisons that keep you guessing until the story's mind-blowing ending."

-Lisa Smith Molinari
The Meat and Potatoes of Life

"If you are looking for a story to dive into and not come up for air until you have finished every riveting word, Nancy Roy will become your go-to author....I have seldom if ever encountered a work of this complexity and emotional depth. I was totally mesmerized by the skillful storytelling, poignant scenes and jaw dropping ending. As an added plus, the supernatural elements intrigue and tease throughout, what a great read!"

-Melissa Martin Ellis, author
The Everything Ghost Hunting Book

"Suspenseful, tense and moving...*There Was A Fire* is a riveting tale of terror, love and raw emotion--relentlessly paced and balanced with great characters...all shot through with the sheer excitement of great story-telling!"

-Mark Ellis, author of
Mack Bolan, Doc Savage and creator of the best-selling *Outlanders* series

THERE WAS A FIRE

NANCY ROY

WALT the DOG PRESS

Book & cover art & design by Melissa Martin Ellis
Walt the Dog Press logo design by Fred Roy

ISBN: 0692459871
ISBN-13: 978-0692459874

For Michael –
"Writers write."

No one walks through life unmarked. Damage may come in many forms, but it always comes. There is damage from war, from loss, from heartbreak and damage from love. There is no life lived that doesn't court the scars of its living. But it is in the wearing of those scars, whether in grace or despair, that one's character is known.

CHAPTER 1

The tendrils of fire licked the Thai silk as they tasted, then hungrily devoured the draperies framing the window she lay looking through.

Beneath the pristine panes of glass stood a dressing table holding photographs. She watched as the pressed linen coverlet caught fire, the starch inviting the flames' even spread. In her mind she could hear the soaring notes of a soprano singing *Ave Maria*. The Bach, not the Schubert. The soundtrack her ever-in-denial subconscious had chosen, was as disconnected from the surrounding horror as her physical body was. She watched, a spectator to her own demise, the adrenaline of fear gaining no favor in her prostrate limbs.

As the fire gained fuel and fervor, the photos in their matched silver frames began to bubble and melt away. She had lined them up chronologically, never thinking that one day she would watch her life dissolve as the flames consumed her memories year by year.

Ave Maria...

The first to burn was the one of her as a nine-year-old 4-H-er, holding the bridle of a perfectly groomed yearling Holstein in one hand, and a Second Place ribbon in the other. Though she stood in the middle of a dirt arena, her white jeans and shirt were still pristine. The exposed old photo paper flamed quickly. The young girl was gone in a flash.

Then, she and her proud parents on the afternoon of her graduation from college. The three of them standing, arms linked; three sets of sunglasses and smiles. It was the only frame of the collection that still had its glass. The rest had been broken over the years in different skirmishes. At first the glass reflected the flames, then as the heat intensified, smoke charred the outside as the photo boiled beneath.

Next came a smaller frame of her kissing—well smooching really—the cheek of a young girl. She was pretty, with bold eyebrows and a pixie cut. The girl was flinching, eyes closed, but with a toothy grin. A moment caught before a shriek of laughter. The photo blistered, then melted away.

The soprano's voice soothed her.

Dominus tecum...

Finally, the largest frame; an 8 X 10 of the perfect wedding. She was radiant in a jeweled headdress and a pearled satin bodice with sheer sleeves. The groom was dashing in his morning coat, both of them gazing straight into the camera, eyes shining in anticipation.

From above the picture, a piece of drapery dropped onto the photo's leaning face like a small fire bomb. It burned from the center out to the edges, like the opening credits of *Bonanza,* revealing yet another wedding photo beneath. It was her again, but younger and with a different man.

At this wedding she wore a simple white dress and short veil that touched the ground as her handsome groom dipped her backward into a Hollywood embrace. He was smiling as he kissed his young bride. Her arms wrapped around his strong shoulders. He wore no tie. The old photo, revealed for the first time in years, burned and curled like the rest.

Now, all around her the room was being ignited; the walls catching link by link, a chain of flames.

On the floor were the remnants of the evening that was. Her black d'Orsay pumps strewn, the cocktail dress ripped and crumpled by the bed where she lay prone, face turned toward the window above the vanity. Her left arm hung limp over the side, the numbed fingers hovered above the plush carpet that had helped muffle the sounds of the violence from an hour ago. It was on this hand that the six-carat diamond had lived these past fourteen years. Even in paralysis she could imagine its weight. It had always felt so heavy.

Ave Maria...

She lay, virtually lifeless on the bed they had shared since they married, since the now incinerated top wedding photo was taken. In her mind, the soprano's sublime notes swam in her ears, building, climbing to their brilliant crescendo.

...in hora mortis nostrae!

Through the window, her wide eyes stared out beyond the now charred dressing table, and locked on a face.

His face.

He stood motionless on the manicured backyard lawn, beyond where the heat could touch him. The fire's glow reflected his expression. It was ecstasy.

Amen.

Amen.

There was a loud crack, and then...nothing.

He could see her through the window, framed in flame. The strings of Christmas lights dancing in the eves from the updraft of the fire's heat only added to his festive mood.

He could almost feel the air-conditioning leaking out into the heavy Atlanta evening air. He knew he was alone. He had seen to the landscaping design personally, creating a secluded sanctuary on his oversized Ansley double lot.

He hadn't known when he married her that she would end up pathetic. She had been so vibrant, full of light. The perfect complement to his beautiful, unending darkness. But she had become what he most despised: weak, and even worse, average.

He saw them everywhere, the people that settled for whatever they were given, not a vision or an ounce of style among them. They shuffled about in their bargain clothes and ate food that allowed their bodies to all but explode. They were wide and loud.

Both traits should have made them a formidable presence, but in the end, as far as he was concerned, they didn't really exist.

As a surgeon treating these miserable people, he often toyed with thoughts of putting them out of their misery. Alas, that wouldn't do. Society wasn't ready to embrace his version of the world, the last thing he needed was some middle class law enforcement yokel having the last laugh.

It was their ignorance that bothered him most. Maybe they weren't born to be educated and take part in the cream of society like he was, but really, surely there was *something* they could do to raise their station in life. He had a name for them, *The Invisible Mediocres.* Like the walking dead, he regarded them with disgust.

If he were honest, he knew it was her weakness that had attracted him. He had first met her when she was in her deepest despair. How he had devoured her then; soaking in her anguish, being her sole harbinger of hope. But he had lost his taste for her sorrow, her tedious neediness. This past year had left him relentlessly bored. It was time for a fresh start.

Of course he had considered divorce. Really, how mundane. *Unimaginative.* He would never tolerate the gossip, leaving his perfect existence open for the raised eyebrows of The Mediocres. He would do what he must to preserve his precious perfection. Granted, he had little interest in Julia sexually or otherwise, but he found the thought of another man's hands on her abhorrent. She was his and that wouldn't change, even now, when he had decided he was done.

Inexplicably, she had fostered a certain level of fondness from his elitist crowd. People were so easily swayed. Their adoration of her had always annoyed him. Oh, she was *so good.* Before her spark had been all but extinguished—*a job well done,* he inwardly smirked—people had been drawn to her. Hell, he was drawn to her in the beginning. But she wasn't strong enough in the long run; couldn't stand up to the force that was Dr. Justin Richards.

Then the game was on. She was his to whittle away at, until there was nothing remotely compelling left. He had broken her. Piece by piece. Bite by bite. Now she was one of them. The Invisible Mediocres had a new recruit.

Yes. *This is the answer,* he mused, as he saw the flames grow in intensity. The black smoke billowed from beneath the roofline. He allowed his eyes to meet hers one last time, when with sudden violence, the roof collapsed on top of her.

So perfect! He clasped his hands together in glee and had to fight his impulse to burst out laughing.

His Blackberry buzzed in his pocket. Fishing it out, the caller ID revealed the number of the woman he was currently fucking. He smiled at the memory of their activities the night before. She liked it rough, but he wouldn't be seeing her again. Even though she was in her twenties, after closer scrutiny, her body wasn't as firm as he liked. Not wanting the time-stamp to mar his alibi of frantic husband, he let the call roll to voicemail, then deleted every trace of it.

He would need to have the house redone. Insurance would pay for the damage and replace the smoky furnishings. He would commission Penley to paint another portrait of him. It was sad to see the first one burn, but he'd always felt it didn't quite capture the strong cut of his jawline. He was ready to modernize anyway; her taste had always been pedestrian—not that he'd ever let her make a decision. The thought of an all-white interior with Extractionist paintings like those he had seen at an opening a couple weeks ago piqued his interest.

Of course there would need to be the mourning period. He grinned as he thought about the parade of eligible socialites that would flock to his side, feigning support in his time of need. He grew aroused just thinking of all the casserole pussy he would harvest as he moved through his flawless performance of grief.

CHAPTER 2

Spit-shined linoleum. Julia's eyelids pried themselves open, only to reveal this ultimate version of what 1952 flooring had aspired to be. Her jaw and forehead hung facedown, cradled in cushions on all sides of her face. She felt weightless and immediately wondered what was holding her up...and when it would let her fall.

The floor tiles where frothy beige with darker shards of gray rafting through. Was she in an elementary school? It smelled too clean. Elementary schools somehow always smelled of cafeteria hot lunch. Not any specific meal, but the culmination of years of hamburgers, sloppy joes and Friday fish sticks. The spongy platform that held her body horizontal allowed for no movement. *Where am I? What contraption is this?* And then another thought sent a shudder of fear through her distant extremities. *Where is he?*

As if in answer, an upturned face appeared between her and the glistening floor four feet away. It was Dinah. Or more accurately, Dinah's eyes. The rest of her closest friend was covered by a pale blue cotton gown, shower cap and surgical mask.

"Julia honey? Are you awake? Are you with us?" Her soft Southern lilt sounded distant, as if speaking to her from the far end of a tunnel.

Dinah turned her head to speak to someone Julia could not see. "Her eyes are open!" she exclaimed. Then craning her neck to meet Julia's gaze again, "Julia? It's okay...there was a fire. You are going to be fine, well—in a bit—you have some burns, but the doctors are taking care of that."

With a forced cheerfulness that was now building to a full-tilt

Dinah ramble, she continued, "But you'll be okay. Don't try to talk, honey—you're on a respirator. Doctors say it's helping your lungs keep up right now—and your hair! Your beautiful red hair is still with you!" Dinah's eyes began to fill, "Thanks to that up-do you always hated...well if that wasn't just a little hair miracle!"

Julia blinked in warm wonder at her flustered friend.

"Oh, I am sounding ridiculous." Dinah huffed to herself, tears beginning to overflow, "But really honey, you're awake and you're still with us, and oh—I have been so worried! You just don't know... and Justin, you should see how he's been fussing over you—he's barely left your side."

At the mention of her husband's name, Julia's eyes widened, she became agitated, but her limbs didn't seem to respond. She struggled harder and a shock of pain jolted through her. She settled again, frustrated and scared. The only thing that moved were her tears falling vertically onto the immaculate, shining floor.

"Oh dear, we're going to need something to catch those," said Dinah, disappearing from view, her tone anguished.

Over the next few hours Julia came to understand that she was at the Grady Burn Center, where she had been placed face down in a position that allowed her back, violently burned to the core, to breathe and be treated. At least she wasn't at Piedmont, not at *his* hospital.

Later, she wasn't sure how long—the linoleum had no sense of time attached to it—Julia woke to overhear a couple nurses conversing behind her. Again the voices seemed far away.

"It's a wonder she's still with us...with these kinds of burns it's so easy to get an infection, not to mention the skin grafts and surgeries ahead."

Then a second voice, "She's in for a rough ride; a lot of pain, bless her soul. What started it anyway?"

"Firemen thought it might have been a candle."

Julia slowly closed her eyes and let the voices trail away.

Days passed, then weeks. The commotion of pain and drug treatments blurred her sense of time and place. Julia's eyes opened to take stock of her sterile room. There were no flowers or cards. Though there were times the nurses positioned her on her side, usually she remained facing the floor, looking out a hole in the padded cradle that held her head. The mattress was some kind of waterbed, shifting beneath her, adjusting to the slightest shift of pressure.

Justin seemed to always be there, but moved only in her periphery, murmuring with the doctors, always just out of view. When they were alone he would pet the back of her head, all the while spewing hatred into her ears. His touch always threw her heart rate into overdrive; the tangible record of her fear displayed on the respirator's digital read-out panel.

The pain was stealthy, always pressing on the boundaries laid down by the haze of drugs. And when it found its way through, it was all agony; excruciating, with a blinding heat. The ventilator would hold her screams at bay. The only signals the nurses had to adjust the morphine gaps were Julia's heart rate and tears.

One afternoon she awoke as the doctors conferred, always faceless, always speaking behind her back.

"It's time to take her off the respirator." The voice belonged to Dr. Westin. She liked him, he took time to bend down and look her in the eye. She found his voice soothing. But that afternoon he sounded anxious, and he spoke with poorly veiled frustration. "Any longer and there could be consequences. The majority of the lung issues have been resolved."

And then Justin's voice, "I just want to be careful. No reason to hurry such a major step along." Instantly, Julia's entire body stiffened.

"Dr. Richards, you know as well as I do, it's time. Stop worrying, she's in the best hands in Georgia. I'll be back with the team."

Julia heard the door *whoosh* close and knew she was once again alone with her husband. She couldn't turn to see him, but she could smell his familiar , nauseating aftershave, a cross between Polo and the hospital's hand sanitizer. He leaned close, his breath hot against her ear.

"Hello darlin'." Justin's drawl always thickened when he was angry. "The good Dr. Westin is going to remove your breathing tube now. You are doing sssso much better," he hissed. "This is such an important step, I can't wait to get you home." He paused to let the implication settle in. "Oh, don't worry, the damage to the house will be fully repaired by the time you get out of here, people won't even know there was a fire."

Then with a small chuckle, he delivered a quick poke to her back, which caused her to involuntarily cry out—the sound nothing but a constricted moan as the breathing tube labored in her throat. "Wish I could say the same for you."

Now he shifted to look directly into her wide and terrified eyes. It was the first time she had truly taken in his face since seeing him outside their bedroom window on the night of the fire. He looked...haunted.

"Let me tell you exactly how this is going to go," he said softly. "They are going to come back in here and remove the tube, and you, *my dear*, you are going to say nothing but *please* and *thank you*—because if you say anything other than *please* and *thank you*, I will leave this room, drive down to Florida to go hunting for that sweet daughter of yours, and believe me, she will suffer for your sins before she goes."

Julia's breathing, now fighting the ventilator, became uneven and her pulse raced.

"In addition," Justin continued, "should you decide to deviate in *any* way from these simple instructions, my little cunt of a whore, I will find a way to end your pain *permanently*. Don't you dare forget who's in charge here."

Then moving so close she could smell last night's cigar on his breath, he whispered, "I know you saw me. Don't make me hurt you again." Smiling, he added, "You are so vulnerable here..."

At that moment, the door swung open revealing to the medical team what must have looked like a concerned husband reassuring his distressed wife. Justin moved his hand to her cheek and kissed the top of her head. "We're ready."

Along with other preparations, she was moved to a more upright position, after which the tube was quickly removed. The initial coughing caused shooting pains as her back heaved with the motion. A nurse offered her a cup with a bent straw protruding. "Would you like to try some water? It might help."

"Please," came the raspy first word from Julia's lips, her hollow eyes never leaving Justin's. He gave the slightest nod of approval.

She sipped and again the coughing set in, spearheading more stabbing pain. The nurse moved in for a second sip, which she took.

"Thank you."

Thirteen agonizing days later, Julia was finally moved from the ICU to a room of her own. It was her first night in this room, and she found herself lucid enough to truly take in her surroundings.

There were still no flowers, no magazines or books, only the cold germ-free surfaces that now made up her world. The nurses had propped her up so she lay on her side. With pillows acting as guardrails, she couldn't accidentally roll onto her back. It was late, the ward was quiet, Craig Ferguson was doing his monologue on a television suspended in the far corner of the room.

Sitting with her back to Julia was Dinah, her feet elevated in a mauve vinyl recliner. She was clad in the required sterile scrubs, booties and shower cap. Julia imagined the designer track suit and Prada sneakers that lurked beneath the steel blue cotton and smiled at the thought of her dear friend sacrificing her puffy-blonde Southern hairdo as she stuffed it under the cap. True friendship indeed. When Dinah saw she was awake, she immediately moved to Julia's bedside.

At that moment the night nurse entered, and came to stand beside her.

"Okay honey." Dinah never used the usual, *hello how are you's*. "I've got it all figured."

"You do?" Julia croaked. She had no idea what Dinah was talking about, not unusual in their long relationship.

"Yes. How I'm going to save you," she said, matter-of-factly.

Julia was quiet, her eyes darting to the night nurse.

"Oh now, don't worry about her. Allow me to introduce Marilee Stanton, registered nurse, and my niece. She's Bernard's sister Elaine's girl, and our secret weapon." Dinah smiled with pride and her eyes twinkled with mischief. "Marilee is officially our partner in crime."

Marilee reached out, squeezed Julia's hand and gently offered, "How do you do?" She had warm, soft eyes and Julia instantly liked her.

Dinah continued, "Okay, I know you're not quite up to snuff yet, so let me do all the talking."

"I always do," said Julia, with a sarcastic smile.

"Of course you do." Dinah paused just long enough for Julia to see the well of worries brimming in the deep blue eyes of her dearest friend. "All right then. We are going to bust you out of here before Justin can take you home and do God-knows-what to you."

Julia's eyes went wide.

Leaning in closer, Dinah took hold of Julia's hand. "Oh sweetie, to think that I was the one who introduced you and brought all this down on your head—it makes me, well—", Dinah bit back the catch in her voice, "I can't sleep, thinking you could be back living with him. Now I know I should've done something sooner—helped you when I saw you sinking—but dahlin', I didn't know. I didn't know what he was doing, how he was hurting you. But we have someone on our side now. Your Dr. Westin, he took a couple of my *suggestions* to heart and did every X-ray and test you could imagine.

"He's been funneling info through our Marilee," said Dinah with pride, "who just happens to leave a chart here or a note there, where I might *accidentally* be able to read it. Bless her heart! She could totally lose her license. So could he, if someone ever really wanted to trace the breadcrumbs—between the three of us, we were on a mission."

Dinah brushed a lock of auburn hair off Julia's forehead. "Oh honey, all the broken bones, the scars I never saw—" Again, she gathered herself, then resolutely continued, "but two plus two equals three plus one, and it doesn't take an Einstein to know there was something strange about that fire, and...oh—" This time she didn't bother to check the emotions as they boiled to the surface. "How frightened you must have been, the thought of you lying there with the fire coming—" Her tears were well on their way, the words rushing together, "And it won't be proven, you know it won't, because he's too *smart* and his family's too *rich* and people are too scared of him—and so I have..."

Dinah paused to pull herself together, then straightened her shoulders and declared, "I have taken it upon myself to save you." She gently took Julia's face in her hands. "Please let me do this... please let me save you."

The two old friends took a moment to give and accept the love coming from each other's eyes.

"I'm in," was Julia's raspy reply, her eyes wide and intense.

"Well here comes the day! Isn't that what you used to like to say?" said Dinah, with arms wide. "Marilee, we got ourselves a jailbreak!"

Hours later, after the initial escape plan was hatched, Dinah left the hospital and slipped away under cover of the Atlanta darkness. With her friend's departure, Julia eased her head down in the cushioned cradle. As she lay exhausted, overwhelmed at the thought of what Dinah was concocting, she couldn't help but muse at the elemental force that was her best friend.

Julia O'Shea had met Dinah Dubois at Agnes Scott College in Atlanta, the class of 1978. Julia attended on an English scholarship and Dinah on her parents' insistence. They were both freshmen and landed in the same sorority. They both hated their roommates. Julia's was Aurelia Suffaker, a lumpy sophomore with a nasal voice, who was allergic to everything. She insisted on sleeping with the windows closed, in the air-conditioning-challenged Post Civil War building. Aurelia couldn't stand the sound of the late summer cicadas when she slept, opting for stifling heat instead.

Dinah's roommate was Stephie Stokley, who was there on a track scholarship. Stephie was a congenial girl, nice-looking in a muscle-bound sort of way. So congenial, in fact, that she seized every opportunity to sleep with any boy who paid her compliments and/or bought her beer.

Needless to say, Julia and Dinah bonded over long nights spent talking on the meeting-room couches. At the semester break they were able to do some maneuvering and became roommates themselves, a condition that stuck until they graduated three and a half years later.

Dinah came from a prominent Atlanta family whose one wish was for her to marry well, have children and to entertain in a way that complemented her station and family heritage. With the exception of children, she had fulfilled their expectations.

It had been a blow when the doctor told her there would probably never be a child. An "unfriendly womb" was the phrase he had used. She had always found her womb to be at the very least indifferent, if not downright cordial. But friendly or not, it bore no fruit. And until the discovery of Justin's true nature, it was the biggest disappointment of Dinah's life.

She met Bernerd Tecumseh Calvert right after college. He was a banker from a family of bankers. He was also twenty years her senior and ready to settle down with the prescribed society wife. Dinah fit the bill perfectly. She was young and beautiful, curvaceous but still slim enough for couture. She was a natural hostess and her warm, vivacious nature could put even the stodgiest millionaire at ease. From the start, theirs was a marriage of honesty and convenience. He would provide her with security and status, all the comforts his fortune could afford.

After the wedding, at Dinah's insistence, they moved into one of the top floors of the newly iconic 2500 Peachtree building in the heart of Atlanta. At a time when all their set were removing themselves, one wedding at a time, to Buckhead or the even more coveted Tuxedo Drive, Dinah opted for a life accessible to whatever action the Atlanta scene had to offer. Of course, all of these neighborhoods were a mere two miles from each other, the upper crust never wanting to be spread too far apart; still, the social strata lines were clearly drawn.

She knew the ever-grounded Bernerd was never going to be the life of the party. Dinah herself was deathly afraid of flying, and she was determined to keep her Atlanta-based existence exciting. So, by choosing 2500, she was able to bring the party to them. And as long as she didn't expect romance or passion (Bernerd shared in the popular opinion that he was, in fact, boring), she would want for nothing. Dinah, for her part, forayed him into the circles of the married elite. She threw his parties, wrote the *Thank you's* and created a home whose style and grace was enviable even to the highest societal crème. Their alliance had proven a fierce one, and while their liaison never shifted into a grand passion, their affection grew, and they became true confidants with a mutual desire to protect the other from harm. Affairs were not forbidden, as long as discretion was strictly observed.

15

It took Julia longer to find her partner. She had spent an additional year getting her teaching credential and after a few years of false starts, finally found her niche as a 6th Grade teacher at Springdale Elementary in the Virginia Highland neighborhood. Sure, there had been dates and even one eight-month relationship, but Julia could never quite make the full connection. Her parents and grandparents had set a strong example for what a true partnership looked like. A marriage based on love, respect and trust was all she could imagine. So, she took her time.

It was 1983 when little Rosemary Brown showed up in her class. Young Rosie had been a handful then, always disrupting and acting out. The other kids would tease her about the fact that her mom had left. The cruelty of children in full cry. But there was something about Rosemary that had captivated Julia. She had the brightest, yet palest green eyes, with full, dark eyebrows. Attributes that worked in tandem to convey her every emotion, if you took the time to read them. Julia took the time, and found that roiling beneath the mountains of bad behavior was an old soul, angry as hell and begging to be heard. Julia had called a parent/teacher conference with her father. The moment Julia met Henry Brown their attraction had been mutual, intense and final. Though it took months to acknowledge their inconvenient feelings, once done, their lives began in earnest.

Henry was a contractor and had a small construction company. He insisted on doing only small projects where his hand-wrought woodworking passion could be fed. He was kind, warm-hearted, funny and loved all things vintage and traditional. He often immersed himself in the history of a project, sometimes to the detriment of the work itself. It was rare to find him out of Levi 501's, a broken-in plaid shirt, boat shoes or work boots that had been re-soled too many times, and a Woolrich jacket with a striped blanket lining. As a younger man, he had bought a home in Atkin's Park, a 1938 Craftsman fixer-upper, which he had been painstakingly restoring since he signed the deed twenty years before. He was known for his craftsmanship, fair dealing and a snail-like pace. It had to be perfect, and that took time.

Rosemary's mom, and Henry's ex-wife, was Delia. She had left a note proclaiming her love for a man Henry knew, but clearly not well. They would be moving to Baltimore where her new man had a job with the Port Authority. She would send for Rosemary once she got settled.

Then Delia had gotten pregnant and she had explained to her former family that the timing would be too difficult for Rosemary to come right then. When the baby arrived, the arrangement became clear, their households were fixed; Rosemary and Henry in Georgia, Delia and her new family in Maryland. The divorce was fairly amicable, Henry got full custody and Rosemary lost her mother. She was eight.

Henry and Julia married in 1985 in the Dunwoody Methodist Church. She was 29, he was 44. Dinah was Matron of Honor and Rosie served as Best Girl. Julia's dress was simple, with a wide neckline and three-quarter lace sleeves that started just off her shoulders. The panels of buff white satin fit her waistline to perfection, and pooled obediently off the back in a demure train. Around her neck, she wore a single pearl given to her by her Grandma. Her veil hung just to her waist and was made of the same lace as her sleeves.

Henry wore a classic black suit, the first and last suit of quality he would own. He wore it at every wedding, anniversary, graduation and funeral in the five fleeting years that followed. It was perfectly tailored to fit his lean but muscular frame. He had a starched white shirt and a silver tie, which he removed moments after arriving at the reception.

Her father had walked her down the aisle, both he and her mom had approved heartily of the match. Don and Doris O'Shea had driven in from Fort Smith, Arkansas. Neither of her parents had been much for traveling and this marked the first time back to Atlanta since their trip seven years prior for Julia's graduation. Their Midwestern roots felt an instant kinship with the Southern carpenter, Henry's work ethic and integrity easily transferring in their minds to that of a good man who would be a solid provider.

As it happened, the gift of knowing that their little girl would be taken care of was indeed a potent one. Six months after the wedding, at 10:30 on a Saturday morning, while coming home from the Fort Smith Fireman's annual pancake feed, her parents were both killed by a drunk driver. Her wedding would be the last time she saw them. Julia would always feel grateful that their final time together was one of such happiness.

Julia and Henry's life together was a golden time, short-lived as it turned out. But Dinah and Julia's friendship had endured it all; a golden thread that wrapped and wove their lives together, shiny and lovely and strong as steel.

As the days wore on in The Grady Burn Center, Julia resigned herself to two states of mind: drugged on morphine so she was always asleep or in a daze, or somewhat lucid but in constant pain. There didn't seem to be an in-between.

With the pain came her fear, it roared in and out in waves as the drugs ebbed and flowed. It was hard to discern if the fear helped distract her from the pain, or if it was the pain that saved her from the depths of her fear. Hard to know which was the better road, but either way, the two seemed to be irrevocably joined together.

The destruction on her back stretched from just below her hairline at the nape of her neck, down to the small of her back. The old skin was angry and exhausted from being pulled taut, being asked to cover much more area than skin cells should ever be expected to. The new skin, mostly taken from different areas on her legs, was angry from the disruption and disoriented in the foreign surroundings. It had been given a new job, when the old one had been just fine. The new cells resisted and fought the old cells, the prejudice evident on both sides.

Julia could feel the war being played out. Each day, in the few hours she was truly awake, she would discover anew the price of the battles that waged daily on her back. Infection vs. Healing, Rejection vs. Cohesion.

She came to think of her back as its own living entity. Clearly she was not in control and it was all taking place beyond her view, as if clandestine plots were being carried out literally behind her back. She found herself calling it The Wound. She knew they were not allies, but thought of it as a ruthless dictator that the larger political picture demanded you treat with respect. And so, The Wound was now her darkest foe and most intimate companion.

The weeks turned to months. So many setbacks as her body and flesh found their way to a détente. The excruciating debriding, the surgeries—five in all, the care and healing of the donor sites, the decompression procedures on developing scabs to alleviate pressure on her internal organs, the two weeks of stillness after each graft and the assaultive physical therapy that followed, all were a singular hell on their own. Together...the pain was fathomless.

Julia lost those days and weeks, suspended between drugs, agony and sheer exhaustion. The Wound kept a greedy tally of every hour it claimed.

Of course Justin was there, making his daily show of over-attentive concern. At first the day nurses all but swooned over his intoxicating aura of power, money and good looks. Julia could sense how he enjoyed their reaction while he manipulated them with his charade of tenderness. At some point in his visit the two of them would be left alone, an opportunity he would seize by hissing in her ear. "Remember Rosemary, Julia," his voice never failing to roll icy waves down her spine. "One word from you, and she's mine." Her fear silenced her screams as he poked and prodded The Wound's most vulnerable spots.

As the big escape drew near, the band of plotters—Dinah, Marilee, Julia and Rosemary—grew serious, fiercely focusing on the tiniest details. Julia was days away from being released. The excitement of strategizing was behind them and the final countdown had begun. They all knew how high the stakes were.

On May 24th, exactly five months after the fire, Julia took her first steps toward freedom. The physical therapy over the past months had left her able to maneuver about with little assistance; however her stamina deserted her at every turn. But it was not lack of fitness that had her knees ready to buckle as she made her way to the large bank of elevators, once again it was fear.

The ward was quiet at 3:00 AM. She stood dressed in Dinah's clothes, wearing a blonde wig and trying with all that was in her to exude the tiniest bit of Dinah-style confidence. She knew that Marilee would be watching from under her lashes at the nurses' station. The real Dinah was tucked away, decoy style, under the thin blankets of her hospital bed.

Julia jumped at the elevator's hopeful *ping* as it announced the car's arrival. The doors made their obligatory slide, revealing to her downcast eyes a pair of pristine Louis Vuitton Monte Carlo crocodile loafers, perfectly polished. The creased grey-flannel trousers resting atop the textured reptile were tailored to a perfect break.

Justin's shoes.

She stood, frozen, her heart beating a deafening knell in her ears.

Still, she stood, waiting to be exposed, to be mocked. Waiting to lose one last time. The shoes stepped forward, moving to her side. She flinched in anticipation of what the initial assault would be. Julia raised her shoulder to her ear to shield her from what words he would spew. But all she heard was, "Excuse me," as the stranger in fine shoes brushed by.

She turned to watch him walk away. *It's not him!* Not Justin. The adrenaline's retreat left her light-headed and loose-limbed, as reflexively she slipped through the closing doors. Her shaking hand pressed the button for the lobby.

As testament to the detail the women had constructed over the past months, the plan executed flawlessly. Rosemary waited for Julia in Dinah's S-Class Mercedes on a side street, and that first night she drove Julia all the way from Atlanta down to Tallahassee. They knew it was crucial to put distance between them and Justin as quickly as possible. It was three hundred miles south. A straight shot.

For the most part, Julia slept, reclining on her side in the passenger seat. Marilee had advised exactly what dosage of pain killers would keep her comfortable and snoozy for the trip. Julia hadn't asked where the drugs had come from, but assumed that Dr. Westin had a hand in it. She was not the only one taking risks here. She felt the responsibility keenly, and fought through the waves of unworthiness that were crashing in her foggy brain. Six and a half hours later, at around ten in the morning, Rosemary pulled into the KOA campground in Chattahoochee, Florida.

Rosemary had rented the one-room cabin two nights before. They had decided on the venue because it was remote and out-of-character. Granted the silver sedan could possibly raise eyebrows, but they could drive straight up to the cabin door and not be disturbed by other guests. They had planned for Julia's exhaustion after that first drive.

As soon as they arrived, Rosemary gently helped her out of the car and got her inside. Once settled, she changed Julia's dressing as Nurse Marilee had instructed. Then Rosemary gave her another painkiller and tucked her stepmom into bed. It wasn't until Julia's brow lightened in the throes of sleep that Rosemary allowed herself a few precious hours to nap as well.

It was early evening when Julia woke, and as soon as Rosemary was satisfied that Julia had eaten a decent meal and was ready for the next leg of the plan, she drove her to the Tallahassee Greyhound station. It was then that the real tears came, neither of them knowing when they would see each other again.

Julia regarded her brilliant and brave step-girl with awe and she leaned back and took Rosemary's face in her hands. Her beloved Rosie. As she gazed into the young woman's transparent green eyes, now brimming with tears, it brought back an echo of Justin's threat from that first day at Grady; the casual tone as he whispered in her ear, *She will suffer for your sins before she goes.*

A violent shudder moved through Julia which raised alarm in Rosemary's glistening eyes. Julia drew her into her arms one last time.

"I'm so proud of you, Rosie," she said fiercely, her voice catching on the emotion. "He would be proud too." With that the tears flowed on both sides. Finally choking out a final whisper, Julia said, "I couldn't have asked for a better daughter." The two stood frozen as they held each other, each basking in the feel of the other's arms, the familiar scent of family and safety.

It was Julia who found the strength. "You better go." Reluctantly Rosemary released her and with a final, "I love you," got back in the car, leaving Julia on the curb outside the station.

Julia watched as her precious girl drove away to deliver Dinah's car back to Atlanta, and fought back the panic. She was now truly on her own. She walked inside the terminal with nothing but the blue tote bag that Dinah had packed for her. She asked the agent where the next bus out was heading, and using a duplicate of Dinah's driver's license for ID, bought a one-way ticket.

Her original destination was Houston, but still leery of anyone tracking her, she decided to get off a couple stops and a side road earlier. Fifteen hours after she had stepped onto the bus in Tallahassee, Julia Richards arrived, ironically, in Liberty, Texas.

CHAPTER 3

Julia's current rendition of the escape wardrobe that Dinah had packed was a taupe velour sweat suit and white Nike's with an aqua swoosh. That was the outfit she wore as she stepped down from the Greyhound and walked into a wall of soupy humidity. The fine fuzz of the velour was instantly sticky against her skin. She walked to the curb and let the overstuffed bag drop beside her. She ate the exhaust as the bus rolled away, its absence now revealing all that was—or wasn't—Liberty.

She looked down the street one way and saw a row of shops and parked pickups; then in the other direction...more of the same. It was Main Street, noon, hot and empty. She spotted the El Camino Motel down on the left, picked up her bag and started walking toward its neon sign, fully lit and blinking stubbornly in the high Texas sun.

Upon entering the motel office, the mustiness of carpeting that had been rarely vacuumed, but daily heated by sun streaming in through dirty windows, was just shy of assaultive. The equally crusty clerk was unruffled by the straight cash transaction and when he asked her for ID, she thought better of showing Dinah's, wanting to only use it when absolutely necessary. This didn't feel like that time. She told him she had lost her ID in a fire and hadn't replaced it yet. He raised an eyebrow, but lowered it quickly when she slid an extra twenty his way.

"Sorry to hear that," was his response as he pocketed the bill. "Just need you to sign the register then. That'll be fine."

Julia looked at him blankly, then noticed the Guns & Ammo magazine that was open on the desk; her eyes lit on an advertisement. She signed herself *Julia Winchester*.

Once in her room, she immediately set about unwrapping her loose bandages, the newly formed leather of pink scars, still so fragile. She awkwardly applied the lotion that Marilee had packed for her, struggled to rewrap The Wound, took an Ativan, chugged some water and laid down on the bed. She fell asleep almost instantly.

Over the next forty-eight hours she repeated the process, zombie-like, eating vending machine food, until she was finally rested.

Feeling stronger and hungry for a real meal, she ventured out to the local grocery, The Liberty Handy Mart. There she purchased water, apples, peanut butter, granola bars, beef jerky, a couple of area maps and the local newspaper. On her way out, just because she knew Justin would have been appalled, she bought a hot dog with all the fixings.

It was midafternoon and the street looked no different from when she had arrived two days prior. On her way back, she passed a pickup with a FOR SALE sign. She walked slowly around it, taking in its multitude of features: a Ford F150 sporting a washed out blue-green color with a bold black and brushed-aluminum stripe across the tailgate.

The camper shell had been white at one time, long ago, but had settled into a hue reminiscent of burnt milk. The dings were evenly distributed with no part of the teal body unscathed. The rear wheel wells had a hint of rust along the edges and the front passenger-side fender sported a dent equal to a Thanksgiving serving bowl. Peeking through the windows revealed a rough and tumble décor that did justice to the exterior package. It was ugly, not quite old enough to be cool again. It was perfect.

Julia found a shady bench further down the same block and pulled out The Liberty Bell daily paper, dated the day before, and started to read. An hour went by before the truck's owner appeared. She approached him as he was loading bags onto the passenger seat.

"Excuse me," she ventured timidly. "Is this your truck?"

"Sure is. Who wants to know?" he said, with full twang. He was built like the truck: strong, stocky and the worse for wear. His lower lip sported a bulge of chewing tobacco. The crown on his hat was tall and his mustache Fu-Manchu. She couldn't be certain, but she was pretty sure the shaggy hair hanging out the back of his hat was attached to a mullet. He turned to look at her, eyed her top to bottom, his brow creased in confusion.

Julia dropped her eyes, realizing for the first time what she must look like. A week on the road in her Designs by Dinah wardrobe, hair in an unwashed ponytail, she was pale and gaunt. Still, she took a breath and persevered.

"I'd like to buy your truck."

"Doesn't look like you're in the position for acquisitions." He smiled at his own rhyme, and continued loading his bags.

"What's your price?" she asked, trying to sound confident.

"$3000."

"Cash okay?" she said, knowing it would get his attention to either get serious or laugh her off as a kook.

The big Texan turned back to her suddenly, and raising his hand declared, "Cash is king!" The phrase rang as if he'd said if before, and repeated it often.

"Excellent." Her voice sounded shaky. He eyed her warily and she fought the overwhelming urge to flee. "What's in the back?"

The Texan scowled, but moved to the rear of the truck and opened the back camper window to reveal a smorgasbord of hunting, fishing and construction paraphernalia.

"I wasn't expecting to sell her today."

Julia gaped as she eyed the load. "I see that." Then mustering an additional spark of confidence said, "How 'bout this...I give you another $500, you clean it out right here, and sign the pink slip."

The Texan raised his eyebrows, looked her over again, not sure what to think.

"You wanted by the law or something?"

His tone was joking, but Julia blanched. She quickly moved to cover her reaction by walking toward her groceries and begin to gather them up. "One time offer," she said over her shoulder. Then, astounding herself with her own cheek added, "I'm sure there's plenty of trucks in Texas that need buying."

When the Texan said, "Hey there, hold on—", she knew she had a deal.

The transaction proceeded from there without a hitch. His name was Jimmy Silveira, born and raised in town. He worked over at the gas station, and of his three trucks, this was the one that most needed selling. Julia didn't take that as an especially good sign, but figured as long as it was running, it could get her someplace—wherever that might be. The truck would eliminate her need for buses, and the camper, her need to check into motels. Suddenly she felt stronger.

As she pulled away from the curb, the view in her rearview mirror of Jimmy Silveira standing on Main Street next to a huge pile of manly crap allowed her a moment of uncharacteristic pride.

Julia had first noticed the ghosts in the hospital, but never thought they would outlast the big drugs. She had assumed they were a side effect of the morphine cocktails she was given day after day. In the beginning, she thought they were real people, sitting or standing quietly off to the side of a room. Some would look directly at her, others would stare out into the void. They would only speak in spurts of dialogue and were never conversational. It was like there was only one tape loaded, and it ran on whatever single loop they had left.

She had figured it out on one of the last weeks at Grady. There had been a kid a few doors down. Quentin. He was sixteen and had burns over two-thirds of his body from a BBQ accident. The right side of his face was bandaged, but he was able to speak and both of his eyes were still alive with expression. Compatriots in suffering, they would keep each other company waiting for their different therapy sessions. He was always positive and didn't complain, ever. He set the bar high when it came to courage and Julia endeavored to match him.

One afternoon, she woke up to find him sitting in the visitor's chair beside her bed. He looked radiant, all traces of struggle and pain gone; he was glowing youth. Julia was incredulous at his amazing recovery. "Quentin, you're better! You're...healed! How? I'm so happy for you!" Quentin just smiled back with the purest love in his eyes. "I'm so happy for you," she repeated. "You can go home now."

"Julia?" It was the senior day nurse, Meg, standing beside her now, holding her hand and pressing gently.

"Oh Meg, isn't it a miracle? Quentin, he's so much better!"

"Julia...dear, you're dreaming. We didn't want to upset you, but Quentin passed away yesterday. You know how he had been fighting that infection...remember?" Nurse Meg's voice trailed off.

"What? But he's right here," Julia said, looking into the eyes of her bright, perfect comrade. Quentin leaned forward on his elbows, still radiant and meeting her gaze straight on. She felt the warmth of his gaze flow over her. Nurse Meg's seasoned eyes darted quickly around the room, then she smiled and gently swept a piece of Julia's red hair back behind her ear, and repeated that Julia was imagining things. Quentin had died, he was gone.

Julia knew enough not to argue with Nurse Meg, who was the sternest of them all; old school, matronly, with a no-nonsense bedside manner. Julia had always appreciated her honesty. You knew where you stood with Nurse Meg and she didn't treat Julia like a child.

Quentin sat with her until she went back to sleep and then would show up occasionally over the next couple of weeks. He seemed to know when she was low, his energy bolstering her, the same as it did when he was alive.

One morning, as the escape drew closer and she knew no one was listening, she told him what she was planning and that she would be leaving soon. Julia thanked him for all of his help. She told Quentin how he had been the difference more than once between despair and perseverance. He got up, shimmering in the fluorescent light, and walked out of her room. She watched as he passed in front of the nurses' station where the only one that looked up was Nurse Meg. *Could she see him after all?* But the veteran nurse went back to her paperwork. Quentin looked back and gave Julia one last dazzling smile, then disappeared through the double doors of the ward.

She had seen others as well, like the old man who had strolled through her room only to turn around twice and walk out again. She hoped he wasn't still lost.

In the ambulance on the night of the fire, she vaguely remembered there had been a young woman who sat on the end of her gurney as they rode. Of course, Julia had been barely conscious at the time. The woman had sat with her hands on her knees, her eager eyes searching for something beyond the back door windows. She didn't seem upset, but it seemed to Julia that the key to the woman's resolution lay somewhere out the back of that ambulance. At the time, Julia was so drugged she assumed that this stranger was another patient being transported to the hospital. Looking back now, Julia realized how ridiculous it would have been to have someone hitching a ride. The woman was a ghost. Had she been able, Julia would have noted her as the first, a harbinger of the life ahead of her; a community that she now found herself a member of.

None of this scared Julia. She accepted these spirits or ghosts or

THERE WAS A FIRE

imaginings, as part of the new landscape she was negotiating, and in a way, she found them comforting.

Then there was the boy who ran up and down the aisle of the Greyhound. Brown-eyed with dark unruly locks, he looked no more than five. He would laugh as he ran. Contagious five-year-old-boy laughter. So much so, that she found herself giggling along with him. She had pushed herself up on the armrests to see who his parents were, then realized she was the only one enjoying his antics. There was no mother or father interested in gathering him back into the seat next to them. After a while, he settled down and would sit in different empty seats throughout the fifteen-hour ride. One time, he plopped down in the seat next to her. She noticed that his fingernails were five-year-old-boy dirty. She leaned over and playfully whispered in his ear, "Time to wash up for dinner."

She could smell his five-year-old-boy smell, a mixture of grass stains, lake mud and bologna sandwiches. He smelled of innocence. He reached out to her with a glittering hand, and rested it on top of hers. She could feel the warmth, but not the weight of it or the touch of his skin. She shuddered. Then he sprang out of his seat to terrorize the aisle with his infectious laughter again, her fellow travelers oblivious to his unmitigated joy.

There were times when she had to question whether someone was real or not. But after a while, she could tell the difference. The ghosts always had a soft shimmering to their skin and eyes that reflected light, as if it was emanating from inside them. She got good at sorting them out and came to accept them as just another layer in her new life. The better she got at identifying them, the more she realized they were just about everywhere. She would play a game in crowds, challenging herself to see how many she could spot.

The ghosts could be mischievous and playful, or pensive, even solemn. But she noted, they never seemed sad or angry. Certainly not evil, like the movies would have had her believe. Overall, they seemed surprisingly content. The malevolent ghost stories of countless girlhood campfires, finally proven false.

She rarely spoke to them, choosing instead to co-exist in a respectful way. And of course, she never spoke about them, not to anyone.

The new truck owner drove directly to the massive self-service car wash she remembered seeing as the bus rolled into town two days prior. Much to The Wound's instant dismay, she pulled in and went to work. First, she dragged out the floor mats that she was sure hadn't been moved since the truck was minted in 1980 and threw them in the trash. The vacuum did its share of the initial debris removal as she archeologically sucked up each stratified layer of Texas grime. The blue vinyl seats worked to her advantage, as she cranked the water temp as high as it would go and blasted a steaming stream on the interior, point blank. From the front bumper to the Texas Truck license plate, she spared no amount of soap and towels, going after every corner right down to the ashtray, *Disgusting!* And the glove box, *Did he keep roadkill in here?* The Wound was pitching a full fit in response to this sudden burst of activity, but for the first time she pushed on, working through the shooting pains.

Finally, satisfied that every speck of filth that could be dislodged was now gone, she next found a drugstore and purchased what equated to a couple gallons of spray cleaner with bleach. There in the parking lot, she went after the truck again, inch-by-inch, finally using alcohol prep pads for the bright work on the dashboard.

Five hours after she had purchased it, she had transformed the battered old truck to an—if not fully sterile—at least livable environment.

The Wound's shrieking could no longer be ignored. It was all she could do to get herself back to the hotel and into her room, the throbbing almost blinding her now. She took a pain pill, dove into the shower and gave herself the same treatment she had just given the truck. Her hair washed, The Wound lotioned and bandaged, she took a second pill and lay down on the bed. Fourteen hours later Julia awakened in the exact position she had fallen.

She rose up sore from head to toe. It wasn't just The Wound protesting now, but all the muscles that had been idle in the past months. She took some Demerol and hobbled around the room to pull together some outfit that made her look less like a cruise ship refugee. Her hair was thick and curly from going to bed with it wet. Wholly unruly, she gathered it into a ponytail, feeling the tight skin stretch between her shoulder blades as she coaxed her thick auburn hair into the elastic.

A couple doors down from the motel, was a diner. She sat at a small table in the back and ordered coffee and poached eggs on toast. The waitress was friendly and Julia allowed herself to indulge in the first real conversation since leaving Atlanta. During their light chatter, Julia realized how isolated she had kept herself, so necessary, but this was nice. Even in anonymity, she liked what little connection it offered. The outcome was some key local knowledge Julia would need to finish the work she had started the day before.

Two blocks down on the right, she found what she was looking for. As she walked up to The Doll House, she saw a stout, well-endowed woman in black stretch pants and black T-shirt with pink crystal studs surrounding its low neckline, as well as outlining the head and whiskers of a kitten. The woman was attempting to unlock the front door.

"Excuse me," said Julia, tentatively.

"Uh huh?" said the woman without looking up, still jiggling the stubborn lock. It was then Julia noticed the hot pink highlights in her flaming red hair. The hair stack was teased and propped up in a manner that made you feel that a hurricane could try, but be defeated in any attempt to blow it down. She fought the urge to flee.

"I heard down at the diner that sometimes you take walk-ins."

"I surely do," she said. The door lurched open from the combination of perfect key position and the weight of her full form pressing against it. She waved Julia in, and turned the sign from *Sorry We Missed You!* to *Come On In!*

"One sec," she said, as the woman walked to the back and flipped a panel of light switches, causing the beauty parlor and its air conditioning to leap to life.

There were six stations with large mirrors, each lit now by a bank of globe lights. The ceiling sported two hanging chandeliers with clear Plexiglas prisms that Julia assumed were meant to pass for crystal. Over the sound system Vince Gill was crooning, *"I still believe in you."* The color scheme was white and taupe with accents of pink and black. The Doll House was open and ready for business.

The woman returned to stand in front of her, hands on her bountiful hips. "Hi, hon. I'm Dolly, what are we doing today?"

"New color. Blonde."

"Oh! *Quelle damage!*" she said, in some cross between Texan and French. "But your hair is such a pretty color now! You realize this is an all-day process, right? Not just a single dye job, but we are gonna have to first get you to almost white in order to get you to blonde."

Julia lied and nodded her head, realizing that in fact, she actually had no idea what the change entailed.

"I've spent many a day trying to deliver your rich red to some of my clients—why, they would hunt you down and shoot you and me too, if they knew what you were up to! Now why would you want to do that?" She sounded very sincere in her love of good hair color.

"Bad break up...need a change," was the rare truth Julia told. And it seemed to be the perfect answer, because Dolly kicked into high gear.

"Well, say no more! What's your name, hun?"

"Ju—," she almost answered, before remembering the name she signed on the motel register. "People call me Win," she recovered.

"Well Win, take a seat and let's see what we've got here."

After the initial consult, choosing a color and some last gushing comments on her pretty auburn shade, Dolly went off to mix her concoction and left Julia to look at herself in the mirror.

She was emaciated. Her eyes had become sunken, and her skin sallow. She was so thin now! Justin had always commented on her weight—never thin enough, never fit enough. She wondered what he would say now. Would it be enough? *Of course not*, came the swift answer in her head. Nothing would ever have been enough.

Six hours later, the transformation was complete. Dolly's version of blonde was a little more platinum than Julia had anticipated, but what did she expect? She was in Texas. The overall effect was jolting when it was all blown out into soft waves that fell just below her shoulders. Julia couldn't quite take in the change, she couldn't see *herself* in the reflection. They took a moment looking into the big mirror, Dolly's highly coifed bright red hair-do directly above Julia's stark blonde tresses. Dolly looked proud of her creation and Julia praised her work, appropriate to the effort and care she had been given.

"Now then, that's done, and beautiful, if I do say so. Now... what're we going to do about the clothes?"

Julia was once again keenly aware of how dowdy and even ridiculous her outfit was. More retirement home than new-blonde-on-a-road-trip. Somehow still game for more changes, she replied, "You know, you're right, Dolly. Where do I go to fit in around here?

I'm going to need some guidance." As she said it, she immediately prayed that Dolly was not going to recommend herself for this cause.

"Say no more!" She was gleeful, anxious for the transformation to be complete. "I'll call over to Baughman's just over on Second Street. Tania should be waiting when you get there. It's the closest thing to high fashion you'll find around here, but if you want to fit in, there's no better place to get outfitted. You'll need to hurry though, they close at six."

Julia paid and thanked her but didn't escape without Dolly giving her a huge hug. The Wound screamed a warning as Julia was almost consumed by Dolly's voluminous bosom. As she scurried her way over to Baughman's Western Wear, she wondered what a "fitting in" wardrobe entailed, and fought the urge to laugh out loud when she pictured her new blonde self in Dolly's pink crystal kitten shirt.

Apparently not much had changed in Western attire since her summers on her grandparents' dairy farm in Wisconsin. She opted for the plainest shirts of soft chambray and plaids; the mother-of-pearl snaps and scalloped yokes being their only adornments. Of course a bra was out of the question. The Wound would never have tolerated the imposition. For the first time, she was thankful for her small breasts and bought the shirts with extra room so they would be just another of her many secrets. The jeans had to be Wranglers and had to be long.

"Down to the ground," Tania had educated her. "That way they still cover your heel when you bend your knees to ride." Julia covertly smirked at the thought of The Wound on top of a horse.

As she walked to the register she paused at the long row of cowboy hats stacked in perfect rows according to fabric, brim and crown. Tania caught her smile and sashayed over. "Hold on. I'm good at this," she muttered. Tania's brow furrowed in deep concentration, before finally choosing a hat and regally placing it on Win's head.

"There," Tania said. "Very punchy. Told you I was good at this." With that, the self-satisfied clerk returned to the check-out counter and continued to ring up the rest of Julia's purchases.

Despite its surprise-landing on top of her head, Julia instantly loved the hat. It was a cream-colored molded straw with a medium crown and a wide brim. *Punchy* indeed.

A half an hour after her entry into Baughman's, Win emerged with an armload of bags, wearing her new favorite hat and cowboy boots. It was then that she felt the true value of the hat; privacy. With her new blonde hair pulled behind her ears, sunglasses on, and crown pulled down tight, she walked the streets of Liberty feeling the safety of its cover.

Win's grandpa was a farmer and her grandma a farmer's wife. He tended the cows, the milking, the handy work and all the heavy lifting. Grandma grew the garden, fed the workers, kept house and raised the children. Win hadn't thought of those summers in years, even though she had always kept that picture of her prize-winning heifer on her dressing table. She had disconnected herself from that little girl who was so self-confident and headstrong. The nine-year-old in the photo would never have believed the events that would bring her to this street in a hot, dusty Texas town. Win was newly ashamed that the young girl's promise had been wasted. She remembered how the photo had burned so quickly, dissolving in front of her. But the naïve exuberance of the red-headed farm girl had died years before.

Huffing and puffing, her wind still not with her, she toted her purchases back to the motel room. It was near dusk now and the day's glow was waning, but still peeking through the dreary, drawn drapes. All was quiet, except the muffled TV sit-com from the room next door. She sat on the bed and couldn't help but peer into the mirror directly across from her.

Its frame held a woman, blonde, thin, harrowed and haunted, who was staring her down. *So this is me now? This...thing?*

The woman was ugly. A stranger. She looked so sad. She held the same pallor as the ghosts that wove their way in and out of her world, except without the inner fire. Had she died along with Quentin? Was this all that was left? The Ugly?

She stared back at the pathetic woman, locked in a test of wills until finally, simultaneously, they both broke, screaming into their fists, dissolving into tears, falling onto the cheap bedding, writhing with sobs of despair. Mourning the death of Julia; the end of her life, her friendships, her home.

The sobs turned angry and she pounded her fists, tearing at the sheets. She had been so *useless*. She had lived with a monster and— stayed! She had done this, and it was born of her own weakness. She had fallen from a life of happiness into one of fear and shadows. She hated Justin, but she hated herself more. She deserved this. The Ugly.

She cried for herself then, letting the self-pity swallow her whole. The Wound relished her torment, agreeing and spurring her on. As she thrashed, it pulled, threatening to rip open at the edges. The tears almost choked her; her body writhed in spasms of grief. She had not killed herself, her weakness wouldn't allow for it, but Julia was dead just the same.

She lay there, until finally she had exhausted all of what needed to come out. Her whimpering finally gave way to sleep. The kind of sleep that harbored no dreams, no relief, only darkness.

She woke in the early dawn to a fog that had settled inside the dingy room. Her eyes were almost swollen shut from the prior night's tears. She crawled into the shower and stood, her arms braced against tiles that had long been in need of bleach and a scrub brush. The Wound felt numb, a lesion attached, but not connected.

Yet even though it bore no senses, no acknowledgement of touch, she could feel The Wound hanging there. It was suffocating. She stood motionless as the water went from hot, to warm, to ice-cold. She stood still as a statue, until her shaking became so pronounced that it was all she could do to shut off the water and stumble back to bed and under the covers. As her body temperature recovered, she found herself diving deeply into the warmth of the threadbare sheets and she slept hard again. This time her sleep allowed for respite and unknowingly, she dreamt of a warm day.

Win's eyes didn't open again until two o'clock in the afternoon. Without fanfare, this time she got up, dressed in her newest Texas attire and without the aid of a mirror, smoothed her hair back and pulled on her cowboy hat. She packed up her room and put her expanding worldly possessions in the cab. Then she fired up the truck for three more errands.

The first was an automotive store, where she bought oil, an oil funnel, a gas can, five gallons of water, new floor mats and sheepskin seat covers. Again she installed the covers right there in the parking lot. The Wound purred in appreciation the first time she leaned back.

Next, Julia pulled into The Bed Barn just south of town on Highway 146. Twenty minutes later she was followed out to the truck by two men carrying a small mattress that they loaded into the truck-bed inside the camper shell. After she tipped them, they eyed her warily as she sped out of the parking lot. They knew, like the rest of the people of Liberty, that there was more to the story of this blonde scarecrow of a woman, dressed now in gear that still sported the manufacturer's shipping creases. The hint of desperation in her tone of voice made them want to help her, but the aura of damage that surrounded her let them know not to ask.

Last stop was Bed, Bath and Beyond, where she bought a small cooler to keep on the passenger side floor to hold provisions for her drive. She also bought a mattress pad, flannel sheets, blankets and a couple of pillows, the anti-bacterial kind. She made up her bed, discarding the packaging in the garbage can next to the store's entrance.

Her time in Liberty was done.

As she drove the F150 down Main Street and out of town, she caught her own eye in the rearview mirror. With her right hand she adjusted it to take in more of the blonde stranger that looked back at her. The crow's feet in the corner crinkled as half a smile crossed her face, one of just a few she had allowed herself since leaving Atlanta. The blue eye sparked an acknowledgement of recognition. Like an old friend, after a long absence. She pressed the pedal down and headed north.

CHAPTER 4

Beyond the fact that she kept the truck cleaner than any of the roadside motels, the camper-truck setup worked like a charm. For the next few weeks, Win just drifted, moving through Texas, the Panhandle and into Colorado.

Texas had been her appetite's wake-up call. She had consumed with abandon the hot guts sausages and slaw in Elgin, then drove headlong into the beefsteak BBQ with deep fried corn in Tioga. In Colorado Springs, she found bliss in an old school hamburger with chopped onions, BBQ sauce and dare-she-do-it...*Velveeta*, alongside the signature shoestring fries which she fortified with mayonnaise and ketchup. Further up the road in Morrison, she swooned over a buffalo steak that made her sad for vegetarians worldwide.

She was rediscovering food. Calories and carbohydrates were no longer something to be counted, but celebrated. She found herself ferreting out the house specialty and diving in with every long-neglected taste bud. Even The Wound was temporarily mollified as the muscles beneath its ravaged flesh rolled in appreciation.

The first time she laughed out loud was driving by one of the many Waffle House restaurants that dotted the highways of Texas. This one had a sign proclaiming: *It's 2AM: Still time for one more bad decision.* The sound of her laughter took her by surprise, she couldn't remember the last time she had heard it. The last time she had dared. At the very least it had been months...*had it been years?*

She would always start out early. The local diners usually opened around 5:30 or 6:00AM. She would fortify herself with some combination of eggs, baked goods and the strongest coffee she could find, then hit the road. Even with the plush seat covers, she had to sit forward on the truck's bench seat, a posture she mastered as the odometer measured the miles.

She was careful to stay on the secondary state roads and rarely traveled the interstates. She would drive until she felt like stopping. Usually by mid-afternoon she was ready to find her roost for the night. Mostly she found herself in campgrounds. They had facilities and no one thought twice about a woman crawling in and out of a camper shell. In the process she had seen some beautiful country, picking her way through the big square states of the central West.

She couldn't help feeling conspicuous in her new blonde hair, which was ironic since in reality she was actually hiding-out. In hindsight, she acknowledged that maybe platinum wasn't the smartest choice when trying to blend in. On the few times she chose to interact, she noticed that people treated her differently, perhaps more sympathetically, as if it was a given that she would need help. All her life as a rich redhead she hadn't garnered that same response. There had been an assumption of independence and smarts, along with the hot temper, of course. At least, until Justin.

At some point she realized that even with her new blonde mystique, overall she barely registered with people. She had a hard time getting waitresses' attention and regularly got seated next to the kitchen. When someone would pass through a door ahead of her, they rarely held it. Men in general dismissed her, younger people tended to go about their business over and around her. Mothers, of course, were too consumed with their children to notice anything or anybody.

It was the older women, her age and above, that she had an effect on. Not to interact, but to assess. More often than not, they would take stock, head-to-toe in a flash, a vague question registering on their faces.

After a time, she realized the truth of what was happening. It wasn't the aura of battered wife and burn victim that turned people away from her; she was middle-aged, she was alone. She was plain (except for the incongruous Monroe hair), still frail from her injuries and fourteen years of severe dieting. She didn't allow for much eye contact and kept conversation to a minimum. This seemed to suit all parties fine. She felt, in a word, *invisible* and there was no mantle of golden hair that would make up for the fact that in society's eyes, she was irrelevant.

She did find a traveling companion. Most unexpectedly, it turned out to be The Wound. She listened as it sang to her with its constant low-decibel level of pain, only yielding to it when it moved into full chorus. It caused her to see things she would have otherwise missed had it not been for it pulling on her to stop for the day. She found herself trusting its guidance and listening more and more intently as their journey wore on.

Win was on Highway 34 just outside of the Rocky Mountain National Park when the ominous sputtering and burning smell began emanating from under the hood. The ride through the Rockies had been breathtaking. The majesty of snow-capped peaks forcing their will against an improbably blue sky was juxtaposed perfectly against the vertigo-inducing drop off the side of the two-lane road. Adrenaline had shot through her with each hairpin turn. Her senses were keen as she made her way down the winding road; attention rapt, every muscle taut. Even The Wound fell silent in reverence to the task at hand.

The old Ford had struggled, but muscled through its heightened endeavor. Until now.

In hindsight, Julia assumed she had missed some dial pointing into a red zone. She limped the truck onto the shoulder and gently (always gently) slid down from the bench seat. Drawing on the memory of her father and then Henry, after some fiddling, she was able to pop the hood. Holding a T-shirt for protection, she released the radiator cap and a geyser of steam was released. Thus resigned, she settled in to wait for a Samaritan.

Initially, help came in the form of a woman, about her age, broad and bold, dressed in her own version of the Wranglers and hat uniform. But she was pressed for time and after calling for a tow truck, left her there alone to wait.

Her true Samaritan arrived with the tow truck. Tony the Rat's Auto Emporium was blazoned on its side. After introducing himself—yes, it was Tony the Rat himself—he worked swiftly and hitched up her disabled home-on-wheels to the back of the rig.

She climbed into the cab beside him and noted the Top-Siders sticking out from beneath his coveralls. In a flash she was thrown back into a memory of her Henry. He had always worn the sturdy boat shoes. For everything. Work or going to dinner, they were his staple. He liked that they were made in the US. They were all comfort and quality, much like the man himself. She allowed herself a rare smile at the memory, then forced her mind back into the cluttered cab of the tow truck.

After a small stretch of road she said, "So, Tony Rat huh?"

"Short for Rathbone. Rat is better for business."

"Huh. I wouldn't have guessed that."

"Anytime you can make someone stop and remember your name, it's better for business. My wife, who considers herself sort of a master of marketing, has assured me this is so."

"So it's working?"

"Hard to say for sure. Don't have anything to compare it to. Not like I have another store named *Tony's* or just *The Auto Emporium*, or *Rathbone's Car Repair, Rat's Car Spa*—if I had all those going, I'd be able to tell you for certain the true way to go. My wife calls that marketing research." Tony the Rat sighed.

Julia gave a small grin. "Do you mind if I ask you why you're wearing boat shoes? Haven't seen many of those out here."

"Well, you're right about that. But they give a good grip on things. I find them the best qualified footwear when perched on a bumper." With that, Julia gave him an out-and-out full smile and settled in for the rest of the ride to town.

As they pulled into Granby, Colorado, they took a left off the main drag and one side street later pulled into the Auto Emporium proper. She saw an assortment of cars and pickups in different states of disrepair. The central attraction was a two-story corrugated building that housed two working bays with an office attached on the side. Both of the bay doors were open revealing a green sports car up on a lift and some kind of a minivan next door. The Tony the Rat's Auto Emporium sign was stilted high on the roof. She estimated it added another story's worth of height to the snug town lot.

As Tony the Rat was taking her truck off the hitch, she got down to business. "So what are we looking at here?"

"Well, let me nose around under the hood and we'll see where we're at."

Suddenly famished, she asked, "Any place to get a sandwich around here?"

"The H Bar B should be opening up soon. Just around the corner. I recommend the pulled pork. I'll come find you when I've got an assessment."

"Can't wait," she mumbled sarcastically. She idly wondered if there would be any single-woman-on-the-road-alone up-charge attached to the "assessment". She went to the truck, grabbed her wallet and pulled her hat down low on her forehead.

Julia strolled back to the main street where the vertical street sign stated, Agate Avenue. She stood before the exterior of the H-B Bar. She would soon find out it was called the "H-Bar-Bee-Bar". Painted on the windows was a list of all the goods and services

43

you could apparently find inside. They were, in order: *Cigars, Live Music, Dancing, Tools, Dry Goods, Post Office, Jack Daniels, Penny Candy.* She sucked in a deep breath and stepped inside.

Taking a moment for her eyes to adjust, she noted a substantial wooden bar that lined one entire side of the large square room. Clearly, the general store content advertised on the windows had given way to a more singular focus long ago. The bar was old-style: brass boot rail, stools, a mirror spanning the wall behind it with shining bottles of booze tiered in front. A couple dozen tables surrounded a worn dance floor and a small stage where a band was wandering in and starting to set up.

She walked to the stool nearest the front door and gently slid onto the worn leather seat. A stack of newspapers sat near her. She reached over, giving a small wince at the stretch and settled in to await Tony the Rat's verdict.

The bartender arrived a few minutes later. "What can I get you today?'"

"Rumor has it the pulled pork is a winner."

"And to drink?"

Win eyed the tap handles. "Anything local? Kind of light?"

"You might try the Wooly Booger, made by Grand Lake here in town—doesn't get much more local than that."

"Sold," she said, smiling at the outrageous name. As she watched him draw the pint, Win squelched the natural question of how it was named, but as usual, she didn't venture in. She closed her eyes as the first sip of frothy amber liquid hit the back of her throat. It was perfect. Cold and quenching. She smiled her appreciation at the bartender, but opening her eyes, realized he was gone.

Beginning to relax, she settled into her paper. First she noted the date—three weeks since she had read the day old paper in Liberty. *Who knew?*

Then a voice said, "I just can't get used to women wearing hats inside."

Julia looked up to see a man standing midway down the bar. She hadn't noticed him come in. Had he been there all along? He stood, still as stone, with one boot up on the rail, reading his paper. She wouldn't have thought the voice was his; he made no acknowledgement of her, yet he was the only one in the room. Well whoever he was, she was too tired to let him rile her.

Without so much as a nod in his direction or a motion to remove her hat, she answered him in the same tone. "I can see how you'd feel that way." She continued to focus on the newspaper, although now she was no longer reading, distracted by his rude—*Was it rude?*—well at the very least, strange comment.

She waited, and when she was certain he wasn't looking she stole a glance, and managed a head-to-toe assessment. He was older, chiseled, tough. He wore a hat—*Of course!*—a grey felt wide brim, a quilted nylon vest, work shirt, Wranglers—*Of course*— and boots. All very worn and dirty, she guessed from at least a couple days work. She inspected his belt carefully. She always held that a man's belt told you his story. His was hand-tooled brown leather, with a simple silver setup and keeper. Not too fancy but of fine quality. He also had a six-inch knife in a sheath on his side.

Assessing cowboys was an old skill that she found easy to dust off. Up until she graduated, the summers she spent on her grandparents' dairy farm had allowed her access, not only to the dairy and farming world, but to the ranch world as well. As a hormone-bursting teen she had honed the skill of determining the difference between rodeo cowboys, working cowboys and drugstore cowboys. He was working. There was a time, a lifetime ago, when that would have sparked her. She was someone else now.

Her non-response hung in the air until she wasn't sure she had even said it. By the time her sandwich arrived—it was as good as rumored—she got interested in eating and actually reading her paper. *Whatever.*

The clock moved like drying cement. The afternoon sifted into evening one minute at a time. Other folks, mostly men, drifted in after a day's work. A spare few gave her a sideways glance; she assumed they pretty much knew everyone in town, and she wasn't from town. *Where is Tony the Rat?* She was just about ready to go find him, when he came bustling through the door.

"Got you all done."

"What? But I thought you would let me know before you started. What happened to the *assessment?*"

"Sure, yes, but they were such little matters. I just plowed ahead."

She eyed him warily, "How little?"

"Well let's see, there were the air hose, radiator leak, fluid fill, oil change—you were way overdue—and fan belt. All in stock, all installed, all working."

Still suspicious, "Really. And how much are you going to fleece me for all that?"

"Parts and labor, plus tax...comes to $184.26"

Julia stared in disbelief.

"Geez, I guess I should have come by and confirmed, but it being Friday and all, the day was sort of runnin' away, and I could see you were travelin' and it had to be done, whether you liked it or not, so I just forged ahead." Adding in a softer tone, "It's a fair price ma'am."

Recovering, she replied, "Yes, it is a fair price. I'm sorry. I expected because of all the things you just listed, and me being from out of town, that there might be some sort of...up-charge."

Tony the Rat smiled big. "Then I'm pleased to disappoint you Miss—I don't think I ever caught your name."

She fumbled for only a flash, she would have loved to return his honesty with some of her own, but instead she put out her hand, smiled and said, "It's Winchester, people call me Win."

"Very pleased to meet you, Win."

Reaching for her bag, she asked, "Is cash okay?"

"The best."

"Yes, I hear it's King." She smiled at her own private joke. She took two one-hundred dollar bills from her bag and handed them over, "Keep the rest." Then added, "So shines a good deed in a weary world." She knew it was a quote from *Charley and the Chocolate Factory*, but hadn't thought about it in years. It had been a favorite, long ago. "Mr. Rat, Thank you."

With a slight bow, Tony the Rat gave back her keys, "Your keys, m'lady. Just leave her in the lot until you're ready to head out." With a last ceremonial bow, he walked quickly out of the bar. His Top-Siders squeaking on the wax of the worn wood floor.

Win gathered herself up and hailed the bartender for her check. She swayed just a touch when she slid off the stool. She had been there a while and it had been months since she'd had any alcohol. She paid, thanked the bartender and walked outside.

Still musing over the virtuous Mr. Rat, she turned the corner down an alley that would lead to the Auto Emporium. She hadn't heard the footsteps closing in.

One arm seized her from behind and shoved her hard against the side of the brick building. The Wound cried out, the screeching pain made it hard for her to focus.

The first voice was high and scratchy in her ear. "We're gonna need your wallet."

She could smell alcohol on his breath. She recognized him from the bar. He stared at her with what seemed to be amber eyes. Their intensity sent a wave of fear and adrenaline through her. His buddy stood behind him. He held what she assumed was a hunting knife in his right hand. His left rested on the first man's shoulder. He stared into her eyes, reminding her in a flash of memory—*Justin*. Her knees weakened, and the alley started to spin as she felt the panic rise. She fought to take in air, but none would come, she realized she was close to passing out—and then...she did.

Win's eyes opened to find herself in what appeared to be an office. A grungy, disheveled office. Facing her directly was the sole of a boot. It rested on a coffee table and was almost worn through. Looking beyond the boot, she met the stare of the man from the bar earlier, The Hat Man. His eyes, were a cool gun-metal blue as he regarded her with an intensity that made her next breath catch in her throat.

He could have been her age or twenty years her senior. His face, as handsome as it was weathered; she instinctively knew the worn creases were not laugh lines.

With a sudden exhale, she remembered the recent events and a fresh shot of adrenaline rushed through her. She sprang up in an attempt at what, she wasn't sure, but some kind of action was clearly required. What she was sure of, was the ensuing wave of pain The Wound delivered in retaliation for the sudden movement. She blanched white and almost passed out again.

"Whoa, now," said The Hat Man, softly. "Hold on," his tone was patient, "you're okay. Just a little tussle. I sent those boys on their way. No real harm done." He held up her wallet. "You are still intact." He dropped it on the table between them. He spoke slowly, the subtle drawl was Western, different from the South, cleaner.

Still on high alert, she stuttered, "What...but...."

"You shouldn't go flashing hundred dollar bills in a place like this—gives people ideas. I had a hunch Lou and Jack might take the bait, so when they followed you out—I followed them. Convinced them to go fishing somewhere else."

"Convinced them?" She remembered the knife she had seen earlier on his belt.

"Yup." Then placing a bottle of water in front of her said, "You're gonna want to drink this."

She took the bottle and swallowed deep, then looked away from beneath the intensity of his stare. A silence fell between them.

She took a moment to absorb her surroundings. The couch

she lay on was made of a scratchy, plaid upholstery that smelled of...well, she thought it best not to define it. She saw a few stacked boxes of what looked like whiskey, and a bevy of old event posters featuring scantily clad models in the throes of enjoying the beer's "refreshing" effects. There was a desk, with files piled high that flowed into the stacks on its chair. She finally concluded she was in the manager's office of the bar she had just left, and The Hat Man had apparently come to her rescue.

"Where's my hat?" she asked, accusingly.

He smiled. "Let's get you a drink."

She was about to say thanks-but-no-thanks, but he was already gone. She got up carefully, doing a quick head-to-toe inventory as she got herself organized. Her head had a bump where it must have hit something. She opened her wallet; Dinah's cash was all still there. The Hat Man was right. *Stupid!* Carrying money around like this, not that she had another option, but she vowed to be more discreet in the future.

She found the ladies room in the hallway outside the office. Typical bar restroom. *Disgusting.* She splashed some water on her face and dried off with a paper towel that could have doubled for fine-grit sandpaper. As she went to leave, she caught a glimpse of herself in the mirror and stopped cold.

She squared off and took in her image; the blonde hair, the fine lines around her eyes, a flight of freckles across her nose, and her own cool blues staring herself down. The Wound had forced her posture to improve, a trait that in other circumstances could be construed as confidence. Not the case here. She remained a shell. How had she gotten here? She was returning from the unthinkable, but where was she now? *Is this what hope looked like?*

Too soon to tell.

She found her way back into the bar which was now bustling with all manner of folks enjoying their post work-week rituals. She fully expected The Hat Man to have vanished again, but there he was, his back to her, leaning on the bar with one boot on the rail. She allowed herself the luxury of appreciating his athletic build from behind. Below the worn grey felt hat, were strong wide shoulders that vee'd down to his hips, and a great ass. Something about a man in Wranglers that fit just right...kind of tight up top and long, all the way "down to the ground", until they bunched up on top of his boots.

She noted no Skoal ring worn through on his pocket, always a plus, and some wear marks where his spurs must rub. All in all, very nice. She felt something shift deep inside her. She put it all immediately out of her mind. Armed and ready with her thanks-but-no-thanks intentions, she stepped up beside him. On the bar, lined up like soldiers, were two beers and two shots of tequila.

"Oh, I see you already—listen...I really can't...shouldn't...I mean...I've got to get back on the road, you've been more than kind, and I know I haven't thanked you properly yet, but...I appreciate very much you helping—"

Suddenly she stopped cold, a white snake of fear crawling up her spine to the back of her neck. She saw him. Justin. *He's here!* By the door, his back was to her, talking to a couple locals. His hair, his body language, the way he flipped the collar on his shirt—*How?!* What would it take to be free of him?

She frantically looked around for an exit. Had she seen one back by the office? She felt the blood draining out of her face, out of her body. The woman with that glimmer of hope from the mirror had been on a fool's errand, thinking there was something left for her other than pain and the resounding stillness of fear.

She realized she had been holding her breath, so she desperately took in air. As if in slow motion, she saw Justin turn toward her and meet her eyes.

It wasn't him.

It's not him!

She heaved in a couple more breaths and leaned on the bar. In sweet relief, she put her hand to her forehead, almost giddy and shaking her head, not sure if laughing or crying was in order. She settled for a bit of both.

As she brought herself back to the present, she looked up and once again met the icy blue eyes of The Hat Man. He had witnessed the whole event. His stare was intense, she felt him, he could see her. She could feel the blood returning to her face and her heart beat slow up. He pushed a tequila shot her way.

"Good for ghosts."

Win looked at him, and with a tiny smile, rocked her head back and took the shot. The tequila fizzled and burned its way through a tour of her upper digestive track, her eyes watering for a new reason now, she wiped the wetness away, sputtering a quiet, "Wow."

The Hat Man slid a beer toward her. She took it eagerly and chased the sting away.

Feeling the warmth of the booze, she pulled herself back together and eased onto the bar stool. Eyeing the other shot, she said, "Your turn."

"Yup." The Hat Man made short work of the shot, then chased it with a swig from his own beer. As he downed it, the band started in on its sound check.

"Testing—Test—Test."

He called to the bartender, "Hey Duncan, another round—and some limes." Then, sizing her up, added with a small smile, "Maybe some water, too."

She wondered if he was judging the hotness in her cheeks as blushing or an alcohol related flush. She mused to herself, it was most likely both.

The next half hour was punctuated by PA squeals, random drum thumps and disembodied guitar licks.

Duncan the bartender brought the tequila, limes and water. Upon their arrival, Win inhaled deeply and took stock of the situation. She already felt a little buzzed and probably shouldn't drive.

After all, she was still occasionally taking her pain meds and whatever lingered in her system was not going to mix well with tequila. The ups and downs of this insane day could use a time-out and strangely, she felt safe with The Hat Man.

She looked at him, met his eyes with an intensity of her own, and with measured words said, "Okay, but we're going to need to slow it down...I don't get out much."

"Okay." A tension descended between them. "So, your name's Win?"

She paused, again fighting the urge to be truthful. "Yeah, short for Winchester."

"Like the gun?"

"Like the gun."

The Hat Man stood up and put out his right hand. "My name is Calder, Win. Pleased to meet you."

Win took his hand and shook. His skin made the fine grit of the paper towel feel like velvet in comparison. "Likewise, and... thanks for helping me out of my scrape...you were right about the money...it was stupid. I was lucky you happened along...you know those guys? The one man's eyes were—I don't know...they were gold."

"Jack and Lou Potter. Local trash. Always looking for a shortcut, still live with their mother, poor woman."

Win nodded.

The band finally sorted itself out and started in with their version of *Amarillo by Morning*.

Calder stood, gave a long stretch, then held out his hand. "Two-step much?"

Win smiled at the thought, and replied sarcastically, "No, not much."

"Ever?"

"About a hundred years ago."

He still had his hand out, as she considered him, hat to boots, deciding. Then she reached over and shot down the tequila that had been lined up. Calder followed suit, they each took a long pull on the limes and then the beers. After giving her wallet to Duncan for safe keeping, he led Win to the dance floor.

She turned to face him. He placed his hand gently on her left shoulder and raised her right hand up in his left. She tentatively took her free hand outside his embrace and rested it on his bicep. Hard as stone.

Without speaking he moved into her while gently but firmly moving her backwards around the perimeter. The floor boards were shiny with wear; years of wax and boot grime. There were two other couples now, moving counter-clockwise with them. She was trying to remember how and when to do what, but they still weren't quite in sync.

"Shhhh. Stop thinking," he whispered in her ear, "I got you."

With that she exhaled, felt a rush of tequila mix with the music and lights now blurrily going by. She let him shuffle her across the floor. The edges of the room softened as she let herself glide. Before she knew it, the song had ended and he was leading her back to the bar. She settled herself up on the stool where she took grateful advantage of the tall glass of water that had been refilled.

"So what brings you around here, besides a blown radiator hose and an oil change?"

Win cocked her head sideways, "You don't miss much, do you?"

"Try not to."

"So you're the manager here?"

"Nope."

"Then you must live around here...you seem to know all the key players...." She raised her eyebrow, an expression she hadn't dared use in years.

''Nope. I just come through quite a bit. Seems like this place is always on my way. After twenty years of passing through you tend to know folks. You didn't answer the question."

Win looked at him quizzically, pretending she didn't know what the question was, buying time. She hadn't formulated an answer yet. Finally she responded, "I'm looking for work."

"What kind of work?"

"I haven't quite figured that out yet." She almost laughed.

"That's gonna slow the process up."

"Most likely." She smiled and looked down at the bar.

"What kind of work do you do?"

Again, Win worked hard on an answer, she hadn't gotten that far in her escape plan. "Hard to say, really."

"Well, what do you like to do?"

Then after a pause and a small realization, "I like to cook."

"Okay, then." He slapped his leathered hand on the bar. "What kind of cooking?"

"All kinds...Thai, Southwestern, French, even Swedish." With the final cuisine she made a distasteful face. "I've studied," she added almost proudly.

"Restaurant? Chef?" He sounded impressed.

"No, no...too public." She caught herself, realizing it was an odd response. "I mean, I'm not that good."

"Well, hell, I know a place in need of a cook. You might not get to use all those fancy cuisines, but if you can muster the strength to fill the bellies of nine smelly, hungry cowboys, three squares a day, I'll bet they'd be pleased to have you."

Win made a dubious face. "How do you know about it?"

"I—came through the place about a week ago, they said to keep my eyes open. They've been without a decent cookie for months." Conspiratorially, he added, "You'd be a shoo-in."

"Is it far?"

"A two hour's drive toward Saratoga up in Wyoming, about a half hour outside of town." He took a pen off the bar and wrote down the address on a cocktail napkin. "Don't be late." His eyes never left hers as he folded the napkin and slowly slipped it into her front pocket.

She would have asked him what he meant, but suddenly her heart was beating so loud that she couldn't imagine speaking over its drumming. She felt her cheeks flush bright red.

Just then, the band launched into *She's Country*, clearly a crowd favorite, a real grinder and she and Calder were just drunk enough to do it justice. They pressed together in a slow burn, him holding her close, moving her with him, moving as one. At one point Calder put his hand square on her back. The Wound took immediate offense and protested under the pressure. She moved his hand down below her belt line, which he took as encouragement. He slid his fingers inside her back pocket and pulled her in even closer.

As the alcohol took on a larger role, the evening became more a sequence of vignettes than a stream. There was more dancing, more tequila, his hand on her neck, he moved a blonde stray hair away from her forehead and tucked it behind her ear. Then moving his mouth in behind it whispered, "Like spun gold."

She threw her head back to laugh, a response that seemed to surprise them both.

Win pulled him close again, not revealing that her blonde hair was as much a novelty to her as it was to him.

It was late into the night when Calder led her from the dance floor, through the crowd and toward the door. As they passed by the bar, Duncan handed over her wallet and from somewhere produced her long-lost hat. They walked, at first unsteadily, out the front door, down the street and toward her truck.

The cool night air washed over them, calming the levity they had been feeling inside the bar. Their footsteps fell easy and, without intention, matched the other's stride. They passed under the soft glow of the streetlights without conversation. The only shift was his hand tightening around hers. With both heads slightly bowed beneath the brim of their hats, they walked in quiet tandem to what the night would offer next.

Win stood behind her truck, raised the window, then un-latched and lowered the tailgate. Calder glanced inside. Even in the poor light of the auto-yard sign, he would see how meticulous it was. Clean, sterile even. His brow registered the question, but he didn't ask. Instead he took her by the hips and lifted her onto the tailgate. Again, his hands felt their way into her back pockets and with his eyes never leaving hers, gently pulled her into him. Obligingly, she wrapped her legs around his waist. The fire that had been smoldering since the first tequila shot finally broke the surface and from there on, it was a race to see who could touch, taste and need the other more deeply.

Calder was the one to pull away, catching his breath. He held her shoulders at arms-length, his eyes searching hers. Though she knew his eyes were the coolest blue, they now shone black in the pale light.

He took a step back. She could feel his stare pushing hard into her, and she knew, without doubt, that he could see all of her. Win shuddered and fought to take in air. For a moment, she feared he would turn and go.

Then, with animal grace, he leaned in and caught the back of her ankle with one hand and the toe of her boot with the other. He easily slid it off and tossed it inside the camper. Without hesi-tation the right boot followed suit. Next, Calder effortlessly gath-ered and pulled off her socks, then left her legs to swing idly off the edge of the gate. The crisp night air licked at her bare feet, the sensation making her acutely aware of their nakedness. His brow was serious now, as his dark eyes still held hers in their steely grip.

"Com'ere." The word spoke the word quiet, but strong.

His two forefingers hooked into her front belt loops and he pulled her forward until her ass rested on the very edge of the tail-gate. He took her mouth again, this time slowly exploring every piece of it; the corners of her lips, the dulled edges of her teeth, the soft texture of her tongue.

As he tasted her, his fingers busied themselves with the buckle, zipper and buttons that stood between him and his target. Her jeans were shimmied off and her blouse hung agape, just exposing the inner crescents of her bare breasts. She was aware of her hard nipples and felt the soft cotton blouse brush against them as it quivered with her every shaking breath.

Calder stepped back again, his look of assessment slowly turned to what she could only construe as admiration. A sly smile tugged at the corners of his weathered lips, and with an easy agility, he hoisted himself up beside her, rid himself of his own boots and slid forward into the shell. He reached out his hand for Win to take hold of and follow.

"Com'ere," he said, with the same gentle force as before. She grabbed on and let him pull her inside.

With the tailgate secure, Win gained confidence in the darkness. In her drunken haze she returned to the woman she had been long before. Before Justin, before all of the sadness. The perfect, beautiful Julia. He kissed her mouth so intensely she uttered a primal groan. It was a sound that seemed to emanate from beyond her, a low voice that she no longer recognized.

Beyond her alcohol-addled psyche, she could hear The Wound's distant shrieking. "*Whore!*" it cried, as it tried to fight through the cracks of her pleasure. But for once she pushed it back, sealing it behind her for a few moments of happiness. She would gladly pay whatever price it would impose tomorrow. Not this night. This night was hers.

She reached for him and tore open the snaps on his shirt, greedily pressing herself against the warmth of his chest. His kisses were everywhere. He sucked her nipples until they ached and caressed her small breasts as if he had never seen such wonders. His stomach and chest weren't the only thing that was stone hard and when he entered her, she cried out as if she were a virgin once again. He stopped when he heard her, his voice husky in the darkness, "Am I hurting you?" She reached for him and answered with her tongue deep in his mouth, her hips moving and urging him on.

Permission granted, he moved hard into her. Her arms bracing against the wall of the truck bed, she pressed against him to drive him in deeper. Her hunger was his undoing and when he let go it was overpowering, accompanied by a noise of anguish and elation, and he kept moving, thrust after thrust until she knew there was nothing left. She clenched her inner muscles to take it all in and keep it. She wanted it all.

He fell, as if wrecked, with his head between her breasts. She wrapped her arms and legs around his back and they stayed that way, their ragged breaths subsiding, until he gathered himself enough to move off to one side. He lifted himself on one elbow to face her, using his other arm to pull her in close.

"You didn't—I couldn't hold out, you had me too far gone."

She didn't know what to say, she couldn't have felt more satisfied. She hadn't even considered her own pleasure. That would require her letting down more walls and fences than even the tequila would allow. She managed, "I'm perfect."

"Hmmm, yup...but—" Stirring and starting to move south, he murmured, "I'm gonna have to insist."

Perhaps her reaction was too quick. Her hand caught him by the arm, so firmly that it startled him and he looked at her inquiringly. Win could see in his eyes that he knew she was serious. Calder moved back up, looking puzzled at what she knew was now a guarded expression. Did he see the fear? Maybe he would chalk it up to shyness. But thankfully, he contented himself with a long sweet kiss. "You sure?"

"I'm perfect," she said, relaxing again. She stifled a small yawn.

"Yup." He pulled her in close and together, they fell into a deep tequila slumber.

CHAPTER 5

When Calder finally started to stir he realized that his head was at an odd angle. It was resting on a cowboy boot and enduring a laser beam of sunshine drilling onto his face through the side window of the camper shell. Camper shell—*What the hell?* Where was he? A fly was trapped inside and banging against the walls of the interior, its buzz sounding remarkably like a chain saw.

He blinked, instinctively rolling to get out of the sun's piercing rays, and found his face buried in the back of Win's tangled golden hair. He inhaled gently, taking in her scent. Sweet, fertile soil and citrus. He found it exotic and felt himself charge again on the unnamed electricity between them. As the events of the last sixteen hours flooded back to him, he smiled in wonderment that it had all led to this moment; hot and hung-over in the back of her truck. With some effort, he raised his head, wincing at the pain that would only be the beginning to a very long day.

He assessed the situation; inside a camper, naked, the debris of the night's escapade scattered on all sides. Within his direct view he noticed a bottle of prescription pills, without thinking he reached over to examine it more closely. Zithromax. The name on the prescription: *Julia Richards*. He looked down at Win, her tousled locks, sleeping soundly, emitting the most feminine of snores. Her soft shoulder…. It was then he noticed what looked like a scar peeking out from under the blanket.

He paused, knowing he was about to cross a line, then gingerly lifted the edge to disclose the full horror of destruction that had been visited on her precious back. He took it in, all of it; the scars, the grafts, the melted edges, the gory patchwork of white and red, made worse now by the wear and tear of recent events. *How had he not noticed?!* How much tequila accounted for this to go missing? *Sweet Jesus.* His eyes softened as he regarded her peaceful slumber. What an ordeal it must have been and what luxury sleep must be, what an escape. He carefully lowered the blanket.

Win stirred, and he watched as she went through the same sequence he just had. She squinted into the light, and with a raspy voice said, "My head." Then, apparently forgetting about her injuries, she rolled over on her back, and gave a small yelp of pain.

It was a moment before she realized he was there, propped up on an elbow, taking her in. "Good morning," he all but croaked, trying to find his voice. He loudly cleared his throat causing them both to wince.

She groaned, "Not so far." She looked at him through one eye. "How long have you been awake?" He knew that it translated to, *How much did you see?*

"Just opened my eyes."

The reality of where she was suddenly played across her face, what she had done, with him. "Right...tequila."

"Yup. How 'bout I find us some coffee?"

"Yes...coffee...good...what a good man you are." She moved her forearm up to cover her eyes.

Calder leaned over and gently picked up her arm so he could look directly into her eyes. "Yup." Then he gently laid it back down so it shielded her view once more. After some searching, he pulled on enough clothes so he was sufficiently clad to emerge from the truck without scaring the locals. He finished the tucking and snapping outside and finally, ever so carefully, out of respect for his soon to be throbbing head, put on his well-worn grey felt hat. As he cleared the side of the truck, he noticed Tony the Rat leaning in the doorway of his shop. He had clearly enjoyed watching Calder disembark to begin his walk of shame.

"Mornin' Calder," Tony the Rat called, with a big grin.

Calder, with just the slightest hitch in his stride from getting busted, kept moving. "Tony."

He was inside at Ian's Mountain Bakery on Agate Avenue when he saw her drive by. He left one of the coffees he had just paid for on the counter, and headed for the door. The lady behind the register called out, "Hey, your coffee!"

"Yup," was his reply.

As he walked out into the bright morning sun, he stopped and looked down the street where Win had just beat it out of town. He smiled an I-shoulda-seen-that-coming smile, shook his head then turned and walked down the street in the opposite direction.

Be safe, Julia.

As soon as Calder was out of sight, Win started her own version of a contortionist-dressing-in-a-small-camper-with-a-hangover act. Once she was dressed enough not to cause a ruckus, she slid out of the back, made haste to the cab, pulled herself in and gunned it out of the parking lot. From the corner of her eye she spied a bemused Tony the Rat watching her go.

The truck screamed down the two lane road, Win was anxious to put some room between her and the mistake she had just made. She hit the wheel repeatedly with her fists chanting, "Stupid! Stupid! Stupid!" Poetically the country station poked at her as Carrie Underwood crooned, *"I don't even know his last name."*

"Oh really?" she asked sarcastically, her voice scratchy. "Okay then," and she cranked it up to fully experience the irony. By the second verse she started laughing, almost maniacally and didn't stop until a sentimental Keith Urban song brought her back to her senses.

About an hour out of Granby, Win pulled into a gas station, her radio still blaring out the open windows. A couple of old guys sitting out front looked up from their papers to see what the commotion was. Actually there were three old men, but one was a ghost. The third man sat contentedly beside his two former companions, his skin radiating the now familiar luminous sheen, his fingers laced across a very round belly, twiddling his thumbs. She smiled at him but his gaze was set firmly on the horizon, his expression one of absolute contentment. It hit her that this just might be the old man's version of heaven; sitting next to his best friends, listening to them swapping stories. All of their lives spent together in this small Colorado town. The thought of one of them moving on before the others, unfathomable.

When she cut the engine, the violence of the sudden silence startled her. She hadn't realized what chaos she had been traveling in. Now the wind took over her senses, a relief in the high June noon. It blew soft and peaceful. Win sighed and lowered her forehead to rest on the top of the steering wheel,

"So this is who I am now? Tequila slut girl?" she grumbled to herself. She looked in the rearview mirror. "No, that's wrong... I'm *blonde* tequila slut girl. Grrrreaaaat," she moaned, under her breath.

The Wound had been screaming since she first opened her eyes back in Granby. She had violated the truce that had been negotiated and it was making her pay for the transgression. For once she was in agreement. She could only imagine what damage had been done, but as always, it was all taking place behind her, just out of view.

With a wince and a sigh, she carefully stepped down from the cabin, put the nozzle into the tank, left it pumping and walked into the Loaf 'N Jug convenience store. Reaching into her pocket to pay for the gas and a cup of coffee, she found the address that Calder had slipped her the night before. She palmed it while she paid the clerk, walked back to the truck, disconnected the hose and crawled into the cab, where she sat for a moment fingering the slip of paper. Weighing out her options, or lack of them, she threw the old truck into drive and with a slight smile said, "What the hell."

Four hours, three Advil, two massive cups of coffee, a full liter of water, three pit stops and one unsettling egg sandwich later, Win arrived at the entrance of the ranch. The entry arch was made of three massive logs; the longest lay across the top and was supported by the other two, their bases ensconced in a matrix of large river rock. Suspended from the top log was a wrought iron sign, rusted but still hanging with purpose. The name that some blacksmith had pounded out nearly a hundred years prior was *SEARS, Est. 1916.* On each side of the name was an "S "enclosed inside a circle. It resembled the yin and yang symbol, but she knew better than to assume an Eastern influence in turn-of-the-century West.

Beyond the arch she could see the terrain that the portal framed. She took in the vista of scrub sage, taking turns with pasture land, and in the distance, the path of a creek outlined with puffs of aspen and Cottonwoods. From there, Lodge Pole Pines took over as the foothills rose from the valley, the earth heaving skyward up to the beckoning heavens with craggy, snowcapped mountains. She let the Ford idle as she took in the unexpected grandeur.

Win was humbled in the wake of the scene's beauty, and suddenly her mind surged with shame. The tears came, flowing uncontrolled, and through their blur she idly noted her hands were shaking. She couldn't find air, her lungs barely had time to fill between sobs. She laid her head hard against the wheel, stretching The Wound to feel its pull.

"Damn you," she sputtered.

The Wound responded with a flash of fiery pain.

"Damn you to hell." She threw herself full force against the back of the bench seat, writhing and grinding The Wound into the sheepskin.

She could feel the spectacle of nature that now surrounded her, judging her. Harshly. She wasn't worthy of such a place. She was all lies and pain and fear and scars. There was no place for her here.

The sobbing ebbed and her breathing slowed. Finally, with a jagged sigh, she pressed the brake down hard, shoved the gear-shift into reverse and did a three-point turn to regain the high-way. When she hit the junction of Route 130, she gunned it north, anxious to put as many miles as possible between herself and the Sears Ranch.

The road stretched out before her like dark, pulled taffy. The ranches, the valleys, all pieced together in a patchwork quilt of overwhelming scale. The cloudless sky, so blue, so opaque, there was no description that her mind could conjure. It hung, closing in, as if by driving through it, she would emerge stained in its deep azure.

She was exhausted from the night before and the emotional storm she had just weathered. She drove mechanically, barely taking in the ever-changing landscape around her. Her defenses were down now, and through the opening cracks seeped scenes from the night before.

Calder. His hands on her, his eyes intense, his touch electric. They had danced, she had trusted him and let him guide her around the floor. *When will I learn?* Trust was not an option for her now, nor ever again.

She chastised herself, disappointed in her epic lack of judg-ment. But again the events played out in her reverie; Calder in the back of the truck, his sweet breath as he told her how beautiful she was, his calloused hands rough but gentle on her skin, holding her face as he kissed her hard, his eyes only leaving hers to close with his own pleasure, allowing a low and husky moan to escape him.

Even now, the thought of it stirred Win deep down, awakening the desire that had led her to abandon all better judgment the night before. She could feel herself flush, her southern regions hot and ready again at the thought of him hovering over her, covering her everywhere with kisses that held sweet longing. She hadn't needed convincing; she had been as hungry as he was, her hips rising to meet him when the time came.

The memory of him taking her made her insides shudder and Win grasped the wheel tightly as she drove over the great sage flats. *Calder.* He had appeared out of nowhere, saved her once, then saved her again. What a risk she had taken—*idiot!*

North she went, up Route 287 until the gas gauge demanded she stop in the small town of Lander. It was late afternoon; seven hours since leaving Granby. A wave of hunger hit as she was filling the tank. Across the street she saw a burger joint, The Dairyland Drive In, the slogan below the sign asking and answering the question, *Who loves you baby? Cheesewheel, that's who.* She headed across the street and parked in the lot. Upon entering she was greeted by a man of very robust stature, he waved her in to take her order.

"Come on in!" he bellowed. She walked to the counter and eyed the menu posted above his head. Over a sketchy sound system Styx was crooning, *Mr. Roboto.*

"What'll it be?"

"A Cheesewheel," she said with confidence, having no idea what a Cheesewheel might be.

"Any add-ons?"

"What do you suggest?"

"Secret, secret I've got a secret!" he suddenly sang out with Styx, and then asked seamlessly, "How 'bout some green chili sauce and guacamole?"

"Great," she said, looking at him with confusion.

"Fries?"

"Sure."

Another outburst, "Somewhere to hide to keep me alive," then, "shake?"

"I'm sorry?" She said wondering if he had some sort of 80's rock Tourette's Syndrome. She realized her mouth was agape; the song's subject matter hitting a little too close to home.

"Milkshake?"

"Sure," she said, pulling herself together.

"Chocolate or vanilla?"

"Vanilla."

He rang her up. Beside the register a red electric guitar was propped up. Next to it was a sign that read, *Win this Mutha!!!* The sharpie script was accompanied by a small smiley face with its tongue sticking out.

He walked back to the kitchen singing at the top of his lungs. "I've got a secret—my true identity."

Seriously, Win thought. She closed her eyes and shook her head, as if the action could make sense of the burger man delivering her life instructions through the prose of an 80's hair band.

Mercifully, Styx subsided but then Mick Jagger took over with *Sympathy for the Devil.*

Win sat down at a corner table and took in her surroundings. All the other diners seemed to be locals with the exception of two couples. They were older, probably in their sixties. It was easy to tell who was with who, because they matched. The first couple had neon-green t-shirts and black leather vests and chaps. The other couple wore their black leather as pants and jackets, he in a red t-shirt, she in a red, white and blue flag blouse.

All were carrying some extra pounds, mostly up front. She assumed they were in the Harley Davidson cruising crowd, but when they got up to leave, they mounted two sort of motor-cycle-tricycles, except that the single wheel was in back. The whole setup was bizarrely un-cool.

Then the neon couple did something that took her breath away. Before putting on their helmets and mounting their weird three-wheeler, they embraced in a passionate kiss. When done, the man lifted his shades and gave his wife a satisfied grin which she coyly dismissed as nonsense, clearly loving every minute of it. When they got on, he was behind in the rumble seat and she was in front. As she drove her man out of the parking lot, Win couldn't help but notice the fleshy white skin of her muffin-top peeking out from under her shirt.

Win stared, awed as the two couples drove side-by-side down the main street of Lander. Between their age and girth, each partner had a dozen physical flaws, and yet they were so clearly in love. The man on the back of the bike—either they took turns, she enjoyed driving more than he did, or maybe he couldn't drive anymore. Win could only guess. But there would be no beatings tonight. No repercussions for disrespecting his manly ego. No indeed. His manner was that of a carefree, con-tented man. She was a woman enjoying her age and an adven-ture. There would be no consequences waiting when she got home.

"Ahhh, get down baby!" the burger man bellowed from back in the kitchen.

A Cheesewheel, as it turned out, was a cheeseburger that had been battered and deep fried, encasing it in a sort of golden doughy shell, rendering a bun unnecessary. She noted some of the locals eating it with their hands, but the wake of juice and sauce-ooze that dripped on tables and down shirt fronts left her reaching for the plastic knife and fork option. The green-chili sauce and guacamole were the perfect complement and she happily slathered them on with every bite.

"Okay, here's some trivia everyone, whoever gets the answer gets a free sundae," the burger man boomed from behind the counter. The diners all looked up in curiosity. "Who can tell me the name of the bass player for The Doors?"

Win wasn't paying attention. The image of the kissing neon green couple still lingered. She had known that kind of love. *Henry.* Her sweet Henry. Her first husband. He had loved her and cherished her every flaw as part of what made her Julia. He would kiss her, holding her face gently in his carpenter's hands, kind of like—she pushed the thought from her mind. There would never be another Henry. She was old now. Old and damaged beyond recognition. What were the odds that any man would ever see her the way Henry did again?

Zero, came the immediate answer in her head. Zero. And no cheap one-night stand with a cowboy was ever going to change that.

She pushed the vestiges of the Cheesewheel away, suddenly her hunger was gone.

"Didn't have a bass player—trick question!!" His boisterous laughter echoed against the shiny surfaces as Win left the diner and the rock 'n roll burger man behind.

Back in the pickup, Win headed to a campground outside of town. She checked in with the host, found an open spot and crawled into the back of the camper shell. It was just as she had left it back in Granby. Her mattress and bedding were completely disheveled, her hat and belt discarded in a corner; they had not made their way out with her this morning as she had beat her hasty retreat.

Everything was out of place. Again, her insides shuddered as the night's memories found their way back into her consciousness. Maybe it was her complete exhaustion, or maybe it was

the memory of the neon-
green couple that had transfixed her earlier, but instead of
taking hold of the disarray and bringing it back to order, she
crawled into the bramble and lay her head on one of the pillows
crammed against the cab wall. She wrapped herself in the crumpled blankets. Win fell asleep almost instantly, but not before she
got what she was hoping for.

She could still smell him. On her sheets and on her pillow.
Calder.

CHAPTER 6

Four days later, Win once again found herself idling beneath the grand archway with its wrought-iron name plate. This time she rolled down her window, stuck her head out and inhaled deeply. Her lungs filled with the sweet smell of sage and pine. This time she smiled at the layers of texture that rolled out before her. She straightened her shoulders with resolve and set her jaw hard against the uneven dirt road ahead as Win drove through the entrance to the Sears Ranch.

She had spent her few days in the campground outside of Lander doing—well, nothing. She would go to town for food and to buy a book or two, but mostly she slept. Win could feel her lungs relax and make the most of the scant eight thousand foot altitude. For the first time since leaving Atlanta, she had stopped moving, stopped pushing forward.

She didn't feel Justin's breath on her neck; that soft spot where her still perfect skin pressed against The Wound. She didn't feel the fear of him finding her. She had been more than careful. Even he, with all of his wiles and resources, could not have tracked her to this place. So, for now, she had stopped running.

As the days went by, the thought of the cook's job at the Sears Ranch had grown into a strategy. She would go in. Lie of course. She would insist that there could be no paperwork to fill out. They would just have to accept that there had been a fire and those documents didn't exist for her. She would get the job, and she would hunker down and try to figure out what was next. It was with that renewed resolve that she rolled onto the rocky drive under the arch.

As she drove down the dirt road, she allowed herself to fully take in the beauty that surrounded her. Again the rolling green pastures, backing up to secondary mountains that built up to large peaks in the distance. She felt the order of the land. All in its place. Beautiful. Her kinship to it was instant.

Win rattled along another mile or so before she found herself at the mouth of a wide circular drive. Inside the circle itself, was a large patch of semi-tended green grass with a thick grove of aspen trees at its center. There appeared to be some sort of statue in their midst. Immediately, her interest was piqued.

She entered at the six o'clock position and turned to the right. At three o'clock sat a grand house in the classic frontier style. Three stories high and made of tightly fitted logs, it had three dormer peaks at the top. There were plenty of gabled windows and a porch that appeared to wrap all the way around. It had a prominent flight of stairs that led up to imposing glass-paned double doors. From the light coming through them, she surmised there must be very large windows on the back end of the house, as well. It was a majestic and beautiful home—probably not the cook's quarters.

She continued on to twelve o'clock to what looked like a great hall. Some kind of rustic multi-purpose building. It was much less ornate, but still welcoming. There were two utilitarian white front doors and another wraparound porch with three rocking chairs on either side. Beside it was a tiny chapel that couldn't possibly hold more than a dozen people. Interesting priorities.

At the nine o'clock position, she came upon what she could only assume was the working part of the ranch. This was a no fuss L-shaped dwelling with high windows on one leg and traditional windows on the other. It looked to be the oldest of all the buildings; the logs weren't quite as tightly fitted as the grand house, so there was wide chinking in between. She figured the wonky structure to be the cookhouse, maybe the bunkhouse too? She spotted a couple of picnic tables out back, alongside what could only be described as a barbeque on steroids.

Beyond that, she could see a couple of big barns with paddocks flanking either side where a few horses idled, enjoying the early afternoon sun. Other than the horses, the circle seemed deserted.

Win parked the truck and walked over to the cookhouse. Her quick knock caused the unlocked door to swing open. She poked her head inside. No one home. Her only greeting was the smell of grease and the sound of flies buzzing unseen overhead. The dirty dishes from whenever the last meal (or two, or three) had been, were precariously stacked next to a dishwasher that looked as if it had long ago been defeated or surrendered. The ceiling was low with logs serving as cross beams to hold it up.

The kitchen setup was industrial and not too ancient. The stove had eight burners, the refrigerator was just short of a full meat locker and every inch of wall that did not hold a window was covered with shelves or hooks, on which a hodgepodge of plates and pots and bowls and utensils were all vying for their place. As for the windows, she regarded with disgust the drifts of dead black flies that populated every sill.

"Yikes," she muttered under her breath.

Down the center, and running the length of the room, stood a wooden plank table and two matching benches. At the far end, where the table butted up against the wall, a chess game was in progress, waiting patiently for its warring generals to return. Next to that, there were two doors.

Not daring to go in further, she stepped back out into the sunlight and called, "Hello?" When no one answered, she resolved to wait until someone appeared. Once again her gaze lit on the grove of aspen in the center of the grassy circle. She strolled over for a closer look.

Win had always loved aspen—they were noisy. She liked the emotion of them, liked the white straight trunks, so different from the other trees. Their leaves, serene and gentle in the warm months, turned hot yellow jubilation in the fall, then fell, leaving their trunks stripped raw in the harshness of winter. Better still, was the white bark melting into the snowy landscape, camouflaged, until the spring rains rescued them once again.

She had once heard that the largest living organism on Earth was a grove of aspen. The grove itself was really one entity, all connected at the root, beneath the soil. Like a family, feeding each other. That grove was so massive that when it turned its fall colors, you could actually see it from space. Such high drama for something so simple. Lovely.

She passed through the perimeter of the aspen centurions to discover that in fact they were guarding something extraordinary. In the very center of their circle was a monolithic granite marker with the name *SEARS* etched in a strong, no-nonsense script. Around it, fanning out like windmill blades, were graves. As she walked clockwise, the granite names and dates introduced themselves.

Dunwood Sears	1895-1960
Ida Olson Sears	1897-1962
Wallace Dunwood Sears, Jr.	1946-1968
Wallace Dunwood Sears	1922-1973
Mary Ava Joblynsky Sears	1925-1975
Dodge Harrison Sears	1925-1980
Hollis Dodge Sears	1961-1966
June Avery Sears	1927-1976

A family.

She could see them. Not like the usual ghosts that kept her company, but more like traces, watermarks on fine paper. She could see their impressions moving in and out of the stones. The dates told a tale of three generations. She couldn't help but speculate how they all fit together.

Ida and Dunbar married and had two sons, Wallace and Dodge.

The sons married Mary Ava and June, but she couldn't tell who married who. Wallace Jr. had died young, and there was another son...later...only five years old. So sad.

As she pondered the calamity of such an early death, she realized she was being watched. There at the edge of the grove, leaning against one of the aspen's bleached trunks, was a woman. Her beauty stopped Win in her tracks. Her skin was porcelain against a full dark mane of hair. Her wide-set eyes were the deepest brown Win had ever seen. The bend of her eyebrows were like archers' bows, keeping guard above the perfect countenance below. The ghost's lips were full and reminded Win of cherries in high summer. Their eyes met, the dark eyes instantly drawing Win in, and she was once again aware of her own inadequacy.

As she took an involuntary step toward the figure, a sudden blast of cold air swept through the grove and chilled Win to the bone. She caught a whiff of rich tobacco and looked skyward at the fortress of trees—not a single leaf was moving. She felt a wave of darkness so acute that instinctively, Win turned and sprinted, slaloming through the trees and into the drive.

Her heart was pounding from the altitude, and she bent over to catch her breath. The Wound gave a smug protest at the stretch. As she focused on slowing her racing heartbeat, two cracked and crusty cowboy boots entered her field of vision. The boots were accompanied by a barking blue heeler.

The dog was mostly salt and pepper with markings like black cow spots. Clear about his obligations, the pint-sized Cujo placed itself between Win and the boots, and continued to bark incessantly. One of the boots caught the dog's underbelly with its top and gently but firmly lifted it off to the side. As she straightened and her eyes panned up, she noted that the boots were topped with a pair of filthy work pants and a snapped, faded denim work shirt, both of which hadn't seen the inside of a washer in many moons.

"Navy, hush up old girl!" the old man barked back at the dog. The heeler sat down and was instantly quiet. Her dog-years most likely mimicked the age of the cowboy, and her working-dog eyes bored holes into Win's very soul.

Underneath a straw hat with a wide brim and serious sweat bands, the old man's face was a road map of creases. Around his eyes were the major interstates, while the rest of his sunbaked skin was covered with all manner of country roads. He had stark white hair and deep blue eyes, which seemed far away, due to the thick, bottle-bottom glasses he wore. The round gold rims that supported the lenses seemed ready to snap from the weighty responsibility of the old cowboy's declining vision.

"You must be Win," he said, taking her by surprise.

Her brain quickly made the calculation that Tequila Bar Calder must have called to let them know she was coming. How could he have been so sure? *Bold move on his part,* she mused, hoping against hope that cooking was her only talent he had revealed; leaving out the part about the blond slut in the back of the pickup.

"I am," she replied warily, her breath finally returned to normal.

"Well, welcome. Did you have any trouble finding the place? We had one fella make a wrong turn and end up over in Sweetwater County—never did get here. I expect it was too much trouble in the long run. Don't *re*member what he wanted—must have needed something. Anyway, here you are! You come to cook for a bunch of orn'ry ranch hands. Can't *im*agine what would make someone like you want to do a thing like that, but I would say your lack of good sense is our gain. Come on over and let me show you the lay*out*."

Win wondered at the old man's speech pattern, the odd way he had of emphasizing unexpected syllables in longer words, it didn't seem to have any real cadence. It felt like traveling on a road full of potholes, and it left her unsettled.

"And your name is?"

"Oh, for good grace in the morning, I got going so fast I missed the main event—you know I do that, get going a mile a minute, and the next thing you know I've *for*gotten where I tied my horse—just an expre*ssion*. Oh and my glasses! I've gotten so I have to sleep with them on, cuz soon as I take them off, well, they are gone! And the trick is I can't see to even look for them! Can you ima*gine?*" He chuckled. "What a crazy state of doin's!"

Win smiled. Still nothing. "So, your name?"

"Oh now I've done it some more! Yes, my name, let's focus here—my name is Christopher Marl*bor*ough. The closest thing you'll get to a manager around here." He gave a genteel tip of his hat and shook her hand. More sandpaper. "Yes, Miss Win, I am The Marl*bor*ough Man. Not that I ever got paid for it or got my picture up on a billboard or in a magazine. But I'd like to think if that tobacky company ever got a load of me, the search woulda been O-V-E-R, over." Arms outstretched and face upturned to the sky, he declared, "Look no further, here I am, boys! Ready to lead the American public down the road to nicotine reli*ance!*" The old man was chuckling again, clearly pleased with himself. "Well it's their loss, wouldn't you say Miss Win?"

Amused, but not wanting to embarrass him, "Yes, clearly. And this is?" She gestured toward the vigilant dog at his side.

"This old curse? Well this here's Navy, been around here for a long stretch, this one. She'll tell you all our secrets for the price of a bone, won't you, you old flirt. Well say hello, she won't bite."

Win wasn't sure if he was talking to the dog or her. Navy circled around behind Christopher Marlborough's legs, her skeptical eyes never leaving Win, clearly trying to decide if she was trustworthy. Win crouched down and extended the back of her hand to allow for introductions. Navy boldly moved in and took a good whiff, then unconvinced, backed away again.

"Hey, Navy," Win cooed in a soft voice, "you just take your time now, no hurry." With that the old pooch conceded, lowering her head, allowing Win to give her a good scratch behind a less than perfect ear. She relaxed beneath Win's touch. Then abruptly, Navy quit the affection in favor of something more interesting in the aspen grove. Win wondered if the dog was seeing the beguiling ghost as well.

"Well I'll be a rich man's daughter, looks like ol' Navy has been charmed."

"This is charmed?" Win asked skeptically.

"You should see what the FedEx man gets." Smiling, Christopher Marlborough walked Win over to the cookhouse and the three of them entered the kitchen she had peeked into earlier.

It was as she first surmised, mostly functional, totally disorganized and in need of a nuclear cleaning. Navy immediately went over to a folded blanket that lay on the floor in the far corner, pirouetted twice in its well-worn center and dropped into its nest in a compact dog ball. Her eyes closed almost immediately. Win had clearly passed whatever test she had been administered. The threat had been aborted and Navy had freed herself to resume what Win suspected was a heavy napping schedule.

The door at the end of the massive plank table led into the bunk house. Win counted twelve sets of bunk beds, not all in use for sleeping, but all filled with some sort of clutter. Even though some of the high windows were open, she could still make out the ambient odor of cigarettes, sweat and perhaps some lingering man-wind. She silently made it a personal goal to never go in there again.

Win and Christopher Marlborough continued their tour, during which he never stopped talking. Effortlessly, a stream of consciousness passed through his lips. His speech pattern somehow hitting off-syllables, bumped along like a record skipping; never quite settling into a groove.

As they left the cookhouse, Navy gave a heavy sigh and begrudgingly got up to follow. They walked out behind the kitchen and passed between the two large horse barns. The close one was aptly named the

Old Barn and the further one, larger with a spacious indoor arena, the New Barn.

Before her guide had a chance to launch headlong into the history of the naming process, Win instinctively raised her hands saying, "No explanation necessary."

Standing between barns Old and New, they were faced broadside with the big hall. Christopher Marlborough seized the opportunity and forged ahead.

"That there was the work of old Dun Sears. When he built this place back in the 1920's there wasn't much around here. No real town like there is today, just a bunch of home*stead*ers, so old Dun built the hall there, and a bitty little church so the neighbors had a place to do their gathering. Wed*dings,* funerals, dances, poli*tick*ing, it all got done here. Never charged anyone as far as I know. Old Dun, he was a tough one, but he was fair, which helped balance out some of his rougher edges. Well and I guess Ida helped with that too, a big woman, stubborn, but always had something sweet coming out of that kitchen... and she loved us kids." His voice trailed off.

"How long have you been here Mr. Marl*bor*ough?" *Great, now I'm doing it.*

"Please feel free to call me Double M, Miss Win, everyone else does." Before she had a chance to acknowledge his request, he forged ahead with his answer. "Oh, my pops came here in 1944, same year their first boy Wally was born. My pops hired on as one of the hands and my moms helped with the cooking and chores. I was eight and thought them Medicine Bow mountains was the most mag*ic*al place there ever could be—still do, by the way. So, when my moms up and left us a few years later, I stayed on and eventually started working the place in earnest. Been here ever since."

As they walked to the north side of the hall, he continued. "When it wasn't being used for local doin's we'd store the local fire brigade engines around the back, that's how it got its name, the

Fire Hall. Used to be there was always something happening, and the Fire Hall was the center of it. These days we hardly ever break the threshold, 'cept once a year there's still a big party right after the harvest, call it The Fire Ball. Doc still makes sure that keeps going, don't know why, never seems to actually show up, let alone enjoy himself."

"Doc?"

"Doc Sears, he's the last of 'em. Ol' Dun's grandson."

"Is he the one living in the big house?"

"Doc? In the family house? Naaaaw." The dusty cowboy made a slight shuffle and looked out towards the hills. "Doc bunks in with the boys and me. There hasn't been anyone in the family house since Dodge died, Doc's father—my good golly Miss Molly, been some thirty years now. Somethin' went on there, not sure what, no one really knows. Of course there's plenty of speculatin' to be had, but it's been this way for so long now, it's kind of just part of the day-to-day. But it must have been somethin' though, make a man walk away from a nice setup like that and bunk in with a bunch of stinking' cowmen such as us. Must have been somethin'—"

"I'd say so."

"See, Doc's the last surviving member of the Platte Valley Sears clan. Famous in their own quiet way. 'Round here anyway. Old Dun built this place and then worked it till it turned into somethin.'"

They had reached the backside of the Fire Hall and come upon a small two-story house, pale yellow, with a red front door. It was encased with yet another wrap-around porch. In contrast to the stark appearance of the previous porches, this one housed an impressive collection of old upholstery and lawn furniture strewn about in groupings. Win imagined on any given afternoon, with the right amount of caffeine and/or alcohol, you and your companions could easily solve the world's problems right here.

"So this would be your place. There's a room up on the second floor, not too small, not too big. Hasn't been used in a good while."

"My place?"

Double M pressed on without acknowledging her question. "You'll be sharing with the Gradys, they live downstairs. Tom and Lucy. Tom was the manager here before me. Retired 'bout 15 years ago, but still caretakes the Big House. He and Lucy been to-gether *for*ever, they're old but don't like too much fuss made over them. I expect they could use you looking in on them from time to time. Mostly, she's an angel, and he's...not. Shouldn't be much trouble. Only come to the cookhouse for dinner on Sundays. The rest they take care of on their own. Just need to check in before going to town for their gro*cer*y list."

During the last word flow, the determined cowboy knocked on the weathered door and as he finished an old woman appeared. She looked to be in her seventies, maybe late seventies, although Win was never good at telling ages. Her skin was the color of hot cocoa made just right. Her wiry grey hair was pulled back in a little knot at the nape of her neck. She sported a simple flowered dress with a man's leather belt cinched in snug to show off her still small waist. On her feet were Birkenstocks with thick white cotton socks. All in all, probably the most comfortable outfit Win might ever have seen, and she secretly wished she was sporting the ensemble herself. Her Wranglers and long-sleeve shirt suddenly felt claustrophobic.

"Well, good afternoon, Christopher, won't you come inside?"

"Why yes, I will Miss Lucy, but before I do that, may I present Miss Winchester? She prefers people to call her Win. She's coming on as the new cookie, and I'm hoping you'll show her your usual kindness, even out the rest of our rough ways, that way she might stick around for a while." Double M had adopted a sort of Eddie Haskell quality to his bumpy cadence. The man was a wonder.

"Well of course, Christopher. A pleasure to meet you, Win. Please come in. My husband is asleep in the back, so you'll forgive if he doesn't come out now, but you'll meet him soon enough." She and Double M exchanged a knowing glance. "Now tell me Win, what part of the country do you come from?"

After a slight pause, she white-lied. "Most recently, Texas. I guess you could call me a Southerner," she offered, trying to lessen the falsehood. She immediately knew that Miss Lucy was someone that deserved the truth.

"Well, okay then, you'll be our honored guest from the South. How nice to have another female on the ranch. I expect some quality girl talk out of you," she said, wagging a bony finger teasingly at her.

Win was moved by her immediate warmth. Miss Lucy's voice was a blanket you could wrap yourself in. She had forgotten how nice a friend's voice could feel. "I'll hold you to that," Win ventured softly.

"Ex*cell*ent! Just ex*cell*ent!"

"Well Christopher, don't just let our Miss Win stand there, go on up and show her the room."

Double M hopped to. "Alrighty-righty-oh, Miss Lucy. Follow me Miss Win." Then waving his arm with a flourish, pronounced, "Your new do*miss*ile awaits!"

The old man began his ascent of the staircase with a sort of stepping shuffle. She assumed he was favoring some old injury, or more likely, injuries. Win followed him up, leaving Lucy Grady below on the landing.

It was all too confusing. Had she forgotten a conversation on that evening at the H-B? Well, she knew the answer to that was most likely, yes. These people all seemed to know something she didn't.

"Mr. Marlborough, can I ask how you knew I was coming?"

"Double M, please Miss Win."

"Of course, Double M...how did you know?"

Her escort looked slightly puzzled, "Why, Doc of course. He called from the road a couple days ago."

"And do you know how he heard of me?"

"Well, hard to say really, don't know if he men*tion*ed it, but most likely heard about you from someone who knew we needed some cooking help out here—sounded like it was all arranged. You mean you never met him?"

"No." She chose not to divulge that it must have been Tequila Bar Calder that had given Doc her name.

"Well, you never know with Doc, he knows just about everyone, just never talks to 'em, that's all. But if Doc says you're the new cookie, then all I know is to get things ship*ped*y shape for you and be happy when you get here. And now you're here, and now I'm happy—worked out just fine, far as I can see."

"I see."

The stairwell walls were a golden wallpaper with vertical stripes of tiny pink flowers, faded and well past its prime, but not tattered. The banister led from the first floor up to the second and wrapped around the stairwell opening. As they reached the landing, Win looked around and saw four doors. Double M, still continuing his constant chatter (she was already learning to tune him out), showed her through the door on her right.

"This here's yours. The two across are for storage and the latrine is there next door. Been a while since we had anybody up here. And been about forever since it was someone of your female gender. Once I heard you was comin', we gave her a quick coat of paint and tried to vacuum and chase the rest of the dust out, ended up just throwing out the rug, so it's a little stark for now, but I'm sure once you move in with all your knick-*knacks* and the like, it'll be just nice as you please."

"I'm not really a knick-*knack* kind of girl," she said, unconsciously mimicking his cadence again. She hoped it wasn't contagious. Her eyes surveyed the newly painted room. It was pink. Five-year-old girl pink. She smiled at the thought of a couple of cowboys coming up with that decision. At least it was a pale shade and she was thankful for the effort and the cleaning. She'd always loved the smell of fresh paint. There were three, four-over-four windows. One on the wall to her right, and two on the long wall in front of her.

Between the windows was an iron frame bed with mattresses. She could feel the lumps from where she stood. In the far wall to her left were double doors that opened into a walk-in closet, which also had a window in its rear. Thinking of her single bag of clothes in the truck, she gave a small laugh.

"I don't know if I'm going to do this justice...I don't have much."

"Oh, don't try and turn that buffalo my way! I never met a female who couldn't fill up a closet, or a room, or for that matter any space worth settlin' into. I expect you'll be sendin' for the rest. Then myself and whoever else, will be in charge of haulin' it upstairs, then there'll be furniture to move around until it finally lands right back where it started—I know how you people operate."

"You make it sound like a conspiracy."

"You bet it is! A conspiracy of the fairer sex. Makes mush out of the mightiest of men. A sad sight to see." He was shaking his head in mock (she hoped) despair.

"Well, Mr. Marlborough—uh—Double M, I hate to disappoint you, but there won't be anything else coming. There's a mattress in the back of the truck that I'll need a hand with, but I can manage the rest."

"Stop! No moving vans? No UPS man shipments? Where are you hiding it all?"

Win stopped for a moment, looked him in the eye and took a breath. "There was a fire." Her voice was clear, devoid of emotion.

Double M stopped talking long enough to take in the statement. Even he seemed to understand that there was more there, and for once didn't push. "Well, you may just be the female that cures me of all my mis-opinions, wouldn't that just be somethin'?"

"Indeed it would."

"Well I'll leave you to it. Let me know when you want to move that mat*tress* up, I'll get a couple of the boys to give a hand." Double M turned and with a slight bow, started to hobble his way down the stairs.

"Wait, please...."

"Yes, Miss Win?"

"I haven't even accepted the position... I don't know what it pays, when it starts, what you expect...."

Double M stopped, turned and squinted up the stairs at her, as he pushed the heavy glasses back up to the top of his nose. He looked puzzled. "Oh my...I was under the mis*im*pression that you were ready, set, go—when I heard you were coming, only thing I was told is to show you around and make you feel at home."

"So you don't know anything?"

"Well," he answered slowly, scratching the back of his head, making his hat slide down over his eyebrows, "in my es*tim*ation, I would expect it doesn't pay city wages...." Then looking at his watch said, "and starts at dinnertime. And as far as ex*pec*tations, well I expect, well...I expect we'll need breakfast, lunch and dinner most days and some kind of direction on the rest. There."

He beamed with pride for coming up with the master plan. "That's the meat of it. Doc will fill you in on the rest when he gets back in a week or so. He's a fair man, I'm sure if you have any concerns, most likely he'll set 'em to rest. After all, the only thing we need more than an increase in prime beef prices is a cook. Lord knows we need a cook!" He raised his hands in the air as if he was testifying up to the heavens.

"The best among us is Petey, and the results of his efforts have been, well, volatile." His hand instinctively went to his stomach, "If you know what I mean. So whadaya say? Gonna give it a whirl? I guarantee you won't find a more grateful group of diners anywhere in the great state of *Wy*oming."

85

He uncharacteristically stopped talking and awaited her response.

Finally, after a beat and a breath, she murmured, "All right, I'm in."

She couldn't help but smile as he whooped and slapped his knee. "Now we're doing the dipsy doodle! I'll let you get settled. I know you'll want to get to the kitchen and start to whip up your first masterpiece for this evening. The fellas usually wander down the hill around sunset. Once they get the horses put up and fed, they'll be coming your way, with what you might call enthusia*stic* appetites."

Win swallowed hard, "Right-oh."

As Double M turned to walk down the stairs he called out behind him, "I knew you'd do us good, the first time I saw you come busting out of those aspen trees. Like an angel sent our way from those Sears folks already gone." Then with voice and finger raised to make his point, "An angel I say, finally coming to rescue our hungry souls!"

From below came Lucy's voice chastising him like a child, "Now settle down, Christopher Marlborough, you'll run her off with all your words. Be on your way now!"

Obediently, Double M made short work of the rest of the stairs. From above she heard their well-worn final exchange.

"Yes, Miss Lucy, you call if you need anything."

"Won't be necessary."

"Anything at all."

"Off you go."

"Alrighty, good afternoon then."

"Good afternoon, Christopher." Win heard the old screen door's *thwapp!* Against the frame as The Marlborough Man left the building.

CHAPTER 7

Win busied herself unloading her few belongings from the pickup. Her escape clothes, her new western rigs (all now in desperate need of quality time at a laundromat), hat, medical supplies (now running low), sheets, blankets and pillow. The rest was just some empty water bottles and assorted road trip debris that she dutifully tossed in the garbage. She brought it all upstairs to her new pink room and stored it against the wall by the door. Then, after thanking Miss Lucy, she ventured out of the house, down the path between the barns and the Fire Hall, and into... *the kitchen.*

It was 4:00, Win guessed she had a couple hours to pull together her first meal as new resident chef of the Sears Circle-S Ranch, just outside of Saratoga, Wyoming. Giddiness laced with sheer terror danced in her head as she took a quick inventory of possible meal ingredients in the pantry and refrigerator. Immediately, she knew she was in trouble. They both suggested scenes from *The Good, the Bad and the Ugly.*

Out of sheer desperation, she was able to cobble together a dish that would have to be named later. It consisted of penne pasta, canned corn and tomatoes, ground beef (there was no shortage of beef), and what was left of various dried seasonings, including basil and some sort of atomic chili powder. She baked it all casserole-style with cheddar cheese bubbling on top. There were a couple dozen loaves of bread, some old and some really, really old. She chose the least offensive, sliced it, then broiled it with butter and garlic powder. The only produce she found was oranges. At least they won't get scurvy, she mused. She peeled them, then sliced them thin, added a little red onion and dressed them with a hint of mayo, OJ and curry powder (a random find in the pantry) for a makeshift salad.

She stacked the plates on the island and laid out silverware and napkins buffet style. She wondered what the usual protocol was, but since there was no one to ask for guidance (the thought of engaging Double M in another dissertation was not a desirable option), she forged ahead on her own.

The garlic bread and the sweet beef smelled enticing. As the sun began its descent, her mind wandered back to her journey; Dinah, her dear girl Rosie and the world she had left behind. She wondered what they were doing, if they were noticing the same sunset, thinking of her. *Will this be home now?* Was this where she would dissolve into the harsh landscape and one day emerge as someone new? At least, for now she would be *Win*, a fugitive, a refugee, an imposter, a ghost of her own making.

Before her path of reverie became any darker, the side door flew open and in tramped a herd of dusty cowboys, boots clomping, spurs clinking, and along with them another heeler dog, this one a reddish brown, a more compact version of Navy.

"Hello!" she said, startled by the sudden onslaught. There seemed to be at least a dozen men, most of them looking as startled as she was.

"Hello yourself," came a strong voice and an extended hand emerged from the pack. "You must be the new cookie."

"I am. I'm Win." The name was starting to come easily now.

"Well, how do you do Win, I'm Jim." He was tall, 6'2" or 6'3", muscled with serious eyes. Kind of the Chuck Connors *Rifleman* type that she remembered swooning over as a little girl. She had always liked cowboys or at least the idea of them. Jim's rough hand all but engulfed hers as they shook. She could tell he was coordinated and lithe in spite of his imposing size. Certainly some of that confidence came from knowing he could take any man, anytime, anywhere.

"Boys," he said, "this here is our new cookie, name is Win, and from the smell of it, looks like we may be in for a decent meal for a change." He noticeably directed the remark to a skinny sandy-haired hand, who instantly looked sheepish. "So I expect you to all behave yourselves—that includes you, Mac." This time he shot a look to a man in the back leaning on the side of the refrigerator. He was clearly the oldest, sinewy with hunched shoulders. His face was all deep ruts that must have started as wrinkles many years before. He did not smile, and looked at her with blatant distrust. He made a grunting noise in response to Jim's challenge.

So there's even a Grumpy, she mused to herself.

Jim introduced her to the rest of the crew, one-by-one, reminiscent of Snow White and her dwarves—except these were not quite as adorable...or clean. "Win, this here's Dix, Hollywood, Dave and Petey Rose—they're brothers, Sticks and Mac." He pointed as he went and each cowboy tipped his hat as Jim said their name. "I expect you already know Double M?"

"Uh, yes, Double M—"

"The Marl*bor*ough Man?" spoke up Mac with disdain, mimicking Double M's cadence.

"Right-oh." As if she needed reminding. "Yes, I had the pleasure this afternoon."

"Pleasure? Huh," sneered Mac, "surprised your ears aren't bleeding."

During the introductions, the spotted red cattle dog had stood at attention, eying her intently and occasionally curling his upper lip, but making no sound.

"And this is?"

"Oh, this mongrel?" Jim said, his affection clear. "This is Army, Doc's dog. Only gives us the time of day until Doc comes back, then he'll drop us like a stone bone."

"Army, huh?" Win cocked an eyebrow and crossed her arms.

Sensing a stand-off, Jim leaned in to speak low to Win, "Just need to make sure he gets his share of any leftovers and you'll be fast friends."

The crew went about hanging up an array of well-worn apparel on a double row of pegs next to the refrigerator. Jackets below, hats above. From there, they went straight to the table and sat down. Only Jim and Dix bothered to wash up. If the rest were already clean, it didn't show. At the far end where the table touched the wall, the Rose brothers sat down on opposite sides of the chess game and immediately became engrossed. The crew seemed oblivious to the plates stacked on her cook's table.

Okay, so the buffet style is out. She moved the stacks of plates, silverware etc. to the cowboys at her end of the table, where they seamlessly distributed the place settings amongst themselves.

And family style is in. Research completed.

She could feel their questioning eyes on her. Win set to transferring the piping hot bread and orange salad onto large serving dishes that she had unearthed earlier. She placed the casseroles on the table with serving spoons sticking out of the still simmering concoctions. All was consumed with gusto.

There was little conversation. Of course they had done this infinite times before, at the same table, with the same company. But this silence felt awkward. She kept busy tidying up the counters, but could feel her face begin to redden as she tried in vain to appear casual.

Seemingly in answer to her distress, Jim unfolded himself from the bench and stood up. After a few words of grateful praise for her first meal, he began the introductions in earnest.

"I may as well get you a little more acquainted with the crew. Starting at the far end, as I said earlier, those are the Rose brothers, Petey and Dave R., both out of Idaho. There used to be another Dave, Dave N., but he left for an outfit down near Denver. We tried to let go of the R., but it wouldn't go. Petey was our cook while we were waiting for you. Strong effort on his part, results were...mixed." Again Petey looked away at the reference to his skills. "Best way to stay on their good side is not to move that game board. Can't recall it ever happening, but best not be the first. Nearest anyone can tell, they been at war at the end of the table there since they got here about six years ago.

"Next to Dave R. is Sticks. He grew up local, he'll try and talk you into stuff. Don't do it." Sticks gave a mock protest, but for the most part he seemed to agree with Jim's assessment. "Doc usually sits next. On the end there is Mac, who you need to pay no attention to at all. I wish I could say his bark is worse than his bite, but in his case they're both bad."

Mac threw Jim a scowl, and Jim gave him a satisfied smile. Win couldn't tell if Jim was teasing or not, but either way Mac's crabby demeanor was clear.

"Coming down this side, across from Mac, you have Hollywood at the end there. He's set on putting the Circle-S on the map with most of the single, and even some not-so-single, ladies in town."

Indeed. Even after a day's work, Hollywood was by far the best put-together and stylish of the crew. He had sun bleached hair that rested on the top of his collar. The dirty-gold locks had somehow resisted the hat hair the rest of the crew was sporting. His eyes were a soft brown and Win was sure he could work those eyelashes like the most fetching Southern belle. His smile revealed teeth so white she doubted he needed a nightlight to read at night. Hollywood was aptly named and seemed quite content with Jim's description.

"Next to him here is Dix," Jim continued, placing his left hand on the cowboy's shoulder. "He's the early riser and our resident artist. Then comes myself and then Double M," he said, noting the empty space to his right. "We put him between me and Petey, cuz Petey's deaf in his left ear and I have a little trouble with my right. Seems to work best that way."

Win acknowledged the clever strategy with a smile. "I under-

91

stand." Then addressing the group she said, "It's nice to meet you all. I know this first meal isn't much...I didn't have much time and there wasn't much to work with. It's been a while since I've cooked for this many—hopefully, I'll be able to get into town tomorrow and go shopping...and at some point, I'll need a list of what you like and don't like, but for the first few days, I ask for your patience while I get my feet under me...."

She realized she was talking fast and about to go into a full ramble, so she shut herself down. Another uncomfortable lull in the conversation ensued, the silence filled with stainless silverware scraping final forkfuls off the thick ceramic dinner plates, some loud chewing and finally a burp from Mac.

The awkward silence was broken by Sticks. "Excuse me, Miss Win? What's for dessert?" The group looked first at Sticks and then, hopefully at Win. Her face flushed. *Dessert! Since when did cowboys need dessert?* She hadn't even considered dessert. The Rifleman never ate dessert. It was just short of a culinary miracle that she was able to assemble the, albeit wonky, dinner, now they wanted dessert? *What kind of cowboys eat dessert?* She could feel her panic rising.

"I'm sorry...I didn't...," was all she could get out before the snickering started. First Sticks, then Hollywood. Then the Rose brothers broke a smile and finally Jim. Only Mac seemed oblivious to the joke, and shoveled down the last bite of his dinner. Then, finally realizing she was being poked at, she took a breath and smiled.

"Right-oh...very funny."

"Sorry Win," said Jim, "you just seemed kind of nervous, so far be it for us to miss an opportunity to make things worse." He shot a look at Sticks who immediately lowered his eyes. "Truth be told, this is the best tasting meal we've had in months. If this is what your cooking tastes like before you get your feet under you, well, I'm sure I speak for the lot of us when I say, we look forward to you settling in."

The *Here, Here's!* And *Yes, ma'am's!* echoed from one side of the table to the other, except of course, Mac, who was now leaning back in his chair reading a newspaper.

"Thanks," she said quietly, her cheeks a full red. Then surveying the empty dishes, "Looks like I might need to up the ante on the quantity, too."

"We're not a crew that sees many leftovers," said Dix in a soft voice, looking sheepishly down at the table.

"I'm getting that feeling...so, what time is breakfast?" At this the men started getting up and moving the dishes toward the sink. *Okay, so they clear the table...I wonder who washes up?*

Her tacit KP question was answered when Dix and Sticks began to scrape the dishes and load the trays into the dishwasher. The ancient appliance came to life with a grunt and continued with a cacophonic whirr that sounded like the dinnerware was caught inside a tempest.

The crew referred her to the job duty list, and all were surprised when they realized it was no longer posted. Apparently the rotation was so fixed that there hadn't been a need to refer to it in years.

"We need to be saddled up and out by around 6:30," Jim said. "Dix here gets the coffee going so we can do the barn feeding and be back in to eat around 5:30. Breakfast is usually something quick, but hearty would be best; it's got to hold us for a while. We're back in the barn by six to tack up and get going."

"Got it." She said coolly. *Holy smokes that's early!* "How do you like your eggs?"

Again silence fell, as they all looked at her and each other, puzzled. She looked to Jim to find out what she had done now.

"We've never really been asked before—it's pretty much scrambled or nothing."

"Oh...well...no reason I couldn't give it a try...anything but poached," she said, with a smile. Win pulled a pencil and paper off the counter. "How about you Jim?" She proceeded around the table, building her list for the next morning:

Jim: Over Hard
Sticks: Sunnyside Up
Hollywood: Sunnyside Up
Dave R: Scrambled
Petey: Over Easy
Dix: Sunnyside Up
Mac: Poached

After the kitchen was clean, the dishes dried and stacked on the shelves, the crew drifted back to the bunkhouse. Exhausted, Win walked the path back to the Grady's and her room. The June night was black and warm like coffee. She paused and let her head fall all the way back on her shoulders. The Wound at the nape of her neck grumbled but let the insult go. She closed her eyes and listened to her own breath flowing; in...and out, in...and out. When at last she opened her eyes, the stars above her seemed to dance in luminous animation; infinite pinpoints of light flowing in layers of time.

For that moment, she felt part of it all—this place, her worth, a new strength. All connected. All safe.

When she quietly stepped inside the front door, she heard Miss Lucy's voice softly call from the front room. "Win?"

"Yes, Mrs. Grady?" Win entered to find her nestled on the couch, reading.

"Lucy, please."

"Lucy."

"How'd it go?"

"Fine I guess...they ate everything."

Lucy chuckled. "Well, they'll do that. I meant how did you like it?"

Win stopped and took in the question. "I did...like it...I guess." Then assuredly, "Yeah, I liked it."

"I'm glad." They smiled at each other. "You should know that I invited Christopher to have supper with us tonight. Consider it a welcome present." She grinned then with a twinkle in her eye. "Won't be able to keep him away tomorrow night, he was just about out of his skin missing your first meal, but he knows better than to turn me down. I thought it might help to ease you in without our lively manager in the mix."

"You thought right. I owe you one," Win said grinning.

"My pleasure."

"Good night, then," said Win, as she turned to go.

"Good night, Win. Sweet dreams." Miss Lucy returned to her book as Win climbed the creaking stairs up to her pale pink room.

The next morning Win bolted upright from a dead sleep, a move that jolted The Wound awake as well, the vestiges of one of her frequent bad dreams dissipating in her head. Disoriented, she took stock of her surroundings, slowly remembering where she was, last night's dinner and even more importantly, this morning's breakfast. She glanced at the small alarm clock she had found in one of the other bedrooms, it was 4:46. She had set the alarm for 5:00. She shut it off.

Opening her bedroom door, she came face-to-face with a sleepy-eyed Army, the dog still blinking from being roused by her entry into the hallway.

"Hello, you," Win whispered her surprise, not wanting to wake the Grady's. "When did you get here?" She had missed the part where they had become friends. His tail flapped a couple times against the floor and took the open door as an invitation.

After taking in some of the new smells, the red dog confidently plopped down on the corner of her mattress. "Make yourself at home," she said, amused. Army sighed in accord and snuggled into the flannel sheets.

After washing up in the small bathroom, she swallowed the last Zithromax that Nurse Marilee had packed. The Wound, not used to the early wake-up call, felt especially taut and was in a full-tilt grumble. She assembled the cleanest outfit she could piece together and made her way downstairs with Army lazily following in her wake.

Once outside the house, Win immediately felt the promise in the late June dawn. All around her the dew shimmered as the sun's first rays reached for and touched each individual droplet. The air was crisp, but with a promise of transforming into a day of summer warmth. As always, she appreciated the lack of humidity. Compared to the oppression of Atlanta's soup, the Wyoming air felt like an open book where any story might still be written.

It wasn't until she rounded the Old Barn that the true brilliance of the Medicine Bow sunrise stopped Win dead in her tracks. Without warning, she found herself with an unfettered view of the mountains beyond, the sky ablaze behind them as the sun crawled up their back sides. Fire red, giving way to the softer hues of daylight. She marveled at its intensity, as it innocently pried into her darkest reaches. Surely there had been great symphonies written to capture this exact feeling. One flawless moment. But she knew even music's great masters could only knock on the gates that would render perfect description. This was not of man's making.

The cookhouse was empty when she entered. Win assumed they were busy with the feeding rituals that Jim had described the prior evening. With the exception of the coffee already being made, *Thank you Dix*, and an open drawer sagging out of the cabinet, the kitchen was exactly as she had left it the night before. She grabbed herself a cup and set to work.

She had previously scoped out bacon and frozen hash browns, and set them to frying in large, cast-iron pans. There were a multitude of six-inch skillets that she then prepped for the various egg choices. She placed the not-quite-stale bread slices on a baking sheet and turned on the oven broiler to toast the first side. She clustered the salt and pepper, jams and butter in the middle of the table. Win stacked the plates and flatware on the end as she had done the night before. All in all, she was already feeling the flow of the setup and knew the process would only get more refined as time went on. She had just turned her thoughts toward lunch when the side door opened and Double M came striding in.

"Miss Win!" came his jovial salutation, "I wanted to personally convey my apologies for missing your first dinner last night, but our Miss Lucy insisted I join them, and well, there just isn't any turning down Miss Lucy. Truth be told," he said conspiratorially, "I think she might be a little jealous, you know, she's been the only female around for so long now, understandable how she might feel the need to keep me all to herself for one day longer, but she couldn't keep me away forever, so here I am."

"Yes, you sure are," said Win smiling, wanting to keep his illusion of desired table guest alive.

Double M looked around, "Mighty good lookin' set up, organized."

"Do you see anything I missed?" said Win over her shoulder, as she turned the bacon for the final time.

"Can't imagine—'cept Dix likes cinnamon and sugar on his toast, and the Rose boys enjoy peanut butter. There are some green chilies in the fridge there, Jim'll put them on pretty much everything."

"Good," Win said with sincerity, and she moved to place the appropriate preferences near the corresponding seats.

At 5:45 the men started coming in from their morning chores. She fired up the eggs and dished up the hash browns and bacon. The men found their places and removed their hats. Some returned them to their pegs, others placed them crown down beneath the benches.

It was then that the smoke from the burning toast began billowing out from the broiler. Win ran to the oven, flung open the door and grabbed for the baking sheet. Unfortunately, the tissue-thin dish towel she was using as a hot pad did nothing to shield her hand from the oven's heat. Halfway to getting the sheet to the stove top, the pain of her searing fingertips registered in Win's brain causing her to wildly fling the baking sheet, jettisoning sixteen slices of bread, white on one side, charred and smoking black on the other.

Had there been the ability to do a slow motion instant replay, the footage would have revealed the flying slices leaving smoke trails like the bakery version of a Blue Angels show; the dark smoke marking their trajectory as they found their landing spots throughout the cookhouse. The baking sheet, however, was the real star. She had flipped it in such a way that it had spun through the air, horizontally, a rectangular aluminum Frisbee. It soared in perfect rotation and would have made it clean out the side door had it not been stopped by the crown of Mac's hat, which it sheared off his head as he unsuspectingly walked in for breakfast.

With the exception of someone shouting, "Fire in the hole!" the men, for their part had stood motionless, mouths gaping, eyes aloft as they followed the squadron of unidentified smoking objects. The sequence reached its climax when the baking sheet, after removing Mac's hat, ricocheted off the doorframe, with a clang heard across Carbon County. Finally, as if to add the final insult to flying toast injury, the sheet bounced off Mac's now hatless, crouching body.

Win stood frozen. The silence that followed was brief, as it was immediately interrupted by Mac.

"I'll be goddamned! Would you look at my hat! Gawwwwww-w*dammit!*"

Indeed his grey felt had a new dent in the rim. Not that it was pristine before, but Win knew enough that this was a big deal. A very big deal.

It was Hollywood that broke the tension, picking up a piece of toast that had lodged on a shelf between the stacks of plates, and with a loud crunch announced, "Just the way I like it."

Pent up laughter kicked in, with the hands simultaneously enjoying Win's embarrassment, Mac's disgust, and the scavenger hunt to recover all 16 slices of the runaway toast. They were having so much fun that finally Win couldn't help but join in and, for the first time in years, let herself laugh to the point of not being able to catch her breath.

As each slice was recovered, the burnt discs found themselves getting flung anew, this time used as ammo, weapons of war for the eternal seven-year-old that lurks in the hearts of all men. The kitchen once again deteriorated into a flying toast war zone. It was Jim who was finally able to wrangle the crew back to some semblance of order.

Amidst the second wave of mayhem, while intermittently ducking incoming fire, Win was able to get the eggs off the stove and onto plates. The air raid complete, the men quickly ate their bacon, eggs and hash-browns. Then surprisingly, got up and set to making their own lunches. Still in a good humor, they thanked Win for the meal and entertainment and set off for their day.

Finally alone, she sat down, stunned. *What just happened here?* She had all but destroyed her well thought out breakfast, lunch was a blur and yet the repercussions were...nil. In fact her screw-up was practically celebrated.

She flashed back to other meal mishaps during her time with Justin. His response had always been swift—and painful. She had gone through the looking glass; what had once inspired fear, now manifested laughter? She allowed herself to linger in the realization, that indeed, yes, she had escaped.

CHAPTER 8

For the mass of provisions the kitchen was demanding, Win decided to forego the local food market and head into the "big city". She had learned that there was a large grocery store in Laramie and since it was June and the pass was open over the Medicine Bow range, Win took off right after breakfast. The sun was strong in the early summer sky and the snowcapped peaks appeared suddenly as she made a turn on the winding road. The road bent and rolled as the terrain demanded and Win found herself anticipating the turns, leaning into them. The wind had kicked up and the trees all swayed at the base of the mountains like raised arms in a revivalist tent.

There was so much life here. She felt the unexpected majesty of it wash over her. It stirred a place within that had been long forgotten. Win's eyes were suddenly blurry with the bold tears that now poured down her cheeks. She had missed it all. This beauty. This fullness of feeling. The controls that had kept her protected from the depths of her despair, had also kept her from the heights of pure joy. She had lived in the middle lands, surviving, never feeling too much of one thing for fear it would take her to her knees. But now, here in the folds of Wyoming, she allowed herself the luxury of taking in this beauty and letting it move her to tears. If she could stay here long enough, hide here, until the storm down in the middlelands had passed her by, maybe....

She squeezed the wheel tightly and the burns from the flying toast incident gave a silent yelp at the pressure. The scorched skin on her fingers had almost blistered. For anyone else it would have been concerning, but for Win it only served to bring her back to the task at hand. The miniscule burns were nothing to her. In fact, it reminded her to stop into the pharmacy and load up on ibuprofen and antibacterial lotion. Granted it wasn't as strong as a prescription of Zithromax and Silvadene cream, but it would allow her to continue treating The Wound without having to explain or raise any small town eyebrows.

After the fiascos of the past couple meals, Win had adjusted her culinary strategy. These men ate. There was a velocity to their intake that she had never encountered. She would put aside the heightened ideals of her fussy cooking classes, and opt for something a bit more user-friendly. Her brain quickly formed an alliance with all things Bisquick and Pillsbury. There may be homemade breads in their future, but she needed to get her arms around the sheer volume of what she was up against figured out first.

She started at the pharmacy and then moved on to the hardware store. Double M had given her a credit card for purchases, as well as names of stores where she could charge goods to a house account. His version of the welcome wagon had preceded her. Once she had introduced herself to the local merchant, she was invariably met with a "So you're her." or "Double M told us you'd be coming." All followed with a warm, "hello."

The shopping list she had built was literally as long as her arm. It took three shopping carts to contain it all.

LIST
Vegetables!! - lettuce, cabbage, bell peppers, cucumber, tomatoes, squash, broccoli, carrots, green beans, corn, potatoes, celery
Fruit! - apples, oranges, lemons, limes, fresh berries, frozen berries
Bread- enough for toast and sandwiches daily
Milk- whole, nonfat, condensed
Buttermilk

Cream- ½ and ½, heavy
Eggs
Flour- self-rising, all purpose
Sugar- white and brown
Tapioca
Honey
Coffee- darker!
Coffee filters
Chicken
Pork
BACON!
Ham
Sausage- hot and sweet
Chorizo
Pepperoni
Pillsbury- cinnamon rolls, pie shells
Rice- white, brown, jasmine
Pasta- elbow, spaghetti, farfalle, penne
Tomato sauce
Spices- basil, oregano, cumin, cinnamon, parsley, sage, rosemary
and thyme :-), chili powders, cilantro, ginger, lavender, red pepper
flakes, coriander, cloves, anise, allspice, salt, pepper
GARLIC!!
Butter
Cheese- parmesan, mozzarella, cheddar, jack
Tortillas
Salsa- red and verde
Onions- red and white
Mayo
Mustard
Ketchup
Worcestershire sauce
Tabasco- red and green
Chilies- poblano, jalapeno, ancho

Vegetable oil
Vinegar- white and cider
Baking soda
Baking powder
Cornmeal
Pizza dough
Bisquick- pancake, muffin, biscuit
Cocoa
Walnuts
Dried cranberries
Hershey bars
Marshmallows
Graham crackers
Saltines
Dish soap
Dish towels
POT HOLDERS!!!
Sponges
All-purpose cleaner
Mop
Plastic wrap
Foil
Sandwich bags
Freezer bags
Detergent

Before leaving town Win was also able to locate a beauty salon. It was in the Curly Q Salon, that she met Nelda Quinones, proprietor and head stylist. It had been over four weeks since she had first gone blonde back in Liberty and her roots were starting to show. She booked an appointment for the following Saturday afternoon.

She arrived back at the ranch by 3:30, time enough to put away the day's purchases and prepare dinner. She was keen to redeem herself from the morning's mayhem. Now that she had found this amazing refuge, the last thing she needed was to get fired. Double M met her as she pulled up to the front of the cookhouse. He stood, hands on hips, a big smile betraying the extensive dental work he required. *A cross between Festus and Uncle Fester*, Win mused. Then with a single clap of his hands, he strode out, opened the pickup door and helped her down from the bench seat.

"Well, Miss Win, you are *re*turned to us! I admit I wasn't sure you wouldn't get into town and just keep going, what with this morning's little events, but here you are, of course! I didn't peg you for a quitter, and once again, I, of course, was right-righty-oh!"

He had followed her around to the tailgate, and gave a small gasp when she opened it. "Well slap me silly, is there anything left in La*ram*ie?!" The truck was packed solid with bag after bag of long overdue provisions. "Dang, if this don't look like the Promised Land, then you'll need to set me straight to what does! Now allow me, Miss Win, I'll get all this inside for you, lock, stock and pickle barrel. I'll do the trans*port*, then you can tell me where you want it all."

For once she was grateful for his attention. The Wound had been whining at her all the way home, and what energy she had left, she wanted to put toward dinner. She had pulled out skirt steak in the morning to thaw. She immediately prepared a marinade of red onions, garlic, olive oil, assorted chili spices and lime juice. She soaked the meat deep within the concoction and placed the large stainless steel bowls in the massive refrigerator to steep. Then she set to making croutons, broiled (dare she dare!) with a coating of ancho chili powder, garlic and butter. They would be the main event in her Caesar salad.

When the crew arrived around 6:30 the steak had been grilled, *Thank you Double M!* And was resting peacefully under a foil canopy waiting to be sliced. The Caesar was assembled and the water for the fresh corn was boiling and ready.

Earlier, after the croutons had been roasted, she had made biscuits from a mixture of flour, buttermilk and shaved ginger. They sat on the back counter, perfectly golden. She would use them as the finale after the main meal, split and covered with cream and fresh strawberries. They wanted dessert? They were going to get dessert.

Her focus was almost trance-like and the moving parts aligned perfectly in flavor and timing. She was upbeat and cordial but not chatty as the meal commenced. She was not anxious to continue the joke from the morning.

In the end, the men fell back from the table satiated, not just from calories, but from flavors. Army and Navy seemed satisfied with the scant steak trimmings. Win had saved the juice left from the cutting board to pour over their dog food. This seemed to quell any of their remaining skepticism, both butts betraying their pleasure in full wag.

Dix and Sticks helped with KP duty while she prepped for the next day's meals. Around 9:30, she excused herself to walk back to the Grady's, her redemption complete and position secure.

The next morning after the men lit out after breakfast, the kitchen clean-out commenced in earnest. She began with all the dinnerware. The interior lines on the coffee cups marked the passage of time, like rings of life on a tree stump. There wasn't a cup, plate, spoon, bowl, platter or pot that would not be cleaned and put away in a different spot; one that made sense.

Three days later, the re-organization complete, Win stood back to admire her work and noticed that the drawer on the far right of the sink wall lay open once again. She had haphazardly closed the thing no less than three times already that day. She cocked her head in curiosity as she approached the drawer, this time giving it her full attention.

The bank of cabinetry filled the side wall, breaking only for the counter, sink and window. It was painted blue and after two days of scrubbing, Win had discovered that it was a vibrant blue at that. The hardware was simple, streamlined stainless that probably had landed there sometime in the fifties.

The drawer in question measured approximately twelve by six inches on the front. Inside was a collection of useful but rarely-used objects, i.e. little yellow plastic ears of corn attached to skewers to keep your fingers from getting messy when eating corn on the cob. Judging from last night's hands-on approach, the crew had not embraced this piece of etiquette. There was also an array of nutcrackers and grapefruit spoons. Clearly this was the drawer of unused utensils.

Win separated them into containers and pulled the drawer the rest of the way out to see if there might be something packed in behind it and forcing it forward. Nothing. The runners were wood, nothing mechanical for it to slide on, nothing that would it allow it to slip forward, without intentional pressure. She wiggled the heavy wooden box back into its worn, over-painted slot and muscled it closed. She stood and regarded it for a moment longer, arms crossed, eyes squinting. Then, resolving to accept the mystery as unsolved, she turned her attention toward a problem she knew she could fix: *the pantry*.

The expiration dates went back nineteen years. The prize going to a can of wax beans that had expired in November 1988. It all got tossed. The guilt of wasting easily subsided at the thought of the botulism poisoning that would now be avoided. She reworked the shelves with what remained and made another long list of goods to replenish, as well as those needed to be stocked up for the colder months ahead.

LIST- Canned
Tomatoes- sauce, paste and whole
Pasta sauce
Baked beans

Corn
Green beans
Apple sauce
Jams- apricot, strawberry
Peanut butter
Peaches
Pears
Cherries
Pumpkin
Cranberries
Mandarin oranges
Pickles- sweet, dill, sliced and whole
Evaporated milk
Jalapenos
Green chilies
Dark rum
Jack Daniels

At the end of her first week, the transformation was all but complete. There was nothing that had not been either scrubbed, re-organized, thrown out, or all of the above.

Saturday arrived and Win rose before the sun on her first day off. The early wake up, she surmised, could be an occupational hazard. Wide awake, she found her feet and rose up from the Liberty, Texas mattress that now lay on her bedroom floor. She had opted out of the bed frame completely, storing it in one of the other bedrooms. Organizing her limbs and testing The Wound's mood, she shuffled through her morning routine. Her new sleeping companion Army, watched patiently from the corner of her bed.

Downstairs in the Grady's kitchen, after a modicum of searching, she found the necessary components for making coffee. Once the water finished its last gasps on the route through the ancient Mr. Coffee, she poured herself a cup and wandered out to the picnic table just outside the backdoor. Facing east, she beheld the sun's rays just breaking over what she now knew was Elk Mountain. The coffee steam tickled her nose and she greeted it by inhaling deeply.

"Here comes the day," she said quietly as she exhaled. The words echoing her mother's from a thousand mornings in a simpler time. They conjured the place in her past when her life was still a promise, and her footsteps full of every high hope. The sunrise's dazzle fought off the dark thoughts that usually fell after any memories from those times. The darkness always following the light, clawing at her betrayal of that promise. But still, her warm reverie held.

Not this morning, she thought, *not this day*. She closed her eyes and let the beams fall gently on her face, warming her inside and out.

Coffee renewal complete, she made her way back into the kitchen, and to her surprise Tom Grady was there. She had rarely been in the same room with him since her arrival, but now here he was, arms crossed, brow furrowed. He did not look happy.

Before she could utter a *Good Morning*, he stated the obvious. "You made coffee."

"Good m-morning," she stuttered, just to let it be said. "Yes... hope you don't mind."

"Well, I do mind."

"Oh...I'm—"

"I make the coffee in this house."

"Oh, I'm sorry...I didn't realize."

"Well, try not to do it again."

"Yes. I'll try." She couldn't help but smile. "In fact I can almost promise."

"Well, good," Tom grumbled, the furrows now mostly gone. "Warm you up?"

"Um...," Win hesitated, wondering if it was a trick question. "Sure," she ventured.

Tom poured coffee in both their cups and they both leaned against the counter in silence.

"Not bad for a first try, though."

"Oh, thanks. First and last try, you mean."

"For sure."

"Right-oh...well, I'm heading into town." Win made her way to the back door. "Have a good day," she said, eager to end the off-beat conversation.

"I'll let you know," Tom mumbled.

Win drove to Laramie to finish up the pantry replenishment and more importantly keep her appointment at the Curly Q Salon. In between, however, she stopped in at a couple of the local clothing stores to update her wardrobe. She was still utilizing Dinah's contributions, but less and less now. The resort style was becoming more and more disconnected—Win hadn't seen a set of golf clubs since she had gotten off the Greyhound. In addition, the hardcore Texas style that Tania had assembled for her weeks ago didn't feel quite right here. Wyoming had a different flavor to it; a little less flashy, more muted, more functional.

She found her way to Mountain Girl Trading Post, a cute little store on the main drag, part western wear, part ladies boutique. There she met Chris, a stunning woman Win's age with white-grey hair and light brown eyes. By the way she held herself, Win could tell she possessed a self-confidence that Win could only dream of. When Win solicited her advice, a bright earnest smile shone against her lightly tan skin. Win found herself dazzled by the woman's warmth and soft ways. Chris set about outfitting Win in an assortment of Wranglers; a couple even had bold embroidery on the back pockets and down the outside seams. She then added a slew of blouses and shirts. Mostly button-down, some snap westerns, all pretty plain, but a couple could be considered just plain pretty. Chris even talked her into a broomstick skirt, pale blue with yellow accents about the tiers.

She had Win in the fitting room for about a half hour, handing her a steady stream of items to try. There was thankfully little time to assess the unclothed specimen she had morphed into, but there definitely were changes to be noted. First off, the jeans she was trying on were a whole size bigger, and with no room to spare. The weight gain had a pleasing effect on her chest size as well. What few curves she owned had rounded up. Nothing seemed to fit anymore. But strangely she didn't feel fat...just full. Amazing what good food and a lack of fear could do.

As she was bagging the stacks of new clothes, Chris casually inquired, "I hope you don't mind me saying, but that burn on your back? I...I just can't imagine."

Win stopped cold. Of course she saw, the fitting room only had a curtain, it would be plenty easy to catch a glimpse through the crack.

"There was a fire," she said, her eyes darting for the door, escape instinctively in her mind. Win was instantly shamed. She lowered her burning face and her eyes filled. Through her blurry vision she saw her hands that had been tightly gripping the edge of the sales desk, were now covered with Chris's. The shopkeeper's were tough but smooth, their skin brown from the sun, her fingers adorned with many silver rings.

"Please," whispered Win, fighting the tears, not knowing what she was asking for.

"I know how you feel," said Chris plainly as she looked at Win, her pretty brown eyes conveying the depth of her sincerity.

"I doubt it." Win looked away.

"We all have something, Win—"

"No," Win interrupted

"Yes," said the shopkeeper. Win met her gaze, questioning, and saw that Chris's eyes were filling as well.

"You know we don't get here, where we are in our lives, because it's always so easy. Some people maybe...but most not." She looked to the side, thoughtful, seeing something beyond the racks of western wear. "No one gets out of here without scars." Absentmindedly Chris placed her right hand over her left breast and then looked Win dead in the eyes. "I'm sorry about yours, truly I am." Then with both hands she squeezed Win's fists tightly. "Don't ever forget who you were before they landed. We're still those girls." And finally, with words both gentle and fierce, "You are still her."

Reflexively, Win stepped back from underneath Chris's grasp. The honesty of the woman had completely disarmed her.

"How much do I owe you?" was all she could muster, her eyes locked on a single point of minutia on the counter.

Chris smiled softly. "I'm sorry, I overstepped...I'm probably talking to myself more than you."

She went about finishing up the sale as Win stood wooden in front of her. *You are still her.* The words echoed off the sharp edges inside her. She wanted to take this stranger in her arms and thank her, to tell her the whole story, not only of his treachery, but of her own vile weakness. She wanted to ask this white-haired angel for forgiveness. The Wound was of her own making, could she be redeemed still? *You are still her.*

Instead Win, as if in a trance, slowly gathered up her bags, and quietly offered, "You didn't overstep," then fumbled her way out of the store.

Still a little shaken, she stowed her new wardrobe in the pickup and walked the two blocks down to the Curly Q. The sun was high and the breeze cajoling. She felt her jaw and her shoulders release. She stopped for a moment and leaned her head back to take in the warmth, allowing her head to clear out the drama of the exchange, but the message softly remained, whispering on the Wyoming breeze, *You are still her.*

Nelda was waiting for her and waved her into the only empty one of the four swivel chairs. The three other clients were in different stages of their appointments. All smocked and engrossed in various magazines, completely settled into what Win assumed was a well-worn ritual quest for better hair.

Nelda introduced the other stylists. There was Dee, a petite younger woman, vibrant, probably mid-thirties, she had a blonde spiky short cut with a shock of blue coming out of the left side. Very edgy for what little she knew of Laramie. Win instantly liked her spunk. Then there was Joany, a classic brunette, sprayed and stacked high. She was about as wide around as she was tall. By the hue of her skin and her raspy voice, Win could tell she was a smoker, but from the twinkle in her eyes, Win could also tell she was the life of the party. She wore bright and mismatched colors, even by Midwest standards. Win placed her around sixty, and when she laughed, which she would do often, it all shook—her middle to the top of her circa 1965 hairdo. The third hairdresser was Sue, her style was quiet. Her hair was short, salt and pepper, with a small up-spike in the front. She was slight and pretty but with little expression. She worked like a piston in an engine as she foiled the highlights on her client's head.

Then there was Nelda. She was short, maybe five feet, but most likely not. She was a dark brunette, with just a few warm highlights. She styled her hair in long layers and Win sensed it was a style that had worn for many years. She had deep brown eyes and her tanned skin showed off the fitness of her exposed biceps. Win figured Nelda to be about her own age, but whereas Win was still timid and closed, Nelda exuded health and vigor. Win envied her that ease and confidence. She instantly embraced the inconsistency of the four businesswomen and sensed it was a group she could fit into easily. Who wouldn't?

Introductions complete, Nelda ceremoniously wrapped the towel about her neck and snugged the smock in tight around it. They had talked about what Win wanted the day she had made the appointment; the same, just toned down a bit. Without further ado, Nelda went out back to mix up the dye recipe.

Win could feel the locals' eyes upon her as she waited for Nelda to return. Supertramp was playing on the overhead system; it was probably one of the few times during the day without a blow dryer to drown it out. In the interim Nelda's cell phone, that she had left sitting at her station, rang. Win couldn't help noticing the screen saver that was now illuminated. It was a black and white picture of a 1960's Paul Newman, even through the greys of the photo she could make out his blue eyes, hot and sexy. *Nice*, thought Win, smiling at her hairdresser's classic choice.

It was Dee who asked the question dangling in the hairspray heavy air. "So Win, we hear you're the new cookie out at the Circle-S. How're the boys treatin' you?"

So again, her situation had preceded her, the small town's rumor mill was fully functioning. Just as well, she thought, knowing they would wheedle out her story one way or another.

"Okay, I guess," replied Win. "I think we're still sort of sizing each other up."

Joany piped up, "Well don't let 'em tell you anything but 'thank you'. They haven't had a real cook out there since last year when old Cabot died. You could serve them fried cardboard dipped in shit juice, and it would be an improvement over what Petey was comin' up with. Some of his experiments are legendary," she said with a chuckle that set everything on her in motion. "So even with that toast thing last week, you are way out ahead."

Deflated, Win asked, "Does *everyone* know about that?"

"Honey, everyone knows pretty much everything around here. We're a teeny tiny town with a whole world's worth of wonder. Pretty blonde women don't just show up and settle in very often."

Pretty? Win thought, shocked.

"Oh yes," Joany continued. "The men are talking, the women are talking, especially the wives are talking. You *are* single, aren't you?"

Win practically choked at the question. "Uh, yes, but really...no one need worry about me, I have no interest in doing anything besides cooking."

"Oh you say that now, but I'd imagine there's some cowhands that wouldn't mind putting that to the test."

"Mm-hmm," was the collective response from the stylists and clients alike.

"No really," she said dead serious, wanting to squelch any fluttering drama, "*No* interest. Zero."

"Are you a lesbian?" Dee chimed in, completely innocent of the etiquette breach.

"Dee!" squawked Nelda, coming out from the backroom, practically dropping her root erasing mixture. "What on Earth!"

"Jesus!" chimed in Joany.

Dee looked puzzled. "What?"

Sue just kept on working.

"You just don't ask a stranger—" Nelda said, exasperated. "I'm sorry, Win."

"Don't be," said Win. She was smiling not only at the surprising question, but the instant ruckus it caused. She saw her opportunity and made a point of not responding directly. "Suffice to say, the wives can rest easy in Medicine Bow tonight."

"Well, of course they can," said Nelda soothingly. But the knowing eyes, ricocheting looks from mirror to mirror let Win know that the message had been received. As far as Laramie was concerned, the new cookie at the Circle S was a lesbian. Perfect. Her disguise was now complete. The only potential wrinkle was that now Sue was somehow foiling her client's hair without taking her eyes off Win.

"Easy does it, Sue," said Joany, good-heartedly. The salon erupted with laughter, and Sue's face burned crimson as she went back to her task in earnest.

Apparently Win wasn't the only gay woman in Laramie.

Two hours later, and after booking appointments every five weeks for the next six months, Win emerged into the Laramie sun, root free, now sporting a blonde color that could actually be found in nature. Her step was lighter as she walked to her pickup and she smiled, allowing for the possibility of four new friends.

CHAPTER 9

A few weeks down the line on a soft July evening, the sun was fresh into its descent and eager to find its nightly respite behind the Sierra Madre range. The breeze was so delicate that the aspen paddles swung in silence. Win had her routine down now, a strategy that allowed the kitchen to maintain its new order and an epically cleaner demeanor.

She was in the process of preparing dinner: baked chicken thighs in Harissa sauce, steamed rice, tossed green salad...and pie. She had begun to incorporate pie and coffee for dessert. Yes, as it turned out, cowboys *did* eat dessert. With fervor! It was her new signature, a round pie period at the end of the dinner sentence.

Just as the cooking was finishing up, the backdoor opened and the band of dusty, tired cowboys came rambling in. Army, now Win's constant companion, met Navy at the door and both went to wait by their respective bowls to see what goodies might come their way.

Everyone had figured out the drill; filthy hands were washed, hats came off and were hung on the pegs above their jackets. A couple of them, usually Sticks and Dix, helped transport the steaming serving dishes to the table. The conversation was always sparse at first, giving way to their hunger, but as their stomachs started to fill, they turned to talk of the day, telling stories; a few of them new, but mostly old and worn. Joking and jibes were the rule.

Once the platters were empty and the dining frenzy complete, small plates replaced the dinner plates, a piece of bumbleberry pie on each.

Win was in the pantry pulling the baked beans for the next

morning's breakfast, when the front kitchen door opened and Doc Sears walked in.

"Hey, boys."

"Doc!" Greetings came from all around the cookhouse. Had the crew been paying attention, they would have known his arrival was imminent. Army had been waiting expectantly at the door for a good half hour.

With a nervous twinge, Win peeked through the hinge crack of the pantry door to view the legendary *Doc*, only to discover to her shock, that standing in the kitchen doorway was *Calder*! From-the-H-B Calder! Sex-in-the-back-of-her-pickup Calder! *Blonde-tequila-slut Calder*.

As her mind swam in dazed circles, trying to gather the pieces that she had missed, two things were clear: the legendary Doc *was* Calder, and at some point she had been had. She didn't know if anger or laughter was in order, so she decided to concentrate on just breathing.

After the general greetings, Double M was the first (of course) to speak up. "Take a load off and we'll find you some*thin'* to eat."

"Smells good in here," said Doc.

"You bet it does, let me in*tro*duce you to the maker of those smells you're smellin'. *Re*member a few weeks back, gosh almost a month ago now, you called and mentioned a new cookie would be comin' our way? Well a couple days later, whaddaya know, Miss Win here shows up, and with some gentle per*sway*sion by my fine self, she agreed to stay on and keep this sorry bunch in gov'ment feed! Well, she's been nothin' short of a mi*ra*cle, we all never ate so good."

"Doc," said Jim interrupting, Win was now standing in the pantry doorway and he beckoned her forward. "Allow me to introduce Win—but you must've already met somewhere along the line." His head swiveled, looking from one to the other.

Win blanched at the thought that Doc, or Calder, or whoever

he was, would reveal that in fact they *had* met and had a steamy one-night stand in a drunken stupor—a revelation she was not interested in seeing played out on the men's faces. She was proud of her status on the ranch, although it had only been a short time, she liked being just one of the boys. Thanks in part to the local rumor mill, no one seemed interested in anything further than her cooking. They treated her with respect (well, with the exception of Mac) and she had no interest in them thinking of her in any other way.

"Hello," said Win, her eyes anywhere but his.

"Actually," said Doc with a sly smile, "I remember you very well." With a bigger smile now, he let the moment linger as all went silent. Win could hear a night owl call as she envisioned herself bolting for her truck. Finally, she looked into his eyes and steeled her gaze, her message a mix of pleading and fear; a sadly familiar combination. Her heart sank.

"You see, Win here saw some trouble in Granby with a couple of the local low-lifes. I happened to come along in the middle of it, nothing to report really...at some point she mentioned she was a cook by trade, and well—here she is." He gestured toward her. It was all so nonchalant. "Weren't we supposed to get a cup of coffee or something?" He looked at her innocently, but his eyes held a hint of mischief. "Anyway, good to see you again, Miss Winchester." He extended his hand, which she warily took.

"You too...*Doc*." She said his new name with an extra bite, then playing along added, "Thank you again for the assistance...and for the recommendation." With a sweep of her hand around the kitchen she said, "So far, so good."

She forced a smile at him that he met with one of his own, only his was warm and easy. Win felt an unwelcome shot of heat roll through her. She prayed the moment went unnoticed by the crew.

With the help of Sticks, whose turn it was this week, Win went about getting the dishes washed. She felt as if she were watching the scene from outside herself. She could see herself scraping, rinsing, loading and rolling the dirty dish trays through the rumbling dishwasher. She was glad to have the cacophony of the ancient appliance, running water and disposal; her ears filled with something other than her labored breath going in and out.

She noted Doc settled in next to Sticks and across from Jim, in the bench space that had always been empty up until now; like a false tooth filling in a smile. Win couldn't recall anyone ever sitting in that spot since she had arrived, not even casually outside of meals.

Pie was passed, coffee poured. The men gave Doc the latest updates on the stock, calving and fence. He listened and responded when asked, yet all the while, he could feel her there. He knew her every move without having to look her way, conscious of every clink of silverware and clatter of plates. Though he never allowed himself to glance over to her side of the kitchen, he could sense her every breath.

The conversation slowly turned to stories and gossip. A bottle of whiskey appeared from somewhere. A card game of hearts started up and the Rose brothers resumed their chess game.

"We were getting worried you'd miss the Fire Ball," said Dix during one of the lulls.

"Not likely," said Doc. He groaned inwardly at the thought of yet another Fire Ball. His family had been putting on the event for three generations. What had started as the yearly celebration of the end of harvest, had transitioned into an all-out party whose celebrants crossed all age groups, vocations and counties of the Platte Valley. He had carried the tradition forward with great care, the proceeds now going to a couple of charities he felt strongly about. However, without a doubt, Doc's favorite day of the year was the day *after* the Fire Ball, when the whole commotion was put to bed for another year.

Win finished the last of her cleanup. "Okay boys, that's it for me. Dix, I left a new grind out for tomorrow morning...a bit stronger, see what you think."

Dix nodded, still intent on his cards. "Sounds good."

After closing a drawer that had been hanging open since he got there, Win headed to the back door. With her hand on the knob she said, "It's nice to have you back with us, Mr. Sears." He looked up and found her eyes for the second time that night.

"Just Doc is fine."

"Right, *Doc*...." Then turning away, she said softly, "Good night then."

Good night's were returned all around with the exception of Doc.

"Don't be late," he muttered as he watched her go. She had changed since he had met her, softened up a bit. There was a color to her cheeks that had been missing. *Medicine Bow*, he mused.

"Your turn, Doc."

"I'm thinking, hang on," he said, returning to the present, then played the wrong card which Jim immediately picked up to win the game.

"Thinking, all right," Jim said, "just not about cards." There were good-hearted chuckles all around.

Doc stood up, stretched and smiled, "Good night, you sad excuse for a ranch crew."

He walked into the bunkhouse and closed the door.

The next afternoon, Doc came around the corner of the New Barn just as Win was stepping off the Grady's porch to head down for the dinner shift. He eyed her from top to bottom, and though he showed no expression, Win felt the same unspoken current run through her that she had experienced the evening prior. The feeling was not only unspoken but unwelcome, yet she still found her-self pinned by it, her feet now glued to the ground at the bottom of the stairs. Without any further acknowledgement, he walked over her way.

"Hey," he said lightly, as he got closer and jammed his hands deep in his pockets

"Hey," she replied, crossing her arms and looking down.

"Sorry about the surprise last night, I guess I thought that you would have put two and two together by now, and since you were still here...."

"You know you could have mentioned this was your ranch," she said, surprising them both with her peevish tone.

"Would you have come?"

"Sure," she said unconvincingly.

"Sure?"

"Sure." She repeated the word with coolness.

"Seems like the only thing you were sure about that morning was not sharing a cup of coffee."

"I had to get on the road."

"Yup."

"I did!" she said defensively.

"Not saying you didn't. But had you stayed, I'm pretty sure I would have layered into the conversation that this was my place."

"Really?" she asked skeptically.

"I'd like to think so."

"But you're not sure."

"Never had the chance to play it out." Doc looked out toward the back acres. "You saying you would've come here if you'd known you'd be seeing me again?"

"So you admit it, then."

"Admit what?" he asked, his brow wrinkling beneath the brim of his hat.

"That you got me here under false pretenses." Win surprised herself again with the accusatory tone.

"False—what?" Doc was becoming exasperated. "Look—Win— we needed a cook, you said you could cook. Maybe I didn't spell it all out, but it's not like we did a lot of talking that night...."

Win flushed and looked away.

Doc gave a slight wince at her embarrassment. Then in a softer tone, he offered, "I swear, I never meant to mislead you...mostly."

Doc had to know his case was thin, so he wisely tried a different tack. "Anyway, forget all that." He took in a clarifying breath. "Seems like you like it here. The boys can't stop talking about your cooking. Looks like it was working fine—'til I showed up. Wouldn't be the first time something like that happened," he said under his breath, then continued "But if you can't stand being here—now, with me here—just because we—or for whatever reason you want to pick, then...."

"Then...." She was looking at the ground again, her confidence wavering.

"Then...you should think about going," he said quietly. "I mean, well, since I was the one to coerce you, the right thing to do would be for me to bow out and leave, the problem is that I kind of own the place." He looked at her then, squinting into the sun with a slight smile on his chiseled face. "You realize, my life wouldn't be worth a single cent, if the boys find out I was the one that ran you off. Boss or no boss, they would most likely string me up. I wouldn't want you to have that on your conscience—be an awful thing, that." He was now looking everywhere but her.

"It's so kind of you to consider the hardship on my conscience," she said sarcastically.

"Just looking out for you." He found her eyes again. His steely blues boring into her, she felt a distant tug deep inside. "You know I—we—could look out for you, a little bit anyway, never know, might be a good thing."

"I can take care of myself Calder...or *Doc* or whoever you are. I don't need looking after—and I don't need you to make apologies when you're not sorry. What I need is a job, and whether you like it or not, I think I'm doing a good job here. So, unless you want to fire me, I'm staying. For now." With that she made a sharp pivot on the heel of her boot and strode off down to the cookhouse.

"Well, good then, glad we worked that out," she heard him call, as she stomped off. Damned if she couldn't hear the smile in his voice and she pictured his grin growing under the brim of grey felt.

Where did that come from? She marveled to herself, her mind whirling just shy of a head rush. Before she reached the cookhouse, she doused the smile that had bloomed beneath her own hat.

After those first encounters, Doc kept his distance. He was polite and appropriate during the meals, doing nothing that would raise an eyebrow on how he regarded her one way or the other.

At first Win was proud of herself. She had stood up to him and he had taken her at her word. But as the days went by, it was clear to Win he couldn't be less interested in her, and she began to feel sheepish about how harshly she had treated him. After all, what did he have to be sorry for? He had saved her from a couple of thugs, taken her to a level of escape and pleasure that she wouldn't have thought possible—an activity in which, by the way, she had been a very willing participant—then had the *audacity* of finding her a job and orchestrating her arrival here in this small corner of paradise. All the while, he had not judged her and had been nothing but a gentleman. There was no crime. No treachery had been committed. Win felt herself bristle at the realization.

The next afternoon, she sought him out. Win knew he had stayed behind from the day's ride, to look after an ailing horse. She found him in one of the stalls in the Old Barn. As she drew nearer, she was surprised at how nervous she had suddenly become. She approached him quietly, the horse between them was hooked up to a huge IV bag of fluids.

"Hey," she said quietly.

"Hey." His head popped up over the horse's withers, his eyes alive and questioning.

"Who's this?" she asked, looking at the droopy-eyed rust-colored horse. His head hung lower than it should.

"Him?" he said, petting the horse's neck underneath its mane. "This is Speedy." Then he stepped back, crossed his arms, and with concern in his voice said, "Though, not so much right now."

"Is he going to be alright?"

"Too soon to tell. Bad case of colitis." Then stepping in to pet him again said, "Would help if he put up more of a fight—kind of given up."

"How can you tell?"

"Just can. Speedy's been through this a few times now...it's hard going, takes its toll. We all have our limit." Then focusing anew on Win, Doc's eyes now revealed his own fatigue. "What can I do for you?"

"Oh." She had been so taken with the sad-eyed Speedy, she had to regroup her thoughts on her purpose for being there. "I thought...I wanted to...thank you."

"Thank me?" Doc raised his eyebrows, confused but definitely interested.

"Yes, thank you...for not saying anything...I mean, about how we met."

"Never an option," he said sincerely. "No one's business." He set about continuing his work.

"Well anyway, thank you. It's just that...that night, I don't know what got into me...I haven't really...ever...I hope you don't think...."

He sighed and looked at her again, resting his forearms on the back of the horse. He gave her half a smile, his eyes gleaming with a hint of mischief. "I don't think either of us really thought that one through."

Win blushed crimson and her eyes suddenly glued themselves

to the top of her boots.

"And no," he continued, "I don't think...."

"Oh." The slight disappointment in her voice seemed to confound them both.

Doc gave her a puzzled glance, then returned to the business of tending the ailing chestnut horse. The silence built between them with Speedy's every labored breath. Win felt embarrassed. Clearly, their one-night stand was just that, and whatever he had felt that night in Granby, had stayed in Granby. She turned to leave him to his work.

"Do you ride?"

She turned back, but didn't see him. She looked around to see where his voice had come from. Tilting her head, she realized he was bending down behind the horse holding one of its hooves on his knee.

"I'm sorry?"

"Do you ride?" His voice strained as he dislodged something stubborn.

"Um...no, I guess."

"You guess?"

"Well I used to, when I was a kid. My grandparents had a dairy farm in Wisconsin and they raised Belgians, kept them around even after they didn't need them to work the farm anymore. Grandpa 'usually had a team for sale'. That's what his business cards said." Win smiled at the memory of the gentle giant that was her grandfather. "I spent my summers with them, and he'd throw me and the neighbor kids up on their backs. In the beginning, our legs barely cleared the tops of them. They were huge! I was probably seven or eight, so everything seemed big back then. So I would grab onto their mane and try not to fall off. It was fun."

Win realized she was rambling. She had allowed herself to get caught up in the memory, then realizing her audience, immediately felt like an idiot. Another awkward silence ensued.

"Well, since you're here now, you should probably know your way around a horse." Doc was back in his vet mode, her presence no longer seemed to register with him.

"Oh...I don't think—"

"I'll have Dix teach you. He's patient."

She checked her disappointment again. Had she assumed that the owner of the Sears Ranch was going to take time out of his day to give her riding lessons? Even so, his hand-off stung a bit. In addition, apparently his assessment of her skills revealed that her instruction was going to need untold *patience*. He was bringing in the patience specialist. She moved from feeling stupid to being annoyed.

What did she expect? She put aside the snub and focused on the positive. She had a job. She felt safer than she had in years. Surely those benefits far out-weighed some alcohol-ridden tryst in the back of a pickup. Having said all that to herself, the thought of dealing with The Wound on the back of a horse did not feel like a remotely good idea.

"Anyway...," she started her excuse anew, "thanks, but—"

"Good. I'll let him know." Doc walked into the tack room.

Effectively dismissed, Win just stood there, not knowing what to do next. Clearly he wasn't interested in actually having a conversation. Yes, *annoying!* She turned on her heels, shaking her head as she strode out of the barn.

Through the slats of the tack room, Doc watched her go. He marveled at the effect she had on him. He wasn't much of a talker, ever, but even so, he practically suffered lockjaw when she was near. She did need to learn how to handle a horse out here, if only for safety reasons, but he wondered if the trauma on her back would let her ride. The destruction he had seen that morning when he stealthily peeked beneath the covers had haunted him ever since. He saw it when he closed his eyes at night. Whatever the cause, it must have nearly killed her. But somehow she had survived. She had beat it, as much as she could, and now she was on the road, clearly alone, using a different name. Whatever had happened had made her run.

Even as she feigned normalcy in her day-to-day world, he sensed her fear. She was skittish. She jumped a little too much at a loud noise or unexpected movement, her face blanching white. Though she would quickly recover, Doc never missed the subtle shifts.

If he were the one to teach her riding, he would be too careful; revealing what he had seen, what he already knew, what she was desperate to hide.

Dix was the best horseman on the ranch. He was born to break them gentle, guiding them, making the right things easy and the wrong things hard. He had a way with horses that the rest of the crew could only dream of. Doc knew he'd have to tell Dix about her injury, maybe not the full horror of it, but enough that he would be mindful of her limits. Doc also knew that Dix would keep her secrets. Dix was a deeply honorable man. He would keep her safe. Above all, she must be safe.

Doc knew the intensity of his feelings would only frighten her away. If she knew how that night had stirred him; in the forgotten confines of his heart, his gut—she'd run. She had put it all in motion. Even as he replayed that night over and over in his memory, he was amazed at how it continued to grip him.

It wasn't just the tequila, though in the end, he knew it had greased the evening's wheels. The moment he had seen her, the exact moment, he had instantly felt her pull, and with it his world had tilted, with everything sliding toward her. The strange thing was, it all felt easy, not complicated, even with the Potter boys' escapade, him being able to step in and help felt like the most natural thing in the world. He was drawn to her and with stunning clarity, he knew they would be together. He knew that just this once, circumstances would work in his favor.

Crazy.

And now she was here. Now she was here and he couldn't put two words together to make her feel welcome, to make sure she stayed, to let her know that her every move beguiled him.

Again, he rationalized, at least she was safe here. He would make sure of that. He would give her time to settle in and let the magic of the Snowy Range work its spell on her, as it had on him all these years. And in the interim, he would try not to rile her with his inane lack of conversation skills, to the point that she ran away from here, too.

CHAPTER 10

"So you got stuck with me, huh?" Win asked, with an apologetic smile.

Dix looked perplexed.

"I know Doc pawned me off on you. I'm sure you've got better things to do than teaching the cook to ride."

"I can't think of what that could be. I was delighted when Doc asked me." Dix always spoke in a measured sort of old-world cadence, articulate and understated. His dress code reflected his speech pattern. He always wore a vest, tweed or wool, plaid or solid, buttoned and fitted tight to his lean form. Dangling from a center button hole was a braided gold fob that scalloped into a lower pocket. It connected to an elegant timepiece that he cradled with respect every time he referred to it; which was often.

He was standing in the walkway, between the stalls and the arena, holding a lead rope. At the other end of it was a sorrel horse that looked like someone had sprinkled powdered sugar from one end of him to the other, the look was accented by a dark red mane and tail. *The horse version of Army*, she mused. What little she knew of horses was enough to know this one wasn't going to win any beauty contests.

"Win, allow me to present Beau," said Dix, beckoning her in. She approached cautiously, reaching out to him, intimidated by the sheer size of his head. Her touch was tentative as she petted the length of his Roman nose. The freckled horse graciously lowered his head and rubbed it up against her.

"Oh!" she said, as the simple gesture pushed her back on her heels.

"He likes you."

She eyed Beau skeptically, scrutinizing his big brown eyes. They were calm, the lids hanging heavy and soft.

"Doc picked him out special for you," offered Dix.

"I bet that was a short conversation," Win muttered under her breath.

"Hardly." Dix looked at her with a puzzled smile. "We must have talked through the pros and cons of every horse on the ranch, and even a couple on the neighbor's places. Their gaits, their size, age, attitude—"

"Their patience?" Win interrupted, sounding more bitter than she intended.

"Sure, that too." Dix went on, unfazed, "Beau here emerged victorious."

Dix scratched him behind the ears and Beau leaned into him. If he had been a cat, Win was sure he would have purred. The horse-choosing process confused Win. Doc couldn't have been less interested in her the other day. She quickly put the puzzle out of her mind. She had more important issues to deal with, like the crazy idea that The Wound would ever tolerate being on the back of a horse.

"Look Dix, I appreciate all this, but you should know...I'm not so sure this is a good idea...I—"

"I'm certain we haven't determined that yet," Dix interjected, not allowing her to continue. "Let's see what Beau's got to say about it."

She eyed the sleepy-looking horse, still wary, then took a step back and looked sideways for the exit, an old habit.

Dix took a step backward as well, giving her room. His God-given gift for reading animals and people alike, was now homed in on Win. Doc had told him about the burn scars that she bore and no other details, but he sure as hell could guess.

He had been watching her—occupational hazard—furtively reading her since she had arrived. She shied easily, moving *around* people, quietly calculating just enough distance so she wouldn't, couldn't, be touched. Her eyes didn't maintain contact and her smiles were most times empty, barely connecting to her eyes, rarely exuding real warmth. He had worked with horses that showed the same signs.

Sometimes he knew their dark histories, other times he'd let them tell their stories in their own way, letting him imagine the details, but always there was a common conclusion. Abuse. Some were broken beyond repair, their trust shattered. He could get them going, get them moving under the saddle, but there would never be anything but fear just below the surface, the bond between horse and man irrevocably broken.

On the few occasions Dix had witnessed Win's smile break through whatever fences she was riding, she was brilliant. Dix could see the true Win, at least who she had been once. On those occasions, she damn near *sparkled*. An aura of light yellow and pinks surrounded her. He noted the sheer beauty of it...and the effect it had on Doc. Then the fences would mend up again, quickly repaired by her need for self-preservation, and the glow would fade. Dix regarded her now, his road map set.

"Today's just about introductions." Without asking, Dix stepped gently toward her and handed her the lead rope, then seamlessly stepped away. "Why don't you guys take a walk?"

"I...." Win fought her panic as she felt the lead rope heavy in her hand.

"Just keep it easy, no running just yet."

"Running?" She could hear the panic rising in her voice.

"Just a figure of speech." His voice was smooth, slightly amused.

She took a breath and tried to relax her shoulders. "Right-oh."

"For now, it's one boot in front of the other. I promise wherever you go, he'll follow." Dix's voice was low and soothing. His eyes looked directly into hers and seemed to beam with anticipation.

Win took a step and looked back at the doe-eyed horse; he didn't budge. She looked skeptically at Dix. "Just walk, give the lead a little jiggle, a little tug, so he knows he's with you."

She took another step and gave the slightest shake to the lead rope that connected below his chin and to her surprise, Beau followed, causing her to stop in her tracks. He of course, stopped too, eying her now, interested but patient. When she stepped forward again, this time he went with her, not needing the extra tug. Together, Beau gamely trailing behind the death grip she had on the lead line, they walked down the aisle. His shod hooves echoed as they *clip-clopped* along the concrete. Win smiled at the noise.

Having let himself inside the arena, Dix eased up alongside her, quietly giving instruction over the partition between them. "There you go. You got it. He'll follow you anywhere. Hold the lead out to the side a bit, give him some room." Win adjusted her grip. "When you're ready say *Whoa* nice and low, then stop."

Win did as she was told and Beau dutifully stopped at her direction. "That's it now, that's all, why don't you take him outside for a walk around the barn. I've got work to finish up in here."

"Alone?" Her alarm was evident.

"Sure. Take a stroll, enjoy the day."

Win looked at Dix for reassurance, but Dix was already walking to the tack room. She looked again at the huge animal on the other end of the lead line.

"Okay Beau," she said under her breath, "here we go." She walked the horse forward again, through the opening at the end of the barn aisle and out into the sunlight.

As soon as Win turned the corner at the end of the New Barn, he was watching her, mirroring her progress around the building, as he stalked her, stall by stall, from the inside. Dix knew that this first time would tell the tale.

When Doc had told him about the damage on her back, the expression on his face told Dix all he needed to know. The fact that Doc didn't offer details meant that Dix didn't ask, and the fact that Doc had asked him to do her training and not undertaken it himself, told him the rest of the story. Somehow, Doc had gotten himself in deep.

Dix had worked Beau on the lunge line for an hour before Win arrived, and made sure his belly was full. Beau had always been the King of Cool, but he wanted insurance that this wouldn't be the one time Beau decided to spook at something random. He wanted this for Win...and for Doc.

Dix's wiles paid off and half an hour later Win returned to the barn at a strong pace, stood at the door of the tack room and waited for Dix to look up from whatever he was pretending to be engrossed in.

"Hey."

"Hey!" he greeted her, feigning surprise, "How'd he do?"

"Fine. Good, I guess." Her eyes held a brightness he hadn't seen much of. "What's next?"

"Next? Well unfortunately, that's it for today. I've got to shoe two horses before the boys get back."

"Oh." Her disappointment was apparent. Dix could tell she was bewildered at her own response and it caused him to fight grinning ear to ear.

"How about tomorrow?" he asked.

"Tomorrow?"

"Tomorrow, let's say every day around 2:00. We go and do a little something more, and get you back in time to do that magic you do in the cookhouse."

"Um, sure...." She was tentative again, the fence mended up for another day. "See you at dinner."

Dix smiled at her. "Absolutely. Thanks for taking Beau out, he gets lonely out here."

"Lonely?"

"Well, he's a bit of a retiree. I think he misses his buddies when he gets left behind every morning."

"Oh." She looked at Beau, sympathy clearly registering on her face. She took her hand and petted him down the satin coat of his neck. "Bye, Beau. Thanks." She whispered it close to his jaw. Then she gave Dix one of her false smiles and walked out of the barn.

Dix's smile wasn't false at all as he gave his complicit partner a good scratch high above the ears. "You did well, good sir," he said softly. The horse leaned into the scratching. Dix would have a good report to give Doc tonight.

After dinner, the cleanup complete, the men settled into their pre-bunk routines. Win had made her pork loin with apricot glaze. It was a recipe she had perfected back in Atlanta and pulled out to impress guests. Tonight she had tripled it, replacing the single shot of bourbon with a full cup of Jack Daniels. It was a hit. She had saved the gooey glaze, figuring it might be fun to add it as a syrup option the next time she plied the crew with Swedish pancakes.

Doc was nowhere to be found, again. Win said her *good-evening's* and exited through the back door. However, this night, instead of her usual path up to the Grady's, she took a small detour into the New Barn.

All the stables were full now with the horses that had been out working during the day. The munching of alfalfa, occasional snorts and shuffling hooves were the only sounds that filled the stillness of the vast space. She inhaled deeply, the still air emanated all aspects alfalfa, redwood shavings, horse sweat and the rest of their bi-products. It all mingled into a heady aroma, transporting her somewhere new. She felt her heart dig in and her insides open wide. *Terra firma.*

Small wooden placards hung from each stall door proclaiming its tenant. *Dutch, Old Jet, Diesel, Surprise, Texas, Speedy, Millie, Curly, Geronimo.* There were only a few lights casting pale circles on the cement aisle as she made her way. Without thinking, she walked around their perimeters, the spotlight still somehow threatening.

Suddenly, tears pricked the corners of her eyes and she stopped abruptly, quickly wiping them away. Not sure what had provoked them, she touched a wet fingertip to her tongue, the salt calling to her from another place. These tears were not from the usual well filled with fear and helplessness. These came from somewhere new. A fresh spring was flowing inside her. She closed her eyes and inhaled the New Barn's perfume again. The tears of relief flowed anew and a guttural sound of release escaped from the back of her throat.

The noise echoed off the hard edges of the walkway, bringing a couple of the horses' heads up from their meals. Win grinned at their inquiring faces, their ears cocked in her direction. She wiped her eyes again, this time with the heels of her hands. "I'm okay," she cooed softly to the interrupted diners, and they returned to their meals.

Pedro, Argument, Sterling, Big Guac, Flipper, Sundance...at last she found the name she was looking for.

"Hey, Beau," she said softly, as she approached his stall. Instantly he raised his head, interested in his late evening visitor. "I brought you something." As she said it, she held out her hand, revealing a small green apple. The old horse nickered his approval and eagerly bit it in half using her flat palm as leverage. Then he made short work of the other half, leaving nothing but slobber and apple juice in its wake. She wiped it off on the back of her jeans and tentatively reached up to pat his forehead, then drew her hand down the length of his long, sloping nose. When finished, she stood there for another moment and whispered, "See you tomorrow."

Then Win turned and strode out of the barn, her footsteps echoing stronger than when she had entered.

From across the arena, Doc looked up from where he was checking a horse that had showed a slight lameness earlier in the day. He had heard the footsteps, and though she never passed beneath the overhead lights, he instinctively knew it was her. He had stayed silent, watching. As usual, he was struck by her pull on him, surprised anew at how her every move seemed to turn him inside out. When she stopped and was suddenly wiping tears away, he had fought the urge to go to her. So much sadness in her still. His gut wrenched hard as he felt it with her.

Just as he was about to make himself known, she had gathered herself, squared her shoulders and continued down the aisle. He watched as she stopped in front of Beau's stall to offer up an apple. Then after a time, she had turned and strode back down the walkway, disappearing from his view as she was enveloped by the cool July night.

"Good girl," he said behind his teeth, his jaw set. "Good girl."

That first week all Win did was walk with Beau; he on the lead line, she slightly ahead, but still off to the side. She would appear around 1:30, between lunch and dinner. Dix would have him out and ready. Beau seemed eager to comply, perhaps anticipating the carrot or apple she always brought. They would walk around the ranch, occasionally stopping to allow him to graze on some sweet summer grass.

On the sixth day, as she was leading Beau back into the barn, she noticed a large wooden box inside the arena. It measured about two-by-two feet, was inverted, bottom up, and nestled into the soft dirt. As usual, Dix met her in the aisle, but this time instead of walking Beau back to his stall, took him to stand in front of the tack room and connected Beau's halter into the cross ties. Without explanation, he placed a pad on the horse's back and then gracefully heaved a saddle on top of it.

"Are you going riding?" asked Win, glad that Beau was going to get out of the barn again.

"No," said Dix without looking up, "not me."

He pulled the cinch snug, unhooked the cross ties and led Beau through the mid-aisle door and into the arena. Once inside, he made a direct line to the wooden box. He stopped and tightened the cinch again, this time buckling it and threading the long strap through a flap on the saddle. Dix then turned to Win, and with a twinkle in his eye said, "Okay, Win, let's get you up here."

Dix turned back to the horse busying himself with the stirrups. Win looked down at her boots; they suddenly felt nailed to the ground. Of course, somewhere in the back of her mind she had known this was coming. Beau wasn't a dog, after all. She wasn't going to just walk him forever. Dix acted like it was the most natural thing in the world, which of course it was. As she took a step, a wave of nausea swept over her, always a precursor to her fear. Then another step. Now Dix was beside her at the arena gate. He spoke quietly, matching her step by step, but at an arm's length, giving her room, looking anywhere but at her.

"You know old Beau's sweet on you, right? Don't you worry a minute, he'll take care of you."

"I...." She struggled to form the words. Even though Dix kept his distance, she was aware of him somehow moving her forward. "I don't think...," she continued, still at a loss. They were there now, standing next to the wooden box. Somehow, Beau had doubled in size and she practically swooned as she looked up at him towering over her.

"Here we go," said Dix, as he handed her up on what she now understood was a platform. From this vantage point, Beau shrank back to his original size again. She stood stock still.

"You should know Dix...," she stumbled, thinking of The Wound, "I can't—"

"Look Win," he said, interrupting. "There's nothing going to happen here that you can't do. I promise." He looked deep into her wide eyes. "This part here will be the hardest. But I know you can do this. Beau's ready, and you are, too."

He was holding the halter lead in his left hand and with his other, gently reached for her left foot. Win took a deep breath, bidding her insides to settle, then exhaled and allowed Dix's sure hand to guide her boot into the stirrup. Instinctively, she grabbed the saddle horn for balance. Feeling the slight pressure in the stirrup, out of habit Beau squared his weight off on all four hooves. "Good Win," Dix cooed, "now just step up and over."

"I—" she stammered, still unsure, yet a hint of excitement was starting to take hold.

"Just hold onto the horn and swing your leg around."

She closed her eyes and followed his instructions. When she opened them, she was sitting in the saddle, feeling a stretch and her weight beneath her in a new way. The Wound awoke and gave her a warning tug.

"Now, how easy was that? Next time we'll try it with your eyes open." Dix's eyebrows were raised in surprise, clearly amused. As she settled into her seat, she took a couple of deep breaths, consciously trying to lower her heart rate. Dix was checking the length of the stirrups. "Seems right. How do they feel?"

"Um...okay, I guess."

"Looks like I guessed right. Ready to go for a little walk?"

"I—" But before she could say *Wait!* Dix was leading Beau away from the platform and walking around the arena.

The movement was bigger than she remembered from the monster Belgian draft horses on her grandparents' farm. The saddle seemed to move side to side, backward and forward all at once. She was gripping the horn for dear life, her knuckles white. The

Wound uttered constant dissensions, griping at being stretched in this new way. For once she ignored its protest, more concerned with not falling off the, once again, towering Beau.

"Don't let go!" she called urgently.

"Oh, no fear of that. The three of us are in this together."

"Don't go outside!"

"All right." His voice was even and soft, the counterpart to hers, which was now nearing hysteria. As they walked around the arena, Dix kept a steady stream of encouragement and instructions flowing. "That's right. Easy now, Win. Just relax. Let Beau show you where to be. Move with him. Settle into your seat."

The moment before her distress peaked, mercifully, Dix brought Beau to a stop. He waited while she closed her eyes again, and willed her breathing to return to just the nervous side of normal. When she was ready, she opened her eyes to see Dix standing patiently, regarding her with a gentle expression.

"Okay," she said, and the three of them walked on again.

The days after her initial ascent into the saddle found Win increasingly at ease. Dix had shifted from a short lead to a long lunge line. He would stand in the middle of the arena and pivot around as Beau carried Win according to Dix's soft commands. She got used to his voice, low and strong. Once she was fully comfortable with walking, Dix slowly introduced her to Beau's other gears.

There was a gentle slow jog that didn't cover ground any faster than walking, but she found the movement easy to take. Beau's lope, once she finally relaxed into it, was equally smooth, gently scooping her along as she felt Beau's muscles rolling beneath her and the barn blurring at its perimeter. She found it exhilarating and could never contain a huge smile whenever Beau really got up to speed.

The trot was the gear The Wound refused to tolerate. On the many occasions she lost her seat, her behind would pound the saddle in opposition to the movement. With every collision, The

Wound spewed profanity, threatening to tear itself away in protest. Though she tried to hide her discomfort from Dix, she knew her blanching face betrayed her. Apparently, Dix could read her the same as he did the horses, and he would invariably slow Beau to a jog or cluck him into a lope before she had a chance to wince further. Though the *Whys* were unspoken, trotting was out.

Dix, again with patience and clear instruction, circumvented the punishing trot by teaching her to post when Beau moved through that gait. He taught her to read the movement of Beau's shoulders, letting the saddle push her up so she would rise using her knees and thighs, going up and down in rhythm with the two-beat gait. Again, new muscles were required and Win would lumber out of the sessions with a full John Wayne shuffle.

She liked the feel of her muscles' burn and the tightness that begged for a two-day recovery—though they rarely got it. Her lungs were also adjusting to the high altitude, and riding was the first time she had put them to the test. Her body was becoming strong again. No longer just an accommodation for The Wound, it had other things to do now.

The afternoons in the barn started to melt together, with Dix layering in skills so subtly she rarely felt stressed, in fact she found herself looking forward to the next challenge.

At some point, the lunge line came off and Win took up the reins. Dix remarked at how good she was at keeping the light pressure on the bit without jerking. Win was keenly aware that this was her connection with Beau, how she would talk to him, gently asking for what she needed. She could feel the horse's pull against the thin leather with her fingertips, eager to respond, showing her the way to make it easy. Win felt Beau's wisdom and guidance deeply, and returned his patience with a gentle hand.

On the third week, Win summoned another round of courage and asked Dix if they could go on a ride outside. Dix's eyes practically danced, accompanied by a grin wide with pleasure. "Don't mind if we do." Dix efficiently tacked up his favorite mare Millie and before she could lose her nerve, they were sitting side by side in the arena.

Riding out of the barn and into the sunlight was a revelation. The high afternoon sun was just beginning to stretch the shadows, the sky crystal clear and wide. Beau moved out easily, nickering his pleasure.

CHAPTER 11

T he days shortened, August waned, and the annual preparations for the Fire Ball heated up. It always took place on the first Saturday in September. With no warning, Win found herself at the center of what at times seemed like a hurricane. Two weeks prior, the ranch had begun its transformation, which didn't end until the first cowboy arrived, spruced up beyond all recognition.

She had been to the Curly Q twice since that first visit. Her blonde hair finally felt like it belonged on her head, instead of some Marilyn impersonator. Nelda and the ladies had given her the lowdown on Fire Balls past, and what to expect. It never failed to amaze her how easy and open they all were. They held the secrets of Medicine Bow firmly in their hands. Although they reveled in a good story and strong gossip, Win could see that they drew a firm line between good natured gabbing and hurtfulness. Somehow, they had taken to her and Win felt a kinship to these fine, fun women.

It was at the salon that she did the majority of her laughing. Between Dee, Nelda and Joany, there was never a dull moment. Sue was still the quiet one and always at some point during the stay, Win would feel Sue watching her. She felt a pang of guilt at misleading all of them on that first visit. Now that she knew them, she knew her lies were a betrayal. Such was the line she negotiated every day; the more she fit in and felt at ease, the more her former world slipped away, and the more she had to fight to remember why she had come there in the first place.

With singular focus, Win took on the challenge of making this

Fire Ball the best in Sears Ranch history. As the preparations started to consume her every waking moment, she very quickly found
herself running short of food storage space. After bringing it up
to Double M one morning, he suggested she use the deep freezer
in the back pantry of the Big House. "The old beast will need to
be cleaned and plugged in, but should refrige*rate* your fixin's just
fine."

That afternoon, before the dinner prep, she and Army walked
across the compound to check it out. Since Doc's return, Army had
been splitting his time between them. Most days he would follow
Doc out to assist in whatever work needed to be done, but nights
found him nestled in with Win upstairs at the Grady's. Today Doc
had gone into town and not invited him along, so he dutifully, if
not begrudgingly, followed Win through her day, both clear that
this was his second choice.

Win had never been in the Big House. It loomed large on the far
side of the circle drive, but was mostly blocked by the aspens that
stood between it and the cookhouse. It was rarely, if ever, referred
to and up to this point she had never required entry.

Of course she was curious. Here was this grand home, clearly
built with the highest quality and care, that stood, virtually abandoned, while its rightful occupant wedged his way between the
bunks of the men he employed. Yet, it wasn't the elephant in the
room. It wasn't a subject that was avoided, it was as if the house
didn't exist at all. Indeed, there were times when she would be entering or leaving the circle drive, that she found herself surprised
to see it there. Yet, there it was, three stories of well-maintained
real estate. A perfect house in perfect symmetry with the rugged
beauty of the land that embraced it, that no one cared to acknowledge, let alone live in.

The stairs up to the porch didn't creak. Instead, they seemed to
gently give way beneath her weight as she made her ascent. The
porch was devoid of any furniture, the antithesis of the Grady's

flophouse setting. The pretty woman ghost that she had seen occasionally, now sat on the rail at the far end. She leaned against one of the bark-stripped log pillars that served as a sort of colonnade to support the awning roof that wrapped around the entirety of the house. Her one foot was atop the rail with her leg bent at the knee, allowing the soft fabric of her green dress to pool in her lap. Win gauged the styling to be somewhere in the 40's or 50's, maybe rayon, maybe silk, nipped in at the waist, maximizing the effect of her pin-up perfect figure. Her exposed thigh was as firm as it was fair. Her other leg dangled, idly swaying, as if moved by a slight breeze. Win noticed that an extra button was undone at her décolletage, looking for relief from the dry heat of the late summer sun.

Army sat calmly, looking directly at the woman, his tail wasn't wagging but the intensity of his stare left no doubt that the old dog saw her as well. She sat looking vacantly out at the aspen, her arms crossed under her ample bosom, her cleavage even more impressive as it shimmered in the afternoon light. As always with the ghosts, Win made no effort to interact. But doubly so in this case; she didn't want to disturb the pretty woman's reverie.

The burnished-bronze door hardware moved with the slightest pressure, and she entered the foyer in well-oiled silence. Win had left Army on the porch, still enthralled with the beautiful ghost. The entryway spilled out into a great room straight ahead. Its center opened up to the second story. At the far end stood a mammoth fireplace built of large river rock that encased a massive granite slab that served as its mantle. She judged that she could stand up inside it without soot rubbing off on the top of her blonde head.

The hearth was flanked by banks of massive windows which went from floor to ceiling, composed of two-by-three foot panes. They faced west. Even now with the sun just beginning its trip down from the top of the sky, its beams, all confidence, were flowing into the room. Win dared to think of the heady show it would put on with the nightly sunsets. The amazing vista revealed a spectacular connection with the hills and sky beyond; the space felt more like a cathedral than a living room. Whoever built it had felt the land deeply, and had taken pains to ensure the boundaries between inside and out were as slight as the seasons would allow.

The fireplace held the attention of three deep-maroon mohair couches with worn leather seat cushions. There were three large Navajo-looking rugs, the far one laid wide in front of the hearth beneath the couches, the other two placed long-ways and side by side, at Win's end of the room. On one rug was a large dining table, with seating for fourteen, the other defined an additional seating area with deep leather chairs and a game table.

A bannister at the second-floor level curved out from each side of the far windows and met above where Win stood to form a horseshoe-shaped balcony. Beyond its railing she could see doors, all symmetrically arranged across from each other. She assumed they were the private rooms, very closed off, so different in feel from the vast space before her.

Win walked to a door beyond the dining table and logically found the kitchen. It ran the whole length of the south side, and incorporated another large table. Heavy oak. She instantly knew that this was where the majority of the meals and business of the day had been conducted. Beyond the table, through one final door, she found the pantry and therein the fabled freezer that Double M had spoken of.

She dared not guess the year it had been minted, but hoped it was within her lifetime. She found the plug lying idle beneath the wall outlet, as if it had just been disconnected yesterday. As she placed the three prongs back into their home, she closed one eye, not sure if she was about to take down the county's entire electrical grid. The old machine coughed and shook as the current resuscitated its long-dormant wiring. After waiting while the clatter settled into a semi-healthy whine, and confirming there was no smoke rising, she backed away and closed the pantry door.

Having accomplished her mission, Win sauntered over to the window above a large but shallow, porcelain sink. From there, and over the porch, she could see the west side of the Fire Hall and most of the Grady's house. Off to her right she was treated to an expanse of country with nothing but the earth and sky to frame it. She wondered how many hours the women of the house had spent looking at that same vista; if it had moved them, as it did her in this moment. She wondered if they ever felt as whole or as small, or if they took it all in stride, as if they deserved it.

She turned around to take in the kitchen and it suddenly hit her how clean it was. In fact, the entire house was clean, practically pristine, down to its deep shining wooden surfaces and its silent hinges. It was then Win heard the faint whistling.

She re-entered the main room and located the source as coming from behind one of the doors upstairs.

Quietly she followed the raspy whistle up the staircase until she located the room it was emanating from. She took a breath and lightly knocked on the door. The whistling abruptly stopped. There was no sound. She knocked again, even more tentatively.

"Hello?" she said, almost a whisper.

Win was suddenly aware of how vast and hollow the space felt. Her next instinct was to run. She turned to begin her flight and came face-to-face with the woman in the green dress, deep brown eyes drilling into her own. Her skin seemed illuminated from within as it shimmered in the light from the wall of windows. She smelled of perfume and cigarettes, her expression was...*what was it? Eager? Hopeful?* The woman didn't speak, she didn't smile, but Win could feel the ghost urging her on.

"Win?" She heard a low voice. *She knows my name!?*

"Yes?" said Win, still mesmerized by the beauty's dark eyes.

"You okay?"

She whirled then to face the voice coming from behind her. There in the doorway, with a concerned look on his face, stood Tom Grady.

"Oh, Tom..." *Of course!* "Sorry," she mustered, as she regained composure. She turned back again and found the green dress ghost gone.

"What brings you in here? No one ever comes here, especially to this room. Gave me quite a start when I heard you knock, thought you might be...well...."

"What?"

Tom was silent, sizing her up.

"What?" she prodded.

"Nothing that an old creaky house couldn't account for."

"You mean ghosts." The adrenaline from a moment ago was making her brave.

"I suppose you could make that argument, if you were the type that believed in such."

"Are you?"

"I've had my moments. Something's always going bump in the night in this old place. I confess that's why I do my work here in the middle of the day. Always gives me comfort to see the sun," Tom said, looking thoughtfully out the tall windows. "They're a mischievous bunch, I give you that."

"Really?" said Win, instantly intrigued. "How so?"

"Oh the usual—lights, doors, drawers, windows open when they should be closed and vice versa. Sometimes I even smell them."

"Cigarettes?"

He eyed her, surprised. "Sometimes."

"I've seen—smelled it too," she said, catching herself.

"No kidding?"

Not willing to reveal any more of her secrets but wanting to continue this new alliance she said, "Hey, Tom, how 'bout a tour? It's my first time here. I only came in to see about the freezer downstairs, then I heard you whistling, and...well, can you give me the lay of the land?"

Without another word, Tom walked away from her toward the stairs and left her wondering how she had offended him this time. Without stopping or turning, he said, "Come on, then. We'll start at the beginning." Win eagerly fell in step behind the rickety old man, which was easy, since his walk was sort of a slide and roll, clearly favoring a hip or a knee, she couldn't be sure which, and she knew enough not to ask.

For once she wished that Double M was her guide instead of old Tom, whose tour consisted of what she already knew. "This here's the big room—the fireplace—the kitchen—the stairs."

Win didn't push it, just glad to be in the house and feeling legitimate. She realized that up to that point, she had felt like an intruder. When they arrived back on the second floor, he led her room by room. He would open a door, let her stick her head in, then abruptly close it again. From one side of the fireplace, around the horseshoe, the rooms fell into succession. There were eight.

"Wally's,—Mary Ava's—Wally, Jr.'s—Calder's—Dun— Ida's—Young Hollis." Tom said the boy's name with a sigh, then moved on. "June's—Dodge's."

"No one shared a room?"

"Oh, there was *sharing*—" He stopped himself. "After all there was the boys. Calder and Wally, Jr. didn't arrive by stork." The old man gave Win a patronizing look.

"Right-oh," she muttered, a bit embarrassed. "But...,"

Then as if in answer, he said, "Lucy and I came here from out East as caretakers back in '51. Dodge and Wally were both married, Calder and Wally, Jr. were turning wild, and Dun and Ida were getting older. Most of the focus was out on the land, so they hired us to look after the insides and keep an eye on the boys from time to time. By the time we got here the rooms was already sorted out. Always thought the *Whys* were none of my business." He looked at her squarely as he said it. Win got the message.

"So you're the one that keeps this place so perfect."

"I keep it up. Been doing it for years now. It suits me to work on my own. And it suits Lucy to have me out of the house some."

Despite his surly ways, Win liked Tom. You always knew where you stood with him—usually in the don't-bother-me category. But now she found herself growing comfortable with the cantankerous old man. They had never exchanged this many words one-on-one before.

"Doesn't it get lonely?"

Tom looked deeply into her eyes. "You know as well as I do, there's no lonely here."

"Yes, but I work in the cookhouse."

"I'm not talking about the fellas—I'm talking about the family... the ones still with us."

Realizing what he was saying, she asked cautiously, "Do you see them?"

"*See* them?" he said, surprised. Then with a small self-aware chuckle, "You mean, am I crazy?" And finally with a broad smile said, "No, I just see their handiwork. Always undoing what I just done. I used to try and come up with believable stories, but after a while I ran outta excuses." Then serious again, he muttered, "I don't talk about it cuz there's nothing to be done. But to be sure, some of those Sears folk are still about and take their turns raising a fuss."

"Do you know who?"

"Naaah, who knows. Sometimes it gets quiet for a few weeks, or months even. It gets so I miss them." Allowing himself half a chuckle, he added, "I know it sounds nutty, but I find them good company. I always know when they're about, even when they aren't up to something. I can feel them around."

"And today?"

"I saw your face when I came out of that room. You tell me."

Win paused, "Yes, there was...she's beautiful."

Tom stopped. "Beautiful? You *see* someone?"

Tentatively she nodded, unsure she should have revealed her secret. Tom went abruptly into the room he had originally appeared from and came out a moment later with a photograph.

It was a black and white picture in a small oval frame. *It's her!* The beauty in the green dress, except now she wore a dress with large tropical flowers on a pale background. Her hair was pulled up into a soft bun, and even without the benefit of color, Win could tell her lips were still painted a deep, lush red. On her lap was the perfect blonde toddler with bright eyes. He was pointing at something that held his fascination outside the picture frame. She looked straight into the camera. She looked contented, happy. A very different expression from the one she carried now. Win's finger gently traced the outline of the Wyoming Madonna and child.

"Yes, it's her."

Tom looked at her hard, but didn't need convincing. "That's June, and with her is Hollis."

"June...," she said absently. Not since Quentin, back at the burn unit, had she known a ghost's identity. She remembered the names from the circle of stones inside the aspen. "How—"

But before she was able to finish the question, Tom interrupted, "Not my story to tell."

When he held out his hand, Win obediently handed over the picture. Tom returned it to wherever he had found it back in the room, then purposefully shut the door behind him. "We best be gettin' on with our days," he said curtly.

Win, taken aback by his sudden change of demeanor said, "I'm sorry, I...."

"No reason to be and no reason to talk about it, neither." Then with less abrasion, "No one's going to appreciate a cook and a caretaker swapping ghost stories."

"I understand," she said, realizing now how much Tom had revealed and how out of character it was. "It can stay just between us."

"No one's business," he said, descending the stairs.

"Of course," she agreed, following him down.

As he ceremoniously opened the front door to facilitate her exit, Army appeared, tail wagging and eager at her return.

Win took one last glance over her shoulder into the great room. On the upstairs railing across from the bedroom door that Win now knew was hers, sat June, her inside leg slightly swinging as it had on the porch. Still her gaze met and held Win's. In a moment that captured Win wholly, she felt June pull her in, needing her, but without a word as to how or why.

Even with all the preparation for the Fire Ball, Win still found time to steal away for a ride on Beau. She was out from under Dix's wing now, and she relished her time alone. Beau never seemed to mind her ever-cautious pace, moving out smoothly beneath her. She liked to ride the trails out behind the New Barn. The ground was red and rocky, full of scrub sage that rolled to meet the foothills to the north and the horizon to the south.

The terrain was broken up by a couple of streams that Beau would gamely navigate. Along the banks grew cottonwoods and further out, the aspen groves grew deeper. These were her favorite. She would enter in and weave Beau through the close-knit trunks.

It was a Sunday afternoon and a thunderhead had just rolled through an hour before. The iron-rich earth smelled of sage and rust. Win loved that smell. Once the giant raindrops had abated, she never missed an opportunity to get outside and inhale the unique perfume of the Snowy Mountains; a musk, earthy and sensual.

At first she had kept its impact at bay, knowing that it would move her too deeply, but the aroma pulled at her, knocking insistently on all her closed doors. Begging. In the end she had found it so intoxicating, she had succumbed. She would inhale the heady smell, her greedy lungs welcoming it inside. The scent infiltrated all the hardened parts of her and for that moment, in that breath, she would regain herself: Julia of the red hair and warm heart.

She felt part of this Wyoming earth. Her eyes welled as she smiled contentedly and gazed out into the pale blue sky.

"Hey?"

The word jolted her back to the here and now, the doors inside her slamming soundly shut.

It was Doc riding up from behind her. "Didn't want to startle you."

"No...you didn't." Then she confessed, "Well, maybe a little."

Win smiled, knowing she had almost jumped out of her saddle. He was wearing his usual uniform of work shirt, lightweight quilted vest, kerchief, working chaps, gloves and of course, his grey felt hat. His cool blue eyes squared off on hers, which caused her next breath to catch in her throat.

"What can I do for you?" she asked, feigning nonchalance. But the words came a bit too quick, giving her away.

Doc sat still as stone. She was aware of him taking her all in, sizing her up. She tilted her head, repeating her question, this time without words.

"Wanted to show you something. Up for a ride?"

His eyes were on her again. They felt hungry.

"Sure," she said tentatively. "But...um...I don't go fast."

"I know."

"Right-oh." She looked down. Of course he would know, there wasn't much that happened on the ranch that Doc missed.

Without another word, Doc moved Dutch around her and walked out eastward across the sage flat. They walked along, her trailing a length behind, Beau ably keeping up with Dutch's animated pace, his ears perked forward, seemingly enjoying the company.

Dutch was a pretty paint horse, white with big black patches. He was one of Doc's frequent choices when heading out for a workday. "Just about to get good," was how Doc described the young horse. The affection was clear on both sides.

The only sound beyond the hooves' work was the *oola-oola-ool* of a lone Sand Creek crane calling down the sun.

They rode up into the foothills and did cutbacks until they were fully into the Lodge Pole pines. They wound through them, always going higher, until they finally breached the top and entered into a clearing. Doc stopped and leaned forward on his saddle horn. Win moved Beau up to sit beside him. The two horses nuzzled each other and exchanged snorts.

From the clearing Win had a bird's eye view of the spread that was Sears Ranch; the archway off the highway all the way to the ranch proper, the circle drive with its treasured aspen, the buildings that fanned out from its core in harmony with the breathtaking country beyond. The cattle herd seemed like so many ants scattered across a checkered tablecloth of fields. The hay had mostly been harvested and from this vantage point the massive rolls looked like wine corks strewn across the land. *Must have been some picnic*, she mused to herself.

"It's beautiful," she said, feeling the inadequacy of the word, overwhelmed by the bounty stretching before her.

"Yup," said Doc as he exhaled, not moving from his perch.

They sat in silence, gazing out on the vista. For once nature and man's effort seemed in full accord.

"I come here sometimes," he said casually, as if they were in the middle of a conversation. "Clears my head."

"Does your head need clearing?" she asked sincerely, not in the mood to banter.

Doc turned to her, eying her keenly. "Yup." Then he returned to the view in front of them. The sun was starting its descent, the long shadows threatening to combine and overtake them.

"What do you call this place?"

"Doesn't really have a name, not officially. I always think of it as The Rise. No one comes here much, so no reason to name it."

Win smiled to herself. He was right of course. It was a human characteristic, to see something, to name it, to possess it. It was that trait that was at the very core of the conflict between humans and nature. It started kingdoms as well as wars. It allowed men to marry and claim their women as their own. To name them. To possess them. Win felt herself start to wind down a dark path.

As if he could read the darkness beginning to brew in her mind, Doc gave a soothing, "Shhhh." His eyes were on her, concern etched on his brow. Win instantly lowered her gaze, concentrating on the hand-tooled leatherwork of her saddle. "Don't want to miss the show." He nodded his head toward the west.

Following his soft suggestion, Win looked up to see the sun dipping below the ridgeline of the mountains just beyond the ranch. The spectacle was disarming, immediately drawing her out of her morbid memories and back to the wondrous display before her. Doc reached over and gently took her hand. At some point, he had removed his glove and work-roughened palm folded around her clenched fist. Immediately, she felt his heat transferring to her. Through his strong fingers, so gentle on her, she felt the dark musings of a moment ago dissolve. The contact of his skin against hers jolted her senses from the vista in front of her, to being completely focused on his touch.

Instinctively, she released the saddle horn and turned her palm to his, tenderly wrapping her fingers around his hand. When she did, he ever so slightly increased the pressure of his grip which caused her heart rate to fly. Her face instantly flushed, and in that moment she was thankful for the cover of the glorious dusk that enshrouded them.

Win sat frozen, not wanting to break the spell. Though she longed to lace her fingers between his, she didn't dare, as if it would be too intimate. She fought the urge to bring the back of his hand to her lips and gently kiss the tanned leather of his skin. Instead, she sat, immobile in the heady sensation that was Doc's hand holding hers.

The sky was on fire! The yellows and heated pinks were descending into a blaze atop the silhouetted dark cuts of the mountains. The snowcapped peaks glowed, ghostlike as the sun finally dissolved into their immovable feast. As darkness finally overtook them, Doc just as gently withdrew his hand and casually replaced his glove.

"We should get back." Torn from the daydream she had been basking in, she noted with despair the return to his standard tone. Business as usual. Suddenly, she realized that with the sunset's show all but over, the night was quickly overtaking them.

"It's so dark."

"Horses know their way," he said evenly. "Got the moon on our side, too."

Win looked up over her right shoulder and gasped when she saw the Harvest Moon rising behind them. Bold and orange and massive, challenging the sleeping sun by throwing shadows of its own.

"Oh," she said awestruck, then looking at Doc, his face now barely visible in the shadow of his hat, "it's beautiful." Again the word was glaring in its inadequacy.

He nodded and wheeled Dutch around to start the downward trek back to the ranch.

As Beau followed without hesitation, Win's anxiety re-surfaced. "Are you sure this is—"

"Shhhh," he softly soothed her again.

She took him at his non-word, let her mind go quiet and trust both Doc and Beau to get her down the mountain safely. He was right, of course. The horses found their way back with expert agility, little guidance required. When they finally found themselves back in the New Barn, they dismounted and Doc took the reins of both horses to lead them to their stalls.

"I got this."

"I could help," she offered hopefully, wanting to prolong their time together.

"Nope," was his ever succinct response.

Once again she was taken aback by his curtness. "Right-oh," she sighed under her breath, realizing that whatever it was that had happened up on The Rise was now over. "Well...thank you," she ventured as he walked the horses away from her and down the side aisle.

"Yup."

The barn's darkness enveloped them until all she could hear was the *clip-clop* of eight hooves and the shuffle of his well-worn boots.

CHAPTER 12

The Fire Ball was ready. The grass cut, walkways swept, hedges trimmed, shrubbery pruned and fences painted. The floors of the Fire Hall were scrubbed and waxed so that a dress boot could slide over them like ice. The brass doorknobs and hinges were polished and hung on their freshly painted doors like fine jewelry. Overall, the ranch was feeling festive, anticipating the onslaught of neighbors and townfolk.

The expected turnout was around two-hundred fifty, but that headcount always included some dogs. The men's attire was a pressed shirt, their best denim, spit shined boots, belt with a silver trophy buckle—only if they'd *earned* it—and their best hat. The ladies usually wore a simple dress or a broomstick skirt or Wranglers themselves, with boots and hat as well. There were lights strung from one end of the ranch to the other, and the farolitos lining both sides of the circle drive shone like a diamond necklace cradled in the seductive bosom of the Snowy Range.

The to-do list that had originally overwhelmed Win, had finally been conquered. All in the name of, as Double M put it, "Dinin', drinkin' dancin' and debau*cheery*." It all had her mark and the end result was nothing short of a feast with all the trimmings.

There was BBQ beef and pork ribs for days, slathered with a sauce that only Doc knew the recipe for (his sole contribution to the menu), cheesy cornbread with jalapeños, two kinds of coleslaw, fresh squash with roasted red bell peppers and four kinds of potato salad.

There were baked beans with bacon and brown sugar that had been slow bubbling for the past twenty-four hours. And then there were the pies. Thirty-two to be exact: apple, apple-blackberry, bumbleberry, peach, pecan, cherry, cherry-blueberry, pumpkin, chocolate-pumpkin, and strawberry-rhubarb. Win had started baking when the beans had been put to simmer and pulled the last four from the oven a half hour before the party started.

There was a bar set up near the door at the back right of the hall with beer, whiskey and tequila. Across the other side was lemonade, ice tea and strong coffee. The party was slated to start at 6:00, and the band kicked in at 6:02.

The eight-man combo played a variety of country-western and blues with the occasional round of bluegrass thrown in. As was the tradition, it was determined to include every song that contained the word "fire" in the title that had been penned in the last fifty years. *Fire on the Mountain, Fire and Rain, Firecracker, The Fireman*—the list went on.

The crowd moved seamlessly through two-steps, waltzes, ten-steps and riotous swings. There weren't a lot of wall flowers. If you were in the hall, you were either waiting at the bar or on the dance floor, doing what the lead singer proclaimed, "a-scootin' and a-swingin'!"

Win found herself outside the hall in a tent the boys had constructed over the food tables in case of the sudden downpours that were common in September. She and Miss Lucy along with Nelda and Sue (whom she had recruited from the Curly Q), headed up the effort to keep the bowls full and the buffet organized. They moved in clockwork to each other, as if they had been doing this for years.

"Never underestimate how much work can get done by four women with something to talk about," was Nelda's response when Win commented on their amazing efficiency. All had laughed in agreement. It felt good to work beside women of good humor again. She had missed the ease and warmth of being in female company.

Both Army and Navy pulled sentry duty guarding the succulent trays of BBQ. Their diligence was rewarded often by the dripping, spilling and overall sloppy nature of the meal and its diners.

For Doc's part, once the party started, after all the hard work and expense he had put into bringing the ball to life, he all but disappeared into the sweet smoke of the BBQ. He was nowhere to be found.

At some point in the evening, Win noticed a familiar face in the line-up for the food spread. It was Chris, the woman from the small boutique in Laramie. Their eyes met and both women smiled a warm acknowledgement of the other. Chris was sporting a straw hat with the broadest brim Win had seen. Very punchy indeed. The handsome cowgirl's words returned to her then, *You are still her.* Win upped the ante and gave her a mega-watt-old-school-Julia smile which Chris answered with a conspiratorial wink over her shoulder as she and a heaping plate of ribs exited the tent and returned to the crowd.

Despite the perfect evening air, Win could feel the perspiration dripping from beneath her ponytail. The Wound didn't allow for her to feel the rivulets as they rolled down her leathered back, but everywhere else she could feel the wetness of her cotton shirt as it clung. She was hot from laboring over the steaming plates of food. The Wound felt hot as well, like an old army blanket strapped to her back. She knew that she would pay for the exertions in the morning. The Wound always kept score.

Around ten o'clock, with the majority of the guests either uncomfortably full or fully intoxicated, things started to quiet down in the cook tent. Win and her helpers filled up the grub dishes one last time for whomever else might still need a bite, then wandered over to listen to the band. When she stepped into the Fire Hall she was met by a wall of sound and human humidity. A passable impression of Johnny Cash crooning *Ring of Fire* filled her ears. The bar was only two-deep now and the remaining dancers were the hardcore crew; sweat-soaked shirts and red glistening faces, only stopping when the band took a breath.

Win could feel the levity in the air, the release from the day-to-day stresses. This party only came around once a year and she could see folks were making the most of it.

She was thinking it *couldn't hurt* to join in when Sticks came up and threw an arm around her shoulders.

"Cookie!" His breath held the sour combination of beer, beans and tobacco. "Cookie!" he declared again, this time moving a clumsy hand to her waist, pulling her in tight to his side. "How-bout a dansh, Cookie?" He slurred in her ear.

Her point of view instantly changed from *couldn't hurt*, to *couldn't possibly*.

"I don't think so, Sticks." She shrugged her shoulders while extracting herself from his arm. "Still on the clock," she said, tapping her watchless wrist.

Undeterred, he swooped her up again, this time more force-fully and held her tight so they were face-to-face. She could feel his wiry strength and knew she was no match for it. The panic and memories unfolded in her—the many times when Justin had held her, helpless, due to the simple fact that she was weaker, in body and in mind. Weaker in spirit. How he loved it when she felt small. He would make her beg for mercy, and once he felt her full contrition...hurt her anyway.

With her next heartbeat, she felt adrenaline shoot from her boots, up her spine and out through the crown of her hat. In one fluid, ferocious motion, she raised her arms up, broke his grasp, placed her hands hard on his chest and pushed him away. To her shock, he literally flew through the air and collided with the backs of three cowboys waiting at the bar, laying them out like so many Stetsoned bowling pins. The ensuing clamor of men, breaking bottles and profanity brought the hall to a sudden standstill, the band ceasing in mid-song.

Win stood paralyzed. The only sound was her pounding heartbeat, now deafening in her ears. *THUMP-thump!* She knew the crowd was staring because they could hear it too. *THUMP-thump! THUMP-thump!* It boomed inside her skull, slicing through her brain.

Then everything started to slide. She could vaguely make out Sticks at the end of a blurry tunnel, standing, re-organizing his long limbs, "Well a simbol 'no' would'a dunnit." Then making a useless attempt to save face, pointed a bony finger at her saying, "Okaaay, an dunt spect me to askya agin, neither."

There were a couple of chuckles and heckles from the crowd, and the band decided to stop gawking and start playing again. But for Win, this last part was all in slow motion. The hall's edges were growing softer, the pounding in her head, though still raging, was becoming muted. As Win tried to process what had just happened, she felt a hand under her elbow, gentle but firm.

"Come with me." It was Doc's husky voice in her ear as he guided her on shaky knees to the door.

"I'm sorry," she said instinctively.

"Easy now." Steadily moving her down the front stairs, he whispered, "I got you."

She could scarcely feel herself walking as he ferried her around the side of the hall and without protest, she found herself being lowered gently into one of the worn-out chairs on the Grady's porch.

Doc sat down across from her on a couch and propped up his boots on a beat-up end table that all but filled the space between them. She remembered those same boot bottoms from that first night in the H-B office. They sat in silence. Win concentrated again on her heartbeat, but now with its alarm subsiding, she became aware, as if waking from a dream, of where she was and what had just happened.

"Oh God," she said quietly, focusing on the soles of the boots facing her. Then looking beyond them, she met Doc's luminous blue eyes. "Oh God," she said again, dropping her head and covering her eyes with her hands. "I'm so sorry."

After a beat had passed she quietly ventured, "Am I fired?"

"Nope."

Win lifted her head but wouldn't meet his eyes. She fixed her gaze on an unknown point, over the Grady's porch railing off into the inky night. "I don't know what happened. I've never done that before." She could hear the familiar pleading in her voice and her stomach turned. "I'm so sorry...poor Sticks! He must be so mad at me...."

"Pfft. Nothing to feel sorry about. He had it coming. Had it coming for a while. He tends to lose his manners after a certain amount of whiskey."

"Oh...." Not knowing what else to say, her embarrassment truly taking hold, she sighed heavily and turned her head to finally meet his stare.

"So," Doc said, in a measured tone, "what happened?"

There was a long pause, then carefully she began. "Well, I'm not sure...he was asking me to dance...next thing he's lying in a pile across the room." She looked at Doc incredulously. "I did that, right?"

"Yup, I saw all that." Doc slid his boots from the table and leaned forward resting his forearms on faded denim thighs. He bowed his head, showing her the top of his hat. Win willingly distracted herself with how perfect the felt looked in the party lights that floated above the porch awnings. What she knew to be a pock marked, sweat banded grey, now shone like so much velvet. She fought the urge to reach across the table and trace its shallows, but snapped back to the present when Doc's shoulders squared. He raised his head, revealing haunted eyes. Instinctively she leaned back, a pang of fear registering in the back of her brain.

With weight on every word, he pressed, "What really happened?"

"Oh—" She realized now what he was asking. She looked at him, balancing the moment, trying to figure what there was to be told, what he would do if he knew it all, and if she could trust him with the truth. Was she ready to remember, to live it all over again? She weighed it all out. He sat waiting, quiet, patient, but never easing his gaze.

"There was a fire."

"I know."

Her eyes widened, her senses sharp as a blade. *He knew it all already? How?!* The panic from earlier resurfaced full force, and she looked for a route out of the maze of strewn furniture.

"How did you find out?" she blurted. "How long have you known?" Win rose quickly and slammed into the coffee table. "Ow!" She flopped down again hugging her shin. Then with a note of defeat in her voice, she said, "How could you?" She could see he was taken aback by her outburst. His surprised look transformed into one of concern.

"Easy now," came his soft response. He gave her time to settle, never letting her eyes leave his. Doc took a deep breath. "I know because I saw the weeping scars that night in Granby. I know," he continued, his cadence labored, "because you had hospital grade Silvadene and painkillers in that camper of yours that was so clean you could about do surgery in it."

She sat quietly, listening to his admissions. "I know, because I was a corpsman in Viet Nam. I know what burns look like, and I know what they cost."

She could see then in his eyes the vestiges of his own scars— he was telling the truth; he had seen that destruction, that unique pain.

"So," he continued, this time in barely a whisper, "what happened?"

"There was a fire," she repeated stubbornly, silently begging him to not ask more.

"And there was a man." It wasn't a question. Though he whispered, the words held a fierceness that spoke to her deepest core.

She looked at him dead on, her jaw set, her voice small, "Yes."

"A man that did this."

Win felt her reserve falter and looked away. Tears suddenly in her eyes, she quietly uttered the bravest word she would ever say, "Yes."

They both gave quiet sighs; his of resolution, hers of despair.

"Where is he now?"

"I don't...."

Doc pressed, "How could you—?"

"I wasn't strong enough," she blurted, interrupting him. She cast her eyes downward with shame. Before she let herself see his disappointment, Win stood abruptly, causing Doc to pull back in surprise. Growing more frantic, she quickly scanned for a clean way out of the overstuffed and sagging upholstery.

With eyes welling, but a voice deceptively light, she said, "It's too much. All this intrigue, it was such a nice party...I'm sorry again for disrupting...hopefully the whiskey will blur the details for the folks that saw. I'm just so sorry...." Finally, climbing over an ottoman to freedom, she offered over her shoulder, "Well I'm going up...big night...."

Without a glancing back she disappeared inside the screen door. *Thwapp!*

Doc could hear her taking the stairs two at a time.

He had pushed too far. God, she had a hair trigger. Once again his coarse ways had made her bolt.

He was desperate to know her story. Not just curiosity, but he could sense her pain came out of some violence; a darkness that had sent her on the road. How could he keep her safe if he didn't know what it was? The danger that had made her run wasn't resolved yet. Maybe it remained only in her mind, but it still stalked her. If it was the last thing he did, he would free her from those shadows.

168

Not strong enough?! Her words, finally registering, staggered him. From what he had seen she could take anything. She was a survivor. Hell, she had escaped whatever had happened and the smart, brave woman, had made her way totally alone with injuries that would have broken any man.

She not only had saved herself, but damned if she wasn't saving him in the process. Hell, the whole damn ranch had practically bloomed under her care.

The courage she showed in mastering Beau downright humbled him. He extracted nightly accounts from Dix of her progress. The stories he painted—of her working through her fears, one-by-one, well—he didn't have the words.

Nothing new for him. He rarely had the words.

Women had always been a fairly easy equation for him. They responded to his strong and silent cowboy ways, and he wasn't above working it when the situation required.

He was good at getting a woman into bed, and even better at a soft exit the next morning. The ever-wagging tongues of the tattling town usually had his conquests informed ahead of time, which made his tactics all the more seamless.

It had all changed with Win. Jesus, what she did to him. Now suddenly, his shuffling cowboy routine wasn't working. Hell, he might be more lost than she was. She had been forced to face her demons; had the guts to take action. A wave of unworthiness overtook him. His one-word conversational skills weren't going to be enough to hold her.

"Yup," he said, under his breath.

Doc looked around the porch and relocated himself into an ancient La-Z-Boy to the side of the front door. It was one of Tom's favorites and he made a mental note not to get caught in it come morning. He flung the lever back and reclined with his feet in the air. The party was truly waning now, just a few last revelers with something to laugh about. He lowered his hat over his face and began the night watch.

Around four-thirty, pre-dawn, Win held her boots in her hand, her escape bag once again slung over her shoulder. The Wound protested under its weight. She could feel it poking at her, like a gun muzzle to her back, urging her forward. A hostage once more.

Warily, she made her way down the creaky stairs. With every sound she froze and listened for anything stirring besides herself. She passed the bedroom where Lucy and Tom were trading snores. As if giving a blessing, she placed her hand gently on the door. Win closed her eyes, lowered her head and whispered, "Thank you."

It took an eternity to silently open and close the screen door on its rusty springs, but once done she had nothing left but a straight run to the truck in her bare feet. But before she cleared the porch, Win caught something out of the corner of her eye. Turning, she saw Doc stretching and repositioning his hat on the top of his head. She froze in place.

"Mornin'," he said, smiling in the darkness. He reached for the recliner lever, and flung it to sit himself upright.

Win stood still as a statue, her limbs cement. She felt the blood drain from her face.

Doc recognized the look. It was fear. He immediately changed his approach. He rose slowly, hands up in surrender, and spoke softly, like he would to a green horse. "Hey...not my meaning to scare you. Not this morning...or last night. I...figured you might be wanting to be on your way, so I thought I'd settle in to see if I might talk you out of it."

Her demeanor remained unchanged. Her eyes darted to where the truck was parked down by the cookhouse. She made a small move toward the porch steps.

"Look," he began, measuring each word carefully, "I know you aren't here because you were dying to try out your cooking skills on a bunch of smelly cowboys. Someone like you wouldn't be here if they weren't running, hiding or crazy. But Win, it seems like it suits you, being here...and well, it suits me—us, fine too. And frankly I don't care if you robbed a bank or shot someone, you have a home here now. You're *safe*." He let the word hang in the air between them before continuing, "And we don't ever have to talk about...*him*."

Win raised her eyes when Doc's breath hitched and caught on the word. Then exhaling and releasing his clenched fists, he went on. "I don't know what the word is that describes a man like that, but you don't have to worry about me bringing it up again. As far as I'm concerned, you're just someone I met in a bar in Granby, who knows how to dance, shoot tequila and work downright miracles in a kitchen. Win, you're the best thing to happen to this place in a long, long time. I know I speak for the whole crew when I'm asking you to stay...and for myself, I say...." In the pause that followed the only sound was the sole of his boot shuffling over the grainy porch floor. Doc looked away into the distant dawn, "Please stay."

It was more words than he had used since he met her. Combined. He was instantly afraid that once again he had gone too far. She looked dazed. He could almost see the warring factions battling for territory inside her. Still she stood there, stone-faced with fear, but when he saw her stance almost imperceptibly shift, he knew he had her turned. He saw her shoulder sag slightly under the weight of her bag, and she gave a sharp wince as it idly began to slide down her arm. Before it hit the porch, he was there to catch it and when he stood they were face-to-face. As Doc looked into her pre-dawn eyes, he saw them brim with tears.

It was the second time that night he had seen her eyes fill, both times at his hand, and the shame of it gutted him. He saw how hard she fought them back, and it broke his heart to see her struggle. Her tears would never be something he would stomach. He reached up to catch the first drop, but she quickly turned and walked down the stairs.

"Where are you—?"

"Start the bacon," was her simple reply as she slid off into the dark morning barefoot, still holding the boots in her hand.

CHAPTER 13

The cleanup after the Fire Ball took a fraction of the time it had consumed to put it together. By the following Tuesday the only evidence it had taken place was the well-manicured landscape and Sticks' daily apologies.

"Enough!" Win finally stopped him short as he stood shuffling after the morning meal. "Please Sticks, as far as I'm concerned it never happened. We're good. Please—enough."

"If you're sure, Miss Win."

"Out!" she shouted, surprising them both, pointing toward the door. "If you bring it up again, I'll put you on pie restriction for a month!" That seemed to do the trick. Sticks slid out the door and never brought up the transgression again.

As summer broke down into autumn, Win could feel herself rebuilding. With each passing day and turning leaf, she felt herself growing more settled and confident. Inside, she was quiet;, the sharp edges softened, the walls slowly eroding, and with the exception of a stubborn inflammation on The Wound's shoulder blade, Win felt her world falling into a new order.

She couldn't recall when the crack had happened. Most of the time now, the tissue that defined The Wound had no feeling at all. It was vacant now. Dead. But somehow she had bumped something, hooked it on a sharp edge, deep enough to open up the leather of scars, but shallow enough to go unnoticed.

At least until now. Win took pains the night before to take a look at it in the bathroom mirror. It had become red and puffy. Immediately she had scoured it, applied antibacterial cream and covered it with a bandage. With any luck it would heal quickly and wouldn't require antibiotics. She had gone this long without needing a doctor to intervene and she had no intention of changing that.

She threw herself headlong into her work, nourishing herself and the cowboys. Her recipes shifted as the produce changed in the local farmer's markets. She had gained entry into the community of local growers down in Encampment. The season yielded squash and late tomatoes. She stockpiled and dried herbs as they made their last stands from the ground. She despaired over the rich summer fruits and vegetables that she had missed early in the season and made plans about when she would gather and put up next year's crop.

The crew settled into the routine like she'd been there for years. Five AM, Dix's coffee, she would be next in to start the bacon, sausage, ham or some kind of hash. She remembered camping with her folks as a young girl and waking up to the smell of coffee and bacon. The best way to open your eyes. When her mom caught her blinking away her dreams, she would smile her pretty smile and say, "Here comes the day!" The crew didn't know that this was her gift to them, but every morning it secretly pleased her that they woke up to that same aroma of sweet and savory promise.

From there it was eggs to-order and pancakes, or toast that they made on their own in the toaster on the side counter; the decision to abandon the broiler strategy having been made on that first morning. She was always sure there was a good selection of local jams and fresh butter from a dairy down over in Carpenter. She even perfected the Waffle Taco, which consisted of a warm waffle folded in half around a hot sausage, an over-hard egg and the slightest drizzle of real maple syrup.

Most mornings Petey went to work on the eggs, something he had tried once, actually succeeded at and decided he liked. He was beginning to make a name for himself with his creative omelets; cheese and BBQ beans, or chicken, cheese and broccoli. Mostly he just made use of the leftovers from the previous night's dinner and then added cheese. But overall he had a flair for turning questionable ingredients into something edible. His taking on the eggs every morning freed Win up to start the *Sandwiches*.

Every day nine saddlebags were piled at the end of the worktable from the day before. On an average day she would pack each bag with two sandwiches, an apple, beef jerky (Dix's contribution), a large water bottle and a thermos of coffee. She would throw in a Polar Pak to keep the mayo from going south. She tried to mix it up the best she could, with different meats, cheese, veggies and bread, but at the end of the day there was only so much you could do with a meal that would most likely be eaten one-handed. She even packed a lunch for the hands that didn't stray far from the ranch, finding it saner to limit the destruction of even one cowboy coming into the kitchen to fend for himself.

She had put her foot down early on the special order sandwiches. Making eighteen sandwiches required more of an assembly line mentality than made-to-order finesse, but little by little she bent to Jim's aversion to tomatoes, Hollywood's preference for potato chips *inside* the sandwich and Dix's passion for PB&J. With each morning the work got smoother, faster and more detailed, and in the end she didn't mind all the one-offs. She knew how hard they all worked, and her toils in the kitchen by contrast, seemed more like a privilege than drudgery.

Doc never made special requests and seemed pleased with anything that came his way via table or saddlebag. Still she found herself adding an extra helping here and a larger slice there, enough so that the crew eventually took notice that the cook was playing favorites.

An early fall day in a far field, Doc had just unveiled that day's sandwich; a solid four-incher, piled high with ham, swiss cheese, lettuce, tomato, and artichoke hearts. It was Hollywood that finally made the comment. "Hey Doc, if those sandwiches get any bigger, Dutch is gonna go on strike, citing heavy load conditions."

The rest of the crew gave a good ribbing chuckle, then seeing that Doc was not amused, all fell silent, and waited. He took his time as he finished chewing, finally stating, "Good sandwiches don't come along every day." Then with a smug smile he walked off over the crunchy remnants of harvest to enjoy his masterpiece alone.

For his part, Doc was up to the reciprocity; one small gesture for another. He took it upon himself to change out the wild flowers in the juice glass she kept on the windowsill. As the flowers became fewer with the encroaching fall, he would find a small branch of turning leaves or a handful of hulled wheat grass left behind by the thresher. He would also collect things along the trail that he found beautiful. A perfectly striped river rock, a tiny rough garnet or a golden aspen leaf on its way to turning fire red. He never actually presented them to her, but instead would carefully place them somewhere she too could discover them; inside a kitchen cabinet, on top of a jar of preserves in the pantry, on a stair going up to her room.

They never openly acknowledged the simple gifts garnered from the other, but from time to time their eyes would meet and soften. In those moments a friendship was building, and trailing closely behind waiting patiently, was trust.

It was a Wednesday in late September when Doc awoke with a start. Something was off. He looked at his watch.

5:15.

5:15 and no bacon. He swung his feet over the side of his bunk and perused the slumbering crew. Only Jim was awake, eying him. Apparently, the rest of the crew had grown to rely on the bacon as their wake-up call as well. "No bacon, no wakin'!" was Double M's pronouncement a few weeks back.

The postulate now proven, Doc pulled on his jeans and boots, then grabbed a clean shirt from the top bunk that doubled as his closet. As he stepped into the kitchen, he saw Dix standing at the sink, a cup of coffee in hand, looking out through the window.

"Where is she?" asked Doc, noting the irrational wrench of fear now running through him. Almost before he got the question out, Dix interrupted, moving toward the door, "Here comes Miss Lucy—and she's running."

Doc swung the door wide just as she got there. He reached out and held her frail huffing and puffing body up by the arms.

"She's sick," was all she got out. Without a word he gently passed her to Dix and took off running down the path to the small house, its pale yellow just on the verge of glowing in the sunrise. He wouldn't remember how fast he ran, or how he almost knocked Tom over who was waving him in from the porch. He wouldn't remember flying up the stairs, but he would never forget her face as he lunged through her bedroom doorway.

Her pale skin was damp with sweat, her eyes desperate, locked on his. She lay on her side and was shaking with fever. He eased over to her soft but swift, held her burning face in his hands and urgently asked, "What?"

"Infection," came her small voice.

He carefully rolled her on her stomach and lifted her soaked T-shirt to reveal awkward bandages that she had clearly applied herself. The tape and gauze struggling in vain to contain what was now roaring and out of control. Trying to be as gentle as possible, he worked to release the adhesive and she let out a small, keening wail. He had heard that sound before; a calf caught in barbed wire. He fought the urge to answer her with a moan of his own.

"Easy now, I got you," he cooed in the most soothing voice he could muster.

As he peeled the soaked gauze away, he saw The Wound, now in all of its furious glory; a hurricane of red and white heat that had swelled in one spot to the size of a child's fist.

"Dammit," he said, covering his mouth and nose from the stench of decaying flesh. He sat back on his heels to take it in. It was bad. As bad as infections get, right before they kill you. He had seen many of these during the war, poisoning their victim soldiers, but he never expected to see one at home—not on her.

"Win...this isn't good," he measured his words. "I need to get you to the hospital, and we need to go now."

He looked up to see Miss Lucy, Dix and Jim in the doorway. Their faces stricken with the horror of Win's desecrated back. Doc moved himself to block their view, instinctively still protecting her secret. "Jim get my truck, better yet, get Win's truck, we'll put this mattress in the back. Get a couple fellas and move fast. Miss Lucy, call Doc Seymour and let him know we're coming." He turned back to Win.

"No," she said, the word quiet but firm.

"No choice." Doc scanned the room for something to wrap her in.

"No," she repeated, her conviction clear.

"Look, I'm not gonna argue here. You go, or you die." His eyes told her the true story, but she remained resolute.

"Then I die." She uttered the simple statement without a hint of stress.

"Win, you've got a fever, you don't know what you're saying."

"Please...I know I can't fight you, so I'm begging you...If you take me...it'll all be done. They'll find me...he'll find me...I can't go back, it'll be the end. I'll run. I'll find a way. Please don't put me back there. I won't be lucky next time...I won't be lucky."

She reached for him, and buried her clammy fingers in his muscled forearm. "Promise me...." She was starting to fade. "Promise me!" Her fierce red-rimmed eyes desperate on his, he was helpless against her.

"Okay." The word came out as a sigh of anguish.

"Promise." Her voice was growing fainter.

"I promise." He surrendered, knowing he would keep his word

and praying it wouldn't mean the unthinkable. As he yielded, she gave the smallest smile and he fought a wave of panic as she floated away from him down a burning river of fever.

Doc sat quiet for a full thirty seconds, taking in the scene. There was Win, splayed and passed out on the mattress, The Wound seething, daring him to take it on. He weighed all of his experience and finally went to work. There was a clamor in the stairs. Jim and Dix, now joined by the Rose Brothers, had arrived to help with transport.

"Change of plans, boys. Too sick to move. Dix, find me a pen and paper. Jim, get Doc Seymour on the phone again and tell him we need him here, now. But don't let him leave until I talk to him. He needs to bring supplies. Petey and Dave, I need you to fill a big bowl with ice water and get me a pile of washcloths. Miss Lucy, I'll need clean towels and you'll need to get a big pot of water boiling."

They set about their urgent tasks without question. Doc got on the phone with Doc Seymour, told him the situation and gave him the list.

"Are you sure you can't get her to the hospital?" The two Docs had known each other for years and held an unconditional respect for each other.

"Yup," said Doc, and the discussion was over.

Doc went back to the eerily quiet room and arranged Win so at least she looked more comfortable. He gently brushed a lock of sweat-drenched hair from her forehead.

"Hold on Julia," he whispered.

The next forty-eight hours were a blur of activity. Doc and Lucy kept her cooled down with the cold wash cloths to try and fend off the fever from overtaking her completely. Once Doc Seymour arrived with supplies he and Doc set up an IV to keep her hydrated, and then began sterilizing the environment for what needed to happen next.

They worked in tandem to lance the bulging fist and relieve Win of the toxins it held. Then after the final draining, they scrubbed the remaining compromised tissue with peroxide. They gave her antibiotics to help her gain a foothold against the advancing infection, and a good dose of morphine in case she decided to wake up during the fight.

Three hours later, with the makeshift surgery complete and all other strategies exhausted, they covered The Wound's latest volley in Silvadene cream and swaddled it in sterile bandages. Doc double-checked her fluids and settled in for the long wait.

As day turned into night, still the fever held. She would fluctuate through layers of consciousness, most of the time out cold, her breathing labored. But other times, she would awaken, only to be present in some alternative world where her shrieks cut Doc to the bone.

"I see you!" she would cry out. "Don't leave me here! No! I'm on fire!! I SEE YOU!" Then she would scream in agony, scream for her very soul. She would look in his eyes, but seeing someone else, plead with him, "Please...." She would reach her arm out to him, and then collapse back into her dark sleep, "I'll be good...."

Her terror sickened him. Whoever, whatever this monster was—how could a man—*to her*—to anyone! He had seen enough of war to know the answers, yet his insides continued to churn with the thought of anyone laying a hand on her.

On Friday morning, as Doc lay beside her half on the mattress and half on the floor, fast asleep, he was awakened by a cool hand on his forehead.

"You look awful," said a concerned voice, as Win's face came into view. He was instantly awake.

"Hey," he said with a full smile.

"Hey." Her eyes were foggy, but her lips slightly lifted at the corners.

He felt her face. It was cool. The burning had passed. Still soaked from the broken fever, she smiled. "You should get some sleep," she instructed. He grinned as her eyes closed again into a relaxed slumber. Before getting up, he checked The Wound. The red lava of the infection was mostly replaced now with a robust pink; new cells being exchanged for sickness. He cleaned and re-dressed it.

When he finally stood, Doc felt like he'd aged thirty years. Every joint creaked and every muscle protested. As he passed the mirror, he got a glimpse of what she was talking about. His eyes were as red as The Wound had been, accentuated by two days growth of his mostly salt beard. He looked haggard.

Miss Lucy met him at the top of the stairs. "Heard you movin' around up here, how's our girl?"

"Fever broke."

"Oh thank the good Lord!" She nearly cried as she took him in her arms. He stood and let her envelop him, allowing himself to lean against her fragile frame.

"I'm going to take a shower. Would you sit in for a while? Morphine's still dripping to keep her comfortable. At some point she'll need cleaning up, fresh T-shirt and sheets, you think you could find something?"

"You know I can. You take your time. I'll sit in as long as you need. Why not go and get some sleep, heaven's sake. I'll wake you if anything changes."

He only nodded as he negotiated his suddenly ancient bones down the stairs and out into the crisp morning sunlight.

The bunkhouse was empty, so he showered and shaved in blessed quiet. When he laid himself down for a twenty minute refresher nap, his body took over and didn't allow him to wake until three hours later. When he groggily opened his eyes and re-membered, he sprang up and beat feet back to Miss Lucy's. Burst-ing through the door, he found Win sleeping peacefully in a fresh nightshirt and crisp clean sheets. Miss Lucy, looking amused, was leaning back in a chair reading the newspaper.

She shushed him. "She was awake for a while, seemed clear again."

"Good. Sorry I was so long."

She just chuckled and shook her head. "Yes, you are a selfish, selfish man." She got up slowly from her chair, and kissed him firmly on the cheek as she walked by. "I'll bring up dinner in a bit... for both of you."

Doc took her place on the chair, closed his eyes and allowed himself a moment when all he could hear was Win's soft and steady breath.

Days passed as The Wound steadily healed, and for the first time Win found herself angry with her former traveling companion. Hadn't she given The Wound enough patience and submission? The infection was a betrayal, the last she would tolerate. The Wound seemed to take her at her word and healed itself with a fervor that Doc marveled at. "Whatever you're doing, keep doing it," was his instruction. Win continued her admonishments of the once-beast behind her back with daily vigor.

Her strength returned with every voraciously eaten meal and every sound sleep. Some days her convalescence found her and the ever-present Army on the porch ensconced in one of the overstuffed sofas. She would bundle up in sweats and a blanket and snuggle in for a crisp autumn day. She read and wrote in a journal. The big event was doing the daily crossword in the Denver Post. It only delivered into the ranch on Friday's, so she got seven at once. She would stack them chronologically, not allowing herself to begin the next day's until the last one was completely filled in. There were even times she *created* a new word out of desperation just to get on with it. She always felt better with all the squares full.

Along with The Wound's new daily song of contrition, Win had another companion when she lazed on the couches. Most days June would be there, her ghostly form stretched out on one piece of furniture or another. Mostly she would look wistfully off into the distance, at times smiling at an unknown source of amusement. But at other times, not often, her gaze would bore down upon Win, pulling her into those dark brown pools. Win could feel her desperation, compelling Win to action. She implored Win to do something. *But what?*

Win would allow the ghost to stare her down, trying to understand, but the message wouldn't come, the words could not be spoken. Then in an instant, June would shift and be peacefully marking the distance again. As frustrating as it was, Win tried not to dwell on it. June would come and go, her mission never clear, but Win felt a kinship with the beauty in the green dress. She liked when June was there. All in all, she was good company.

A few days after the fever broke, Doc had reluctantly relinquished his bedside vigil and resumed his daily routine. Up and out with the boys early, last one in from the barn. However, instead of rolling into the cookhouse he went straight to check on Win, making it clear that she had been on his mind all day. Once satisfied that she was still as he left her that morning, if not a bit better, he walked back to the bunkhouse for a shower and dinner.

It was during this time that Win made a curious discovery. The far right drawer in the kitchen was not the only far right drawer that found itself in need of closing. In fact it was joined by the same drawer of the bureau in her bedroom, Lucy's kitchen and the sideboard in Lucy's living room. Never all at once, but occasionally, every few days, there it would be, the far right drawer of whatever piece of furniture or cabinetry that held it, open, agape, requiring it's mistress to close it on her next trip by.

One late afternoon as Tom made his way up the creaky porch steps after working in the Big House, Win stepped outside their usual pleasantries of the weather or her recovery. "Tom, can I ask you something?"

"If you must."

"It's about what we talked about when you showed me around the Big House."

"Okay...." He sounded unsure now.

"It's the drawers. Always the one on the far right...on the top... seems like they're always open. I used to think it was just in the cookhouse, but since I've been laid up, it seems like it happens kind of, all over. Do you know what I'm talking about?"

"Course I know."

"It happens to you, too?"

"Sure...most every day, one or another needs shutting. Depends on the room...I figure it's their way of letting me know they're there."

"They?"

"Well, I guess—you're the one who sees them—you tell me."

"I've only ever seen June, except in the aspen. Seems like there's more there...I don't know."

"Makes sense, I guess. She was always the odd one. They could never figure each other out. Though why she'd want to stick around is beyond me."

"*They* who?"

"All of 'em! June was a city girl." As if that was all the explanation needed, he threw up his hands and walked into the pale yellow house. *Thwapp!*

The crew took over the cooking chores as they had before Win arrived, with the exception that Petey had gained some actual skill in the kitchen. He now completely oversaw the breakfast, and organized a make-it-yourself sandwich bar that always looked like a deli had detonated once the crew was finished. He attempted the daily cleanup with mixed results. Dix always tacked up Petey's horse so their makeshift chef could ride out with the rest of the men.

Dinner rotated between them, each taking a turn with varying degrees of success. Especially challenged was Double M, who was confident that Cheerios along with baloney sandwiches was an appropriate meal any time of day. On such occasions many of them opted for the thirty minute drive to Centennial and the special at Shirley's Gentle Cafe. Unfortunately, they then rolled next door to The Line Bar, where beer and whiskey took center stage. This made for a less than agile morning after. After all, they were grown men, and could certainly manage to feed themselves. But it was on the post Line Bar mornings that Win's absence was truly felt.

As The Wound repaired itself, Win became more and more restless. All the laying around was making her soft and left her too much time to think. On a morning exactly three weeks after the fever hit, Win rose at four-thirty and made her way over to the bunkhouse. By five o'clock the air was swollen with the fragrance of coffee brewing and sizzling bacon. One-by-one the aroma tickled the noses of the slumbering crew and they stumbled out to the kitchen with smiles beaming on their faces.

Sticks: Well thank goodness!
Dave R: Hey, Win.
Petey: I still got the eggs!
Dix: You beat me to the coffee.
Double M: Halayjaluyah!!
Hollywood: Awwww, but it was Mac's turn.
Jim: You sure, Win?
Mac: 'Bout time.

Then Doc stepped in. "Too soon." His clipped tone stopped the chatter cold, but Win wasn't deterred.

As she moved fluidly between tending the bacon and pulling

plates down from the shelves, Doc was there to help before the plates hit the counter. "If I lay around one more day, I will go crazy. I'll take it easy," she assured him. "It'll be fine."

The boys slipped back into their old routine, gratefully and without a word. Toast was going and Petey rolled out the eggs. Meanwhile Win set to work on the Sandwiches.

Doc was silent and moved through the meal, clearly unhappy at the turn of events. As they grabbed their saddlebags to leave, Doc caught Petey by the arm, "Not you Petey, you stay and watch out for things here." He leaned in close, looking the surprised cowboy cool in the eyes, "I don't want her lifting or bending or carrying— you get the idea. If that scar goes south, I'll know the reason why."

"Yes sir, Doc."

Doc and Win's eyes met, hers in frustrated affection, his just frustrated. He stuffed on his hat and headed out.

Petey took Doc's words to heart and there was barely a task that Win attempted to do, that he wasn't under foot and doing it for her, or in some cases a step ahead of her.

By midday after cleanup and making a foot long shopping list of the sorely depleted pantry, she was exhausted. Petey leapt into action. While she napped he went to town and hunted down the groceries. Around three o'clock, she rose to the sound of her truck returning and did the prep and cooking for the dinner meal. But she was down again before the crew was back. This was going to take longer than she had thought.

At about six she could hear Doc charging up the stairs, but as always, he checked his force before entering. He was good that way. He took in the scene of her sleepily reading. "Good."

"I know. You were right. Too soon. But honestly, you put the Fear-of-Doc so deep in Petey, I think we could be on to something. He hardly let me lift a spoon...frustrating really."

Doc smiled. "Good."

"Thought you'd like that, *and* I think he kind of enjoyed it, kind of has a knack."

"Good. He's hired. Consider him your new sous chef."

"Deal," she said, surprised not only at how easily she agreed to the compromise, but that he would know what a sous chef was. But Doc always found a way of keeping her guessing. She realized she still knew so little about him.

"Now let's take a look at the damage." Doc knelt beside the floor mattress and peeled back the dry gauze bandage. No irritation or swelling, still okay.

"Told you." she said, and he looked at her sideways. She just smiled.

"By the way...," he ventured, as he leaned back on his haunches, "what's with the mattress on the floor? I know Miss Lucy had a bed in here, and what's up with the closet door? Most folks appreciate a good door on their closet, hides the mess."

"Are you saying I'm messy?" she said, with mock offense.

"No, I'm saying I don't see why you went to the trouble of removing a heavy as hell oak door from its hinges."

She looked at him and after a moment resolutely said, "I wanted to be able to come in here and see it all from the door."

Of course, he thought. It made perfect sense and he kicked himself for having asked.

"I didn't want there to be any place someone could hide," she continued, "no checking for...."

"Ghosts," he finished for her. She remembered him saying the same word to her after she thought she had seen Justin in the H-B.

"Yes." She smiled softly, allowing for the ease with which they now navigated the once forbidden territory.

"I'm sorry. I didn't realize...and I promised."

"It's alright. I know it looks strange...but it helps with the peace of mind," she smiled again to let him off the hook.

She took in the moment. It was the first time when faced with the past, she hadn't recoiled and run. She simply answered the question and didn't plunge into despair. Something had changed in her. Whether it was her new found détente with The Wound, Doc's constancy or the oncoming winter...she was settling in. "And anyway, you haven't exactly been forthcoming about your past...."

"Open book."

"Really? There's a fascinating ring of stones not a hundred yards from here, that I have spent many hours conjuring stories about, none of which, I'm sure, are remotely close to the truth, because no one here ever really talks about who was here before. It's as if this whole place just sprang to life when I drove the loop for the first time, like it was waiting for me to get here and someone yelled, 'Action!'"

He took a quiet moment, realizing how close she was to the truth.

She laid back and sighed, tired out again, then rolled to look him in the eye. "Sorry...you take me as I am, I need to do the same. But so you know, I understand curiosity...." She let the statement hang in the air.

He got up to go. "Guess I'll check out your assistant's first effort."

"See you in the morning."

"Don't be late." he called from the hallway. Doc's boots fell hard on every step that took him further away.

CHAPTER 14

Saturday morning rolled around and Win busied herself with the Sandwiches so she could get on the road to the Curly Q. With her being down for so long, she was way over her every five week regimen and her strawberry roots were increasingly evident. The ranch only worked a half crew on weekends, just basic feeding and care of the stock, so she was surprised when Double M burst in the side door.

"Hey Miss Win, I hear you have a new shoe chef?"

"You mean sous chef."

"Sue? You sure?"

"Yes."

"Maybe just call him your assis*tant*—you know what Mr. Cash said about calling men Sue."

She laughed. "Right-oh. How 'bout we just call him Petey."

"Ex*cell*ent idea!"

The oven buzzer rescued Win from yet another nonsensical conversation with Double M, but as she swapped a fresh batch of baked cookies for a sheet of raw dough, she ventured a question. It was rare for her to encourage discourse with the verbose old timer, yet she knew he would have the answers she was wondering about.

"So I'm curious...."

Double M immediately looked at her with anticipation, and she already regretted her question, but against better judgment, persevered.

"How did Doc's grandfather start this place?"

"Ol' Dun?" His blue eyes sparkled behind his bottle-bottom lenses.

"What was he like?" Simple questions, yet Win knew they would incite a deluge of information. She settled in for his response.

"Ohhhh, he was a goodun," the old cowboy said, with reverence. "He always had the vision, always knew where he was going. He grow'd up ranching down in Colorado, and when that Home*stead* Act ripened up, he took hold of it with full force. He'd already married Ida and knew he'd have to get an outfit of his own to take care of her right, so north they came. On about 1916, it was. He always talked about seeing the val*ley* for the first time, coming over Bar*nett* Ridge. It had him gut-hooked from that moment on. He started with a couple parcels, one for him, one for Ida, then home-*stead*ed out using the workers names, then buying them back, always giving them a nice profit, giving them a chance at making a foothold for themselves somewhere.

"I expect the ranch was about seven thousand acres and count-ing when the big drought hit in '31. That's when a bunch of them *home*steaders fell down. The water dried up and they couldn't make the payments, couldn't hold their stock. Dun bought'em out, each by each, at what was *con*sidered a more than fair price for then. He let 'em have a nest egg for their next go 'round, as well as keep their dignity in a tough time."

Win slid the plate of warm cookies toward Double M to keep him talking. He absentmindedly took the bait.

"You see, Dun had done the water right. He'd been patient when he came. Damming wide and high in the mountains and down the Platte river. He dug a maze of irr*ig*ation ditches, going beyond what the local knowledge would have him do. The wa*ter*ways wove him a web of control and in the end, it's what saved him from the Dirty Thirties." Win raised her eyebrows in question. "Sort of our version of the Dust Bowl," he qualified. "Most of the old timers won't ever talk about it. Must've been somethin'." Double M shook his head in empathy, then after a tick of time he took another bite.

"The land was harsh and the weather changed on a dime—well,

still does, but for those early-century folks—to say it was un*for-*giving, doesn't really cover it. After he laid the water*ways* he went to burning out the scrubby sage and then scarfed through the top soil to even it all out. From there he planted our sweet hay to keep the herd fat and hearty. It was Herefords in the beginning and it looked like that would always be our trade, until the Angus craze hit in the eighties. The ranch moved with the times, so over the next years we rolled to a mix of Black Baldies and were finally fixed as being one of the premier *pro*ducers of prime Angus in the state."

The old man paused again in the telling and looked Win square in the eye. "He did it right." His words held more emotion than Win was prepared for. "Anyone that really new Dun, knew he had a toughness and a goodness that the rest of us only dream on."

Win took it all in, for the first time not wishing for a swift end to one of his stories. "What about his sons, Doc's father?"

Double M's demeanor changed. The reverent emotion was gone. "It wasn't that he wasn't a good father," he said thoughtfully, measuring his words, "he just never really had the time. You see around here, it's a full-time go. You have to be ready for it all or it'll beat you.

"'Course I wasn't around in the beginning, but you could tell, even in the later years, there just wasn't much of a bond there. Wally and Dodge respected him same as the rest of us, but as far as I could tell there was never that arm-on-the-shoulder-I'm-proud-of-you-son stuff that I'm sure they coulda used. Plenty of stories that roll around an outfit like this, I know plenty and been told the rest." Then he defensively shot out, "Dun may not have been the greatest Dad, but he did alright, that didn't make him any less of a man. Sometimes you just gotta make your choices, and those choices aren't easy."

The old man had grown agitated. He shifted on the bench as he nervously pulled hard on his two-day growth whiskers. Win

191

had never seen him like this. Gathering himself, Double M took a moment and continued, "Most of their raising was set on Ida, but there weren't any hours lying around after her chores, either. I think back now, and I know she said a lot of her *I love you's* through the food that came out of her kitchen. She took care of them—and all of us in that way. I know she loved them boys, but maybe the mo*ther*ing thing was just not what she was gonna be best at. Those boys, Wally and Dodge, started working the ranch as soon as they could stand up and be reasoned with."

Then Double M smiled. "Doc's Uncle Wally was something, he was. I was just a kid, six or seven, but I remember him. You should have seen him then—hand*some* like the Clark Gable, he was. He had that spark, that *char*isma—us kids just wanted to be around him. He took to ranching okay alright, not that he had a choice, but you could tell this wasn't what he was dreamin' about.

"He took to drinking better—early, and it took to him right back. He was the one who started the party when he walked in the room. Then the war came and kicked it all out of him. All except for the drink. Whatever those war me*mor*ies were, I think he drank to drown 'em, but then he found out his sufferings could swim."

The old man looked at Win, his blue eyes distant behind the thick glasses.

"Now Dodge was a different story, he took to the ranch like his Daddy had. He saw beyond the grind, he could see the same beauty in the val*ley* that Dun had that first time he laid eyes on the place, and Dun took him under his arm in that way." Double M gave a slight smile revealing the crags in his teeth now filled in with melted chocolate chips.

"Dodge got the Har*vard* of ranch educations at the foot of his daddy and for the most part, he lived up to that legacy, but hard choices came knocking on his door, too." He stopped and sighed, and Win saw him make a decision not to go any further. *A first!* She looked imploringly into his tired eyes framed by the warped golden rims.

As if in explanation, Double M offered, "The work load here was relentless, everything had to be created, made, broken twice and made again. It's not like it is now; we're just topping on what they built for us. What we do is easy. We're not building fences and barns and digging irrigation. We don't live and die by a field going sallow or a virus where the medicine hadn't been invented yet. We inoculate, we spray the fields with chemicals so the beetles don't know what hit 'em. You know we're still using fence that was built by his hands?"

The old man pulled hard on a cuticle with his chocolate-laced teeth. "Ol' Dun—to Dodge— to Doc...you can't know what you don't learn."

Win cocked her head, trying to make out his meaning.

"Fathers and sons." Double M sighed, as if his words held all the answer she would need.

Win was surprised to see water pool in the corner of his eyes and threaten to overflow into the deep crow's feet. "Double M—" was all she got out, before he sprang from the end of the bench he had been sitting on.

"Gotta run, Miss Win, there's still plenty of chores need doin' in these modern times." With that he simultaneously threw open the door and swiped a cookie from the sheet she had just taken from the oven. "More love from the kitchen!" he declared. Then with a chivalrous bow, and a grand gesture of donning his hat, he was gone.

Army, as always close by, cocked his head as he watched the dramatic exit. Win leaned over to scratch her red-headed friend between the ears.

"Whatever you're thinking...you're right."

Win had to gun it into Laramie to make her appointment, Double M's story still playing in her head as she drove. When she walked in, Nelda was sitting in her chair talking on her cell, which she immediately hung up.

"Come on in you! How are you feeling? Heard you were sick as a dog out there for a while." She got up and gave Win a huge hug. "Well, you look okay, little skinny still—we were keeping close tabs on you through our sources."

Joany piped in with raised eyebrows, "Sources? So that's what we're calling it now, *sources*?"

"I'm right as rain, thank you. Way too much fuss for what it was." Win quickly shifted the subject, "So what're we talking about... sources?"

Nelda busied herself in prepping Win with her smock. "Pay no attention to them. They think they know things about things. But really, they know not much about nothing." Joany and Dee exchanged amused glances. Win just looked at her, expressionless. Between Double M's take on sous chefs and now Nelda talking in circles, she decided to immerse herself in the latest *People* and wait for whatever this crazy wind was, to just go ahead and blow through.

She returned around four o'clock and thawed out some of her spaghetti sauce. Once a month she would make a huge pot of sauce and freeze quantities to get them through the next three Saturdays. Saturday's were always a mixed bag anyway. Half the crew was out doing the basic ranch chores, the other half was either lazing around or who knows where. She didn't spend much time wondering what they were up to, as much as some of them could use someone to guide them along, she didn't want to become their mother. They seemed to respect her privacy, so she reciprocated. What they knew was every Saturday at five o'clock there was sauce on the burner, spaghetti noodles in the side pot and garlic bread in the oven. They ate when they wanted, cleaned up fairly well and she needn't be back in the kitchen until Monday morning. Sunday was her day off.

So it was on that October Saturday at around five-thirty, she fixed herself three plates and walked them over to Miss Lucy and Tom (another part of the Saturday routine). They were already sitting at the kitchen table, both with big smiles on their faces.

"Perfect! Very good!" was the overzealous response, as she laid the plates in front of them.

"Yum," Tom gushed, inhaling deeply.

She gave them a suspicious look. "You realize this is the same spaghetti we had last Saturday."

"And the Saturday before that," said Tom.

"And the Saturday before that," said Lucy. Both grins got bigger.

"Alright, what gives?" said Win, as she sat down.

"Nothing," said Lucy.

"Less than nothing," said Tom. As they started eating, she saw them exchange glances, co-conspirators.

"What?!" Win said, exasperated. What was it about this day? Had everyone gone giddy?

"Tell you what," Lucy said, with a now ridiculously big smile, "if you let me borrow that shawl you have to fight off this chill in here, I might let you in on the secret."

Without so much as an, *I'll be right back, you crazy old people,* Win ran up the stairs to get the wrap. As she entered her room, she stopped in her tracks. Her floor mattress was no longer on the floor. It now rested on a wooden platform, solid as granite and most likely as heavy. Her bed was now a height that regular, normal people could get in and out of, and there was not even a remote chance that anyone or anything could hide underneath.

She went to it reverently, gently lowering herself to sit on the end. It met her exactly thirty-one inches from the floor. She laid back and let her legs kick up and down like a day-dreaming school girl. *This is good.*

She got up, found the shawl and leisurely made her way back to the kitchen. Upon entering, she was met with the bright eyes and dental work of Tom and Miss Lucy.

"Well?" they crooned, in unison.

"Here's the shawl, so what's your news?" She sat down, straight faced.

"What's the news?" echoed Miss Lucy, incredulous. Then Win smiled and laughed, and as she unfolded, so did the Grady's.

"Oh you! So what do you know about that?" cried Miss Lucy.

"Who? When?" were Win's knowing questions.

"Who do you think?" said the old woman, with a mother's pride.

They all gave each other a smile and dug into their spaghetti, now stone cold.

Like all quality kitchens, the cookhouse had a window over the main sink that kept its mistress connected to the outside world. From there, Win could see the front entrance to the Old Barn, the walk that led to the Grady's, the east side of the Fire Hall and anyone coming around the circle drive could not help but cross her view. On any given day, as she stood sentry at her sink, she could pretty much track all of the ranch's comings and goings. She knew when the boys rode in from their day so she could time the meals, and she could monitor all visitors welcome or not. It even allowed for her to prepare an exit strategy if Double M was striding up the lane with a particularly talkative bounce in his step.

Next to the sill sat an old AM/FM radio, sturdily constructed of avocado-green plastic, circa 1972, she guessed. She kept it tuned to the local country station where the DJ regularly proclaimed, "Four out of five cowboys agree, the best country music in Southern Wyoming, and we're pretty sure the fifth one's dead." She smiled wide each time she heard it.

Every morning she cleaned out the black fly carcasses that had gathered from the previous day. She had discovered early in her ranch tenure that this was a never ending project.

Win loved this window. Most evenings she took the time to absorb a piece of the sunset through its glass portal. In the shortened days that warned of the approaching cold, she would pause in her dinner preparation, and wipe the steam that had gathered there to reveal the latest display of perfect glory as Mother Earth prepared to close down another day. Occasionally it was so beautiful she crossed her arms and cocked her head sideways in awe. "Okay, now you're just showing off," she would warmly scold under her breath, "save a little for tomorrow."

In these small moments when she was alone and filled with something other than her memories or the work at hand, she felt a gathering hope for the future nudging up inside her. The hope was quiet. Stealthy. She could feel it sidling up beside The Wound, and was amazed when her former traveling companion allowed for its company.

The steam would gradually fill in from where she had wiped, and the evening inevitably commenced with the entrance of nine cold, hungry cowboys. Their coats smelled of the coming winter, pine needles and cigarettes. As they peeled their outer rind of layers and the warmth of the kitchen ovens started to permeate the remaining flannels and denim, she could see them softening. Their posture, their voices, their eyes all seemed to get whittled down. By the time they had washed and settled in for dinner (which set land-speed records nightly) they were almost civilized.

Along with the fading warmth of the shorter days, Win and Doc had moved into a sweet yet silent friendship. He continued to leave her his tokens; a perfectly formed pine cone or a smooth stone from the riverbed. Her heart would jolt each time she found something new on her windowsill. At day's end she would take each offering with her and arrange it carefully amongst her other found treasures on the top of her dresser.

She would replace a button on his shirt when he wouldn't see. She took pains to accidentally brush the back of his hand when placing a bowl on the table. In the mornings, he lingered just long enough to be the last one out to the barn. Just long enough to catch her eyes and take her all in, before he turned and was gone for the day.

She took in each gesture, feeling them deeply, but now bittersweet. She remembered him taking her hand that evening on The Rise. How her heart had leapt in her chest. But whatever had prompted him then had somehow mellowed. His attention remained caring, yet when she looked for something more in his eyes, she came up empty.

Although there was truly nothing to tell, Jim kept the gossip in check and while the crew might have felt a shift between the two of them, the men showed their undying respect for Doc in their restraint. The subject never came up.

In those last weeks of autumn, more and more, Win could feel Doc's pull on her. She found herself running the memory of their first meeting that afternoon at the H-B, and the night that followed. It played through her mind on a continuous loop. She would bury herself in work, and try steadfastly to take her mind somewhere else. She knew he was far away from that torrid first memory. Though his tender gestures continued, he never took it any further.

She knew why of course. He had seen The Wound. Though she had never given him the details, he must have created some scenario in his head, and whatever it was, she knew the truth would horrify him even more. After all, she was a walking lie. *Win*. The lie had somehow carried her to safety, and now? She was not worthy of a man like Doc, not anymore. To think that they would never be lovers again, that their chaste encounters would be all they'd have—before, this thought would have been a haven of comfort, now it unfolded as yet another sadness whispering in her ear.

The wind bit him hard as he walked down to the cookhouse from the Old Barn. He was done. There was only so much that a man could take and Doc had taken it all. Damned if he could let it continue. He had been patient. *Patient?!* He had been a god-damned saint.

God, she haunted him. A ghost in every thought. He had seen her literally bloom in front of him. So brave. So much stronger than she thought she was. Her fever had almost broke him. Then seeing her make her way back, again, finding the strength to save herself—he was humbled. The woman owned him.

He strode solid, his muscles tight from the cold. He could feel her with him. It wasn't just her pull on him anymore—now, they pulled on each other.

He was exhausted. There was no sleep, for thinking of her beside him; his arms around her soft shoulders, inhaling her rich scent. The men were starting to notice the mistakes; the lack of concentration when his daydreams collided with the task at hand.

He knew whatever her demons were, they wouldn't let her come to him. So, enough. He would risk it all. Heaven help them both, he prayed she was ready.

As fall officially waned, an unseasonable cold snap wrapped it-self around the Sears Ranch, giving Win her first true taste of the Wyoming winter that lay ahead. The steam was thick on the sink window as Win busied herself finishing up the last of the evening's dinner work. She had served Sloppy Josie and Beer Bread, a crew favorite. Army and Navy had given a collective sigh at the lack of leftovers.

The men drifted into their usual pastimes. The Rose brothers soldiered on in their chess game. Dix had taken Hollywood on as a whittling apprentice and they were deep into their next project. They had decided to make a full set of chess pieces to replace the worn set that the brothers used. Win wasn't sure if this would be a welcome gift.

The figures were slowly being shaped as characters from the ranch. The pawns were cows (harder to carve than one might think, as the results looked like a combination of cows, dogs and a couple of cats, all with horns). The rest were cowboys; on horseback for the knights, leaning on a fencepost for the rook, holding a six-gun as the bishop. Win couldn't tell if there was any specific subject in mind when being rendered, but she noted the queen on both sides was wearing a wide straw hat.

As usual, Double M was talking her ear off on KP duty, and Mac was doing a New York Times crossword that had been left over from a passing delivery man. His cursing was getting on Win's nerves.

On the radio George Strait was crooning, *"How 'bout them Cowgirls"*. She remembered it being played at the H-B, so long ago now, that Doc had held her close in his arms. She didn't allow herself to let the memory flow further.

Between the cooling ovens and cleanup, the air hung steamy and fragrant from the meal that had just passed. Doc had gone out into the cold to check on an ailing steer. More and more he kept his distance now. The process had taken almost imperceptible steps, but she noticed. It gave her starts of melancholy and twinges of heartache. *A country song in the making*, she smiled to herself. She had let him in, he had seen too much, and to his credit, he was trying to let her down gently.

The kitchen had emptied out. One-by-one the crew had opted for their bunks. Only the brothers remained and heaven knew when they might stand down their silent battle and find their way to a few hours of sleep. Long ago the crew had gotten so they barely noticed them there; solid and still at the end of the table. Carved statues, like the pieces they occasionally moved as they waged their fraternal war of kingdoms. The men talked over them, moved around them, and in every way left the brothers to their nightly battle of wits and wile. It was a blood feud, and though all witnessed it playing out nightly; only the Rose boys would ever know why it gripped them. And they weren't talking.

The door blew in ahead of Doc from the force of a bitter gale that had kicked up early in the day. The blast of cold air seemed to awaken the brothers from their current death match and they each took turns stretching up from the table and muttering a "Good night, Win," on their way into the bunkhouse. Surprisingly, Doc didn't follow. Instead he poured himself a cup of coffee and sat on the end of the table facing her, his heavy packers dangling loose above the floor.

Win sighed inwardly, sensing this would be the conversation that she had known was coming. The one she was dreading.

A wave of anxiety began building inside her. She gave him a half smile before turning her back and busying herself with the last of the sink cleanup. He said nothing. Still he sat, slightly swinging his boots, sipping his coffee. She could feel his eyes boring into the back of her. Was it anger? Something wasn't right.

Get it over with! she cried on the inside, while outside her extremities mechanically moved through her work. She felt his scrutiny upon her, the judgment so tight it threatened to cut off her air. Her breathing grew deeper as she struggled to focus. She heard the clunk of the ceramic mug on the table.

"Win." He said it low, she felt it more than heard it and the word stopped her cold. She stiffened her back and let her rigid arms support her on the counter. With a loud creak of protest from the oak table, she heard him ease himself off, his heavy work boots hitting the floor. She gauged the length of his stride and knew the number of steps it would take to reach her. Five.

One.

Two.

Three.

His footsteps fell gently, yet with conviction, as he came toward her. *Four.*

She still hadn't moved, but her every nerve was on its prickly end. *Five.*

He stood behind her, an inch between them, his breath on her neck, his scent in the air she was trying to take in.

"Win," he repeated. She could hear his desperation, and with a sigh she closed her eyes and leaned back. All of her, against all of him.

His lips found her neck below her ear, urgently pulling her shirt collar aside as he moved down to her shoulder, tasting her. His breath harsh against her throat as he threaded a course of hungry kisses and soft bites.

"Doc," she gasped as his left hand found her breasts while his right made the journey down to the waistband of her jeans. "I..."

"Remember that first night? Win, do you remember?" She froze. *Do I remember?!* The night she had been obsessing about ever since? Her brain was racing to catch up with her body's response. He was waiting.

"Yes," she finally choked out.

"Me too." He continued as if that was all the explanation required.

She let her body ease into his hands, feel their pressure as they moved over her sensitized skin.

"Win," he said again, this time resting his brow on the top of her head, his words soft in her ear. He took a deep breath. "Might have been a ragged start for us, but I remember all the pieces that count. I remember your eyes, your lips on mine, heart beating under my hands. I remember your scent—" he inhaled deeply, breathing her in, "—same as now. Tangy oranges. Sweet soil. God help me, I've craved it every hour since." Doc's hands pulled Win's hips back into the pressure behind her. Those same hands worked in tandem as they undid the rivet button on her jeans and slid the zipper all the way down.

His words fought their way through her fears and fences, planting themselves deep inside her. "I remember it all, Win. Never gonna let it fade." Then moving his hands deeper inside her jeans, "I remember what didn't happen, too."

He let the statement float, while her thoughts soared back to that night, searching for what had been missing. Realization hit when a his fingers found their target.

"Oh!"

"Yup. *Oh.*"

"Doc, I...."

"It's time Win. Let me in. I've been waiting for you. I'm not going to spend another day pretending like you don't mean more."

Her mind whirled. The crew slept in the next room. She had been so distraught over the certainty of rejection—had she misjudged his intention entirely?

Wouldn't be the first time, The Wound rose to spew venom in her ear.

Right-oh. For once she agreed with its judgment. Could she trust herself to make the decision? She had chosen so catastrophically before. She could never let herself take that risk. Never again? But then she knew. She let herself see what was right in front of her. What she did know for sure. *He's a good man.*

She may not trust herself, but she could trust him.

"Calder." She said it clear as a ringing bell.

She was awake. Whatever else she might still need to prove to herself, she had no doubt; this man, Calder Sears, was a good man.

"Yes," she said, the water from that fresh well, flowing again inside her, brimming in her eyes.

"Unfinished business." His voice was warm and light. Immediately, her knees started to give way as he began in earnest the task he had come for.

Both hands found their destination, soon discovering just how ready she was; one circling and kneading the spot where every last nerve-ending in her body was now focused. The prodding was as urgent as it was intricate. He was breathing with her now. There was no time to overthink, to analyze or anticipate. There were only Doc's hands and his breath in her ear.

Her hands, still warm and soapy, reached up behind her, to the back of his neck. Craning her head sideways, she pulled his mouth to hers. Their tongues collided, and she recognized his taste. She clung to him forcing his hard chest to cradle The Wound, while his fingers claimed every last piece of her below.

"Please—" was his fraught whisper that allowed her to let go. She could feel the heat spreading out like warm oil, as his touch unlocked the flow to every extremity. When the waves began to crest, he seized her by the waist with one arm to keep her from falling. "I got you," his words an echo from that first night. She let the waves break over her, crashing through her body, her brain fizzing with white light. She let go. She let it all go. Her release so complete, in spite of the sleeping crew in the next room, she cried out.

With the cry came a sleepy voice from the bunkhouse, "Win, you okay?" accompanied by a rustling that meant someone was coming to check on her welfare.

With fluid precision, Doc stood her back on her feet, kissed the back of her neck, and zipped up her jeans.

When Petey poked his head out the bunkhouse door, he saw Doc sitting at the table sipping his coffee and Win at the sink where he had left her.

"Thought I heard a shout," he said, with a puzzled look on his face.

Without turning, Win and Doc answered simultaneously.

"Cut myself."

"Saw a mouse."

CHAPTER 15

The cold snap behind them, the last perfect evening of the Indian Summer made its appearance. The night was really *too* nice and made Wyoming folks leery of what bad weather lurked around the corner. Such weather would always be regarded with suspicion in the Platte Valley, assuming they would pay for it sometime in the harshness of February.

But this night was perfect; warm with just a nip of cold to keep it honest. The night was clear as water with stars beginning to shine through the liquid velvet. Rising in the east over the Snowy Mountains was a moon so white and bold, it would soon cast shadows on all it regarded.

Doc showed up as Win was buttoning up the kitchen after dinner, her latest effort at perfecting her aptly named Sears Ranch Chili. It combined the season's butternut squash with Italian sausage and buffalo meat that she had traded for some of the ranch's best sirloin. She had found a green chili source online out of Santa Fe and cheated with black beans from a can, full lead, which meant they were cooked in lard. With each innovation the dish was steadily climbing the crew's Top Ten list, with a bullet.

Doc leaned against the refrigerator and regarded her with his usual intensity, but Win sensed a rare tone of uncertainty when he said, "Take a walk with me."

The events of that night a week ago, had paved the way for new forms of affection; the meeting of eyes, the touching of fingertips, the stealing of kisses. They conducted their affections in private, thieves stealing time. She knew he was thinking of her in *that way* when he lowered his head and all she could see was a sly smile beneath the brim of his hat. Then she would make her way to be somewhere secluded, knowing he would find her.

She hung up a damp dishtowel, put on her faded trucker and walked through the front door as he held it open. "Where are we going?"

"Not far."

He took her hand and led her to the middle of the circle drive, through the guardian grove of aspen, now bright yellow in their last gasp of Autumn. He brought her to the ring of graves and stopped directly in front of the two most weathered markers.

Dunwood Sears
1895-1960
Dearest Husband
Father and Rancher
Wyoming Son

Ida Sears, née Carlson
1897-1962
Minnesota Daughter
Wyoming Wife
Devoted Mother

"Curiosity," he replied, to her questioning look. "My grandfolks, Dun and Ida," he said, as if introducing them. Then realization set in as to why they had come, and Win fought back a wave of emotion. "They built this place," he continued, "Dun was one of the first to take advantage of the Homestead Act. They started with 1280 acres between them, two bulls and fifty seed cows. They first built the cookhouse, then the yellow house. Dun built that for Ida when the hands made living in the first house too crowded. I'm sure you can imagine," he said with a smirk.

"Next came the Old Barn. Ida was the one who thought up the hall there...she felt like folks needed a place to gather that didn't have God looking over your shoulder—pretty radical thinker for back then—of course they built the chapel too, 'gotta give the Lord his due,' but you can tell by the difference in scale...." Doc let the point make itself, then continued, "They would have all sorts of gatherings; dances, grange meetings, the ladies would gather to do their good works, that old hall saw everything that required four walls and a roof."

Doc didn't look at her, concentrating on the stones in front of him. He spoke in a stream of words that flowed forth the way water poured from an open spigot. Cool and steady. He continued, "They were strong people, wouldn't say warm exactly, but good to those around them and good to each other. The Big House wasn't built until the boys came along, Wally and then Dodge... my father."

Win strolled over and stood between three graves and found herself facing the marker of a woman.

Dodge Harrison Sears
1925-1979

Mary Ava Sears née Joblynsky
1925-1975
Devoted Mother
Cherished Friend

Wallace Dunwood Sears
1922-1973
Son and Brother
Veteran WWII

"Was Mary Ava your mom?" asked Win.
"Nope...Wally's wife...."
"And your mother?" she said, continuing around the circle, fi-

nally stopping two stones away.

June Avery Sears
1927-1976

"June...," she said, giving nothing away.

"Yup."

Then noting the grave between Dodge and June, the smaller marker shaped as a heart,

Hollis Dodge Sears
1961-1966
Sleep now, Angel

"Was he your—"

"Brother," he finished for her.

"Only five years old. Oh, Calder." She could see an old pain flash in his eyes. "Calder...you don't have to do this."

"It's time."

He took her hand and led her to the grand center stone and sat her down at the base of it. He walked back over, and standing between Dun and Ida, he began to tell the tale. As he moved through the telling, he would walk and stand before the stone of whoever he was speaking of, as if asking them to witness his testimony of their story. As the characters rolled in and out, he would point to their stones or lay his hand on the smooth granite tops.

"Dun and Ida built this place," he said again. "Dun had ranching in his blood, never thought of doing anything else, and from the minute Ida met Dun, she knew she'd be a rancher's wife. They built the ranch, made a home, lived simple, lived honest, built a community of friends and the other odd folks bound to be found out here...all were expected and welcome at their gatherings.

"First came Wally in '22. Three years later came Dodge. Two

strong boys to carry on after Dun was gone. And he left early enough; had a heart attack when he was sixty-five." Doc sobered and took a breath. "Not a day, hell, maybe an hour, goes by when I don't think of him. He sort of took me in when my father's interest lay somewhere else. I was a sixteen-year-old greenhorn. I didn't know until that day what losing someone really meant." He took another deeper breath. "She went along a couple years later—could never get over being here without him, got the flu, didn't care to fight it."

He walked the few steps between Dun and Dodge's graves. Setting his shoulders, he stared the marker down. "My father...Dodge, was fifteen when Wally was eighteen and got drafted into the tail end of the war." Doc moved to stand again between the two brothers. "Dodge met Mary Ava when they were just kids. Grew up together, came of age together, were always sweet on each other. Everyone knew it was just a matter of time before they were married and settled in here at the ranch.

"Until one summer, Mary Ava went to live with one of her relations in Cheyenne. She was helping out with a herd of children while their mother was sick, or something along those lines. That's the summer that June Avery came to live with her aunt down in Riverside. June was a beauty. The kind of beautiful you find in the city. I'm sure it was exotic for my father...working hard every day, Wally in the war, Mary Ava away, and ol' June shows up, pretty as a pin-up, smelling like perfume.

"From what I can figure, they probably had a great time, until September, when things started happening fast. June was pregnant, and back then that meant a wedding. They got married and I was born five and a half months later. A lot of first babies had a habit of coming early back then," he said it with a bite of chagrin, "and somewhere in there, Mary Ava came home and got her heart broke.

"I don't know when or how their affair started, but Dodge didn't let his marriage to my mother keep him away from Mary Ava for long, and they continued their romance, one that lasted until she died some thirty years later. Soon after they took up again, Mary Ava discovered that she was pregnant as well. About that time, Wally came home from the war and after some persuasion, not sure what that entailed, he and Mary Ava married, and some months later Wally, Jr. was born. Early.

"After the war, so the story goes, Wally was different. Still easy going and the life of the party, except now he was a drunk. He drank every day, some days all day, and passed out most nights right after dinner. Fathering duties fell to Dodge, which, I guess, goes without saying, he didn't mind a bit. Of his two sons, he saw me as the reason he couldn't be with his real family, Mary Ava and Wally Jr.. Of course June saw it all and became more bitter and mean each day.

"I was around fifteen when Dodge actually moved to divorce her, right after Dun died—I suppose on the grounds of *Just Too Mean To Live With*, and who could blame him? But suddenly, June was pregnant, how, I don't know, since I don't remember them ever sharing a bedroom, but ol' June was a wily one, and in 1961, she gave birth to Hollis."

Win's mind was whirling, so many questions, but she knew he had to tell his story his way, and she made herself as still as the center stone she leaned on. As Doc addressed each memory, the watermark of that ghost would ripple and move around him. None of them came to *life* like the ghosts Win usually saw. Even June made herself scarce for Doc's testimony. Win couldn't help wonder why, but Doc's low voice brought her wandering thoughts back to the present.

"Up to that point," he continued, his eyes glazed, "I always thought that Dodge didn't like me because I was June's child. There wasn't anything I did that he said couldn't be done better. Hell, he was my *father*, I tried hard to please him. But he never failed to put making my life miserable at the top of his list; just behind Mary Ava's happiness and keeping the ranch afloat. Then

Hollis showed up, this little angel child; happy, clear-eyed, gentle little spirit, so good...everyone, including my father, instantly took a shine to him. I had to finally accept that it wasn't that I was June's kid—it was just *me* he didn't like.

"I won't pretend that wasn't a tough go. I was seventeen. But at least it made things clearer. I stopped trying so hard. I didn't let his harsh words cut into me like before. I guess I kind of gave up on him, something I should have done early on. Dodge must have sensed the change, and for whatever reason, maybe it was Hollis that changed his ways, things sort of settled down for a while."

Doc bent and dug a hand into the hard dirt of young Hollis's grave. He stood slowly clenching the soil in a tight fist.

"Then, it was Christmas Eve, 1966. I was twenty-two, home from college on winter break. I was in my first year of vet school. Dodge was out punching and June was in town shopping...I thought Hollis was in his room, but he had snuck out, probably to see his favorite foal in the barn, except the barn door was frozen shut so he went to climb the fence...to get in through the rafter door... something we did in the summers when we wanted to hide up in the loft...." Doc's narrative was becoming more and more labored. "He must have slipped...." Doc stopped then and Win could see him drawing deep breaths, but silently, nothing moving but his chest as he stared at the cold stone heart at the head of his little brother's grave.

"He must have slipped...." Another pause. Win didn't dare move, she didn't want to take him from wherever he had gone in his mind. "We found him...on the ground below the rafter door. He'd frozen where he lay from the fall." Doc stood still as the stone he confronted, then finally continued, "Must have just gone to sleep... Doc Seymour said he didn't suffer.

"At the funeral, as we carried his casket...it was so small...down the aisle out the back of the church and loaded it up to take it here to be buried, my father came over to me. I was crying, I had given up trying to hold it back, I thought, finally, maybe, he would take hold of me and we could speak some comfort to each other, instead he drew back and slapped me square—hard."

Doc bent down again and returned the handful of dirt to where he had pulled it from. He patted the earth softly before he rose again and continued. "The next day, I enlisted to fight in Viet Nam. I thought at least there I could fight a war with a possibility of winning...was wrong about that, too."

Wallace Dunwood Sears, Jr.
1944-1968
Beloved Son
PFC US Army • Vietnam

He walked a couple graves over and stood before his other brother. "Wally Jr. got drafted a year later. Everyone begged him not to go, get a college deferment, or sit it out in Canada, but he said he was proud to go. He was killed on August 18th, 1968 in the Tet Offensive. I didn't come home until late the following year.

When I saw my father, we shook hands and I told him how sorry I was, about Wally Jr...I remember he stared out past me as he said his peace, 'He never would have gone if you hadn't enlisted. He was always trying to beat you at something—he looked up to you, I'll never know why—he was such a good boy, no darkness in him, the best of all of us combined.' Then he looked me in the eye and said, 'It should have been you.'"

Doc took a couple steps back to the edge of the ring, "Within a six year span, they were all gone. Uncle Wally died first. Too much drink, finally got the best of his liver. 'Til his last day he was a good-natured drunk, but his charm had worn out years before. Mary Ava was next, breast cancer they didn't catch in time. Dodge nursed her around the clock until their final vows.

"June died two months later; car slid off the road in a blizzard, but she was already sickly with a heart condition. We didn't find her for three days. Most that knew her figured she stuck it out until after Mary Ava had passed, either from a sheer force of will, or probably, more accurately, spite.

"Dodge went last. Older than his years, and tired. He'd worked this ranch every day of his life and never got what he was waiting for. He never forgave my mother, or me, for keeping him from his happiness. He hated me and never missed an opportunity to show it. After we laid him out here, I moved in permanent to the bunkhouse. I didn't, still don't, have any interest in being Dodge's son in the Big House." Doc spat out those last words, the quietly said, "He never saw it that way, and neither do I.

"In the end, they were four people that spent their lives breaking each other apart."

At last, the telling complete, he re-focused on Win, still sitting quietly, tears in her eyes. He walked to the center stone, pulled her up by the hand and led her out of the golden grove of aspen, then alongside the Fire Hall and up the front steps of the Grady's yellow house. At the front door he stopped and gently placed a kiss on each of her closed eyelids. "Thank you," he said, and then even more gently, kissed her lips.

"See you tomorrow," she said softly.

"Don't be late," he said, as he turned and walked toward the bunkhouse.

That night, a luminous Hunter's Moon took its time rising in darkness so opaque, the stars seemed restless, as if counting the hours for dawn. Its beams finally breached the protection of the surrounding aspen, once more illuminating the deep cuts of a mason's chisel;

SEARS
Counsel, Solace, Grace
The Land gives and takes all.

213

CHAPTER 16

Autumn's big show had come and gone quickly that year. The leaves' perfect shades of fire had all been extinguished, and one-by-one fallen to the ground. The first snow laid itself down on Halloween night, heralding winter's arrival in earnest. As with all first snows, there was a festive feel in the air. The ceremonies of snow boots, shovels and plows, were re-launched and the new calves from spring bounced and ran with excitement as their green and brown world suddenly turned white. With the winter's official return the ranch shifted effortlessly to the hardships of cold.

The stock had already been moved in from the higher pastures and what was once an unending series of grazing land had now shifted into a patchwork of feed lots. The huge rolls of grass stood fenced in and ready for the crew to dole out the herd's daily meals. Riding fence still continued but was accompanied by the chore of breaking ice on the drinking system, ensuring the cattle could get to water.

After the time-change in the first week of November, Win started using three oil lamps she had found in the back of the pantry. The overhead fluorescents had always felt garish in the evening, making everyone look even more tired and ragged than they felt. Now the sun was setting around four-thirty and the lamps' soft light provided a much-needed respite as the unrelenting darkness came in hard. On the first night of lamp light, she endured the anticipated response:

Sticks: Did we blow a fuse?
Rose brothers: (didn't notice, went straight to their game.)
Dix: Nice.
Double M: How *Ro*mantical!

Hollywood: Don't get any ideas, old man.
Jim: Very nice Win.
Mac: More horse shit.

By the end of the week they had survived this, yet another earth shaking change to their routine. Win noticed the difference right away. They all seemed to soften with the light and dinnertime became a more genteel affair. Even Mac was less critical, saving his input for the larger issues, like whether there was too much salt in the stew or not enough sugar in the pulled pork.

Win and Doc's romance was settling in for the winter, as well. Most nights found them together in her room, nestled on top of the bed platform he had built. Other times they slept apart. Both were careful to give way when room was needed, already understanding each other's subtle shifts. They didn't make an announcement or hide the fact that their friendship had grown into something more. The boys and the Gradys were plenty sharp to figure it out. However, they kept their private life, just that, private. They rarely showed affection in front of the crew.

With Miss Lucy and Tom, things were a bit more relaxed. Both Gradys were tickled that Doc had at last found someone to care about. And it was clear that Doc was a balm to Win's troubles. So, it was now a foursome that sat down to spaghetti on Saturdays and that same four gathered for coffee and Miss Lucy's cinnamon rolls on Sunday morning.

Her body had also changed in the past months, a combination of honest food and riding Beau, had filled her out and made her strong. Even after The Wound's last stand—the fever that had all but broke her—she continued to bloom. She was lean still but with real curves. Doc's approval was secondary to her own, and she felt the power that her body had over him. How it called to him and how his would answer. The electricity that had connected them that first night in Granby had become even more potent.

She reveled in the attraction, the way her insides would seize when he walked in for dinner each night, how the memory of his hands on her from the night before could make her lose her way mid-sentence. She would smile then, treasuring the sensation of his pull.

Beyond their seasoning romance and in addition to the early sunsets and snow, November brought forth another big event; Thanksgiving, and Win was gearing up. After conferring with each of the crew, the dinner attendees were fixed:

Sticks: Attending solo, but holding out for the option of a guest (preferably female).

Rose brothers: Driving 300 miles to Sheridan to have dinner with their mother.

Dix: Accepted, "With pleasure."

Double M: An *en*thusiastic, "Yes, yes and yes ma'am!"

Hollywood: Dining in town with the family of a girl he'd met two weeks prior.

Jim: He would be bringing Nelda(!). Apparently they had struck up a friendship since the Fire Ball. It looked like Jim was the *source* of all the innuendo from her last visit to the Curly Q.

Mac: Dining elsewhere, "No one's business where."

The Gradys and Doc would fill out the table to nine with an outside chance of ten if Sticks got lucky before November 22nd. Win fleetingly considered talking to Doc about having it in the Big House, but then thought better of it. Even though the grand room would add untold ambiance compared to the cookhouse, she respected Doc's boundaries. It was his house. If he wanted to pretend it didn't exist, well that was his right. But ever since the impromptu tour with Tom, she had felt a connection there.

Accessing the ancient freezer had caused her to go in and out a few times since. Each time she would see June, always off to the side, lazing about, but staring Win down with her daring eyes.

Win lately felt chilled under her gaze, and would have to fight the urge to flee. As intrigued as she remained with the secrets the Big House held, she was always relieved when she closed the silent front doors behind her and made her way through the aspen, back to her side of the ranch.

As the preparations progressed, for the first time Win felt her old life tugging at her. Not Atlanta, and certainly not her life with Justin, but her precious Rosie and dearest Dinah. They would be heading into the holidays too; for the first time without her. What she would give to take her headcount to eleven and see them at the cookhouse table. She fantasized briefly about what that meal would look like, the cowboys and her girls, both sides fascinated with the other. Some lively conversation would definitely ensue. Dinah would hold court. Rosie would be her usual shy and dazzling self. Oh, and they could meet Dix and the Gradys, and of course, Doc.

She stopped herself mid-reverie. Hers was an escape, not a sabbatical! There was never going to be a Hallmark homecoming. She had made her bed with every wrong decision since Henry's death, and now it was hers to sleep in. She swallowed down the longing to hear her girls' voices, hold them in her arms and share her secrets. *You are still her.* The whisper of hope from an all but anonymous saleswoman, still called to her. But for now, she was still someone else.

Thanksgiving dinner went off without a hitch. Well, almost. The cranberry mold didn't set up, and the yams that Nelda had brought to be reheated, had been forgotten in the oven. Actually Nelda called them "Orgasyams" due to what she proclaimed as their "over-the-top-ultimately-transportive deliciousness." Whatever their powers were, the extra time in the oven had added "blackened" to their description.

Besides those slight trials, the turkeys (she'd made three, knowing that leftovers factored critically into the Sandwich strategy) were succulent and golden brown, the gravy as smooth as choco-late syrup and the pumpkin and pecan pies took their place of hon-or with even more pride than usual. The wine was poured during, and the whiskey flowed after with the coffee and pies along with the stories of various ranch exploits. Their bellies were so full it pained them to laugh, yet as the post-dinner revelry went late into the night, a second round, now officially leftovers, was consumed.

The kitchen held them all, a steamy terrarium. The oil lamps' soft flame, the only light, illuminated a space only as big as the table and the faces their glow fell upon. The tales of ranch glory fi-nally died down around one o'clock, with Jim and Nelda being the last two standing. The diners had finally given way to the couple's furtive looks and gave their clearly budding *friendship* some late night room to bloom. Miss Lucy (she and Tom had left, succumb-ing to their age and the drink around 9:30) had her guest room at the ready.

"Far too late and too cold to be driving home," she had insisted.

Nelda gladly accepted the hospitality, what combination of who would be using the accommodations remained to be seen.

On Friday morning, Black Friday to the retail world, the Morn-ing After to the revelers of Sears Ranch, Win awoke quietly and slowly extricated herself from under Doc's spooning arm. His light snores continued without pause. She stood by the platform bed, marveling at his peaceful slumber, the rare instance of his sleep-ing in. Normally she would wake to find him already up and get-ting dressed, his mind occupied with the priorities of the day, but when he would see her eyes open, he would come over and kiss her awake the rest of the way. Then, satisfied he had her full attention, he would leave her, carrying his boots in his hand so as not to wake the Gradys.

But on this morning he slept. Win spent a moment longer ad-miring him. He looked so much younger without the worry lines that striated his forehead. She could imagine him as a young man, and even a boy, always handsome with his strong jaw and blue eyes. She wondered how their lives would have been different if she had met him...she stopped herself. She grabbed her boots and stealthily padded out of the room and down the stairs.

The cookhouse looked like a scene from an interrupted Roman feast. What had been an intimate gathering by lamplight had morphed into a crime scene of gluttony by the harsh light of day. She excavated the coffee maker (apparently Dix was sleeping in as well) and fired up an extra dark pot of liquid salvation. Bacon would require two empty burners which she would need to dig for. In fact, every square inch of stove, counter, table and some of the benches, was piled high with Thanksgiving debris. *How many of us were there?* Surely the destruction far surpassed the headcount.

She allowed the coffee to drip directly into her mug before replacing it with the pot. It took three deep sips before she could feel the warmth easing into the parched crevasses of her insides. Three more sips before she could begin to formulate a strategy, and two more before she began her assault. Gather. Scrape. Stack. Repeat.

Petey showed up first, then Dix and Dave R.. All three blindmanned their way to the coffee pot. Once their own caffeine fix kicked in, they pitched in on the cleanup. Though the conversation was sparse, with four of them working, the traction was swift and the kitchen was pulled back into a functioning entity. The rest of the crew roused and appeared, as usual, with the smell of the bacon.

Doc showed up in the middle of breakfast and got the boys organized for the day. Just the minimum to keep the livestock alive. All else would be left until after the holidays. The crew wandered off to either the meager chores, a trip into town or back to their bunk. Once again, Win found herself alone in the kitchen with Doc. They worked silently to finish the final vestiges of cleanup.

Doc was drying one of the big serving dishes.

"Do you mind if I ask you something?" she ventured.

"Nope."

"So, what was with the hat?"

"The hat?"

"You know, the hat." Then she quoted him from their first meeting at the H-B in her best impression of his husky low drawl, *"I just can't get used to women wearing hats inside."*

"Hmm."

"Do you really *care* if a woman wears a hat inside?" Win turned to him and crossed her arms. "Doesn't strike me as something you'd spend time on."

"Well no, I don't care about it." He jammed his hands in his pockets, looking uncomfortably out the sink window.

"No?"

"What?" He looked as if he didn't understand the question.

"What did you mean then, I mean...about the hat?"

"I think you wear it well."

Win tried again, slightly exasperated. "At the bar, that first night...you...."

He looked at her, seemingly perplexed, not giving her an inch, but with the slightest smile at the edge of his mouth.

Now fully irritated, Win held her hands up in surrender. "Fine, forget it."

"Forget what?" Doc feigned confusion, but was now smiling.

"Fine."

"You know, that first night—might've been the tequila talking."

"It was before the tequila started talking," Win snapped. "You were there, suddenly," she remembered then how it seemed he had just sort of appeared, then regaining her annoyance, said, "and giving me a hard time about my hat."

"You wear a fine hat. Can't imagine why I'd say otherwise."

Win glared at him, then after a beat, went back to wiping down the counters, this time with fervor.

"Fine."

"Yup."

"Fine."

"Well...good then," Doc concluded, with a grin and a tip of his hat. He exited quickly out the back door.

"What the...?" she said, under her breath, bewildered by the irritating exchange. She had already closed the top right drawer twice and now found it hanging open again. Whether it was her now pounding headache, the irksome conversation or finally reaching the end of her patience with an ongoing prank, she went to stand directly in front of it, and with all her strength, slammed the heavy wooden drawer shut.

"What?!" she yelled in exasperation. The entire bank of cabinetry shuddered with the force. The echo from her outburst hung in the air and instantly embarrassed her. She turned toward the bunkhouse door, assuming she had disturbed the sleepers inside, but nothing stirred. When she turned back around, her blood ran cold.

The top right drawer was still snug in its slot, but the rest of the wall of cabinets, drawers and cupboards alike, stood open wide; the drawers out as far as they could go without falling off their skids, the cupboard doors gaping open, displaying the porcelain, stainless and glassware in all their glory. Win realized she wasn't breathing and took in a desperate breath to keep herself from swooning. The ghosts had made no sound in their reply, but the message was a *scream*.

The kitchen's insides glaring and exposed no longer felt like mischief from a restless spirit. Instead, it marked the first time she felt fear from the energy that was her parallel world of icy winds and shadows. The spirits had felt her frustration and matched it with their own. Suddenly, it was clear that the drawer was not a prank but a message. A message she didn't understand, but now, at least, she would try.

The top right drawer. She had examined it inch-by-inch and found nothing. But there had been others; the bureau in her room, the sideboard at the Grady's. Maybe the kitchen was just where they had found her most often, perhaps it was time to think beyond the cookhouse. In her head she began to go methodically, room by room, building by building, taking a mental inventory of all the furniture and built-ins that had drawers. Not that many, really. She could hit them all by the end of the day.

Then she froze again. Through the window of the cookhouse door she saw her, standing barefoot in the icy gravel of the circle drive with her green dress moving in the cold pressing wind, the figure of June, her gaze fixed on Win. For the first time, along with those dark piercing eyes, June was smiling.

CHAPTER 17

Even from that distance June's eyes seemed alive. Dancing. Hopeful. She was radiant.

"Okay," said Win under her breath.

She grabbed her down jacket and lit out from the cookhouse straight to where June had stood. Win caught a glimpse of her green dress as it moved through the aspen and saw her next in front of the glass doors of the Big House. As Win approached, again June was gone in an instant.

The Big House stood silent as a tomb in the grey chill of the Black Friday noon. Win's urgency dissolved to reverence the moment she stepped inside the voluminous room. Her movements became fluid, with every noise she made echoing back on her in soft waves. Without hesitation she climbed the side stairs and glided down the hall until her hand rested on the burnished bronze doorknob of June's bedroom. The lock mechanism moved with the softest click and the door swung open, silent on slick hinges.

The light from the side window revealed a time capsule. This was her room, as it had been, unchanged from the moment she had died. But she hadn't left. June lay idly, diagonal on the bed atop a lavender satin coverlet that complimented her illuminated porcelain skin. She lay there, strewn, with an arm resting on the pillows above her head. Her face was as peaceful as Win had ever seen her. Her full lips partly open with half a smile. But this time her eyes didn't bore into Win's, instead they rested on the grey horizon outside the window. They were wet with tears, yet sparkling with what Win could only construe as either rapture or hope.

When Win drew her eyes from the spectacle of June in her languid repose, she located what she had come for. There on the side wall was June's vanity. Two banks of drawers that framed a low desk with a mirror centered above on the wall. The wood was veneer, and sloped off the front in the finest deco style. Like everything in the room, it was different from the décor in the rest of the Big House. It was feminine and stylish. Win could easily imagine June spending hours perched on the skirted stool, gazing at her image, knowing that she, like her pretty dressing table, would never fit in.

Win went now and sat on the stool herself. The mirror reflected her blonde image back with startling vividness. Her hard edges now gone, replaced by someone more round, feminine. Her complexion was flushed from the winter wind and the steam heat of the kitchen. Her blonde locks were still full, but contained as always in a ponytail. Absently, she reached for the band and pulled it off, setting her hair free. She took both hands, and starting at her temples, ran her fingers slowly through the strands now shining like spun gold. Instinctively she reached for the lipstick standing next to the tortoise-shell brush and comb. She undid the lid and twisted until the cylinder of red wax extended. Win closed her eyes and moved the tube gently. She felt the cherry-ripe color of the old wax pull and bump along her parted lip; thirty years of waiting since its last application melting away as its stain grew brighter with every coat.

When she opened her eyes, it was *June* she saw in the mirror. June, with her dark eyes and soft, wavy hair. Her red lips in the mirror exactly where Win's had been. Win was entranced. She could feel June with her now, inside her, and Win resolutely let go of the reins.

June took over then, and took her time; brushing her hair, admiring herself angle-to-angle. She smoothed the bodice of her green dress and lightly pinched her cheeks for color. Then without taking her gaze off her own image in the mirror, she let her hand drop and gently hooked her fingers into the handle of the vanity's top right drawer. June released it from its holder slowly, not stopping until it was completely freed and fell to the floor. With the crash of its fall, Win was jarred back to reality. June's image now gone, replaced with a lipsticked, blonde, fifty-year-old cook, hiding out on a ranch in Wyoming.

Win sighed as she gathered the many trinkets and ancient cosmetics back into the drawer. All so personal, she arranged them respectfully back into their space. She sat for a moment before sliding the drawer back home. So this was it? One last look in the mirror for a beauty the world never knew outside of the Platte Valley? But Win had difficulty sliding the drawer into its slot. Something kept it from closing.

She found the letter taped to the bottom.

The Wound had grown mostly silent. Like most bullies, when faced down by something stronger, its bluster had slunk away. Win carried the leathered scars like armor; a souvenir shield from a battle she had won. A shield of pink and marled flesh, deadened to the sense of touch.

But there were other kinds of scars. Invisible. The ones she held just below the surface. With December, came the memories of a year ago. And now with each passing day, those memories threatened to burn holes into her internal defenses, fortifications that were still easily breached.

Win's body memory contracted involuntarily as she was faced with the trappings of the season. Granted, the Sears gang didn't do much in the way of holiday decoration, but the single string of colored lights that someone had taken the time to outline her sink window with, made her blanch every time she took in their cheery glow when entering the cookhouse. Though her conscious mind dismissed the connection, her body remembered. It remembered how the terror had spread along with the flames. One year ago. She had lain looking out the window as the colored lights danced in the eaves, their festive glow oblivious as she braced herself for the horror that would soon end her life.

A week after the sink window lights had gone up, they came down. Win couldn't help the sigh of relief that came when she entered the cookhouse that morning.

"Better?"

She turned to find Dix regarding her over a steaming cup of coffee.

Win's eyes welled. She quickly looked away and started in on her breakfast prep. "Much," she said.

For Doc, the holidays had died along with his little brother forty-one years earlier. He endured only the minimum of Christmas rituals, for the crew but beyond that, it was a season to be endured rather than celebrated. He drove himself hard in these weeks, trying to miss the inevitable. But the surrounding argument of all that was that afternoon, the length of the day, the place of the sun in the sky, the crisp cut of the air, the snow blanket waiting to catch the small body once more. His senses knew, and dutifully informed his mind that this was the time, the day, the hour...Christmas Eve, and Hollis was another year older in the ground.

Win found herself in equal straights, the first anniversary drawing her back, her whole being seemed intent to relive the events of a year ago. She grew uneasy, skittish, the tears lurking just below the surface. She too, immersed herself in projects old and new. Idleness was her new nemesis, the keeper of the floodgates, the waters pressing hard against them.

The Wound had been silent for months. But now, as if it sensed a lowering of her guard, it stirred to greet its birthday. A small infection under her left shoulder blade had appeared. Doc attended it with unparalleled attention.

Though Win and Doc's world was now intertwined, they proceeded through their days without acknowledgement of the heightened, yet unspoken, angst. They knew enough about each other's history and timelines. They hunkered down and endured the season together.

Christmas morning dawned and Win awoke to find Doc dressed and entering the room with two cups of steaming coffee.

"Oh, you lovely man," she said, eagerly reaching for the offered mug.

"Merry Christmas," he said quietly, looking into her sleepy eyes.

"Merry Christmas," she replied, with grateful affection.

Then clumsily from his back pocket, he pulled a small parcel wrapped in brown paper and tied with twine. It looked well worn, as if it had been traveling in that pocket for a while.

"Here you go," he said, with a slight shuffle of his work boot.

She took it reverently. "You didn't have to—"

"I know," he interrupted, clearly uncomfortable.

"I mean, I never expected...."

"I know," he said, now with an edge in his voice.

She stared at him, puzzled by his sudden sour mood, then undid the string and began to pick at the tape. Doc shifted on his feet, hands now jammed in his pockets. *He's nervous*, thought Win, with wonder.

"Don't have to make a meal of it," he said, impatiently.

She stopped before the final revealing to beam a smile at him.

At last the contained object fell free from its wrap and onto the blanket that still surrounded her. It was stellar. A hand-chased silver belt buckle with the letter W scrolled and engraved deep in its center. The surrounding surface was a mélange of leaves and flowers that came alive in the pale pink room's morning light.

The tears she had been harboring over that past weeks finally found their escape route and drove her into his arms, her kisses interrupted by her thank-you's, the thank-you's giving way to her tears. He held her tight until she was ready to let go. She sat down on the edge of the platform bed, cradling the buckle in her lap with both hands. She was quiet for a time, taking in the beautiful gift. Finally she looked up and said, "I have something for you, too."

Win went to her bureau where she placed the buckle among the various other tokens he had given her. She opened the top drawer and took out a faded envelope from under her socks. Then, she went to Doc, put her hand behind his neck and pulled him into a deep kiss. When she released him, he looked down, surprised to find the envelope in his hand.

"I found it in June's room. The top right drawer," was the only explanation she gave. Then she left for the bathroom down the hall, to brush her teeth and give him room.

Doc stepped over to the rosy light now streaming through the window. The envelope was yellow, the adhesive defeated long ago. Inside, he found the letter.

Christmas Eve, 1967

Dear June,

There haven't been many words between us, good or bad, this past year. So I'll write a few down here.

Whatever words I might come up with won't start to speak the sorrow inside of me now that Hollis is gone. Our Hollis, June. I figure a mother's sorrow has got to be at least twice that of any man, even a father's. I wanted you to know that I see that.

There never really was much between us, at least until our boy came along. A lie is no way to start a life together, but I guess you've paid, probably more than was fair, for that lie. Calder too.

I remember when we brought him home from the hospital. Such a perfect boy. Maybe he wasn't conceived exactly from love, but he showed up just the same, and in a way he redeemed us all. You and I finally had something real between us. June, I'll never understand why you did what you did back then, but with Hollis, I thought there might be a clean start, I want you to know that I was trying. I'm sure not enough. It was a year ago tonight we came home from the hospital again. This time without him. I never knew there could be pain like that.

Now Wally Jr.'s gone off as well. I feel the loss of my other boy is surely a minute away. I don't know how, but I knew when I sent him off on that bus, it was the last I'd see him. I mostly spend my days now just waiting for the call or the letter, however they let you know that the only son you have left is gone.

As for Calder, he was born to blame. The wrongs I've put against him can't be undone. I can't be forgiven for what I'm not sorry for, even though I know how I treated him never was right. I don't care to know what kind of man that makes me.

My sorrys are running deep in me tonight. So deep, I don't know where they begin and end. But Juney, just for tonight, I wanted you to know, I always did the best I could, and I'm sorry it wasn't ever enough.

Dodge

When Win returned to her room, she found Doc sitting on the bed, motionless, quiet. The letter, held loosely in one hand; his other lay palm up, cradled in the sheets beside him. He stared long through the window and didn't move when she came and sat beside him.

"Where did you find it?"

"It's a long story...but I know June wanted you to have it, and somehow she knew I was the one who could get it to you."

She then went on to tell him about the ghosts, about June, all the times she'd seen her, the top right drawers, all of it. For his part, he stayed still, keeping his vigil. She knew he was probably only taking in pieces, but the story filled the space that had opened wide between them. She finished up. "I've had it for a couple weeks...I didn't know when would be the right—"

He stood abruptly, went to the window and bowed his head.

"I wasn't his." The words hung in the air. "I was never his son." Doc raised his eyes to the hills beyond the window glass. "She trapped him with someone else's son inside of her. Maybe he knew or maybe he found out later, but I was never his. He had two sons, Wally Jr. and Hollis, and as far as he was concerned, I was the reason they died. I kept him from Mary Ava and I killed his boys." He turned to Win and raised his eyebrows. "No wonder he hated me."

"Calder, you can't blame—"

"I don't. Now, anyway." He looked away again. "I had to figure that out a while ago."

Doc squinted into the sunlight and gave the beams a half smile. "Life takes its victims, living and dead. When I came back from the war, I had to hold onto what little—Dodge and his anger, was never going to be something I could change—I knew I had to let him go if I was going to survive. The thing was, I could never make peace with why he loved the other boys so deep and treated me like the enemy. It never occurred to me that, I was...."

"Oh Calder, I didn't mean for—"

"Don't," he interrupted, his eyes holding hers. "It's a gift." He moved to her in a single step, his mouth finding hers, he kissed her, hard. "Win," he exhaled, as she became lost in his intensity, his raw need for her. She always slept in one of his old t-shirts and Doc seamlessly slipped it over her head and pulled her in him once more.

His kiss was fevered, and the sensation of the worn cotton of his jeans and un-tucked shirt against her naked skin fueled her. She snuggled close and inhaled, wrapping herself in his scent. She felt vulnerable but safe as he held her fast, his kisses urgent, his ever-protective arms enfolding her, grasping, wanting. Suddenly hungry to feel his flesh, the snaps on his shirt popped easily as she all but tore it from his chest. His jeans came off with equal authority, and when at last they both came up for air, he turned her away from him and gently laid her down atop the platform bed. Doc reached around her waist and pulled her up into him, filling her as his fingers once again found their target, circling and teasing. His rhythmic thrusts only increasing fervor until she hovered on the brink.

"Calder?!" His name came from deep within her, expressing her need.

"Win," came his answer, a plea of his own.

With her release growing, he shifted, turning her to face him, then lowered them both onto the bed. As he hovered over her, their eyes locked, blue on blue, connecting far beyond the small insignificant room.

She moaned deeply as he once again buried himself inside her, forcing white heat to fly from the source of where he now moved to the tips of her extremities. She let him drive her all the way to the threshold, holding her there, where desire and heat was all that remained. Then with one last thrust, he took her over the edge, spilling into a zenith of stars, her open eyes seeing nothing but luminous color. Her heart beat like brilliant timpani, above which she vaguely heard him calling her name as he found his own release.

Doc collapsed on top of her, his head between her breasts. She wrapped her arms around his sinewy shoulders, the muscles still pulsating with his every breath. Win held him close, her spent body stretching beneath the length of him. Still swept up in the depth of his desire, her tears, unbidden, began to fall.

Sensing the shift, Doc stirred from his euphoria and raised himself up on his elbows. His brow perplexed.

"Hey?" he rasped, "What's this?" His hands cradled Win's head and using his thumbs, he wiped her tears.

Pushing his hands away, she turned her head and covered her eyes, trying to escape his concerned gaze. As he eased off of her, she rolled from beneath him and curled herself into a ball. Doc gathered the strewn blankets and wrapped them around her. She pulled the satin border up tightly to her chin.

Her tears continued and soon turned into full sobs, her body convulsing with the raw emotion. Doc instinctively knew that these weren't idle tears. These tears had been lying in wait, choosing carefully the moment to fight their way out. He spooned around her, lightly holding her to him, making way for these deepest sorrows to finally find their way to the surface. He waited silently, patiently, until the last drop had been offered up. Then he took her into him, holding her close and whispered into the back of her tangled hair, "Easy now...I got you." He marveled once more as she let herself relax and finally doze in his arms.

They stayed that way until noon. All the while the sunlight, reflecting off the walls, surrounded them in a rose-colored glow.

THERE WAS A FIRE

CHAPTER 18

Win was at the sink window when she saw the unfamiliar car coming around the aspen. It was a perfect crisp day in the heart of January and the luxury silver sedan looked out of place in the plowed, yet snowy circle. The men were out working in different parts of the property, so it was just her and Petey finishing up the breakfast work. The car stopped in front of the hall. Win's inner alarm went off and she felt the hair on the back of her neck stand at attention. As the doors on both sides opened, a moan came up from her toes. "No!"

Petey looked up to see Wins face drain of color. "Win? What?!"

"Oh no!"

The load of plates she was in the process of unloading from the dishwasher went crashing to the floor. Petey tried to catch both them and Win as she ran for the door, but neither could be stopped.

The two bundled figures now were now facing the kitchen door, which had burst open with her shriek. "NO!" she cried, as she ran straight for them. Their cries intermingled as she fell straight into Dinah and Rosemary's arms.

"My God, you're here!"

"Julia honey!"

"Mom!"

"You're blonde!"

"How can you be here?" Win cried.

"Oh dahlin' it's a long story! You're blonde!"

"He's dead!" blurted Rosemary.

"Rosemary Brown!" Dinah scolded.

235

"What?" asked Win, suddenly stopping.

"He's dead Mom—Justin is dead. He killed himself," she answered, searching her stepmother's eyes to be sure she took in the full impact of the news.

Not daring to hear Rosemary's words, Win took a moment to drink in her stepdaughter's striking features anew. Her hair was darker now, and offset her bright eyes with even more power than before. How she had missed those eyes. Win stared at her, disoriented, then finally bringing herself back to the present, mustered her voice to repeat what had been said. "He killed himself...."

Dinah jumped in. "Honey, he jumped off the Chattooga Bridge, left his car, left a note, the whole deal. But the headline is, he's gone!" She took Win's face in her gloved hands. "He can't hurt you anymore." Dinah let the statement set in, then with a huge Southern smile, said, "You can come home."

Win's mind was swirling. "Come home...." She repeated Dinah's words as if tasting something for the first time. *"He killed himself. He can't hurt you anymore."* She couldn't take it in. Her breathing grew labored.

"Julia, honey?" Dinah's eyes held worry, but her voice sounded distant.

It was then she saw Petey, with a puzzled look on his face, he was standing in a small snowbank halfway between them and the cookhouse. She immediately gathered her wits and her women and herded them up toward the yellow house. She called over her shoulder as she went, "They'll be two more for dinner!"

She hustled them straight past a surprised Miss Lucy and up the stairs to her room. Upon entry, Dinah, of course, was the first to speak. "Oh, dear. This is where you've been living?" Then noting the whisper of hurt on Win's face, she checked her tone. "It's very nice. Very minimalist."

Win looked around as if for the first time, seeing it through their eyes. She saw what it must look like; a flop-house room, more in-patient than bedroom. There was the thin mattress that suddenly looked suitable for a crack house laid on top of a crude wooden platform, next to it a short stack of books with a flashlight on top. She still used the blankets she had bought back in Liberty, which now had been joined by two more and accompanied the mismatched sheets from Miss Lucy's linen closet. There were four shirts in the closet with no door, an extra pair of boots on the floor and two pairs of jeans folded on the shelf above. The pink walls were just that, pink—nothing hanging, no mirror, just pink.

The top of the small chest of drawers was empty with the exception of a strange collection of stones, branches, leaves and a bouquet of dried flowers in a jam jar. *Is this my home now?* Up until that moment, it had been her hiding place, safe haven, escape hatch, a nest for her and Doc; whatever name she chose, home had not been among them. But then where was her home? Back in the chilling perfection of Justin's would-be fortress? Or back in Atkin's Park, where her sweet Henry's memory still haunted her until she couldn't breathe? *Home* just wasn't on the menu, or hadn't been until that afternoon.

"It's been a good place for me," she murmured in response.

They settled in on top of the bed and slowly unfolded into each other's arms as they told their tales. Indeed Justin was gone, the story spilling forth from Dinah and Rosemary as they filled in each other's version of the story.

After she had disappeared out of the hospital, he had raised hell, forcing an all-out search from the local police, who finally brought in the FBI. Big mistake. The deeper they dug, the more people started talking, the more it became apparent that Dr. Justin Richards wasn't the model citizen he had portrayed himself to be. There had always been rumors, but now as folks were faced with an FBI badge, those rumors came to light. Not only did they suspect him of abusing his now missing wife, they wondered if there might be foul play regarding her disappearance. This last detail Dinah told with unprecedented glee.

"To think that our little escape plan could have such a delightful consequence!" Dinah continued, "A couple months of investigating and still no sign of you, and Justin was still *a person of interest.* They couldn't prove it, of course." She leaned in and winked at Win. "No *body.* Eventually the search went cold and though he had started all the fuss, Justin seemed just as happy to let it quietly drop.

"So our poor old Justin, his precious reputation scarred forever, turned quiet. He stops going out for anything. The hospital said good riddance, so he sort of pulls a Howard Hughes, doesn't want to see anyone, except his slimy lawyer—you remember ol' Darren Poole? The cleaning staff gets dismissed or more likely just ran for the hills, gardener gone. You should see the house, it's like those ladies from *Grey Gardens* moved in, you know, Jackie's people? Weeds, vines, the works. You wouldn't recognize it."

Dinah was on a roll now and Rosemary had to bow out of the story, conceding to Dinah's unbridled enthusiasm in conveying the tale.

"And the thing is, though everyone else now thinks he's a killer, he knows he's not! I mean he could have been, but he screwed it up, so now he's taking all this pressure, and he knows you are still alive out there. It's just too good!" Dinah gleefully clasped her hands together. "And the few times we came face-to-face since then, he made it clear that he knew I had something to do with it. I know, that he knows, that I know where you are. Even though I didn't. Not *really.* And there was nothing he'd have liked more than to get me somewhere to squeeze the truth right out of me. But with all the heat all over him, that just wasn't going to be something he could get away with.

"So he lost! He lost and we made him lose. He lost and he couldn't take it, so he took to himself and got so pathetic and depressed that he drove that beautiful black beemer to that bridge out there at Exit 76 out over the Chattooga, and jumped."

"I can't believe it...he would never...."

"Oh, he did," said Rosemary, edging back into the telling, "that loser left the top down in the middle of winter, so people would notice. He left you a note!"

"A note?"

"Yes," said Dinah interrupting again, "and oh, by the way, he left everything to you."

"What did it say?"

Dinah continued, "Oh just a bunch of pigshit about how you were the love of his life and he couldn't go on without you, and how misunderstood he was, and blah-blah-blah. I suppose some folks bought it, but not anyone who really knew him. I say good riddance—he was garbage in a pretty package. I hope he enjoys his time in Hell."

Win just sat, looking deeply into Dinah's eyes, taking it all in. "So...it's over?"

"Yes dahlin', it's over."

"He's gone."

"Yes, honey, he's gone." Dinah cradled Win's jaw in both her hands. "He's never gonna hurt you again. You can come home now, that's why we're here—you can come back to your life."

"My life." Win let the words hang in the air, then in a small voice said, "Guys, I'm not sure, but I think this might be my life...here."

"Here?!" squeaked Dinah, looking around. "Here? Out in the middle of nowhere, down dirt roads, to a room that's more like a cell than a bedroom? Here?" She looked deep into her friend's eyes. "Help me understand."

Win smiled at her friend's perception, of course she couldn't see it. Then she noted the time. "Come on down to the kitchen, I've got to get supper going—you must be famished...and I need to introduce you to some friends."

"Friends? What, you've known them for about a minute now,

and they're *friends*? Not like me friends, I mean you haven't been here *that* long."

Amused at Dinah's insecurity, Win got up from the bed, reached her hand out to pull Dinah up and enfolded her in her arms, inhaling the sweet Southern scent that was uniquely her best friend's. Win whispered in her ear, "No, my dearest Dinah, nothing or no one, would or could, ever compare with you."

Dinah pulled back and held Win at arm's length. "Well alright then, of course not, I mean really, how could they?" she said, striking a pose. "So let's go see these friends of yours. The cowboys, the barbarians—let's take a look." With that, she strode off down the stairs, full of loyalty, love and life.

Win shook her head at the thought of her two worlds colliding: the Snowy Range and Atlanta, the Crew and Dinah, Calder and Justin, Win and Julia.

She held out her hand to Rosemary to head down, but instinctively they both locked each other in a deep embrace.

"God Rosie, I've missed you," Win whispered desperately in her ear.

"Me too," was all her small voice could offer through her now freely running tears. "Sometimes I thought I'd never see you again," she choked on the words, "you know you're all I have left of him."

"Easy now," said Win, softly rocking her side to side. "Together or not, you'll always have me...and he's always with you. You have to know that, right?"

"I know, it's just—this whole thing's been...."

"I know...hard." Win sighed softly.

"Hard," Rosemary echoed, her voice calming to match Win's.

Then from downstairs came Dinah's twangy call, "Ladies, let's get moving. I'm starving and I want to meet some cowboys!"

"Well, this should be interesting," Win said, with a grimace that made them both laugh and they tramped down the stairs to join their impatient, yet favorite, Southern belle.

Arms linked in an unbreakable chain, the three women made their way down the icy path from the Grady's to the cookhouse.

"By the way ladies, while you're here, you can call me Win."

"Win?" they asked, in unison.

"Win," she stated with finality, staring straight ahead, not missing a stride.

She could feel both sets of eyes on her; Rosemary's questioning, Dinah's in loving wonder. With the exception of their footsteps crunching through the frigid earth, they walked the rest of the way in expectant silence.

Petey had witnessed the reunion unfold. At first Win's screams and breaking plates had terrified him. Then he watched in disbelief as she ran into the strangers' outstretched arms, the three of them in an airtight grasp as they literally jumped for joy in the foot-high snow. And that is how they stayed, intertwined as they had moved from drive and up to the Grady's. Even though he knew, obviously, that these women were a good surprise, and would be staying at least as long as dinner, he wasn't sure what had just happened. He knew enough though, that Doc would want to hear about it.

He skirted out the bunkhouse backdoor and up to the Old Barn where Dix told him Doc was on the far end of the North pasture, most likely in the crew shed working on a "busted something or other." Petey opted for saddling up, thinking Doc could use the mount if he wanted to get back fast. Plus, Petey had begun to miss riding out every day with the boys and it was a chance to feel a little more Western than was allowed for in the cookhouse.

As expected, he found Doc going over the books and waiting to be sure none of the boys were left unaccounted for in the merciless cold. The crew shed was a rustic, stripped wooden box, big enough for some equipment, a work bench and a couple chairs. A wood-burning stove was stoked and glowing as it spewed heat into the room and out the less-than-perfect seams between the eighty-year-old planks. The crew used it for respite from the elements, clomping in between tours of riding out to feed and make sure the water was still moving in the lines.

Army, once splayed out in front of the stove in a deep afternoon snooze, had leapt to attention at the sound of the horse coming. Doc had heard it as well and had stood ready to hear what news brought the kitchen hand this far out on such a bitter, cold day.

"Hey Doc!" called Petey, as he came in the wooden latched door. Army, unimpressed with Petey as a guest of interest, sighed and laid back down in front of the stove.

"Hey."

"Something kinda weird's happened...It's Win—"

"Define weird."

"I figured you'd want to know—I don't think it's anything bad—"

"Petey," said Doc, impatiently, "define weird."

"Well I didn't get to meet them, really, but she saw them drive up and started hollerin' 'No! No!', which I don't mind telling you scared the bejeezuz outta me, then she ran out the door like to save her life, and by that time these two women had gotten out of the car, and next thing you know they was all crying and holdin' onto each other. Last I saw, they were rolling up to Miss Lucy's. That's when I came to find you."

Doc stood staring out the small paned window that looked out over the icy pasture.

"You know it's funny," Petey continued, feeling a little uneasy with Doc's silence, "she never mentioned having people of her own. She never talked about it, so I just assumed she was alone. Anyway, if you want to ride Texas back, I'll catch a ride with Jim when he drives on through."

Doc's next words surprised him. "Thanks for coming out to tell me, but I need to finish this up. Go ahead, get on back, I'll come in with Jim later."

"Oh." Petey looked at him, puzzled. "Okay then, well I just thought you'd want to know first."

"And now I do," said Doc, ushering out the confused hand.

"Well, alright. See you at supper, then. Looks like we'll be having company."

"Yup," said Doc, as he latched the shed door behind Petey.

Doc pretended to go back to work as Petey rode off. When the horse was long into the snowy land, he straightened up, leaned on the raw wooden window frame, and stared out across the frozen mud of the pasture.

"So they found you." His words found no one but a sleeping dog and the four crooked walls of the old shed.

Army answered with a whimper in his sleep.

Doc had never been much for family reunions, but this was one he'd been dreading. It had taken him a lifetime to find her, and now her past had found her, too.

So the battle begins, he thought, knowing all the while he would defer to what was best for Win. *Or is it Julia now?* He had always known this day would arrive.

He took his time coming in from the barn. As expected, the crew was milling inside the cookhouse when he came through the heavy dutch door. Of course Double M was the first to greet him with the news.

"Doc, *oh* Doc! Well, guess what the cat dragged in?" he exclaimed, not clarifying if he was referring to Doc, or Win's new friends. "Allow me to make some in*tro*ductions. Mr. Doc Sears, may I *in*troduce to you Miss Win's dearest friend, in from Atlanta, Georgia no less, Mrs. Dinah Calvert, *and*—you might want to settle in for this one—Miss Rose*mary* Brown, Win's daughter."

"Stepdaughter," Win interjected quietly, her eyes never leaving Doc's, his steely stare meeting hers.

243

"Right, whatever, Win's kin! Whoever knew that, I don't know!"

Mac let out an audible groan at Double M's rhyme.

Doc shifted his gaze to meet the two sets of curious eyes sizing him up. Both women hadn't missed the connection between Win and Doc and their radar was immediately piqued. Doc took off his grey felt hat and reached out his hand to shake theirs. "Ladies."

"Hey," said Rosemary shyly.

"A pleasure," said Dinah, looking back and forth between him and Win. "So Doc, these fine men say you're the one in charge around here."

"He surely is," piped in Double M. "It's his family what built this spread and it's cuz of Doc here that it's still alive and kicking."

"Oh, how lovely," Dinah said, looking back from Double M to Doc. "It's so important to carry on those family traditions. You can never underestimate the pull of blood on blood." Her eyes met Doc head on.

"Well, you know that's true, and there just aren't enough folks that think that way anymore. Why, Doc here is carrying on that *pi*oneering spirit that his Daddy had and his Daddy before that had when they first saw this land from the top of Barnett Ridge. It's been ranched under the name of Sears since 1916."

"I see. And do you do all the talking for Doc, as a rule?"

The crew gave a chuckle, but before Double M could retort, Doc firmly put his hand on Double M's shoulder and said, "Mrs. Calvert, I think you'll find that Double M here does most of the talking for everyone." More chuckling and agreement rumbled through the ranks. Double M shuffled and his sheepish expression acknowledged that his enthusiasm had overstepped once again.

"Never mind, Mr. Marlborough, I have always found people who over-communicate to be of the highest intelligence and the kindest of heart. I should know, I have been guilty of the infraction myself." She gave a big smile to Double M who accordingly lit up like a Christmas tree. Turning to Doc, she said, "And you may call me Dinah."

With that, Win broke in. "Anyone hungry?" The crew voiced their *Yes, verys,* and all were quickly settled in around the table. Double M insisted Dinah sit by his side, attention she didn't seem to mind. Rosemary squeezed her slight frame in between Doc and Mac. Win as always set about keeping the food moving and if anything, kept even busier than usual.

The dinner had been makeshift, due to the reunion which had cut into her usual prep time, and Petey seemed to be running behind as well. What was planned to be breaded chicken breast over Fettuccine Alfredo, turned into her fail-safe short-prep concoction she had coined Cowboy Chop Suey: a variation of the casserole she had made on that first night. Truth be told, it had a striking resemblance to Hamburger Helper, but with a few more bells and whistles. The men never had a problem eating every last elbow of macaroni, and even the finicky Dinah had seconds. Win accompanied it with her fallback, simple green salad and garlic bread, and finished up with some left over gingerbread and mulled cider, which most of the men chose to lace with brandy from the sideboard.

Overall, the Sears Ranch wasn't much of a drinking outfit, just a beer or two in the evening. Mac, of course, had his own bottle of whiskey that he kept stashed separately. He drank a couple fingers every night as he read the newspaper. But tonight was special. The spiked cider went down easy, as those gathered at the table started in on the tales they were famous for. It had been a while since they had fresh ears to ply with their adventures and exaggerations, and Win found herself basking in the moment where her two worlds seemed to co-exist in harmony. To say it was a dream come true would have been a lie, for she had never allowed herself to dream of such a night. It was too much to hope for, but now, tonight, this day, her luck had shifted. Hope had been added to the menu.

The mulled spices hovered heavy in the steamy kitchen and hours later, one-by-one, the story warriors bid their good nights and lumbered off to their bunks. Finally, it was just the four of them: Dinah, Rosemary, Win and Doc.

Though he had been the butt of a couple of good punch lines and certainly played his part in more than a few of the tales, Doc had been quiet throughout the evening. He had held back, laughed just enough, participated just the minimum. Win could feel him waiting. Waiting with all his questions.

Win got up, went to the sideboard and pulled out a bottle from way in the back. Not exactly top shelf but a far cry from the rot-gut Mac drank. She sipped on a small glass every now and again after the final wipe down at night. Win blew out two of the oil lamps and softened the third that lit the end of the table where the three of them still sat; Dinah and Doc across from each other, Rosemary at the head. Win put the bottle between them.

"Come on Rosie, let me walk you up, wouldn't want a moose to get you."

"*Moose?*" Rosemary said in awe. Win smiled, her eyes dancing with love for the still so-innocent girl.

"Don't worry, I've got you," she said, with a soft look at Doc, as they busied themselves with coats and scarves. Doc and Dinah sat quietly. The bundling complete, Win and Rosemary moved arm-in-arm toward the door to face the cold night. Before they ventured into the darkness, Dinah said softly, "Dahlin', how much?"

Win stopped and considered for a moment, then turned taking them both in.

"All of it. Every last thing."

Dinah acknowledged with a nod, her eyes welling for just a

moment, then mother and step-girl stepped into the icy crush of the January night.

NANCY ROY

CHAPTER 19

With the closing of the heavy door came a realized silence as Dinah and Doc faced each other in the dim lamplight. Never being one to dance around a subject, Doc went first.

"So, you're here to take her." He didn't pose it as a question.

"Yes. If she'll go," Dinah answered. Clearly they were both ready to speak the truth.

"Should she?"

"It's her home. It's where she belongs."

"A home she took great pains to disappear from."

"Yes. But things have changed since then."

Doc challenged the statement with his silence.

"Just how much has she told you?"

"As much as she could."

Dinah eyed him with a smile. "Something tells me that wasn't much."

Now it was Doc's turn to smile. "Nope."

He went on, "I know her name is Julia. I know that she has scars way beyond whatever hell played out on her back. And I know when she showed up, this place needed her as much as she needed it. Beyond that...." With a sigh, he shrugged.

Dinah looked at him and squinted her eyes as she sized him up. "Well, I guess tonight it all gets told, those blanks get filled in. You ready to settle in for a stretch?"

Doc rose and got a couple juice glasses from the cupboard. He placed one in front of Dinah and poured them both a couple fingers of the dark amber liquid. He raised his glass. She met him with a *clink* mid-table.

"To all of it. Every last piece," he said, echoing Win.

"All of it," Dinah repeated, shooting it down in one pull. Doc

249

raised his eyebrows in amusement, then shot down his own glass. He refilled both.

"By the way, my real name's Calder."

Dinah's eyes softened and smiled. "Nice to meet you, Calder. Okay then," Dinah paused, "where to begin?"

She placed her palms on the table and sighed. "I guess I want to ease into it a bit. She's so much more than this last part...you know she wasn't always this way. She was happy once you know, really happy. When she married the first time—"

"The first time?" Doc interjected, surprised.

"Yes, there were two husbands, the first was a good, good man. The other," she halted, "we'll get to him later." Dinah sighed again and started her telling in earnest. "Julia married Henry a few years out of college. She was twenty-nine and he was, gosh, mid-forties, forty-four, I think. And he had a daughter."

"Rosemary."

"Rosemary. Henry was divorced, and even though Julia was young, it was like they, the three of them, were just meant for each other. Even when Rosemary was in those evil adolescent years, writing poetry and lighting candles, Julia found her way to her. See, Julia was sassy then. Not like what she became...later. So sure of herself, she created a much needed bridge between Rosemary and her father, and the three of them just built this little family that felt like it could weather just about anything.

"He doted on Julia. He was smart enough to recognize salvation when it was given, and in return she idolized him, he was her everything. Looking back now, maybe that's where the bad seed was planted...being that wrapped up in someone else's world is fine if that person is a worthy man, but if you put that same devotion toward someone devoid of all human kindness—" Dinah sighed, "well, then...."

She stopped and sipped, her demeanor changed. She closed her eyes. "Henry died on January 15th, 1990. I remember because it's

Martin Luther King's birthday...so nice to have a national holiday to remind you of the worst day of your life. Henry came home from work early, thought he had the flu. She had made him some soup. After, he went and laid down, had a heart attack and died in his sleep. She discovered him a couple hours later. When poor Rosie came home from school, she found them together. Julia had wrapped herself in his arms one last time, her head laying on his silent chest.

"Seven years was all they had, all they were given. Julia was devastated. Six months later Rosemary went off to college and Julia was even more lost. Oh, she kept up appearances well enough, but I knew. She was desperate with grief and empty as a church basket during Mardis Gras. That's when Justin showed up."

"Husband number two."

"Yes, the anti-Christ, as I like to call him when I'm feeling charitable. Dr. Justin Highland Richards, graduate of Duke Medical, cardio-thoracic surgeon, the youngest to ever be elected to the board of Piedmont Hospital, and from one of the finest families in Atlanta. The ultimate bachelor, man about town, all the appropriate debs and socialites had given it their best shot, but it wasn't until he met Julia that his head could be turned.

"He had seen her at the hospital when Henry was brought into ER. He saw her on her darkest day, as her weakest self, and there was something there that hooked him. Maybe it was the way she wailed when they wheeled Henry away. It's sick to think about it, how it started, but we didn't know then how it would all go—how could we have known what a sadistic-piece-of-shit-bastard he was underneath that chiseled jaw of the Old South? He had a cleft in his chin, just the right spot, people would always talk about it...," her voice trailed off, then looking at Doc, perhaps for absolution, she added, "We just didn't know.

"Justin had asked me to make an introduction after he met her in the hospital, after a couple months, so it didn't look odd. My husband and I were benefactors, so Justin and I would run into each other at events. He had seen me with her in the hospital and made the connection." She looked up again at Doc. "Yes, I was the one who introduced them. Don't think for a minute I don't live with that every hour of my day."

Doc replenished their juice glasses. Dinah obliged by taking in another deep drink.

"Oh, he courted her," she continued. "Subtle at first—the thought of moving on for Julia was unfathomable. But he was smart, so cunning. He started in as a friend, a shoulder. They went on walks, met for coffee, he listened and supported and comforted. From the outside, we all thought he was an angel sent to save her, and when things started shifting from friends to something more, we encouraged it! Finally, karma rewarding the goodness in her. So we thought.

"She started relying on him more and more. He influenced her decisions from wardrobe to what she had for breakfast, and she was devoted to his every need. He even took over Rosemary's college costs. You see Henry was not a wealthy man, used his money to live well today, which in the end, since he went so young, wasn't a bad idea, except it didn't leave his family in a good position financially when he passed. Early on it was clear Rosemary's continued tuition would be far beyond Julia's salary as a teacher. Again, Justin *the hero* to the rescue.

"Two years after Henry died, she married Justin in the perfect ceremony at our Philip's Episcopal. Three hundred of the Atlanta elite gathered to watch one of its favorite sons walk from swinging bachelorhood into upstanding privileged middle age. Never mind that she was recently widowed, middle class, the daughter of an electrician and a church secretary. Julia never cared about society, that level of wealth was never on her radar, but she was a quick study on all things that her new social position required. She held up her end. She was a radiant bride. Those that were there still speak of her on that day as if they were in the presence of one of God's angels."

Dinah ruefully shook her head. "It happened very slowly, over time, you know? It took forever for me to catch on. I was so stupid! I was caught up in the same euphoria that everyone else was. Justin the *savior*! He moved her into his place, oh—he had built this house, or should I say museum to his machismo a few years back. Just off The Prado. The only house in Ansley that had the gall to take up two lots. Mid-century modern," Dinah sniffed in disdain, "just another name for *cold* if you ask me."

Dinah shifted in her seat and looked squarely at Doc with haunted eyes. "We hadn't realized then that it had already started. The over-protection, the isolation, the weight loss! Julia was always a curvy girl, you know, the right kind of curvy, but after the wedding she started getting thin. 'Justin doesn't like that I'm so fat.' she told me once when I questioned her. She was already skin and bones at that point.

"All those signs were just the above-the-surface face of what was going on at home. To this day, I still don't know what all he did to her but the X-rays finally told the story she never could. He was skilled, as you might imagine a surgeon would be. Beyond that...I expect the head games were even more sublime—otherwise, why would she stay?!"

Dinah was becoming more agitated. The whiskey was having its effect but not in a calming way. Doc kept their glasses full and braced himself for what was next. But Dinah fell back to a safer time, seemingly needing to bolster her resolve before getting to the end.

"In the beginning they were glorious. She was so pretty, you know? I mean she's still pretty, but back then there was a spark about her. People would notice when the couple came into a room. He, so handsome and successful, you know, that kind of power that's easy to mistake for charisma? He ate up the attention she gave him, he never missed a step in public. They attended everything. The balls, the symphony and ballet openings, charities, you-name-the-disease fundraisers, they were there.

"There were two pregnancies, both ending in a miscarriage. About that time Rosemary graduated college and left for Florida permanently. After that, things seemed to shift. He would still be out but she was with him less and less. He always had good excuses, but after a while it got awkward and people stopped asking, and she sort of slipped into the background. It wouldn't be the first time a perfect union became more of an *arrangement* than a love affair, and Atlanta society is good at reading the signs. And then the behind-her-back chatter: '*After all she was middle class, not really cut out for her role*'— They turned on her so fast." Dinah shook her head.

"He would always be protected and she knew it. Finally, it was accepted that he flew solo...and all that that entails. I don't know if he even tried to be discreet, or if he got off on humiliating her with his one-night stands. If she knew, she never told me. Every now and then I would drag her out to lunch, or to go shopping, but she never said a word against him. Always going on about how hard he was working at the hospital, how devoted he was to his charities and patients. And she had all the privileges too; that monster of a house, the cars, the clubs, designer clothes, but really, none of it seemed to excite her.

"I think of her now, so alone, in that perfect prison. The last few years she just seemed empty, always tired. I assumed she was on anti-depressants, but who knows what all he had her on. I expect she might tell me now—I guess if she could endure it, I can bear to hear it. It's the least I can do." Dinah traced one of the worn ruts of the table planks with a perfect polished nail. "The very least."

Dinah stopped and took a long breath. She looked at Doc with eyes that had seen a horror, searching his for answers. Doc stayed quiet, but reached both hands across the table, palms up. She studied them for a moment, then gently placed hers in his.

"Finish it," he said.

She squeezed his palms and lit into the rest of the story in a rushing of stream of consciousness. Her eyes now focused over his shoulder, off in the distance.

"What I know is this: It was Christmastime a year ago. She called me out of the blue to tell me she had decided to leave him. Well, I of course was *so* relieved, and she was talking like her old self again. Full of plans. She was going to wait until after Christmas proper and then, when he was on a long shift at the hospital, simply walk out. She had stashed some money aside, but asked if I could help with a suitcase and a ride to the airport. She didn't say where the flight was going. I was so happy for her! I urged her to go right then, I'd come by, I'd help her with it all. But she was adamant. She said she'd waited this long, and he'd be so busy that she would barely see him. She even told me then that she knew he was spending his nights elsewhere and that was just fine with her.

"So I hung up." Dinah took a quick gulp and cleared her throat, her voice low. "The next call I got was early the following morning. She was in the hospital, intensive care, with burns. The house had caught fire. It was bad. I don't even remember getting there, but I got there quick. And there he was, hovering, whispering in her unconscious ear, so sweet, so concerned, so distraught!! It was a disgusting performance. Of course they all ate it up. 'Poor Dr. Richards. What a tragedy.' Please. At least now I was onto him.

"She almost died a couple times that day, but they brought her back, and at some point her precious, broken body decided to fight. So that's when I started fighting, too. Almost immediately she was transferred to the burn ward at Grady across town. Finally out from under his jurisdiction. He hadn't counted on that—he hadn't counted on her surviving. He was very aware that I was not attending the little pity party he was throwing, and was clear with the staff that only family should be allowed in. Of course Rosemary was around by then, but he even managed to keep her at bay unless he was in the room, too.

"What he didn't know, is that I figured out a way for my husband's sister's girl, dear Marilee, my niece, to be the one working the night shift on Julia's floor. She would break me in for a couple hours each night. I did some asking around and found out who in power on the burn team might not be drinking the Justin Kool-Aid, either. And finally, I had an ally.

"Dr. Robert Westin! He was the one I was able to talk to about my suspicions. He was the one that ordered the full X-ray series that would finally expose the damage.

He took a chance on me, a huge risk for him, that breach of confidentiality. Justin's family is very powerful, and after secretly talking to a detective friend of his, all agreed to wait to file a police report until Julia was stronger, and that the hospital, for now, was the safest place for her. He worked her meds with the help of Marilee, to keep her drugged up during the day, but then allowed her to be fairly coherent at night when I would visit. If she was to have a chance at all, I needed to get her talking.

"One night, some weeks after she first regained consciousness and the drugs didn't have her in la-la-land, she was finally able to tell me about that night.

"He had come home unexpectedly that evening after her call to me—knowing him, the bastard probably tapped her phone. He had told her that he knew she was unhappy, and that he was willing to let her go. Well, as you can imagine she had cried with relief. So grateful that he had been the one to say the words. 'Let's go out to celebrate!' he had said. 'Let's show Atlanta what the perfect divorce looks like.'

"Well, she bought it of course, and went to go get dressed for dinner while he called their favorite restaurant so they could have a last night together, 'Just like we used to'. She remembered putting on that little black dress he always insisted she wear, even though she always felt it showed a bit too much. She didn't want to do anything that would set him off and change his mind. When she was ready, he had poured them each a drink and proposed a toast to their time together, to their new futures. She'd fought back her tears of relief and drank the concoction down.

"As they were getting ready to leave, suddenly she was so tired. It was then he hit her with the needle. She remembers it was a tiny thing, barely noticeable, but immediately she felt the numbness spreading up from her toes and fingertips. She remembered slumping to the ground, unable to move, but she was still aware of what was happening.

He gathered her up, no problem for him, she was nothing but skin and bones by then, and carried her into their bedroom. She remembers him ripping that dress off, and him on top of her—the animal!" Dinah was in an alternate state now, quivering with anger. "He drugged her, and raped her, and lit a fire and left her to burn!"

She squeezed Doc's hands so hard, he felt her fingernails starting to dig through his flesh, but he stayed still, allowing her to get whatever was left of the horrors out. "And the part that makes all the rest of it seem small in comparison—" Dinah suddenly took her hands from his and frantically wiped her tears. She stood up violently from the table, the entire bench scraping on the floor, and started pacing back and forth.

"Look at me crying, like I've got some right to cry—after what she went through—never complaining, the pain of the cleanings and the grafts, she never cried like this, like me, so fucking weak—I could have saved her, from it all—but I was afraid of him, too! What he could do to me in our *precious* social circles—I knew something wasn't right—I betrayed her along with the rest of her so-called friends. All for appearances, all for the *show*. I'm just as much of a monster as he was."

Doc came up to her and grabbed hold of her arms with his gentle strength. He looked at her straight on and softly repeated her words of a moment ago, "The part that makes the rest seem small...."

Her shoulders crumpled and she started to sob. But he held her up, still at arm's length, he leaned in to catch her eyes again with his.

"Tell me."

"She was awake!" she blurted between her sobs. "The bastard gave her a drug that instead of knocking her out, just paralyzed her body, so she would be awake as she *burned*! She told me she saw him—outside, through the bedroom window, she could see him from where she lay on the bed, and he was...smiling. She knew that he had set it. She knew that he had played her one last time, that he had won."

Finally, looking into Doc's eyes, now wide and burning the fiercest blue, Dinah whispered her final horror. "She said she could smell her flesh burning."

With that, Doc took her in his arms and stood still until her sobs ebbed to quieter tears. Eventually he set her back down at the table and she leaned forward, holding her head in her hands. Every last piece had been told and she had crawled ashore from the tempest of truth, exhausted.

Doc set about making a pot of coffee. Immediately the aroma and gurgling water was comforting, as it moved through the industrial system. Dinah sat quietly. Once the coffee was brewed, Doc poured two cups and sat down to join her again. They sipped in silence, until the first vestiges of caffeine fought their way through the heavy fog of whiskey. The oil lamp still burned steady, but somehow seemed brighter now.

Dinah looked up for the first time, her face still puckered and red from the trauma. Then with a perfect Southern air, she lightly brushed away the hair that lay disheveled around her face with the back of her hand, and with a small tired smile asked, "Sir, would you have any cream and sugar?"

Doc smiled in kind, and moved to accommodate his genteel guest. After a few more sips, she continued, "It was Dr. Westin who was the real hero. Once I had confided to him my suspicions, he went to work. He X-rayed every bone in her body and showed me the places he had hurt her. The little hairlines, the full fractures. A lot of ribs, some fingers, a shoulder socket that was worn from being repeatedly dislocated, same with the knuckles...."

She gathered herself further. "Even with the evidence, his police friend said unless she would corroborate it, he most likely wouldn't be prosecuted, and with Justin hovering around her all day long, we figured she'd be afraid to tell the authorities what we already knew. Honestly, I think the good Dr. Westin figured out ways to keep her even longer than what would have been the usual, whatever *the usual* would be. He knew, like I did, that the longer she stayed away from Justin and that house, the better chance she would have.

"He was also the one who arranged for my niece to be transferred in on the night shift. Prior to that, she was working in an ER across town. She commuted an extra forty-five minutes each way to do this for Julia, even though she didn't know her well. But once I told her the reason, Marilee was there, and watched over Julia like a hawk.

"Even though I swore her to secrecy, I know she told a couple other nurses, she felt they were trustworthy, I guess. I only know that Julia got the best care a patient had ever seen. Never underestimate a few strong Southern women with a good cause. Anyway, Marilee and her crew always saw to it that I was undisturbed when I would sneak in nights and sit with her. She was pretty doped up most of the time from the pain, but like I said, Dr. Westin fixed it so she had a lighter dose during the hours I was there, so when she was ready to tell her story, she could.

"When she did talk about it, it was kind of like tonight, a single light to tell horror stories by...I don't think she'll ever be able to really say the whole truth. I begged her to tell the police but she outright refused, convinced that his connections would get him off, and once free he would track her down and kill her. Probably right.

"That's when we had the idea that she would need to simply disappear. Oh, we had plenty of time to plan it—she still had two months of nightmarish treatments ahead of her. During that time I did the legwork and research. When the police did question her, she stoically denied any such accusations. Justin played the dutiful caregiver. How she could stand to have him near her was a daily Oscar-worthy performance.

"We had the route figured out early on. Rosemary was waiting in one of my cars a block away from the hospital. After final rounds I walked in with my usual signature style around 2AM, when everything really settles down. I always carry a big bag, so there was nothing new there. Immediately we swapped clothes. Marilee and I dressed her to look just like me, including a blonde wig. You know she used to be a redhead, right? Anyway, as far as the hospital surveillance was concerned, I was leaving the same as I did every night. I'd even come up with a quirky wave that I did each night to the lobby guard, and we made sure she did it to perfection on her way out.

"I had outfitted the car with everything she was going to need. A copy of my own Georgia driver's license, medical supplies and drugs, enough to last at least a couple months. A couple changes of clothes, nothing too flashy, and about twenty grand in mixed bills I had been collecting over the past months. A withdrawal here, cashing checks instead of depositing. I didn't want to raise any eyebrows with any big money activity or withdrawals. Good thing I've always been a strong spender," Dinah said with pride, smiling for just a moment. "Bernerd never even noticed, bless him.

"I took up residence in her bed so there would be someone under the sheets when people walked by and Marilee made sure there weren't any unexpected visitors. At around 5:30, before the morning shift change and after my sweet niece said the coast was clear, I snuck out using a stairwell we knew had no cameras and hopped in a car I had parked around the corner. From there I drove home and waited for the phone to ring."

Dinah was becoming more animated as the adrenaline of that night pumped through her veins anew. "That first night Rosie drove straight through to Tallahassee, and stayed at some low-rent motel outside of town. She made sure Julia was still doing okay, health-wise anyway, and kept watch while she slept for the next six hours straight. Then she drove her to the local Greyhound, where Julia, still so weak, bought a ticket to—well, I still don't know where. We decided no one would know, not Rosemary, not me, no one. You can't tell what you don't know.

"After saying their good-byes, and don't think that wasn't a hard one, Rosemary drove straight through to the Atlanta airport, where I met her, and she caught the next flight back to Florida. I drove my car home and parked it back in the garage as if it had never been gone."

Doc found himself squinting, trying to envision all of what was being told. But Dinah reassured him, "I know, a lot of moving parts, but trust me, we had it trussed up like a Thanksgiving turkey with extra stuffing.

"By the time I met Rosemary at the airport, the police had already come and gone to my house to question me. I told them how I had been sneaking in against Justin's wishes, most nights around 1AM, and that the night before I had done just that, leaving around 2:30. They were already sniffing around Justin's role, smart boys, asking about the marriage, signs of abuse, all of it. Clearly they had already interviewed Dr. Westin. I wasn't even on their radar, so I was able to get that last car swap done without raising any eyebrows.

"And our coup de grâce...," she leaned forward with a sparkle in her eye, "our innocent little nurse, Marilee, mentioned that she might have seen Justin going into a stairwell early in the morning. She told them she couldn't be sure, but she thought it was odd since he always used the elevator. Of course Justin was home sleeping, so he had no alibi. It was never proven of course, since it wasn't true! But it got their minds working in the right direction just the same.

"I mean really, it was something—us meek, obedient little ladies, just smiling and plotting, smiling and plotting, for months! We never wrote a thing down, no one could ever have known what we were up to. She was the amenable victim, wife, and I—I was the invisible friend. There were times where it was almost...fun... at least, it was a way to infuse hope into the insanity of what had happened.

"Dr. Westin couldn't believe how fast she was healing. Her delicate skin was working double time knitting itself back together, because she knew as soon as it was even remotely safe, she would go. She would go and have her chance to start again, to leave him and his treachery behind, all the fear and the pain...and try again.

"During the plotting months, yes, I do call it *plotting* not planning. Plotting is much more crafty, don't you think? I like the sound of that." Taking a brief respite from the horror of her tale, Dinah allowed Doc a glimpse of her mischievous side. She was tickled with herself for pulling off their plan and she deviously rubbed her hands together. "Anyway, the first thing I did was rent out P.O. Boxes. We would only communicate by letters through the mail, anything else could be tapped or hacked or traced or whatever they do. I ended up with six different locations. We figured she could send me word every two weeks, to a different box and at the end of the note tell me what PO she'd be sending it to two weeks later. It was always random, no pattern, just not the same box twice in a row. That way no one could possibly intercept.

"She sent me this address about four months ago, and said she was settled in for a while and wouldn't be writing for another six months. She gave me a date and said where the next letter would show up. We had agreed that once she felt safe, we should disconnect for a while, the less contact the safer she was. I memorized the address and burned the letter."

"And him?" It had been so long since Doc had spoken, his words landed heavy in the air.

"Dr. Justin Richards, I am *not* sorry to say, is no longer with us. The police came after him like locusts and everyone assumed he had murdered her. His career was in ruins, reputation destroyed. He decided to grace us with his permanent absence and jumped off a bridge. So that's why I'm here...Calder...I know, I can see...she wouldn't have me telling you all this if she didn't care for you. And you should know, it's not my intention to cause either of you any heartache, God knows she's seen enough sadness, but she had to know...."

"Yup."

"You know before all this, before Justin and all of it, you should have seen her...she was a shiny penny. Shiny and new. People were drawn to her. Of course she was pretty, but she was wise, too. Honest. On any given day she would tell you her truth, and keep your secrets when you asked her to. She was something...," her voice trailed off. "And we've—I've missed her."

Doc smiled. "I understand." Something told him he was about to feel the same way.

"You know, just being with her today, she feels a bit like that again, like she was, maybe not all the way back, but really, that's probably not even possible anymore. Maybe she was too green, too happy, and bad people can smell that, and the really bad ones want to destroy it.

"She seems to fit here somehow, not just with you, but this place. It reminds me a little of how she used to talk about her grandparents' place she'd visit as a kid in the summers. Dairy farm I think, somewhere in the Midwest, maybe that's why she

263

feels at home here."

The dawn light was just starting to scratch at the east windows and Doc moved to start a fresh pot of coffee for the boys. "She should be along shortly...Dix's coffee's usually going by the time the rest stumble out. Though after last night, might be getting a late start."

With that, as if on cue, the pantry door opened and out wobbled Mac. His hooch bottle wasn't visible, but Doc was sure wherever it was, it was empty. Doc leaned back on his seat, stretched and looked at Mac with suspicion. "You get a good earful last night?" He knew the pantry door was thin.

"An earful of Double M's stories, more than too much, I had to sleep with the goddamned canned beans to get any quiet." Not sure if it was an explanation or a statement, Doc gave him a sideways look. Mac moved on to the coffee pot.

Before getting up, Doc leaned across to Dinah and in a quiet voice asked one last question. "Did they find his body?"

"No, but there was enough evidence to know he's dead. Even though it's going to take a while to get legally set, the detectives are calling it a clear suicide. There was an obituary and everything. He's gone. I know for sure, or I wouldn't be here."

"Good. Right." He smiled reassuringly.

As the men started drifting into the kitchen in different states of disrepair, Doc made note of the hair on the back of his neck standing at attention, and the ice now running through his veins.

"I'll be in town," he said, and was gone before the men had a chance to ask the question.

CHAPTER 20

As morning broke full, sunlight streamed in through the windows, filtered by the buildup of yet another season's grime. Win found herself contemplating just how long it had been since they were last cleaned, and why she had not noticed their sunlit shroud before. She vowed that she would not leave the day without lifting their filmy veil with a worthy scrubbing of soapy water and ammonia. For now though, the gauzy light fit perfectly with the crew's haze of hangover and fatigue. The coffee steam rose out of their individual mugs like campfires marking the landscape of a large encampment. The streams mingled with the dust specks that hung, illuminated by the sun's muffled rays. The particles danced like tiny snowflakes caught in a light beam on a windless night.

Rosemary had easily folded herself into Petey and Win's routine, and assisted in the eggs, bacon and pancake production. Doc had left before Win had gotten in, some appointment in town, they said. She figured he needed time to process all he had heard. Win knew it had been a risk sharing the burden of her story, and from the look of Dinah it had been a rough ride. Now it would be up to Doc whether he wanted to be part of such sordidness. She also knew that this day had always been on its way and, though she feared the repercussions, she was relieved that it had finally arrived.

Dinah, though exhausted, kept up her end of the amicable chatter. Somehow, Rosemary had become the object of Hollywood's attention, a twist that Win had not foreseen and found herself instantly disliking. Rosemary was holding up her end of the flirting, and Win's maternal instinct kicked into overdrive.

It was not going to be the most productive day in Sears Ranch history, but the crew gallantly tried to find a way through their internal fogs. They finished their breakfasts, took a last spin through the latrine, layered up and set out for their day. Finally, it was just the three women left at the end of the table and instinctively, they let out a collective sigh.

Win was the first to speak.

"So?" she said, looking at Dinah.

"So," Dinah replied looking at her friend with her tired, make-up-cried-off eyes.

"How did he take it?"

"He seemed okay...it's not an easy story to hear...hard to tell too," she said with a weak smile. "I'm sure you know he doesn't talk much. But I'm sure I did enough for both of us." Dinah paused, her eyes soft on Win's. "He loves you, you know."

"No," Win surprised herself at the fervor of her response. "I don't know that."

Dinah, amused at her friend's denial, spoke calmly. "Trust me. The man loves you. Maybe not like Henry, but he's a different man." Dinah took Win's hand. "And you're a different woman, but I know for sure dahlin', he has you in his heart, and he has just heard a story so horrible, that's made him feel so angry and so helpless, that it's gonna take a man like him awhile to put it all in order in his mind. I saw your face when you realized he'd already left this morning. Have some faith and give him some time."

"Besides," said Rosemary, "you need to come home, at least for a little while, all your stuff—you still have a home there, you still have people—"

"Really Rosie? A home?" Win was suddenly flustered. "The thought of walking in that house again...." She shuddered. "I wish it would just disappear. I wish I could just go back in time before Justin, before...." She reached out her hand to Rosemary. "Before he...your Dad was gone...we were so happy then."

Rosemary instantly teared up. "Yes we were...but it could be okay again. I could even move back for a while, you wouldn't be alone. The bad part's over now. It's time to come home." Win sat a moment and pondered her words, still not sure what they meant to her now.

Doc had driven straight into town and parked in front of the County Sheriff's office, just south of Main Street. He strode inside with a confidence of someone that knew his way around the place. Sheriff Angus Waters was third generation law enforcement in Medicine Bow. Just a few years older than Doc, the two men had interacted on every issue that running a ranch of unruly cowboys might entail. They had a mutual respect for each other, both knowing where the line was between their friendship and their duties.

"Hi Doc," said the girl at the front dispatch, unfazed by the unannounced visit. "He's in the back." She waved him through.

"Yup," said Doc, with a tip of his hat, never breaking stride as he went by.

"Hey Doc!" said Sheriff Waters with surprise. "What brings you in? Mac still minding his business?"

"Nothing like that." Doc didn't take the chair in front of the desk like he usually did when discussing matters with his old friend.

"So what is it like?"

"Angus, I'm gonna need you to keep your eye out for someone."

"That so?" Sensing Doc's serious tone, the sheriff raised his eyebrows and leaned back in his chair. "Who am I looking for?"

"Dr. Justin Richards." As he said the name he walked over and closed the office door. If there was a way to keep her secrets and still protect her, he would find it.

The dispatch girl took note of the private meeting and wondered which of the Sears boys was in trouble now.

Doc spent the rest of his day up on The Rise overlooking the front fifty of the ranch. He had come back after talking to the Sheriff, saddled up Dutch and rode out straight away. He only stopped by the kitchen to grab some lunch and found that Win had left out his saddlebag packed with a sandwich and a thermos of coffee. He assumed she was off with her girls. *All the better*, he thought.

He rode out on one of the fence trails, then circled around to the front acreage.

It had been a dryer than usual winter and the snow was fairly easy for Dutch to navigate. All the horses were feeling pent-up from the cold and Dutch was frisky to get out of the barn. The young paint kept a spirited pace as they moved over the frozen ground.

When Doc arrived at his destination he had a full vantage point of the entrance road under the Sears Ranch sign, as well as traffic coming along the road in either direction. He settled himself in the midst of the Lodge Pole pines, and with his binoculars, waited.

Doc knew most every vehicle that might have a reason to drive past on Route 130, and he certainly would know anyone that might turn into his drive. He figured if ol' Justin was indeed alive, he would have to strike quickly, otherwise someone was bound to notice a Southern city-type nosing around, and Justin's opportunity would pass. He also knew this man was smart, and the odds of him just rolling in through the front gate were slim. Still, he couldn't just sit and do nothing. Angus would make the inquiries, and he would sit here, waiting, nursing his coffee, and figure out what to do next.

The sheriff had pulled up photos from the different Atlanta news services on the Internet while Doc was in his office. There were plenty to choose from. The good doctor with—and then without—his beautiful auburn-haired wife. He smiled at the thought of her blondness, another remnant of her past covered up. As for Justin, the doctor was handsome, clean-cut with a toothy smile. The stories had played him all the way from victim to maniacal murderer within the span of a few weeks. The most recent photos showed the wear and tear of stress, especially around his eyes. The smile now forced, his haircut fraying at the edges. After close inspection, though, Doc could still make out the cleft in his chin.

The Sears Ranch spread out over the hills as far as he could see. It felt odd to view the entry sign now. Now that he knew he wasn't a Sears. Not by blood anyway. The letter had told him what he had always felt, but never could have known. It gave logic to Dodge's eternal dismissals. Explained, but not forgiven. In the letter, Dodge said he didn't care to know what kind of a man all that anger had made him. Doc could tell him now. It made him weak. So June trapped him into raising some other man's kid. So she stole the love of his life away from him—all the terrible deeds—still didn't justify treating a kid like dirt. To always tell him he was less-than. Never enough. Yes, Doc could tell Dodge now just what that made him. Dun and Ida didn't raise a child to hurt a child. They deserved better and so did the land they gave their lives to. The Dodge that had plagued his every move had turned to dust now. The breeze that would ripple through the aspen come spring, would carry that dust somewhere far away from where he stood.

His reverie was suddenly broken by the snap of a branch. By sheer instinct he wheeled around, simultaneously pulling his Smith & Wesson .357 revolver from the high pocket of his duster. Through the pines came Win on top of Beau.

"Shit!" she cried, when she saw the gun pointed at her.

"Shit," he said in disgust, as he urgently un-cocked the gun and stashed it away. "I wasn't expecting company."

"You sure about that?" she said, still shaken as he helped her dismount from Beau's fifteen-two hand stature. "For someone that doesn't want company, there's plenty of pretty tracks to follow you up here." She gathered herself, then looked around.

"What're you doing?"

He had no intention of telling her his suspicions. Hadn't she been afraid for long enough? Besides, he might be just borrowing trouble, an old and ugly habit of his. No need to drag her into that. "Thought it might be a good day to get out and clear my head...been a couple of wolf sightings up here, thought I might keep an eye out, let 'em know they're not welcome."

Win seemed satisfied with the story, and Doc breathed a silent sigh of relief.

"So, clearing your head, huh?"

"Yup."

"About last night...."

"Some."

"I hope you know that I—"

"I know."

"I never wanted to lie to you. I mean, I guess I did want to lie, to you and everyone else, in the beginning—"

"I know."

"But then you became...something else, and for a while I thought, well maybe I could just go on like this, you know, forever...so stupid...." She looked down, her face burning, "I didn't count on it all coming out so soon...I'm so sorry." She reached for his crossed arms. "Please forgive me...I never meant for you to get dragged into all this...nightmare." Her tears of frustration and sadness had broken free. "You have to know—"

"Win, I know."

He reached out and held her shoulders with straight arms to control the distance between them. His eyes took her in. Then, after a long moment and a singularly deep breath, he took her into his chest, his leather-gloved hands cradling her face and then kissing her hard, both of them taking up the space of one. Their hands frantic to draw the other closer through the layers of winter clothing between them, finally they paused to catch a breath.

"I'm so sorry," she repeated, now breathless from their tryst and still distraught at what she had wrought on his world.

"Shhhh, not your fault."

"Maybe not. Maybe not in the beginning...but then I knew, you know?" Her eyes searched his. "I knew what he was and I stayed. I wasn't strong, so weak...." She said it with disgust in her voice. "Too weak to stand up and walk out. What does that make me?! I brought this on, the fire, the pain—it's all my punishment...for being...nothing."

Doc spoke up sharply, "Don't say that."

"Did she tell you about the babies?"

"The babies?"

"The pregnancies."

"That you lost them—Win, I can't imagine...."

"Well imagine this, I lost them alright," and with eyes filling with violent tears, "I—got *rid* of them!" She backed away, crunching through the knee-deep snow. Her clumsiness was no match for his stride as he caught her arm. "I killed them!" She spewed the words as she shook off his arm. "He wouldn't have it. Wouldn't have my body *distorted*. He called it a *distortion*—disrupting our perfect lifestyle...*perfect?!*" She spat the word. "So he made the appointments, all the arrangements—made sure I was drugged up and wouldn't cause a fuss, and I—I just...went along with it. I showed up and let them take my babies. My precious...." She was gulping hard, trying to find air. "I laid there and let them tear them out of me. What does that make me?" Then quietly, choked with emotion, "I don't even think there's a word for what I am."

"Do. Not. Say. That." His voice was ferocious but barely a whisper now.

Win took his cue and lowered her voice to a whisper as well. "I have such shame...." Her eyes pleading. "This is my shame." Then shaking her head, "I don't expect you to understand."

"Julia," he said plainly, the weight of her true name hanging between them. "You were a prisoner of war. I understand that more than you know."

"TWICE?!" She suddenly howled. "I let him do it TWICE!"

Then with the ramblings of a woman possessed, she spewed, "He never used protection—didn't like how it felt—and I couldn't, my body wouldn't—always fighting it—so he knew full well—after the second time, that's when I just shut down...gave up...took whatever he gave without a fight, without all the tears—they only made him angrier anyway. Deep down, I knew he'd never let me go, no way he would allow a divorce, but I went along, knowing the odds...but however it went, I knew I was done, one way or another...I was already dead."

She had finally let the hard words fly, and her shoulders suddenly dropped in exhaustion. The wind took the opportunity to bite into them, and Doc drew her into his arms, whispering in her ear as he did, "But you're free now. Nothing's going to hurt you. You survived...and God help you, the memories survived with you, but it's over now." He held her tight, his cheek to hers, their tears mingling.

They stood on The Rise for a while more. Just holding on, wanting to be close, taking in the white valley that laid itself at their feet, allowing the late afternoon sun to soothe their raw and ragged edges.

Win was the first to loosen her grasp.

"I better get dinner on."

He held her fast. "You're late."

"What?"

Finally releasing her, he gave a resigned smile and removed one of his gloves to wipe clean her tears with his rough hand.

"I mean, I've been waiting for you—in my life—I didn't know you were coming, that I'd find you—and then you were there. I knew it was you—even before the Potter boys—I would have followed you, found a way to you...."

Looking past her out over the land that was his family leg-acy, his words left downy clouds in the icy air. "I'm late, too. It should have been me that found you before...the damage. I've always thought there could be someone. Someone that could see me—I don't know, maybe we both had to be so beat up in order to recognize the other. Not to ask more than we could give. There might not be enough left, but I'll take whatever you got, and I'll give whatever I can—might not be enough...."

It was her turn to hold his face in gloved hands. She kissed him softly, their silent tears blending to create an elixir that, if harnessed, just might heal wounds the world over. Their silence held as they saddled up and headed back toward the ranch.

About halfway down the hill Doc broke the percussion of the hooves crushing through the ice and snow.

"So it was the only thing I could think of."

"What was?" she said wearily, not sure if she had heard him right.

"The hat?"

"The hat," she repeated, still not comprehending.

"The hat."

"You're telling me about the hat." She secretly marveled at the non sequitur to their prior conversation, and yet, *finally*, The Hat!

"It was the only thing I could think of to say."

"The only thing you could think of."

"To say." He said it as if it made perfect sense.

"The only thing you could think of to say was the hat."

"Yup."

"When?" she asked innocently, knowing full well when.

"There any way you might make this easier?" He cocked his head back at her from under his hat.

"Doubt it." She was going to work this for all it was worth.

"Okay." They let a silence fall for another two cut-backs.

"I was there when you came in."

"Where?"

"The H-B, I was there at the bar, so...."

"I didn't see you."

"I know."

"So...."

"So, you were pretty."

"I was pretty...," she said, skeptical now, her tone icy.

"Yup. You were."

"Oh."

"So I had to come up with something."

"Oh, so...."

"Yup."

"The hat was a *line*."

"Yup," His tone was laced with pride.

"You couldn't figure out how to say hello, so, you decided to announce that my hat annoyed you."

"Yup. But when you put it that way, sounds kind of—"

"Lame?"

"Lame?" he said, tasting the word in his mouth. "Don't know that I'd go that far."

"So you don't actually *care* if women wear hats inside."

"Nope."

They both gave the exchange a rest, and let the discourse of creaking saddle leather and ice-breaking hooves take over.

"Okay?" he finally asked.

"Okay," she conceded, but couldn't help being tickled by his ridiculous strategy.

They rode in silence until they reached the entrance of the New Barn. Doc dismounted and took both horses' reins. Win slid off and made for the cookhouse. Just before she turned the corner he called out, "I still stand by 'pretty.'"

She stopped and looked back at him. He was staring at her, his eyes taking her in and saying it all. He tipped his hat and turned to lead the horses down to their stalls. Without turning around he added, "I got that part right."

It was dusk and the sun headed for shelter in the gentle wake of his words. As they walked away from each other down their opposing paths, the wind subtly shifted directions.

Only the horses noticed, and nickered a soft alarm at the change.

CHAPTER 21

J ustin smiled when the silver Mercedes he'd been following from a distance turned off the two-lane highway onto a dirt road that led under a rustic metal arch. The name hanging in forged iron was, *SEARS*.

Dinah was always so sure she would win. Always so confident that someday he would make a mistake—be found out and Julia would escape him forever. So close! He remembered her smug smile when he confronted her the day after Julia disappeared from the hospital. He had called her and arranged the meeting at Goldberg's coffee house in Buckhead. They looked like any other couple sharing a latte. She had met his eyes straight on. Nervy bitch.

He had foregone the niceties and gotten straight to the point. "Where is she?"

"Whatever do you mean?" she said, in a chirpy tone.

"Where is she?" He used more force than intended.

She immediately noted the crack in his armor of arrogance, and smiled.

"Even if I knew, which of course I do not, do you really think I'd tell you?"

He gathered himself. "Oh, I think you'll tell me," then paused, letting her feel the threat, "and when she does come home—"

She interrupted then, with fire in her eyes. "Oh yes, I can imagine. I've spent a lot of time over the past months *imagining*. What would you do to her? Hmm, let's see....You've already beat her and broken her bones, degraded and controlled her every move to the point she's completely paralyzed from making a decision, oh, and rahhh-ight, you tried to burn her alive. So, really, what's left?" She tilted her head quizzically with a big fake smile. "What is the punishment for leaving such a loving home?"

This time it was his turn to smirk at her liquid sarcasm, but he knew he mustn't underestimate her, not again. She had proven a formidable opponent. He could smell her perfume from across the table, the nauseating stench only fueled his anger. He leaned forward and quietly whispered, "She's mine, Dinah. Don't get in my way."

She had leaned in as well, to meet him face-to-face. "Justin, she's not coming back. And Jusssstin," she let his name slither off her tongue, "she was never yours."

With their eyes locked in combat, she had stood slowly, and with that infuriating smug smile, she lightly exhaled, "I'm done here."

"Oh, we're only getting started."

"Rot in hell, you sick bastard," she snapped, her calm façade finally breaking. Then she had strutted out of the restaurant like the peacock whore she was.

He had forced a winning smile on his face, but how he had burned. The adrenaline started at the top of his head and flowed lava-hot down to his spine. He didn't remember rising slowly, returning to his car and driving back to the hospital.

In those first weeks, he could never have imagined that it was going to go so wrong. The police had asked him question after question, at first hanging on his every word as the devastated husband, then as the hours and days ticked by, the questions slowly turned to accusations and the accusations turned to assumed guilt as the details of his personal idiosyncrasies began surfacing one-by-one. So, so wrong.

People he had considered friends, allies, turned on him, one after the other, until finally, the lynch mob was complete. Julia was the victim. He was "The Monster". And he took it. Humiliation by humiliation.

They searched his home that was newly under construction after the fire. In searching, they found some of his little toys and souvenirs, leaving all that was left of his perfect order in shambles. His dismissal from the board, his social circle disappearing, the suspension of his medical license, his dear family cutting off the money flow; without so much as a bead of sweat, he took it all.

He took it because he knew she was alive. And he knew if he could just bide his time, keep himself out of jail, he would figure out how to find her.

As it turned out, his composure had paid off. He never cracked, never spoke of Dinah's role. And in the end, there was no body, no corpse, and so no proof that he had killed his wife. He had just waited them out. Once the investigation was shelved, nothing really changed for him. He was still a social leper and the hospital board voted not to reinstate him. In other circumstances, he would have sued, but he had more important things to do.

He centered all his efforts and energy on Dinah. She was the key. He also knew that even she might not know where Julia was actually hiding. But they must have figured out some way of communicating and it would have to be untraceable. Julia wasn't smart enough to dream up this insane plan on her own, so it was Dinah he watched.

He became a shadow, started dressing like the Invisible Mediocres that he had always disdained. Sweats and a baseball cap. He'd grown his beard out scruffy and donned cheap sports wrap sunglasses. He consciously changed his posture to a slouch and walked slowly with the slightest limp. He abandoned all of his local haunts and made any purchases at strip malls out in the suburbs.

After the police had given up dogging his every move, he spent his waking hours stalking Dinah. It helped that she lived in the heart of Buckhead in a high rise. 2500 Peachtree was one of the most exclusive addresses in Atlanta. The sand colored stucco facade rose in wedding cake tiers from the grand entrance up to her seventh-floor residence. The luxurious lobby always bustled to meet the every whim of its needy residents. He could hang out on the streets and in the surrounding diners and coffee houses with no one raising an eyebrow.

Through the help of Darren Poole, Esq.—his ever-sleazy lawyer—and some new friends, he was able to get a copy of her mail key. Dinah or her boring husband usually picked up their mail in the late afternoon or evening. The mailman always delivered between 10:00 and 10:30. Like clockwork, he would wait for it to arrive and slip in to lift the mail. He would then go home and with his surgeon's skill, steam the envelopes open. He checked her credit card bills, bank statements, phone bills, Peach Pass toll statements, but nothing pointed to Julia. The old bitch was smart. The next morning, same time, he would return it and exchange it for anything new of interest.

As weeks passed, it was clear he was wasting his time. After some re-strategizing he came to the realization that he was going about it the wrong way. He wasn't going to be able to crack whatever firewall she had created. He would have to make it so Dinah would do the legwork. He would fix it so she wouldn't have to slip up to catch her; instead, he would have her physically lead him to where Julia was. He knew the only circumstance in which Dinah would dare go to Julia would be in the event of his death. While he wasn't keen on obliging her with the real thing, he was more than happy to stage a disappearance of his own.

In the month leading up to his *demise* he had taken pains to show the world of Atlanta gossip mongers that he was in a full downward spiral. His house and grounds staff had already left him. Each making their own excuses, but both sides knew they no longer wanted to be associated with the man the papers had christened "The Monster".

After the continued ransacking searches by the FBI, he had opted not to continue the repairs from the fire. The section of the house that had caved in, still had blue tarps anchored with nails to keep out the rain. The grass grew high, the weeds grew higher, and anything that once flowered went to seed. The pencil pines that had once lined up like soldiers around the property's perimeter had grown unruly with the lack of attention, each one breaking ranks in their own way. In a brilliant stroke of nature and luck, a squall blew through and actually detached a gutter from the front of his house. Much to the chagrin of his elegant Ansley Park neighbors, he let it hang.

As with everything in his life, he mastered it. He mastered his own deterioration. There could and would be no doubt whatsoever about how low his star had fallen. He even went so far as to take a hammer to one of the back taillights of his beloved 650 BMW convertible. Where once he took pride in perfectly maintaining its flawless metallic sapphire-black paint job and fastidiously conditioned black Napa leather interior, now he smiled at the mud spray behind the wheel hubs, and grime you could write your name in. This was his new perfect.

As his scheduled demise grew near, the final preparations became all-consuming. He toyed with burning the house to the ground, just to let it all be gone, but as beautiful as the sight would be, he didn't want to give any more fodder to the claim that he set the first fire. It would just have to rot instead.

Again, with the help of his spectacularly corrupt lawyer, he had been carefully and quietly liquidating assets. He would have to survive on a cash-only strategy once the deed was done. It amused him to think that Julia would have had to use the same plan. He was paralleling her moves. He had her scent

now. His excitement frequently led to arousal. With each release, he felt reborn.

On the eve of his ultimate performance, he sat down to pen what
would be his definitive testament. It took all of ten minutes.

12/21/2007

My Dearest Julia,

*It was a year ago tonight the accident that would shape our des-
tiny happened. There has not been a moment where my soul could
rest since you've been gone.*

Where did you go, my love?

*Our home, my life, my heart are all empty. I see your shadow
pass in the corners. I feel you with me, but long to touch you, flesh
to flesh. The way it used to be.*

*Where are you? Who has taken you? The thought of you with
pain in your eyes haunts my every dream. They think I hurt you.
Me! Your love, your husband. If they could only know the perfection that we shared. The perfect connection, so sublime!*

*If you have left this world, then I am coming to you now. I
promise we will be together. Heaven will be mine when I hold you
again.*

Even in death, I am yours and you are mine.

J.

He chose the Highway 76 Bridge over the Chattooga River. It
was two hours out of Atlanta, on the border of South Carolina,
in God and goat country. He had researched it thoroughly and
determined there were no traffic cameras. At 2:30 in the morning
he pulled into the turnout, left the top down to draw attention
on a cold December night, and left his note for Julia taped to the

steering wheel.

He then stole out to the middle of the bridge and dropped one shoe and his favorite coat into the inky waters below. He had added heavy stones to his coat pockets to further convey his intentions. Though the night was moonless, he could hear the strength of the rushing current beneath him. From there, he made his way through the woods on the side of the road and up to the parking lot near Bull Sluice.

He had left a car there the day prior. It was a dark blue Taurus; fantasy vehicle of the Invisible Mediocres. He had paid dearly for the forged registration and plates, but this nondescript tank of a sedan would allow him to travel all but undetected as he began this next phase of his plan.

The trunk was carefully packed to capacity with second-hand suitcases of clothing, food and cash. He drove three hours until he hit Columbia, South Carolina. Just outside of town he checked into a roadside dump of a motel. He slept the sleep of generals, once they knew the war was won.

He stayed there for a week. Only leaving his room to go to the library and use the Internet. He followed the breaking news of his suicide with glee. He had done it, of course. Perfect execution of the perfect plan. He loved perfect.

The search for his body went on for three days and then was called off. The evidence pointed exactly where he had engineered it; Suicide. Ten days after abandoning his precious convertible for the buzzards of authority to consume, he saw it, the article he'd been waiting for in the Atlanta Journal Constitution. It had been an overview of events up to that point; the frustration of not finding a body, but conceding that the all roads lead to his irrefutably taking his own life. The best part was the quote from Darren Poole.

"Dr. Richards was misunderstood and as much a victim as his be-

loved wife Julia. It was not guilt that made him jump off that bridge but the hopelessness that comes when everything you know and love is taken from you. He had nothing to live for and I hold the FBI and the local police ultimately responsible. There's something wrong with a system that tries you in the media long before you see a courtroom. I don't know how these people sleep at night. One of our native sons has fallen on the battlefield of love and loss. This is a sad day for Atlanta."

Granted, Justin had paid him a small fortune under the table to take his side, but God, he loved that guy. He laughed aloud when he read it. The librarian looked up and gave him a chilling glare.

CHAPTER 22

When Win entered the cookhouse she was surprised to find Petey and Rosemary already chopping the veggies for Sloppy Josie. Dinah was busying herself setting the table and had managed to fill two vases with arranged winter greenery. In the soft lamplight Win was reminded that her friend was the consummate Atlanta hostess, and now somehow she had transformed the usual stack of plates and silverware caddies into an intimate dinner party, the place settings only lacking name cards and a seating chart. Win smiled.

"Now don't go spoiling them. I'll have to train them all over again once you leave."

"Not going to be a problem dahlin', cuz I'm not leavin' without you."

Both gave each other their best don't-argue-with-me look, and went on with their business as only best friends can do. Dinah had clearly napped and reclaimed her usual primped and primed self. Win could tell she was enjoying prepping for the evening's festivities. Half an hour later, with the Sloppy Josie sauce simmering, the kitchen door flung open, and like clowns from a clown car, the whole crew seemed to enter at once. Their spirits were high and they set about their business of stripping off layers, general cleaning and warming up.

Hollywood went straight to Rosemary's side and became invaluable to whatever cooking project she was involved with. To Win's knowledge, it was the first time Hollywood ever stepped onto the kitchen side of the cookhouse without begging or shaming. Rosie's wiles were magical indeed. Magical or otherwise, this was not an alliance Win was keen on witnessing. Hollywood was a darling cad, but a cad nonetheless. She knew his M.O. And wasn't interested in Rosemary experiencing it firsthand.

Doc hadn't returned yet from the New Barn, but all was ready and the crew was starving, so they went ahead with the meal. She pictured him taking his time putting away Dutch and Beau then walking the stalls. She knew he was still deep in his thoughts.

Hollywood had sidled up to Rosemary when he sat down for the meal and was in the middle of a charming full-court press when Win slammed the meat cleaver into the hard wood of the table in front of his plate. The razor sharp knife made the *doyoing!* Heard in cartoons, and all conversation instantly came to a halt. Maybe it was the way it severed a 7-inch long tumescent sourdough roll clean in half that got the message across, or maybe Hollywood had a sudden burst of chivalry, but he immediately stood and offered Win his seat. She took it with mock surprise and feigned gratitude while she snuggled in next to Rosemary.

Mac, with the annoyance of an old dog faced with unruly puppies, commanded Hollywood, "Get on down here and set next to me, Romeo."

Rosemary just looked at Win with big eyes and a confounded grin.

"Pass the greens," Win said, as if cleavers flew through the air every day, and after a certain amount of snickering, the conversation returned to its lively pace. Hollywood obediently slid in next to Mac. Win ate her meal right-handed; her left hand firmly around Rosemary's shoulders.

As the dinner came to its usual pie-punctuated conclusion, the gathering loosened up from the benches and began the post-meal routine. The Rose brothers settled into their game, Mac picked up his newspaper and the rest continued their conversation as the clean-up began.

"The barn's on fire."

It was a simple sentence, said without the high drama the situation would normally call for. In fact it was Petey, standing stock still, looking out the backdoor window. Had it been any other four words, it might have been overlooked, trampled by the cowboys' incessant banter, but these words, spoken in quiet shock, cut knife-like through the loud conversation, leaving all to immediately pause and ask the collective, "What?"

Then with one fluid movement, Petey flung open the door and bolted though, repeating as he went, this time with all the fervor in him, "THE BARN'S ON FIRE!"

It was as if they had practiced daily, all their lives, the choreography that followed. The men shot out the open door like bullets in a repeating rifle. Jim instantly shouted directions: "Dix, Double M, Petey, Dave, get to the horses and get anything else out of there you can! Hollywood, Sticks and Mac, pull those pumps over and hook up the hoses! Win, you call the fire department! Ladies, go and make sure the Grady's are out and OK. Stay with them!"

"Oh God—Doc!" Win ran after Jim. "Jim, Doc was putting away the horses!"

Jim swung around and grabbed her. "Tell me."

"He—we were out riding," she blurted, her words flying out of her, "I came in to do the dinner, he took the horses to put them up. That's the last I saw him!"

"Who?"

"What?!"

"Which horses?!"

"Right-oh—" Her mind skipping in her panic, she desperately searched for the names. Finally she spat out, "Beau and Dutch!"

"Got it." Jim released her, and running at full speed yelled over his shoulder, "Don't worry, Doc's been through worse. Now call and get us some help!"

"Okay!" she yelled, but no one was there to hear her. She ran back into the kitchen and made the frantic call. Duty done, she took off again toward the barn but midway stopped short. The memory of that night one year ago flooded over her. She stood riveted and watched the billowing black smoke coming from the upper eves. Horses were running free-range, with white-rimmed eyes that betrayed their terror.

Then suddenly she was on the ground. Hurled there by some force, she fell facedown onto the hard, icy earth. Stunned, she rolled onto her back, eyes closed, trying to catch her breath. The Wound suddenly awakened and sent shots of pain through her extremities.

"Hello, darlin'."

When she opened her eyes, it was Justin's face she saw.

"Did you miss me?" He was leaning over her, eyes crazed, excited.

She attempted to scream, but a hard slap to her left temple took the wind out of her once again. As she recovered this time, she felt the barrel of a gun pressed hard into her neck, just below her jaw.

"Let's go for a walk...so much catching up to do."

"Oh God—" was all she got out before he grabbed a handful of hair and yanked her to her feet.

"Blonde. Hmmm, interesting choice," Justin cooed, his fist still painfully entwined in her hair, while the gun stabbed into the base of her skull. "I didn't think it possible for you to look more like a whore, but you continually surprise me, Julia. Always a surprise." He sighed wistfully.

He began walking her toward the aspen grove in the circle drive. Out of the corner of her eye, she saw the barn becoming engulfed and could already hear the faint sirens in the distance.

"I wouldn't count on him coming." His venom-laced drawl spilled into her ear. "He made one very fatal mistake."

"No!" she moaned, with a despair so deep it echoed within her withering frame.

"Oh yes," he hissed. "He put up a good fight, well, actually not really." He chuckled. "But I expect he's experiencing about now what you did that night. You remember—" He nestled his mouth in tight to her ear. "That night you were supposed to die?"

"Doc!" She twisted hard, thinking only of getting to him, somehow saving him. But Justin's iron grip held her.

"But alas, you did not," he continued, as if he hadn't heard her. "Can you imagine how shocked I was when they pulled you free of the wreckage? And you were *alive*? I have to say darlin', you never cease to amaze me. But I promise, your *boyfriend* will not have such a miraculous ending." He had been speaking as if they were out on an evening walk, but then he pressed his lips hard to her ear. "You have to know darling, I would never allow myself to make the same mistake twice."

Win let out a sob. With the unfathomable loss of Doc beginning to penetrate her brain, the tonic of adrenaline began leaking out of her and her body sank into the dark familiarity of Justin's control.

"So now we find ourselves here," he continued, as they crossed into the aspen grove. "Oh, you and your high bitch friend were actually very impressive in your scheming, but *really*—did you really think I was going to roll over and just let you go?" He gave a dismissive chuckle. "I *own* you, Julia. That's. Never. Going. To. Change."

His long surgeon's fingers bored what felt like holes into her upper arm as the gun's muzzle stabbed deep into her neck. She heard herself whimpering with fear and hated herself for it. She knew how much he enjoyed it. Once again she was powerless. The familiar paralysis of terror swept over her and she silently accepted her fate. The Monster had killed Calder and now he would kill her. She prayed then, the simplest of prayers, yet still bereft of all hope that a greater ghost would hear.

Then let it be done.

Surely this was a prayer that could be answered.

They were deep inside the aspen now, obscured for the most part from anyone's vision. The *SEARS* granite marker loomed over them, while the stones surrounding it felt like passive observers.

She wondered where the spirits of the buried Sears had gone. She scanned the edge of the aspen ring for a sign of June.

Will they see? Please don't let them see.

She didn't want the ghosts of his family to witness her final weakness, the shame already gripping her. It was because of her that Calder was dead.

The sirens were getting closer and she held out a sliver of hope that the trucks might find her through the trees with their headlights, but of course when they finally made it up the gravel road, their eyes were fixed on the flames now pouring out of the New Barn. The trucks screamed around to the back side of the circle and parked as near to the barn as the buildings would allow. She could hear the men shouting to each other, so close, but with all of their energy focused in the opposite direction. They might as well have been a world away.

"Take off your clothes."

"What?!" Her shocked voice was barely audible.

"Take off your clothes." His voice was lifeless, no emotion.

"Justin, I...please...you win." She was shaking, almost convulsing with terror and cold. "I know you're going to kill me...just get it done...I'm through here."

"Well, I'm not. SO FUCKING DO AS YOU'RE TOLD!" he roared, an inch from her head, assaulting her eardrum as the sound waves hit her. Then, resigned that this final humiliation would be an appropriate end to her pathetic existence, she began. Jacket. Belt. Boot. Boot. Zipper. Jeans. Shirt. Undershirt. Underwear. Socks. Finally, there was nothing more.

The silver of the belt buckle Doc had given her just weeks before, glimmered from the snowy ground where it had fallen. The polished metal caught a beam from the three-quarter moon, and reflected the light briefly above her left breast. Her hands reached to touch the light, as if pledging a last oath against her heart. She straightened her spine slowly, her back to him, standing on her pile of clothes in the frigid cold, shivering, naked, ready to die.

"Oh my God—it's beautiful," was his eerie response to this, her newest shame. She heard him step to her with an icy crunch. "It's perfect." He sounded reverent, as he reached out and touched the mélange of scar tissue on her back. The Wound seemed to greet his touch, its response like a baby to its mother; the recognition inborn, the bond of blood.

"I've only imagined up to now, but this...*this* is a masterpiece." Then his tone changed from awe to cold anticipation. "Kneel down now Julia, our time together is at an end."

Obediently she got on her knees, and in doing so, she looked up at the moon, brilliant and almost full in the black sky. The stars danced in and out of the treetops, watching her, resigned along with her. Win's only thought was of Doc and seeing him again in whatever came next. An overwhelming wave of peace came over her and she released her arms from where they had been crossed, covering her breasts. She raised them, outstretched and upwards to the beautiful night sky above her, and prayed for the salvation of her weak soul.

The hammer hit flint. The bullet flew.

Doc awoke, violently coughing in the smoke and haze. He was propped on the side of the Fire Hall where the men had placed him. Double M had been left behind to care for him while the others ran back to lend a hand with the animals and dousing the flames. As soon as he started coughing, the old hand ran off to tell Jim, and to direct the paramedics when they arrived.

The images came flooding back into Doc's consciousness: Putting up the horses after his ride with Win, a stranger had suddenly been beside him. Without warning the man had cuffed him hard, pulled a gun and told him he had come for *his wife*. The gunman was wild and unkempt, bearded. His clothes were new but now dirty and slept in. Doc had realized he was at an extreme disadvantage, until he remembered the Smith & Wesson still tucked in his coat pocket. He just needed to buy time.

"You realize there's a roomful of men that'll come running at the sound of a gunshot."

"Yes, of course." The man he knew was Justin seemed amused. "Which is why I've come up with Plan B." As he uttered the last two words he drew back to pistol whip Doc again, and though Doc tried to deflect it, the fog of the first strike still hadn't completely lifted and his reflexes were too slow. This time the blow sent him flying and unconscious up against a stall, the revolver still waiting for him in his duster pocket.

Now, regaining his senses, a single thought roared to the forefront of his brain.

Win.

Instinctively he knew how Justin's tactics would take form. Like a coyote stalking the weakest newborn in a herd, he would create a scenario that would allow him to cut Win out of the crowd, and take control from there.

"Oh, God—no!" he moaned, gaining his feet. Doc wheezed and stumbled back toward the kitchen and followed the tracks from there. The nearly full moon cast plenty of reflective light in the pale snow to tell the story of the mass of frantic boot steps that must have been laid down once the fire was noticed. There was only one trail that led in the opposite direction, two sets, one steady and sure, he could almost feel the fear radiating from the other.

Doc set off with the stealth of a rival coyote vying for the same prey, sliding undetected through the crisp night air. The tracks seemed to glow in the moonlight, leading him across the circle drive and into the round aspen fortress. Just inside the edge of the grove he caught a man's voice on the breeze, low and seething. Doc calibrated its location and silently moved toward it. Again, the moonlight was his beacon as it reflected off her pale skin. She was nude, on her knees, her back partially to him, arms outstretched in supplication. Terror struck him anew when he registered her expression. It was peaceful.

The Monster stood behind her wild-eyed and moved in to touch the destruction blazoned on her back. He nodded his head in satisfaction, then bent down, saying something in her ear. All the while his other hand held a gun pressed hard against the base of her skull.

The fatal second.

The one where Doc paused to take in the surreal scene. The one where he was deciding how to approach, attack—to free her and kill him. The second it took to reach in his pocket, find the .357, its trigger, and draw it forth. The second it took for The Monster to find Doc in his sights and shoot him down.

At the sound of the gunshot, a crack of adrenaline shot through her body and blinded her. Win crumpled to the ground—yet still she breathed. Panicked and confused, a quick head-to-toe inventory allowed for the realization that she had been spared.

He had missed!

Impossible.

Another one of his sadistic games. She heard his laughter. She was freezing, shaking as she lay naked in the snow. But there was something more now, something new...she was angry.

Win crawled to reach her clothes, her limbs already numb from the deadening cold. She found her jacket and wrapped herself inside it. His laughter increasing now to hysteria.

"*Tsk, tsk, tsk*...oh, Julia..."

She paid no attention. If he was going to kill her, have at it, but she was done with the fear, the games, all of the evil. She. Was. Done. Still fumbling and shivering, she zipped up her jeans and pulled her boots over her frozen, brittle feet.

Justin's taunting continued. "Julia, Julia, Julia, you were always such a slut."

She tuned him out, in a calm strategic trance now. *Is there any way to get out of this alive?* She thought to herself matter-of-factly. She looked up to assess the situation and saw that Justin was no longer facing her—he was transfixed by a dark shape just inside the aspen ring. She knew this was her chance. If she could use the aspen as shelter, she could bolt now and maybe make it to the fire engines and the men for help. It was when she rose to make her run, that she saw Doc's lifeless body lying where he had fallen, where the bullet had thrown him down, his blood, going red to black as it oozed over the ice.

"*Noooo!*" Her scream pierced the frigid silence contained inside the ring of trees. "No! No! No!" Her voice wasn't familiar, more ragged and primal than could have ever come from her. As she wailed in despair, Justin's laughter was the only sound in the forest stillness to punctuate her cries.

She draped herself on Doc to give him what little warmth she held. She took his heavy head in her hands, his pallor like the delicate parchment where proclamations are written. She felt no life.

What she did feel was the gun still in his pocket. She remembered it from that afternoon. Could it have been only a few hours before? Mere hours, when he had held her and kissed her hard, his steady strength engulfing her—she had known then that she loved him. That she would stay. This place was her home now. This place, and this man. And now...

With the elegance of a dancer, in one single motion, she pulled the gun, rose up to face her husband and unloaded, in frenetic succession, deafening rounds into his chest. Dr. Justin Richards, staggered and then fell where he had stood, the surprise frozen on his face. She saw his last vision reflected in his wide eyes. It was of Julia standing with the barn flames glowing behind her, not unlike the first fire, only this time it was he who would do the dying.

Win dropped to her knees at Doc's side. "Calder," she cried softly. He lay cold as stone, his granite complexion now fixed.

"Calder...," she wept, desperation gaining favor with gut sobs and tears. Here again in her arms—the loss unbearable, her mind flew back to Henry, the blackness that followed and now, here—Doc, her rescuer, a promise of love or just the rebirth of hope, once again destroyed and lying cold in her arms.

The excruciating sorrow that had been roiling, finally shot through her as fear's adrenaline waned and she let out a keening wail so soulful, so primal, that any animal within earshot stopped dead in its tracks.

The gun was still warm in her hand. *Strange*, she thought mechanically, for such a cold night. She used to pray, back in Atlanta, she had prayed so many times, begging for respite, pleading for deliverance from Justin's devastation. She had thought God had finally answered, that he had delivered her in all of His mercy, into this world of nature's beauty and the safety of Doc's arms. Had Doc been an angel sent to her? In these past days she had marveled at the gift of the new world she had been afforded. And now...now she folded her hands, the gun between them, and she prayed for the second time that night.

Ave Maria...

She sighed deeply, the soprano's voice from so long ago, now rising again in her ears. Suddenly, she was so tired, her vision blurred, the aspen's white trunks whirled and wove themselves into a cocoon that contained only Win with Doc's lifeless body laid out before her. What was it all for? Her sobs came violently. She closed her eyes and tried to speak through the tears, but instead her head was filled with words that were not her own.

Ave Maria,
gratia plena,
Dominus tecum,
benedicta tu in mulieribus,
et benedictus fructus ventris tui, Jesu.

The notes sublime, weaving with a violin and harp, a lyric voice soaring with the blood in her veins.

Julia opened her eyes and saw with wonder the ghosts of every Sears that lay beneath the ground in that hallowed shelter of aspen, all glistening in the moonlight, now standing around her.

There was Dun and Ida, young again, as they must have been when they first came to the ranch, his well-worn hands fully engulfing hers as they warmly regarded Julia. There was Wally, dashing in his uniform with a rakish smile as he casually rested his arm on the adolescent shoulder of a tow-headed Wally Jr. Next stood Mary Ava and Dodge, young and beautiful as in their high school days, slightly swinging their clasped hands, their fingers tightly intertwined as they stared at Julia in a sort of awe. Then, running and weaving, in and out of all of them ran Hollis, the blonde cherub still five years old, his smile and laughter echoing to the very tops of the trees.

Finally, there was June. She stood at Doc's feet, her son, her face radiating a mother's love. June knelt down and gently placed her ethereal hands on his boot tops, her blazing eyes never straying from his face. Julia knew they were here for him, and was overwhelmed with relief, knowing he would finally have the family he had so long been denied. Indeed, Julia felt a kinship of her own with the luminescent gathering.

She closed her eyes and bowed her head.

Sancta Maria, Sancta Maria, Maria!
Ora pro nobis,
nobis peccatoribus,
nunc et in hora,
in hora mortis nostrae!

With sweet strains of the *Ave Maria* still weaving through her words, Julia prayed, "If You really are all they say...all this world believes...if somehow this was all part of Your *perfect* plan...then please, you will allow me this one...last...small...thing. Dear God... I'm so tired...please...," she paused one more time, gathering herself for what would be next, and last. "Please...let there be one more bullet."

She inhaled sharply and to the circle of ghosts surrounding her and Doc's *Pieta*, whispered, "Take care of him." Then with eyes closed and tears streaming, Win raised the barrel to the crook of her chin and pulled the trigger. She uttered one last word before the hammer fell.

"Amen."

Amen

Amen

Her prayer was answered.

The sound of a gunshot flew above the din of the fire-dousing efforts and alerted the crew that something was wrong. Very wrong. Jim and Dix peeled off from fighting the flames and ran to the bunkhouse. They were met by Sheriff Waters, who had heard the call come through, and with a sick feeling in his gut, had run to his truck and sped the twenty miles to the ranch. "This is not good," was the phrase he kept repeating as he flew. "This is not good."

He had arrived just behind the volunteer fire department that had immediately gone into action with well-oiled urgency. The sheriff went straight for Jim.

"There was a shot!" was all Jim got out, before they heard the chilling wail that had stopped the three men cold. Then more shots, in rapid-fire succession. Without a word the three took off running, each formulating his own version of the event that was unfolding.

Toward the aspen they raced, the snow tracks once again showing the way. Upon entering the grove, they were struck by a quiet so opaque, that the three men pulled up sharp from their headlong scramble, each instinctively understanding that whatever had happened, the danger had passed. They now approached what lay ahead with a reverence that the stillness demanded; Jim and Dix consumed with wide-eyed alarm, the sheriff with a well-seasoned dread.

There in the small clearing between the stark white trunks and the circle of stones, the three bodies lay. The disheveled stranger, his chest perforated and pooled with blood. Then, Doc and Win in their bed of ice and crimson. She lay seemingly cradled on top of him, his body even in death protecting her from the harsh icy world around her. Their devotion as evident in death, as it had been in life.

The sheriff set to checking for vital signs, the innate discipline of protocol, for now, overriding his grief.

Jim and Dix automatically took off their hats in respect for the fallen.

"Jesus," said Dix, losing the fight with his tears.

Jim turned away to give him privacy, walking into the trees, seeking room to gather himself as well, until he heard the sheriff bellow.

"Boys–need a hand here! Got a pulse!"

CHAPTER 23

The aspen grove in the circle drive budded early that spring, seemingly in a hurry to don their perfect paddle leaves. Their ceremonial clatter proclaimed a new arrival to the stones in their charge.

The icy ground that had been broken to accommodate the long wooden box had now softened with the early thaw; the rich soil once in hardened clods, had eased into a single rounded mound, the first sign of new grass pushing through.

At the base of the new granite marker lay a course of perfect river stones, and dried berry branches were held in a mason jar. On top of the headstone lay an antler rack, discarded from a young buck. Doc always kept an eye out for something she might have liked, something he might have brought her and laid on the kitchen sill. That was a habit he kept.

He wasn't there when they buried her. He was far away in Fort Collins Rocky Mountain Hospital, where he had fought his way back from the damage left in the bullet's wake. It had entered his right chest, blown through some ribs, and punctured a lung, before exiting clean out of his back. The snow he had fallen on had turned out to be his savior. He had lain, literally freezing; the ice slowing his heart, thickening his blood, buying him time for the sheriff to discover the faint pulse and call to action the forces that would eventually save his life.

He hadn't been conscious when she had fallen lifeless on top of him, but somehow he knew what had been in her mind; how she had begged for an end to it, the pain of loss unfathomable—the loss of him.

She had already won, twice. Henry. The Wound.

It had taken all that was in her to knit those scars. She didn't have it in her to go another round. Doc understood. A life without love and hope was no longer an option for her. Somewhere in his memory he could hear her voice as she beseeched God and ghost for a reprieve, and then the explosion as the final bullet had bowed to her prayer of destruction.

He hadn't been awake when the bullet flew, but three days later he had opened his eyes knowing that she was gone; the hole in his heart only beginning to tear open into the gaping wound it would become. As his physical body healed, knitting its shredded pieces back together, The Empty simultaneously grew wider. He understood why she had sidestepped this burden. So heavy.

But The Empty was vastly different than The Wound. Doc accepted this new mantle with gratitude for the love he had been briefly given. It was his internal proof that she had been his, the outline of her, now hollowed-out inside him. He knew he would carry it through to his ending days. For her. He knew that this would be his best pain. The only pain he would sign up for again, given the choice to do it once more.

Her stone read:

Julia O'Shea Brown Winchester
1956 - 2008
Beloved Wife of Henry
Mother of Rosemary
Friend and Cook

He had thought long on those words, and knew of course, that they weren't adequate. They all described her in relation to someone else. None told the story that was truly her. Perhaps the essence of who she was still eluded him. She was a ghost in her own life, and now? He couldn't formulate the answer.

He did know that she came to him sometimes right before he slept or awoke, she would sit on the edge of his bed, or stand at the far end of the room. Sometimes they would be walking, he could still smell her scent next to him, her skin radiating light, as if frosted with sugar crystals. She would speak in cryptic commands.

"Easy now."

"Shhhh."

"I got you."

Doc knew they were all things he had once said to her.

And when she came, he would feel himself lifting up, going with her, heavy in the air. He could see the two of them from the top of the room or soaring above the ranch, two figures, tiny against the vast beauty of his family's land. His land now. So many things had shifted in him since she had gone. The anger and grudges from his father had dissipated like a fire's ashes that fly on the wind until all the heat is gone, and when they landed there was nothing left but the dust of what had once been burned.

The anger was replaced now by the dull ache of her lying beneath that stone. He fought the urge to dig in and find her, she was so close...she was right there. But the stoic cowboy went through his days and nights cool and composed, the pain, The Empty, now his traveling partner, solid as the oldest pines on the Snowy Range.

EPILOGUE

The dew on the morning grass dangled like ornaments on a holiday tree. The summer morning pressed hard against the sun's destined trip to the top of the sky. As he stepped off from the bottom porch stair, his bare feet instantly cooled, the ragged hem of his jeans absorbing the verdant wetness as it climbed the denim to well above his ankles. He stepped lightly, so as not to disturb her, and took care not to spill the brimming cup of coffee he held precariously in each hand.

She was there. Sitting on the Grady's picnic bench, her back to him, leaning against the table. She wore a sleeveless sleeping gown made of the lightest white cotton and well-worn lace. It was low in the back and he could see the smooth perfect skin below where her auburn locks hung disheveled from sleep. Her head lay back with eyes closed in worship of the sun's first rays. The skin on her arms shimmered and her face shone radiant as the light kissed her with its warmth.

He took the opposite bench as his first step and the tabletop as the second. He then stepped down to the bench on which she sat, and planted his feet on either side of her. Gently hugging her shoulders with his knees, he sat down on the redwood table. He lowered one coffee down in front of her and she took it greedily, cradling it like a treasure in her shining hands. She hunched over the cup, inhaled its fragrant steam and sipped; the muscles in her back rolling to participate in the pleasure.

"Mmmm," she purred.

She took a second sip and arched her back, stretching, her face uplifted again. She crossed her legs revealing that she was wearing his cowboy boots and with eyes closed, she leaned her weightless head against the inside of his right thigh, sighed in contentment, and whispered, "You're late."

"Here comes the day," was ever his answer, the timber of his voice echoing inside him, always bringing him back from that perfect place, to the room in the Big House where he now slept.

Doc smiled as he woke, his best pain still in front of him.

The End.

AUTHOR'S NOTES

I'd like to acknowledge my fellow writers of the Newport Round Table writers' group; Melissa, Mark, Elizabeth, Devin, Lisa, Wayne, Carolyn, Susan, and Linda. Though the sessions could get heated, there was never a reading where I did not take back something from each and every one of you. It's been a blast. Also, a special call-out to Melissa Martin Ellis, your mentorship and support have meant the world to me. Above all, you really got what the piece was, and your affection for Win and Doc will always touch me.

To my first reader Carole, your patience and encouragement was unprecedented, still not sure how you did it.

This story was largely written in the coffee shops of Newport, Rhode Island. Specifically The Corner Cafe, People's, Starbucks (with apologies to Double D), Washington Square Cafe and Empire Tea & Coffee (the one on Broadway). Yes, I was the one in the corner booth, or at the table along the wall, head down, pulling my hair, chewing on a pen, whose social interaction was maxed-out after begging for refills. These folks are a tribute to the power of what it means to be a true neighborhood merchant.

To Tim and Debbie of the Medicine Bow Lodge, where the wonders of Wyoming went from my imagination to the page, your hospitality is unequalled. I long to go back to "my office" by the fire, in the cushy chair with the perfect ranch dog napping at me feet. Not sure heaven could top what you've built up there. My little cabin, Horse Fly, still calls to me, not to mention the fresh made cinnamon rolls and never-out coffee. Yes, heaven.

A special thanks to my own band of brave cohorts: Jude, LBL, Meesh, T and Katie Scarlet. You've somehow withstood my un-

ending chatter about "the book". The foundation of your friendship cannot be measured.

And lastly, to my husband Fred. I can't fathom there is man
more supportive and loving on the planet. I know that life with
your "own personal hurricane of a wife" never affords you a dull
moment—and you crave those dull moments to your toes—but
knowing you have my back, no matter what, makes all the damn
difference.

This story came to me whole. It was delivered from whatever
force of creativity blesses us in those times of true inspiration; much
like watching a movie, I couldn't wait to see how it ended and I'm
sure I share your feelings about the conclusion. But I promise, if
there had been another way, I would have gladly written it. So, my
final gratitude goes to you, the reader. Thank you for taking the
time to go along on this journey. I hope you fell in love with this
world, as I did, and that whatever scars you may carry are light, and
that you bear them with grace.

Nancy Roy
August, 2015
Newport, Rhode Island

ABOUT THE AUTHOR

Nancy Roy says that entire plot lines, characters and conversations flow from her pen, almost as if channeled from some inexplicable source.

As a corporate executive, she uses her many hours of travel time to transcribe

her remarkable tales and breathe life into her truly memorable characters, some of whom share her early background a western girl in a rodeo town with strong heartland Minnesota roots. Some spring unbidden from that unknown creative source and alternately delight and appall her with their actions.

She now lives and works far from where her journey began, in historic Newport, Rhode Island, an island off the New England coast filled with mansions and surrounded by deep blue seas, where she and her husband Fred have found safe harbor and share their love of sailing, the sea and each other.

She welcomes visitors to her website at:

www.nancyroyauthor.com

Made in the USA
Middletown, DE
21 September 2015